ALSO BY LJ SHEN

All Saints

Pretty Reckless

Broken Knight

Angry God

Damaged Goods

ANGRY GOD

L.J. SHEN

Bloom *books*

Published by Bloom Books, an imprint of Sourcebooks
P.O. Box 4410, Naperville, Illinois 60567-4410
(630) 961-3900
sourcebooks.com

Originally self-published in 2020 by L.J. Shen.

Cataloging-in-Publication data is on file with the Library of Congress.

Printed and bound in the United States of America.
WOZ 10 9 8 7 6 5 4 3 2 1

For Ratula Roy, Marta Bor, and that sliver of hope peeking from every dark moment in our lives.

"We never heard the devil's side of the story.
God wrote all the book."
—Anatole France

THEME SONG

"Saints"—Echos

PLAYLIST

"Gives You Hell"—The All-American Rejects
"Dirty Little Secret"—The All-American Rejects
"Handsome Devil"—The Smiths
"Bad Guy"—Billie Eilish
"My Own Worst Enemy"—Lit
"Help I'm Alive"—Metric
"Bandages"—Hot Hot Heat
"Peace Sells"—Megadeth
"Boyfriend"—Ariana Grande featuring Social Club

CHAPTER ONE
LENORA

LENORA, 12; VAUGHN, 13

You didn't see anything.

He is not coming for you.

He didn't even see your face.

Every bone in my body shivered as I tried to bleach the image I'd just seen from my brain.

I squeezed my eyes shut and rocked back and forth, curled like a shrimp on the hard mattress. The rusty metal legs of the bed whined as they scraped against the floor.

I'd always been a bit wary of Carlisle Castle, but up until ten minutes ago, I'd thought it was the ghosts that terrified me, not the students.

Not a thirteen-year-old boy with a face like *The Sleeping Faun* sculpture—lazily beautiful, impossibly imperial.

Not Vaughn Spencer.

I grew up here and had yet to encounter anything as scary as that brash American boy.

People said Carlisle was one of the most haunted castles in Britain. The seventeenth-century fort was supposedly the home of two ghosts. The first had been spotted by a footman who'd been locked in the cellar some decades ago. He swore he saw the ghost of Madame Tindall clawing at the walls, begging for water, claiming she'd been poisoned by her husband. The second ghost—that of said husband, Lord Tindall—had evidently been seen roaming the hallways at night, sometimes reaching to fix an off-kilter picture, though not moving it an inch.

They said Madame Tindall had pierced Lord's heart with a steak knife, twisting it for good measure, the moment she realized he'd poisoned her. According to the tale, he'd wanted to marry the young maid he'd impregnated after decades of childless marriage to Madame. The knife, people swore, could still be seen in the ghost's chest, rattling whenever he laughed.

We'd moved in when Papa had opened Carlisle Prep, a prestigious art school, a decade ago. He'd invited the most talented, gifted students in Europe.

They all came. He was *the* Edgar Astalis, after all. The man whose life-sized sculpture of Napoleon, *The Emperor*, stood in the middle of the Champs-Élysées.

But they were all scared of the rumored ghosts too.

Everything about this place was spooky.

The castle loomed from a foggy Berkshire valley, its silhouette curling upward like tangled, black swords. Ivy and wild rosebushes crawled across the stone exterior of the courtyard, hiding secret paths students often snuck through at night. The hallways were a labyrinth that seemed to circle back to the sculpting studio.

The heart of the castle.

Students strolled the foyers with straight backs, ruddy cheeks stung by the seemingly endless winter, and taut expressions. Carlisle Preparatory School for the Gifted frowned upon other public schools like Eton and Craigclowan. Papa said ordinary prep schools encouraged weak-minded, silver-spooned, middle-weights, not true leaders. Our uniform consisted of black capes with Carlisle's motto sewn in bright gold across the left breast pocket:

ARS LONGA, VITA BREVIS.

Art is long, life is short. The message was clear: the only way to immortality was through art. Mediocrity was profanity. It was a dog-eat-dog world, and we were unleashed upon each other, hungry, desperate, and blindly idealistic.

I was only twelve years old the day I saw what I shouldn't have. I was the youngest student at the summer session Carlisle Prep had opened, followed by Vaughn Spencer.

At first I was jealous of the boy with the two slits of penetrating, frosty stone instead of eyes. At thirteen, he already worked with marble. He would not wear his black cape, acted like he hadn't the same mandate as other students, and breezed past the teachers without bowing—unheard of in this school.

My father was the headmaster, and even I bowed.

Come to think of it, I bent the lowest.

We were told we were a cut above the rest, the future of artists all over the world. We had the talent, the status, the money, and the opportunity. But if we were silver, Vaughn Spencer was gold. If we were good, he was brilliant. And when we shone? He gleamed with the force of a thousand suns, charring everything around him.

It was like God had carved him differently, paid extra attention to detail while creating him. His cheekbones were sharper than scalpel blades, his eyes the palest shade of blue in nature, his hair the inkiest black. He was so white I could see the veins under his skin, but his mouth was red as fresh blood—warm, alive, and deceiving.

He fascinated and infuriated me. But just like everyone else, I kept my distance from him. He wasn't here to make friends. He'd made that clear by never attending the food hall or any of the social functions.

Another thing Vaughn had and I didn't? My father's admiration. I didn't know why the great Edgar Astalis fawned over some boy from California, but he did nonetheless.

Papa said Vaughn was going to do something special. That one day, he would be Michelangelo big.

I believed him.

And so I hated Vaughn.

Actually, I'd hated Vaughn until exactly fifteen minutes ago, when I walked into the darkroom to develop the photos I'd taken yesterday. Photography was something I did as a hobby, not as art. My art focused on assemblage, making sculptures out of garbage. I liked to take ugly things and make them beautiful.

To turn the flawed into something flawless.

It gave me hope. I wanted it to give everything that wasn't perfect hope.

Anyway, I was supposed to wait for one of the tutors to accompany me into the darkroom. Those were the rules. But I had a feeling the pictures I'd taken were going to be horribly bland. I didn't want anyone to see them before I'd had the chance to retake them.

It was the middle of the night. No one was supposed to be there.

And so, because I was acutely, achingly jealous of Vaughn Spencer, I'd walked in on something that made me feel confused and oddly furious with him.

In bed, I smacked my forehead as I recalled my silly behavior in the darkroom. I'd mumbled "pardon," slammed the door, and run back to my room.

I'd descended the stairs to the second floor, taking two at a time, bumped into a statue of a warrior, let out a yelp, and rounded the corridor to the girls' dorms. All the doors looked alike, and my vision was too clouded by panic to find my room. I threw doors open, poking my head in to search for the familiar white quilt Mum had crocheted for me when I was a baby. By the time I got to my room, nearly every girl in the wing was cursing me for interrupting her sleep.

I dove into my bed, and that's where I stayed, hiding under my quilt.

He can't find you.

He can't enter the girls' dorms.

Papa would kick him out if he did, genius or not.

Then the clank of smart shoes pacing the corridor made my heart jump to my throat. A guard whistled a lullaby in the dark. I heard a violent, loud thud. A guttural moan rose from the ground outside my room. I curled into a smaller ball, the air rattling in my lungs like a penny in an empty jar.

My door creaked open. I felt a gust of wind from its direction, raising the hair on my arms wherever it touched. My body tensed like a piece of dried clay, hard but fragile.

"Pale face. Black heart. Golden legacy."

That's how I'd once heard Uncle Harry—also known as Professor Fairhurst inside these walls—describe Vaughn to one of his colleagues.

There was no mistaking the energy Vaughn Spencer brought into a room because it sucked up everything else like a Hoover. The air in my room was suddenly thick with danger. It was like trying to breathe underwater.

I felt my knees knocking together under my quilt as I pretended to be asleep. Summers in Carlisle Castle were unbearably humid, and I wore a tank top and shorts.

He moved in the dark, but I couldn't hear him, which scared me even more. The thought that he might kill me—actually, *literally* strangle me to death—crossed my mind. I had no doubt he'd knocked out the guard who walked our hall at night to make sure nobody broke curfew or made silly ghostlike noises to scare the other students. No fire was as big and burning as one born of humiliation, and what I'd witnessed tonight had embarrassed Vaughn. Even in my haste to leave, I'd seen it on his face.

Vaughn was never uncomfortable. He wore his skin with arrogance, like a crown.

I felt my quilt rolling down my body, from my shoulders to

my ankles in one precise movement. My two brussels sprouts of breasts—as my older sister, Poppy, called them—poked through my shirt without my sports bra, and he would be able to see them. I squeezed my eyes tighter.

God. Why did I have to open the bloody door? Why did I have to see him? Why did I have to put myself on the radar of one of the most gifted boys in the world?

He was destined for greatness, and I was destined to whatever purpose he'd see fit for me.

I felt his finger touching the side of my neck. It was cold and dry from sculpting. He brushed it down along my spine, standing over me, watching what we both pathetically pretended was my sleeping figure. But I was wide-awake, and I felt everything—the threat wafting from his touch and his scent of shaved stone, rain, and the sweet, faint trail I'd find out later was a blunt. Through the narrow slit of my eyes, I could make out the way he tilted his head as he watched me.

Please. I will never tell a soul.

I wondered, if he was so formidable at thirteen, what he would be like as a grown man. I'd hoped to never find out, although chances were, this wouldn't be our last encounter. There were only so many billionaire-spawns-to-famous-artists in this world, and our parents ran in the same social circles.

I'd met Vaughn once even before he came to school, when he was vacationing in the South of France with his family one summer. My parents had hosted a wine-tasting event for charity, and Baron and Emilia Spencer had attended. I was nine, Vaughn was ten. Mum slathered me in sunscreen, put an ugly hat on me, and made me swear I wouldn't get into the sea because I couldn't swim.

That's how I'd ended up watching him on the beach under a canopy the entire vacation, in between flipping pages of the fantasy book I was reading. Vaughn broke waves with his scrawny body—running straight into them with the ferocity of a hungry warrior—and dragged jellyfish from the Mediterranean Sea back to shore, holding them by their tops, so they couldn't sting him. One day he'd poked ice lolly sticks into them until he was sure they were dead and then cut them, mumbling to himself that jellyfish always cut into perfect halves, no matter which way you sliced.

He was odd. Cruel and different. I'd had no intention of talking to him.

Then, during one of the many grand events that week, he'd snuck behind the fountain I sat leaning against, reading a book, and split a chocolate brownie he must've stolen before dinner. He handed me half, unsmiling.

I'd groaned as I accepted it because I had the silly notion that now I owed him something. "Mummy will have a heart attack if she finds out," I told him. "She never lets me eat sugar."

I'd then shoved the entire thing in my mouth, fighting the sticky goo on my tongue, the rich nougat coating my teeth.

His mouth, a slash of disapproval, had cut his otherwise stoic features. "Your mom sucks."

"My mum is the best!" I exclaimed hotly. "Besides, I saw you poking sticks at jellyfish. You don't know anything. You're nothing but a bad boy."

"Jellyfish don't have hearts," he drawled, as if that made it okay.

"Just like you." I'd been unable to stop myself from licking my fingers, eyeing the untouched brownie half in his hand.

He'd scowled, but for some reason, he didn't seem upset by my insult. "They also don't have brains. Just like *you*."

I stared ahead, ignoring him. I didn't want to argue and make a scene. Papa would be mad if I raised my voice. Mum would be disappointed, which was somehow even worse.

"Such a good girl," Vaughn had taunted, his eyes gleaming with mischief. Instead of taking a bite of his brownie, he'd passed the second piece to me.

I took it, hating myself for caving in.

"Such a good, proper, boring girl."

"You're ugly." I shrugged. He wasn't, really. But I wanted him to be.

"Ugly or not, I could still kiss you if I wanted to, and you'd let me."

I choked on the rich cocoa in my mouth, my book dropping to the ground and closing without a bookmark. *Shoot.*

"Why would you ever think that?" I'd turned to him, scandalized.

He'd leaned close, one flat chest to another. He'd smelled of something foreign and dangerous and wild. Of golden California beaches, maybe.

"Because my dad told me good girls like bad boys, and I'm bad. *Really* bad."

And now, here we were. Facing off again. He was, tragically, nowhere near ugly, and he seemed to be contemplating what to do with our newly shared secret.

"Kill you? Hurt you? Scare you off?" he pondered, exuding ruthless power.

My throat worked around a lump that refused to wash down.

"What should I do with you, *Good Girl?*"

He remembered my pet name from that day at the beach. It made everything worse somehow. Up until now, we'd acted like we didn't know each other at all.

Vaughn lowered himself so his face was aligned with mine. I could feel his hot breath—the only thing warm about him—sliding against my neck. My throat went dry, each breath passing through it like a blade. Still, I kept up the charade. Maybe if he thought I had been sleepwalking, he would spare me his wrath.

"How good are you at keeping secrets, Lenora Astalis?" His voice wrapped around my neck like a noose.

I wanted to cough. I *needed* to cough. He terrified me. I hated him with the heat and passion of a thousand blazing suns. He made me feel like a scaredy cat and a snitch.

"Oh, yes. If you're coward enough to pretend you're asleep, you're good enough to keep a secret. That's the thing about you, Astalis. I can smash you into dust and watch your grains dance at my feet. My little circus monkey."

I might've hated Vaughn, but I hated myself more for not standing up to him. For not opening my eyes and spitting in his face. Clawing his unnaturally blue eyes out. Taunting him back for all the times he'd taunted all of us at Carlisle Prep.

"By the way, your eyelids are moving," he said drily, chuckling.

He straightened up, his finger making a brief stop at the base of my spine. He snapped his fingers, making a breaking sound, and I nearly jumped out of my skin, letting out a gasp. I squeezed my eyes tighter, still pretending to sleep.

He laughed.

The bastard *laughed*.

Was he sparing me for the time being? Was he going to check in on me from now on? Retaliate if I opened my mouth? He was so unpredictable. I wasn't sure what my life would look like in the morning.

That's when I realized I might be a good girl, but Vaughn had underestimated himself three years ago.

He wasn't a boy at all. He was a deity.

Shortly after what happened during summer session at Carlisle Castle, I lost Mum. The woman who was so scared of me ever getting a sunburn or scraping my knee went to sleep and never woke up. Cardiac arrest. We found her lying in bed like a cursed Disney princess, her eyes closed, the smile on her face still small and pink and full of plans for the morning.

We were supposed to board a yacht to Thessaloniki that day, a trip chasing historical treasures that never came.

That was the second time I'd wanted to pretend I was asleep while my life took a terrible turn for the worse—for no other reason than because it could. Diving headfirst into self-pity was tempting as hell, but I held back.

I had two options: break or build a stronger version of myself.

I chose the latter.

By the time Papa took a job in Todos Santos a couple years later, I wasn't the same girl who'd pretended to be asleep when confronted.

Poppy, my older sister, joined him in California, but I asked him to let me stay at Carlisle.

I stayed where my art was and avoided Vaughn Spencer, who attended All Saints High across the ocean. Win-win, right?

But now, Papa was insisting I spend my senior year with him and Poppy in Southern California.

Thing was, the new Lenny didn't turn a blind eye to Vaughn Spencer.

I was no longer fearful.

I'd suffered the greatest loss and survived it. Nothing scared me anymore.

Not even an angry god.

CHAPTER TWO
VAUGHN

LENORA, 17; VAUGHN, 18

I was born with an insatiable appetite for destruction.

It had nothing to do with what happened to me.

With my life story.

With my parents.

With the *fucking* universe.

I was wired in messy-ass knots. Made out of metal cords instead of veins. An empty black box instead of a heart. A laser-focused vision to detect weaknesses instead of pupils.

Even when I smiled as a kid, my cheeks and eyes hurt. It felt unnatural, daunting. I stopped smiling early on.

And judging by the way my senior year of high school had started, smiling was not in the goddamn cards for me in the future either.

Take ten deep, cleansing breaths, I could practically hear my mother pleading in her calm, sweet voice in my head.

For once in my miserable existence, I listened. Driving my fist through every locker in the hallway was probably the dumbest way in the world to get kicked out of school and simultaneously break every bone in my left hand, killing my career in the process.

Not that I was here for the sharp minds of my educators—or

worse, the bullshit diploma. But unlike my shit-for-brains best friend, Knight Cole, I didn't have a red, shiny self-destruct button I was eager to push.

One.

Two.

Three.

F...uck this shit. No.

Lenora Astalis was here in the flesh. Alive, kicking, and in my zip code. In my *realm*. I'd shoved her existence into a drawer in my brain I usually reserved for unsatisfying porn and mindless small talk with girls before they lowered their heads to suck my cock.

But I remembered her. You bet your fucking ass, I did. My little dancing monkey. So agreeable you could get her to deep-throat a baseball bat if you asked, and not even nicely. Supposedly this was a favorable trait in the fairer sex, but Good Girl was too submissive and pure even for my taste.

Back then, she'd had yellow hair like spun gold, shiny loafers, and a terrified, please-don't-hurt-me expression. The Carlisle cape had made her look like Hermione Granger's geekier friend. Voted Most Likely to be Wedgied to Death, Lenora Astalis had the annoying quality of looking perpetually prim, proper, and pathetically righteous.

Now? Now she looked...*different.*

I wasn't impressed with the black shit she'd smeared on her eyes and the goth clothes. They were just camouflage for the fact that she had zero spine and would shit her pants the minute someone dropped the F-bomb near her.

Good Girl was standing by her new locker, her hair now jet black. She was applying an extra layer of eyeliner (she needed that like I needed more reasons to hate the world) while staring at a pocket mirror glued to the inside of her locker door. She had on an OBEY beanie but had corrected it with a Sharpie so the word was now *Dis*obey.

What a fucking rebel. Someone should notify the authorities before she did something really crazy, like eat nonorganic blueberries in the cafeteria.

"Yo, sour-ass kid, what's good?" Knight, my best friend, neighbor, cousin and full-time douche canoe, clapped my shoulder from behind and gave me a bro hug. I trained my eyes on an invisible spot ahead, ignoring both him and Astalis. With all due respect to Lenora—and I had absolutely none—she hadn't earned my attention. I made a mental note to remind her where she stood.

Or in her case, *kneeled.*

I still remembered how she'd reacted when I slid into her room that night. The way she'd shivered under my finger, brittle like a china doll, practically begging to be shattered. Crushing her wasn't even going to give me the usual high. It was like taking candy from a baby. There was no kindness behind my decision to spare her. I was naturally pragmatic.

I had an endgame.

She wasn't going to stand in the way of it.

Risk. Reward. Return.

Hurting her would have been redundant. Astalis had kept her little, pink mouth shut all these years—clearly intimidated. I knew she hadn't blabbed because I'd checked. I had eyes and ears everywhere. She'd kept my name out of her mouth, and when her sister came to live here sophomore year, she'd stayed back in England, probably piss scared of me and what I was going to do to her. Good. Worked fine for me.

But that fragile trust had been broken the minute I saw her here.

In my kingdom.

A Trojan horse with a belly full of bad memories and bullshit.

"Your Cuntness has that extra shine today," Knight observed, looking me over as he glided his fingers through his shampoo-commercial hair, the color of buttered toast. He was star quarterback, prom king, and the most popular guy in school.

Hey, whatever helped him sleep better at night and pacified his adopted-kid complex.

"I'm surprised you can see anything through the mist of your own self-righteous farts," I sneered, stopping at my locker and throwing it open.

Just six lockers away from Astalis, I noticed. Karma really was a piece of fucking work.

Knight propped an elbow on a nearby locker, studying me intently. He unintentionally blocked my view of Lenora. Just as well. Her custom Robert Smith T-shirt didn't exactly add sex appeal to her already bland appearance.

"You coming to Arabella's back-to-school party tonight?"

"I'd rather have my dick sucked by a hungry shark."

Arabella Garofalo reminded me of tiny, inbred dogs with diamond-studded, pink collars and squeaky barks, who occasionally bit your ass and pissed themselves when excited. She was mean, desperate, mouthy, and perhaps worst of all, entirely too eager to offer me blowies.

"Why don't you get your dick sucked by Hazel? She just got old-school braces, so it's practically the same," Knight suggested cordially, fishing his alkaline water bottle out of a designer leather backpack and taking a swig.

I knew there was vodka in there. He'd probably popped a few Oxys before getting here, too. Asshole made Hunter S. Thompson look like a fucking Boy Scout.

"Booze before ten a.m.?" I twisted my lips in a lazy smirk. Love letters and nude Polaroids spilled from my locker in a river of teenage desperation. No girl had the guts to actually come talk to me. I collected and tossed them into a trash can nearby, never breaking eye contact with Knight. "I thought being a virgin at eighteen covered your pathetic quota for senior year."

"Eat shit, Spencer." He took another swig.

"If I will, would you go the fuck away? 'Cause in that case, I'm tempted."

I slammed my locker shut. Knight didn't know about Lenora Astalis. Bringing attention to her wasn't on my agenda. Right now, she was a goth freak with zero reputation or social status to speak of, and that's how she was going to remain in these hallways, unless I showed any trace of emotion toward her.

Which—spoiler alert—I didn't have.

"Don't be fresh, Spence."

"I'm stale as a five-day-old shit." I threw my backpack over one shoulder. *Ain't that the truth.*

"Gross, man. Having Luna, Daria, and me as friends didn't really humanize you as much as your parents had hoped. It's like putting a little hat on a hamster. Cute but useless."

I stared at him blankly. "Are you even talking in English right now? Get your ass something greasy and a bottle of water before everyone gets secondhand alcohol poisoning from your breath."

"Suit yourself. More prime English meat for me." Knight waved me off, a spring in his step.

I shook my head as I followed. As if he'd ever do something about said meat. For all intents and purposes, the guy was a fucking pussy-vegan, more virginal than olive oil. He wanted to dip his dick into one hole and one hole only. It was attached to Luna Rexroth, his childhood crush, who was in college, miles away—hopefully being less pathetic than him and getting laid.

However, there was no doubt the *English meat* Knight had poetically referred to was Lenora, which meant her presence at All Saints High had already drawn attention.

I could see why her older sister, what's-her-face Astalis, was a hit with the dudebros. I'd seen her around. She looked like the kind of attention-seeking, bubbly, mass-made blondie who'd traded her soul for a pair of red-soled heels.

"The only English chick I'm interested in meeting is Margaret Thatcher." I popped a piece of mint gum into my mouth, shoving another one into Knight's without his consent. His Mel Gibson breath was so flammable, he could torch the motherfucking school if he lit a joint.

"She's dead, bro." He chewed obediently, frowning.

"Exactly," I quipped, hauling the strap of my backpack to my other shoulder just to do something with my hands. It was only nine thirty, and already today excelled at sucking all the hairy balls in the universe.

When Knight remained glued to my side, despite not having the same first-period class as me, I stopped walking. "You're still here. Why?"

"Lenora." He unscrewed his "water" bottle again, taking another generous sip.

"Throwing random names in the air is not conversation, Knighty boy. Let's start with an entire sentence. Repeat after me: *I. Need. Rehab. And. A. Good. Fuck.*"

"Poppy Astalis's hotter-than-wasabi sister." Knight ignored my jab. "She's a senior, like us. Gives good-girl vibes." He let loose a devilish smirk, turning around and running his eyes over her black-clad figure. She was only a few feet away but didn't seem to hear us, with the hustle and bustle. "But I can see her pointy fangs. She's a natural born killer, that one."

Poppy. That's what's-her-face's name. Eh, I was close.

Lenora was a year younger than me, and if she was a senior now, that meant she'd skipped a grade. Goddamn nerd. No surprises there.

Knight continued his TMZ report.

"Their dad is this hotshot artist dude—runs that snooty art institute downtown. Honestly? I'm boring myself into a coma by repeating this information to you, so let's just cut to the tea—the black sheep of the family is here for the year, and everyone wants a piece of that lamb."

The meat metaphors were getting creepier by the nanosecond. Besides, I knew very well who Edgar Astalis was.

"I'm guessing this is the part where I should feign some kind of interest." My jaw ticked, my teeth slamming together. He was lying. There was no way anyone wanted to touch Lenora. She strayed too far from the conventional hot-girl look. The black rags. The eyeliner. The lip piercing. Why not jerk off to a Marilyn Manson poster and save the condom?

Knight rolled his eyes theatrically.

"Man, you are really forcing me to spell it out. I *saw* your ass swallowing *Girl, Interrupted* with your eyes." He clapped my shoulder like some kind of old, wise mentor. "You'll be lucky if she ain't pregnant after that eye-fucking sesh."

"She looked familiar, that's all."

She did, because I'd been expecting her to show the fuck up since the minute her sister and dad crashed this town.

At school.

The gym.

Parties.

It didn't even make sense, but I still looked—even at my own parties, where uninvited guests weren't welcome. She was a dark shadow following me everywhere, and I always tried to maintain the upper hand in our imaginary relationship. Fuck, I even rummaged her stupid-ass Instagram and found out what she watched and listened to just so I could understand her cultural world better and crack her, should the occasion occur.

And, well, it fucking had.

I decided on the spot that despite Knight's status as my closest friend, I wasn't going to tell him I knew her. It would only complicate things, pushing my secret one more inch toward the light.

As it was, the truth was clawing at me, leaving welts of uncomfortable reality. Sometimes, on bad nights, I was tempted to tell my parents what had happened to me. They were decent parents, even my dipshit self had to admit. But ultimately, it boiled down to this: no one could take my pain away. No one.

Not even my damn-near-perfect, loving, caring, powerful, billionaire parents.

We come into this world alone, and we die alone. If we get sick, we fight it alone. Our parents are not there to go through chemo treatments for us. They're not the ones losing their hair, puking buckets, or getting their asses kicked at school. If we're involved in an accident, they're not the ones losing blood, fighting for our lives on the operating table, losing a limb. "I'm here for you" is the dumbest sentence I'd ever heard anyone say.

They were *not* there for me.

They tried. And they failed. If you want to look at your fiercest protector, at the one person you can always count on, take a good look in the mirror.

I was in the business of avenging my own pain, and there was a debt to collect.

I was going to get it. Soon.

As for my parents, they loved me, were concerned about me, would die for me, blah blah fucking blah. If my mother knew what went through my head, what had *really* happened that day at the Parisian gallery auction, she would commit coldhearted murder.

But that was my job.

And I was going to enjoy it.

"So you're telling me you don't think Lenora Astalis is hot?" Knight wiggled his brows, pushing off the lockers and matching my stride.

I eyeballed her again. She balanced her textbooks on her hip as she walked toward the lab, not hugging them to her chest like the rest of the preppy damsels of All Saints High. She wore a black denim miniskirt much shorter than my fuse, fishnet stockings ripped at the knees and ass, and army boots that looked more haggard than mine. Even septum and lip rings couldn't taint her shy appearance. She popped her pink gum, staring ahead, either ignoring my existence or not noticing me as she brushed past.

Her beauty—if you could call it that—reminded me of a child's.

Small, button-like nose, big blue eyes dotted green and gold, and narrow, pink lips. There was nothing wrong with her face, but nothing overtly attractive about her either. In the sea of Californian, shiny-haired, tan-skinned girls with bodies made of glitter, muscle, and curves, I knew she wouldn't stand out—positively, anyway.

I arched an eyebrow, shouldering past him to class. Knight followed me.

"Are you asking if I'd let her suck my cock? Possibly, depending on my mood and level of intoxication."

"How fucking charitable of you. Actually, I wasn't asking that at all. I wanted to tell you Lenora, like her sister, is off-limits for you."

"Oh, yeah?" I threw him a bone, keeping him humored. Hell would freeze over before I took an order from Knight Cole. Or anyone else for that matter.

"You can't break any of the Astalis girls' hearts. Their mom died a few years ago. They've had it rough, and they don't need your nasty-ass self shitting on their parade. Which happens to be your favorite pastime. So this is me telling you I'll fuck you up if you touch them. Specifically, the morbid-looking one. You feeling me here?"

Lenora's mother died?

How had I not heard about it when Poppy moved here?

Oh, that's right, I cared about her existence a little less than I did about Arabella's stupid parties.

I knew the mother never moved with Edgar and Poppy, but I'd guessed they either got divorced or she stayed with the talented kid in England.

Mothers were a touchy subject for Knight for more reasons than I could count. I knew he'd take it as a personal offense if I deliberately smashed Good Girl's little heart. Lucky for him, I had very little interest in that organ or the girl who carried it around in her chest.

"Don't worry, Captain Save-a-Ho, I won't fuck them." I pushed the door to my class open and blazed inside without sparing Knight another look. Easiest promise I ever had to make.

When I plopped down and glanced toward the door, I saw him through the window, running his thumb across his throat, threatening to kill me if I broke my word.

My father was a lawyer, and semantics were his playground.

I said I wouldn't fuck her.

I never said I wouldn't fuck *with* her.

If Lenora deserved a public spanking to make sure she stayed in line, her ass was going to be red.

And most definitely *mine*.

The opportunity to corner Lenora Astalis presented itself three days later. I'd skipped Arabella's party and wasn't surprised to hear Lenora hadn't shown up either. But her sister, Poppy, was there—dancing, drinking, mingling, even helping Arabella and Alice clean up puke and cum stains afterwards.

Lenora didn't strike me as a party girl. She had the strange gene, the one that made her stick out like a sore thumb wherever she went, even without the Maleficent wardrobe. I could tell because I had it too. We were weeds, rising from the concrete, ruining the generic landscape of this yacht club town.

The first day, I'd ditched my last class and tailed her car after school to see where she lived. She drove a black Lister Storm—a far cry from her sister's Mini Cooper—and got honked at five different times for failing to take a right turn on a red light. Twice she flipped the other driver the bird. Once she actually double-parked to rummage through her bag and hand a homeless person some change.

By the end of the journey, I couldn't help but smirk to myself. Edgar Astalis had put his girls in a castle by the ocean, with high, white-picket fences and drapes firmly shut.

Nice. Predictable. Safe.

Just like his useless little daughters.

I made a U-turn and drove back to school, where I found Poppy at a marching band rehearsal with her lame-ass accordion, her Prada bag hanging lazily on the back of her chair while her back was to me. I fished out her house key, went downtown, made a copy, and returned just in time to slip it back in before she scooped up her bag and went for milkshakes with the band.

The following day I shadowed Lenora, making a note to see if anyone else was there. Poppy took every extracurricular activity available, including band, peer tutoring, English club, and hiking. (She was *exactly* the kind of teenybopper to make a big fucking deal out of everything she did, including walking.) Edgar Astalis was busting his ass at that art institution he'd cofounded, sunrise till sundown, and was nowhere in sight.

The black sheep, the sweet lamb, was all alone in the afternoons, waiting to be eaten by the wolf.

On the third day—today—I went for the kill. I knew Lenora's routine by now, and I allowed her forty minutes of basking in her own ignorance while I sat in my banged-up truck, my army boots crossed at the ankles on the dashboard, as she went about her afternoon. I sketched a sculpture on my sketchpad in long, round strokes, a half-smoked joint hanging from the side of my mouth.

When the clock hit four and my alarm buzzed, I got out of the truck and made my way onto the Astalis property, unlocking the door and waltzing in like I owned the place. I strolled through the entrance, past the living room with the marble-on-crème accents and antique furniture, and toward the double glass doors. Sliding them open, I glanced down at the kidney-shaped pool, spotting Good Girl.

She was doing laps underwater, moving in small, graceful strokes. I moved to the edge of the pool, lighting up the rest of my half joint and squatting down in my torn, black skinny jeans and frayed, black-turned-gray shirt my mother hated so much. I loathed being rich by proxy, but that was another story Lenora was never going to hear because today was where our communication would end.

Next time I had to make a point, it would be with actions, not words.

Sending a cloud of smoke upward, I watched as Lenora's head popped out of the water, appearing in front of me for the first time since I walked in.

She hadn't taken a breath the entire time, I realized.

She was no longer that kid in the South of France who didn't know how to swim. She'd learned.

And she was completely naked.

Her lashes were curtained with fat water drops that cascaded down her cheeks. She parked her elbows on the edge of the pool, checking the time on her Polar watch. That's when she noticed in her periphery that something—*someone*—was blocking the sun. She squinted up, using one hand as a visor.

"What in the bloody hell are you doing here, Spencer?" She pulled backward from the impact, like my existence had exploded in her face.

"I've been asking myself the very same question, Astalis, since I saw your *good gone bland* ass in my domain and figured you lost your way to the nearest faerie world you're engrossed with."

It was peculiar how, although we hadn't officially been reintroduced since she came here, we still remembered each other in all the ways that mattered. I knew she read fantasy books and listened to the Smiths and the Cure and thought Simon Pegg was a comic genius. She knew I was the type of asshole to break into her house and demand shit, and that I'd been watching her.

This confirmed my initial suspicion. She *had* noticed me at school, just as I'd noticed her. Neither of us found it wise to acknowledge the other. Not in public.

I puffed on my joint, taking a seat on the diving board and slowly lifting her towel robe with the tip of my finger, like it disgusted me.

"Tsk-tsk." I shook my head, watching the reflection of my evil smirk through her shiny, blue-green-gold-whatever-the-fuck-they-were, hypnotizing, Drusilla eyes. "Swimming naked? *Good girls* don't give a shit about tan lines. It's not like you're going to get dicked in this school. That's something I'm afraid I won't permit."

"That's something I won't be asking your permission for," she deadpanned, pretending to yawn.

"Doesn't work that way, Good Girl. When I say jump, they ask how high. And come tomorrow, everybody's gonna know you're damaged goods, so stock up on those batteries because real dick is not in the cards for you."

"Fancy." She slow-clapped, whistling sarcastically. "Top of the food chain now, right, *Spence?*"

She used the nickname I hated so much. She'd heard about me at school, knew about my legion of followers. *Good.*

I cocked my head. So what if she pretended not to give a shit about how popular I was? "Careful. You're not even on the vegan menu, Lenora."

"Bite me anyway."

"Only to draw blood, baby."

"Dying at your hands would still beat talking to you, Spencer."

Lenora leaned forward, trying to snatch the robe from my finger, but I was too fast. I threw it behind my back and stood up, finishing my joint and throwing it into her pool. She smelled of chlorine and cotton. Virginal, pure, and not loaded with teenage hormones and expensive perfume. I was sure Edgar Astalis, who owned half the galleries in London, Milan, and Paris, had a pool boy coming at least twice a week. Maybe the pool boy could give Good Girl the vitamin D she wasn't going to get at school.

"What do you want?" she snarled, her lips thinning even more than their usual lackluster shape.

Really, Lenora wasn't anywhere near the realms of gorgeous. Take Daria, my neighbor, for example. She was a classic, beauty-pageant hottie. Or Luna, my childhood friend, who was mouthwateringly stunning. Lenora was merely pleasant to the eye—and even that only from certain angles. Right now her eyeliner ran down her cheeks, making her look like the clown in *It*.

I smiled. "To catch up, silly Billy. How art thou? Still collecting garbage?"

"Assemblage." She braced the edge of the pool, her skin turning whiter around the edges. A gust of wind breezed through the backyard, and the blond hair on her arms prickled. She was uncomfortable.

So was fucking I.

"I'm making art out of old, unwanted things. The only difference between you and me is that you use exclusively stone and marble, the things your heart is made of."

"And that I'm good." I ran my tongue over my teeth, smacking my lips together.

"Excuse me?" Her cheeks pinked, matching her already-red ears.

It was the first time I'd seen Lenora Astalis blushing since she came to Todos Santos, and even this wasn't from embarrassment but anger. Maybe she had changed, but not enough to give me a decent fight.

"You using garbage is not the only thing different about us. I'm also talented, and you're..." I gathered the ash from my joint and poured it onto her towel. "A prissy nepotist who looks like Bellatrix Lestrange."

"Screw you," she hissed.

"Hard pass. I like my lays pretty."

"And airheads," she snapped.

"Yes, you are." I shook my head. "But you still don't stand a fucking chance with me."

It was a low blow, and I'd promised Knight I was going to keep it clean, but something about the situation made me want to go the extra mile. Her defiance, no doubt.

I walked over to one of their many knitted, turquoise loungers, lying down with my hands tucked under my head, staring back at the sun.

"Dayum. Getting windy out here, huh?"

She was stuck in this pool until I decided to leave or else I'd see her naked, and I was fully planning to outstay my welcome. I thought I heard her teeth chattering, but she didn't cower or complain.

"Get to the point, Spencer, before I call the police." She swam to the other side of the pool so she could get a better angle of me. Splashes of water washed over the gray stone edges of the pool.

"Please do. My family owns this entire town, including the boys in blue. In fact, I'm pretty sure your father is going to have a heart attack if you drag him onto my father's shit list. Your uncle too. How is Harry Fairhurst doing, anyway? Still sucking up to my parents so they'll buy his below-average paintings?"

I wasn't exaggerating. My father, Baron "Vicious" Spencer, was the biggest asshole alive to anyone but my mother and me. He owned the mall in this town and ran an investments firm that turned a profit larger than the budget of an average-sized European country each quarter, so he was richer than God. He also employed a vast army of people from the neighboring towns, donated to local charities, and sent ludicrously generous gift cards to the law enforcers of our town each Christmas. There was no way the police were going to touch him or me.

Even Lenora's father, Edgar, and her uncle, Harry, were under my father's thumb. But unlike her, I had no plans to use my family's connections to get what I wanted.

Of course, she didn't know that about me.

She didn't know much of anything about me—other than the one crucial thing I wished we could both fucking forget.

"I'm sorry to interrupt your little power trip, but could you spit out why you're here and get it over with before I catch pneumonia?" she demanded in her posh English accent, slamming her palm on the patio.

I let out a dark chuckle, still staring at the sun and ignoring the burn. I wished that giant fireball was as good at burning memories as it was burning retinas.

"I thought the English prided themselves on having good manners."

"I thought the Americans were straight shooters," she quipped.

"We are."

"If you want to shoot, shoot. Don't talk."

The Good, the Bad, and the Ugly. I was all three.

I almost let a genuine smile grace my lips. *Almost.* Then I remembered who she was. What she knew.

"About that incident you witnessed…"

"Loosen your knickers, Vaughn. You've got them in a twist." She had the nerve to cut me off mid-speech, her wet mouth moving fast. "I've never shared your secret and never will. It's not my style, my business, or my information to tell. Believe it or not, my not moving to California when my dad and Poppy did had nothing to do with you. I love Carlisle Prep. It's the best arts school in Europe. I wasn't scared of you. As far as I'm concerned, we've never met before, and I know nothing about you, other than the obvious information that's freely volunteered at All Saints High."

She waited for the question. Normally, I wouldn't entertain this kind of behavior. But she amused me. Circus monkey—as I've said before.

"Which is?" I leaned forward.

"That you're a miserable, sadistic arse who enjoys using girls and bullying people."

If she waited for a reaction to my reputation, she was sorely disappointed. I leaned forward, propping my elbows on my knees, narrowing my eyes at her face.

"Why should I believe you?"

She plastered her palm against the ledge of the pool and pulled herself up in one go, rising from the water until she stood in front of me.

No bikini top.

No bottoms.

No nothing.

Good Girl was completely naked, wet and bold, and perhaps she wasn't so mediocre in that particular moment.

Let's just say if there ever was a mood in which I'd let her suck my cock and massage my balls, I was experiencing it now.

Her tits were small but round and perky, her nipples pointy, pink, and begging to be sucked. She had a curvy body, although she did a damn good job hiding all that silky, smooth flesh under the black fishnets and leather pants, and her pussy had a dusting of fair hair. Not a lot, but enough to show me she was a real, virginal blond—not waxed, bleached, and groomed to death, waiting to give some douchebag the full Pornhub experience of a closely shaved cunt.

There was also a tattoo on her inner thigh, but I couldn't get a good look at what it said, and gawking was letting her win.

Returning my eyes to her face, I decided maybe it wasn't so bland after all. Everything about her was small—nose, lips, freckles, ears—but her eyes were huge and aqua. The mass of inky, long hair with the egg-yolk roots did nothing to hide the fact that she was who she was.

Pure, pathetic, and partially insane.

I stood tall, lifting my chin, knowing full fucking well my dick wasn't going to swell in my pants unless I wanted it to. That was one of the best things about my screwed-up condition. I was able to fully control my libido, and I was hard on demand—*my* demand. Most teenage dicks were traitors, and they got my friends into a lot of shit that had nothing to do with anal. Not mine. Mine listened. And right now, I wasn't going to give her the satisfaction of knowing I wanted to fuck her smart mouth.

We were toe to toe. I was a head and a half taller, but somehow, with her chin tilted up in a dead stare and noticeably disobedient posture, she didn't feel so small against me.

She wasn't the same shivering girl who'd pretended to be asleep and begged with her entire silent body for me not to cut her throat that night.

Similar but different.

Innocent but no longer submissive.

"You should believe me," she announced, "because in order to destroy you, I need to acknowledge you first. See, in order to ruin a person's life, you need to hate them. Be jealous of them. Feel some type of passionate response toward them. You stir nothing in me, Vaughn Spencer. Not even disgust. Not even pity, though I really *should* pity you. You're the gum stuck to the bottom of my boots. You are a fleeting moment no one remembers—unremarkable, unnecessary, and utterly forgettable. You are the guy I once believed could kill me, so because of you—yes, because of *you*—I started on the road toward who I am today. Invincible. You can't scare me anymore, Spencer. I am unbreakable. *Try me.*"

I took a step back, still holding her gaze. I knew I would throttle her if I stayed close. Not because I didn't believe she didn't care about me, but because I *did*.

Lenora Astalis really didn't give a fuck.

She knew I was in her school and didn't steal one glance at me.

She didn't talk about me.

Think about me.

Chase after me.

And that was...*new*.

People cared—whether they wanted to give me head, be my girlfriend, my friend, my lab partner, associate, peer, or pet. Whatever they wanted to be to me, they always tried to make it happen. They regarded me with unwavering fascination. And me? I fed the legend. I didn't eat, sleep, or talk much publicly. The only human thing I did in front of an audience was let girls suck my dick at parties. Even that was me proving a point to myself, more than anyone else.

I smirked, grabbing her jaw and jerking her to my body. She thought I'd retreated when really, I just wanted another good look at that sweet ass before making it mine.

"You know, Good Girl, we're going to see a lot of each other the next few years."

"Years?" She let out an agitated laugh, not bothering to fold her arms and hide her tits from me. Which didn't exactly work in my favor. I had full control of my cock, true, but the bastard didn't deserve to be teased.

"Hold off making the friendship bracelets, Spencer. I've no intention of staying here. I'm moving back to England next year."

"So am I," I said evenly.

This had been the plan from the beginning. Get back to England once I graduated and do what I needed to do before opening a studio somewhere in Europe. A fresh start.

"You're moving to England?" She blinked, deciphering the meaning of this. I wanted to dip a hand between her thighs and see what the news did to her.

"Carlisle Prep," I snarled. "They have a pre-college internship program."

"I know. I'm applying there too." She sucked in a breath, panic finally trickling into her system.

Finally. My blood warmed at the sight of her face draining of color. Watching her react to me was like feeling the first rays of sun after a long winter.

The internship was a six-month program, working alongside Edgar Astalis and Harry Fairhurst on a piece of your choice. Astalis was dragging his haughty ass back from Cali exactly for that purpose. He loved Carlisle like it was his fucking baby.

You'll wish you'd kept an eye on your actual baby like you do your prep school, asshole.

She wanted the internship at Carlisle Prep just as much as I did, but for *very* different reasons. She wanted it because she was born for it—a student at Carlisle since the age of six and bearer of her father's legacy. Besides, the intern would get to exhibit their piece at Tate Modern at the end of the six-month term. It offered the kind of prestige that could buy your way to artistic stardom. And I wanted it because...

Because I wanted to feel the taste of blood on my tongue.

There were only two spots available per year, and rumor had it one was already going to Rafferty Pope, a genius, soon-to-be-alumni of Carlisle Prep who could paint an entire city landscape from memory. I'd heard Edgar was rocking the LAX-Heathrow route six to eight times a year to check up on his interns, not to mention disappearing in Europe for the summer.

"Putting the cart before the horse, I see." I took a rolling paper from my back pocket and poured crumbled weed into it, ignoring her nudity like it bored me. "Your chances of beating me at anything are tragically slim. Hope for your sake that you're applying to other places."

"I'm not," she informed me, her voice flat.

"Well, fuck if it's not going to suck when Daddy tells you you're not good enough," I chirped, tapping her nose with my unlit, rolled joint.

"Says you." She crossed her arms over her chest.

"Yes. The guy who deserves the internship. However, winner gets to choose an assistant from the applicants' list. Which means..." I looked up from the joint, rubbing my thumb along my bottom lip. "You could be my bitch for those six months. I like the sound of that, Lenora. Your neck would look pretty with a leash."

"I'm not the one who's going to be a prisoner if you go there," she said softly. "Carlisle is my playground, remember?"

She threatened. Me.

I was about to burst out laughing when she continued.

"Oh, and it's Lenny now," she hissed. "Lenora is an old person's name."

It was the first crack in her façade, where signs of the flaming-golden-haired girl peeked from behind the goth, pasty chick.

"Hate to break it to you, but Lenny is a Gremlin's name." I

stepped back, throwing the towel into her hands, finally showing an ounce of mercy. "Here. Cover up. I'm planning to eat sometime tonight. May I have my appetite back now?"

She made no move to put the robe on, likely just to spite me. I shook my head, realizing I'd been here far longer than I'd anticipated. The Astalis girl wasn't important enough to monopolize my time. I tucked my joint into the corner of my mouth and strolled toward the sliding glass doors, picking up her scattered clothes and throwing them over my shoulder, into the pool. She knew my secret. She had leverage on me, *and* we were competing for the same spot. Seemed like pissing all over my promise to Knight was in order.

Lenora's mother died, and that was tragic.

But what happened to me was terrible too.

Only difference was, my tragedy was silent and embarrassing, and hers, loud and publicly acknowledged.

I stopped at the glass doors, twisting my head around.

"This could get really ugly, Astalis."

"Already is." She flattened her lips, looking unnerved. "But if you look closely, you'll find beauty in the ugliness too."

I left without a word.

Lenora was officially my business, and even though I wasn't fond of complications, the thought of destroying her pierced me with euphoric desire.

She made ugly things beautiful.

I was going to show her my soul was marred beyond repair.

CHAPTER THREE
LENORA

My sister and I were having very different American high school experiences, and that put an invisible barrier between us.

Poppy was head-over-heels in lust with her boyfriend, quarterback superstar Knight Cole. Knight was summer—golden, promising, and reckless, always burning on the edge of something. He led the pack, so she had a temporary seat on the throne next to the king.

Which, I guess, made me the jester. I had the right to spend the time in the cool-kid kingdom's court but only as a source of entertainment.

Poppy never did anything mean to me, but she was too obsessed with fitting in to stop, or even recognize, when I'd been taunted.

For the most part, it didn't matter anyway. A snarky comment here, a Drusilla remark there. I could take it. It toughened me up, and a part of me began to feel elated, like I was above all the teenage bullshit.

The main offenders were Arabella and Alice.

Alice had a platinum pixie haircut, hazel eyes, and huge implants Arabella liked to refer to as "so very nineties." Arabella was tan, with cyan-blue eyes and long, coal-black hair that dangled by the edge of her bum.

They both hated me.

Come to think of it, *everyone* hated me.

My first semester as a senior at All Saints High proved to be the disaster I'd anticipated it to be. I'd spent most of my childhood and adolescence running with ghosts and chasing demons at Carlisle Prep. I had my best friend, Rafferty Pope, and other kids to play with.

In England, I'd always felt welcome and cherished.

Not so, here in California.

The black camouflage I'd adapted to shoo Vaughn away and show him I was not scared made people call me a freak and an outcast. No one but Poppy publicly acknowledged me unless it was to take a dig. Girls detested me for the way I dressed, the fact that I was always cradling a thick book in my hand, and that I answered Vaughn, Hunter, and Knight when they taunted me. Knight and Hunter as a banter, Vaughn more viciously.

They called me *trash* and *weirdo* for standing up for myself.

Even though the first few weeks had brought with them mildly interested guys of the alternative and goth variety, their attention died down once they realized Vaughn Spencer found me repulsive.

Which was literally the word he'd used.

Repulsive.

It had happened in the cafeteria some weeks into the clusterfuck of my American high school experience. Normally I picked a bench and ate by myself with a book, but this time, Poppy had insisted I hang out with her.

She did that sometimes—had a spurt of guilt and made me hang out with her mates. And I, driven by the same guilt as we grew apart, obliged.

I had been sitting with her and her friends Hunter, Arabella, and Stacee—who did their best to ignore me—when Vaughn strolled in and took a seat right between Poppy and Knight, directly in front of me.

Plastic utensils fell on trays with soft thuds and people whispered animatedly. Vaughn never came to the cafeteria. I'd heard all about his legendary antics. Us mortals weren't good enough to keep him company, if you didn't count him letting a select cluster of girls suck his penis when he was feeling generous.

Pretending I hadn't noticed him, I flipped through a copy of *The Night Circus*, taking a bite of my pizza. I was the only student in the entire cafeteria to buy a slice of greasy pizza. In Todos Santos, people treated carbs as though they were war criminals and sugar like it was poison. I was all harsh lines to begin with, with very few hints of curve, so I didn't quite care about losing my figure. Fine-looking things required maintenance, and I lacked the desire to be another pretty face.

I didn't understand the obsession with beauty. We all get old. We all get wrinkles. Life is short. Eat that pizza. Drink that wine. Shut down that bully eejit who tortures you.

Words of wisdom you need to tell yourself, Lenny.

"Vaughn! Why aren't you eating?" my sister purred, fawning over Satan himself.

I hadn't confided in her about his visit to our house the other day. She was the exact opposite of me. If Mum's death made me an angry, unapologetic teen, Poppy made it a point to become the nicest, most agreeable Mary Sue alive—as if being perfect and sweet would prevent people from leaving. From *dying*.

Yeah, once upon a time I'd been a good girl. It had earned me an archenemy. I should have bitten and kicked him when I had the chance, not let him set the tone of our dysfunctional relationship.

"Here, take my Caesar salad. I'm so full from that green shake I had this morning." Poppy slid her tray toward him.

Even as I flipped a page and tried to concentrate on the book, I could tell he was looking at me. I didn't get him. He'd come to my house—*broke* into it—and threatened me not to share his secret. I'd obliged without resistance. Even though I'd played it cool, I'd been mortified by him watching me stark naked. I hadn't spoken to a soul at All Saints High. Not about his secret, not about our history, and not at all.

He'd challenged me to a war I didn't want, but I wasn't going to avoid it at any cost.

Vaughn didn't answer Poppy. And Knight, who had the good sense not to bully me since he wanted to get into my sister's knickers, elbowed his ribs with a frown.

"Say thank you, Lord McCuntson. Poppy was being nice."

"I'm not hungry," he said with his well-practiced icy boredom.

My stomach twisted into deadly knots. I could feel the chill of his pale-cerulean eyes wherever they landed on me, and I suppressed the violent shivers prickling my skin.

"How come?" Arabella drawled seductively, not reading the room.

"I find certain things unappealing to a point of revulsion."

I saw his gaze from the corner of my eye, skating over my lips. He dug at the knee hole in his black skinny jeans. His knee was slightly tan, with golden hair—different than the sickly white-blue he'd been as a child. Smooth and muscular and unfairly perfect.

That was the tragic thing about Vaughn Spencer. He *was* perfect.

The cold shock of his beauty knocked the breath out of you like a supernova. With ruby, bee-stung lips and wild blue eyes framed by thick, masculine eyebrows and cheekbones right out of the comic books.

He was gorgeous, and I was not.

He was popular, and I was an outcast.

He was everything, and I was…

Heat rose up my neck, but I kept my eyes trained on the same line of the same page I'd started before he approached the table. I thought about something I'd read not too long ago about how the world breaks everyone, but the broken places end up being stronger as a result. Ernest Hemingway said that, and I hoped it was true.

I ignored it when the football team chuckled and bumped shoulders, pointing at me. Poppy glared at Vaughn, open-mouthed, furious, but too ladylike to make a scene.

"Vaughn finds life repulsive. Don't take it personally." Knight threw a french fry at Spencer, laughing to lighten the mood.

I could feel Arabella's eyes on me—assessing, taunting, waiting. She never could look at me without turning red. Sometimes she looked at Poppy the same way. I knew how territorial she was about Knight, Vaughn, and Hunter—the third amigo. She regarded them like some impossible prize. Them giving me attention rattled something deep inside her.

"Yeah. You're not repulsive in the slightest. I would fuck you and not even just anal. I would gladly look at your face as I plunge into you." Hunter snagged my can of Diet Coke and chugged it empty in one go.

If Knight was a golden boy and Vaughn was a bad boy, Hunter was a mix of the two, with hair a rich hue of wheat and a cunning smile even his mother couldn't trust.

"I would look into your eyes while eating you like a Del Taco on a road trip. Nasty but worth it," one of the jocks exclaimed, shooting me a wink.

"I raise you looking into her eyes and add an Atticus quote while I wreck her uterus. But that's gonna cost you a cream pie." A third *tsksed* in my direction, dipping his index and middle fingers into a cupcake on his tray suggestively.

Vaughn sat back, an amused smirk on his face.

I yawned, flipping another page without processing any of the text. Vaughn was pushing it. I was honoring my side of the deal between us and keeping my mouth shut, yet he deliberately antagonized me.

None of it made sense. Vaughn wasn't daft. He was cruel when messed with, but if you kept your distance, you were safe.

Why wasn't I safe?

"Thanks for the riveting mental images, dipshits." Vaughn stood up, glancing around. "Where's Alice Hamlin? I could use a blowie right now."

Jesus Christ.

"She's with her new boyfriend." Arabella tossed her hair, sucking her green shake's straw unnecessarily hard.

"Good. He can watch," Vaughn clipped, pivoting and making

a beeline to the doors. I'd almost taken a relieved breath—*almost*—when he paused and turned around, as if forgetting something.

"Lenora."

My name felt like whiplash curling on his tongue. Poppy winced. I had no choice but to look up. I put a little smile on my black-hued lips just to make sure he knew I wasn't impressed.

"You're a virgin, aren't you?" He cocked his head, another one of his patronizing smirks tossed my way.

"Duh, unless Lucifer was feeling desperate…" Arabella huffed, pretending to examine her hot-pink nails.

More laughter boomed across the cafeteria.

"That's *enough*," Knight hissed, pushing his tray until it bumped against a smug jock's abs.

His swift mood change made me think Vaughn had hit a sensitive nerve. As if *the* Knight Cole even knew what virginity meant. He probably thought a virgin was a Virginia-state resident.

"It's fine, Knight. I appreciate you coming to my rescue, but I don't need protection from toothless, ball-less dogs who bark but can't bite for shit," I said serenely, making a point of tucking a bookmark between the pages of my book.

"Whoa…" The guys at the table balled their fists, howling.

I turned to Hunter and the jocks and swept a bored look over their athletic bodies.

"Also, I appreciate the hospitality, but I'm rather adamant on sleeping with men, not immature twats who are only good for drinking, partying, and burning their parents' hard-earned cash, desperate to forget that high school is the peak of their lives. Which says something, because you're at an age when not wanking for a day seems like a herculean accomplishment."

Silence fell across the table. All eyes tried to penetrate the mask of indifference I was clinging to with bloodied fingernails.

Were they expecting me to cry? Cower? Run away?

To ask them why they did this?

Stifling another fake yawn, I licked my finger and flipped a page in my book, taking the bookmark out. My heart searched for an escape route, thrashing against my rib cage. One thing I knew about men like Vaughn Spencer—they either broke you or you broke them. There was no middle ground.

But I wasn't going to be the one picking up the pieces when we were done with each other.

"You should come and see how it's done." Vaughn ignored my comeback, his iron voice slicing the air between us. "Prep you for next year, Good Girl."

I looked up, despite my best intentions.

"When you assist me, silly. I'm sure your father thinks it's a great idea."

No, he doesn't.

But when was the last time I'd spoken to Papa about my art? About *me*? He was too busy, and I was too shy to demand his attention. He *could* think that. He could.

"Never."

"Never is a very long time," Vaughn mused, his voice sweet and faraway all of a sudden. "Pride comes before the fall."

"Don't be so sure I'll be the one doing the falling."

"Considering you can barely fucking walk without tripping over your own feet, I'm hardly shaking."

"Course not, Vaughn. The only things that scare you are feelings and little girls who walk into the wrong place at the wrong time."

I'd been busting my bum for years for this internship. I wasn't going back to Carlisle Castle as an assistant to an intern. I was going to *be* the intern. Assisting a star intern was prestigious, and I'd have loved the opportunity, but not if the intern was Vaughn.

Never the ocean-eyed god.

I felt my nostrils flare as I stared back at him. I hated him with abandon, with passion that seared through my veins. Fury could be either a weapon or a liability, but in my case, it was both.

There was nothing diabolical about him. No. The devil was red, hot, expressive, and desolate. Vaughn was the Night King—cold, blue, dead, and calculating. You couldn't get to him, no matter how hard you tried.

I thought wearing black clothes, eyeliner, and making up elaborate stories about my summer in Brazil for fellow students who didn't care would show him how much I'd changed. But he kept challenging every syllable to come out of my mouth.

It was time to fight back.

"You know what? I think a lesson in oral is an *excellent* idea. And who could teach it better than the *expert*?" I shot to my feet, pushing my tray aside.

I had actually been enjoying my pizza before he arrived, but I wasn't hungry anymore. I also knew my calling him an expert was getting dangerously close to the truth about what had happened in the darkroom that day.

"Shall I bring a notebook to take pointers? Perhaps an iPad?" I smiled, blinking angelically at him.

"Just your smart ass."

If Vaughn was confused and taken aback, he didn't show it. Poppy, however, shot up in an instant.

"Lenny!" She slapped her heart. "Why would you ever—"

"Go back to pretending you have a personality, soul, or prospects that do not include marrying a rich, fat asshole who's going to cheat on you with his secretary and give you ugly-ass kids, Daffodil," Vaughn barked at my sister, his icicle eyes still holding mine. "This is between me and your sister."

"It's Poppy!" she exclaimed, Knight tugging her by the hem of her skirt to sit back down.

"Because that was the entire fucking problem with what I just told you." Vaughn's mouth twitched in menace.

I grabbed my Sprayground shark backpack and followed Vaughn out of the cafeteria, acutely aware that all eyes were pointed at our backs as we exited through the double doors.

Knight's voice rang behind me, gruff, low, and lazy. "Y'all gonna slow dance to a Billy Joel song? If so, don't forget to leave room for Jesus. And Moses. And Muhammad. And also Post Malone, because hey, he's kind of a religion now too."

As we filed into the buzzing hallway, I couldn't help but notice how tall Vaughn had become. Whether he ate at school or not, the boy *ate*, all right. He filled his clothes nicely. He wasn't beefy by any stretch of the imagination but muscular, with sinewy dexterity and the grace of an archer. In fact, there was nothing boyish about him anymore. He was all man, and it was ironic that he reminded me so much of the iconic, imperial statues he carved.

"What's good, Good Girl? I mean, other than your untouched hymen," he asked, gliding along the hall, looking for Alice.

I found it hard to believe he'd be able to rip her from her boyfriend's arms, but stranger things had happened where Vaughn Spencer was concerned. Plus, I knew Alice. She fancied Vaughn for all his eccentric, tyrannical behavior.

"Spare me the bullshit, Vaughn. You hate me."

"Hate you?" he mused in *Thinker* pose, fist curled under his square chin. "No, that requires commitment. I find you embarrassingly disposable. Are you going to chicken out on me, Astalis?"

"No," I clipped. "You seem eager to show everyone your willy. You are aware fifty percent of the world population is male, right? Your cock is not a national treasure."

"Don't slam it before you've tasted it." His jaw twitched, and he seemed done with the conversation.

I'd hit a nerve. Why was Vaughn so fond of having an audience when he was intimate with girls?

And while we were on the subject—why did he choose the *least* intimate way to be intimate with girls? One that didn't require him to touch, to caress, to reciprocate?

A few seconds of silence passed before he rounded a corner and snapped his fingers, motioning for me to follow him.

Alice.

"You really think a girl who is with someone is going to suck you off? On school grounds? While people are watching?" I couldn't help but blurt.

"Yes."

"Is this a game to you?"

"If it were, I'd be dealing you the fucking cards. Now shut up."

I'd heard all about Vaughn and public blowjobs. There wasn't one person in this school—other than me—who hadn't seen the shape and size of his (allegedly impressive) penis disappearing down a girl's throat. Sometimes there were two of them, licking and taking turns. People said it was because he was handsome, unconventional, and the richest boy in town that every girl secretly wanted to marry into the Spencer family, who were royalty by name, assets, and reputation. They were old money—railroads, prime realty, and hedge fund companies—and one of America's top twenty-five richest families.

His ancestors had built this town, and he was going to inherit most of it.

But I thought there were other reasons girls gave Vaughn what he wanted.

Essentially, deep down, we all liked to be sexually degraded, just a bit. The taboo aspect, the helplessness, the part where you're at the complete mercy of someone else.

We're all a little sadomasochistic.

Especially when young.

And powerful.

And beautiful.

And rich.

The numbness of a charmed life was easily taken away by shame, something Vaughn distributed in spades. He liked humiliating people. A lot.

Vaughn stopped in front of a set of black-and-navy lockers. Alice was wearing a sweetheart-neckline flowery dress with puffy sleeves and a slit across the side. The guy next to her was a bit on the short side, and he looked moneyed to death, with an expensive haircut and a smart, nav- blue blazer. He had kind, brown eyes and a quirky vibe.

"Alice," Vaughn hissed, ignoring the guy.

"Oh, hey, Spence." She blew a lock of her short hair away from her eyes, her pink lips curling in delight.

I wanted to throw up when she leaned forward to give him a peck on the cheek, shaking her boyfriend's arm from her waist.

"I can fit in a quick blowjob in the next ten minutes. Rookie here needs to take pointers." Vaughn threw a thumb behind him, toward me.

Alice's gaze collided with mine, and her eyes widened for a fraction of a second.

You and me both, girl.

"Ummm…" She glanced at the guy next to her, biting on the side of her fingernail.

His eyes were widening slowly, shock seeping into his system. She was going to ditch him. The worst part about it, she wasn't even considering telling Vaughn to bugger off. Her eyes said *I'm sorry*, not *Would you mind?*

"Jason…" she started.

I wanted to punch her on his behalf, bile rising in my throat like an overflowing saucepan. He stared at her, agony dripping from his expression, wordlessly pleading with her not to finish the sentence.

"Practice makes perfect, though, right?" I interjected with a chirp, taking a step forward. "And since Alice is oh so kind as to demonstrate her flawless oral-giving technique on Vaughn, would you mind being my guinea pig, Jason?" I unzipped my leather jacket, shrugging out of it and flinging it over my shoulder. I offered him my hand for a shake.

It was perfect, really—the look of horror on Alice's face when

Jason threw a look at Vaughn, whose jaw was ticking, and took my hand, shaking it limply.

"Don't worry. I'll still be watching." I patted Vaughn's back, keeping my tone light as the four of us headed down the corridor to God knows where. "Although, I may have a few tricks up my sleeve." I winked.

Lies.

I'd never given a blowjob before and, up until a minute ago, had no immediate plans to perform the act on anyone but Alexander Skarsgård, who, unfortunately, I had no real prospects of ever meeting. But Vaughn was pushing me, and Jason was trying hard not to cry, even though his humiliation was bloated and hanging in the air like fog.

If I could recover some of Jason's self-esteem, while shocking Vaughn into understanding that I was no pushover, maybe he'd finally back off.

But Vaughn didn't look shocked at all. He looked…*pissed.* His jaw was ticking so hard, I thought it might snap out of his mouth and bite my face off. He tugged at my sleeve, jerking me forward, forcing me to keep up with his pace, a few feet ahead of Jason and Alice.

"What the fuck are you trying to do? Prove a point?" He bared his teeth.

"What point would that be? That I have a mouth?" I smiled serenely, taking weird pleasure in knowing he was irritated. "Maybe I want to get some action too."

"With that fuckboy?" Vaughn snorted, his nostrils flaring. I matched his stride, desperate not to pant. "He wouldn't know how to get you off with four dildos, a magic wand, a vibrator, and the entire football squad."

I would've laughed if I wasn't so nervous about what we were about to do.

"Some like dark, tall, and handsome. I like fair, short, and…sane."

Vaughn yanked a door open and shoved me inside wordlessly with a force that said he was royally pissed. The room was dark, cluttered, and stuffy. It smelled of dust and cleaning products. The janitor's room, I figured.

Enchanting.

Alice and Jason joined us, and Vaughn shut the door behind them. He flicked the light on. Still frowning, he started working his belt in angry, jerky movements.

"I can help you with that." Alice licked her lips, waiting for his okay.

Jason eyed me warily, expecting directions.

What have I gotten myself into?

"Jason, come here." I waved him over awkwardly, gathering my tar-dyed hair and dropping it over one shoulder. He shuffled toward me, bumping his knee on a broomstick on his way. Vaughn's hawk eyes followed us as Alice continued unbuckling him. The sound of the metal clicking made my heart jolt.

Alice cupped Vaughn's groin through his black briefs, but he was still looking at me.

"Lenora." His voice held a threatening edge, cruel and cutting, like broken glass. I knew a warning when I heard one.

Ignoring him, my unstable fingers worked Jason's buttoned trousers. Flashes of me in Carlisle Castle, shaking under Vaughn Spencer's finger like a leaf, ran through the dark corridors of my brain. He thought I was such a naïve, weak girl.

If I had to suck a stranger off to show him I too had a dangerous edge, I'd make the sacrifice and deal with the psychological damage later.

Holding on to all that unchanneled hate would likely give me a heart attack as it was.

Even though I hadn't intended for it to happen, Jason's trousers slid down, the fabric pooling around his ankles with a soft thud. He was in his briefs now, and already hard. I watched the bulge of his penis, plastered to his stomach through the fabric—like a leech, long and swollen and frightening.

Lenny, you daft cow, you really did it this time.

No part of me wanted to do this. The right course of action had to be informing the educational staff and my father that Vaughn had been bullying me. Not that he did exactly that. He hadn't forced me to do anything, but he challenged my every step and made sure I remembered I didn't belong.

This wasn't a movie though. No one would find my actions heroic or acceptable if I came forward and complained. People were going to call me a snitch, turn against me, and seek me out, whereas now, most of them simply ignored me or called me names. All told, I had a little less than one year to endure here in California. I could suck it up.

"*Lenora*," Vaughn said again, his princely voice sharp as a blade.

Swallowing, I put a tentative hand on Jason's...*member*. It jumped. I jumped right along with it, letting out an involuntary yelp.

"Are you okay?" A frown knit Jason's brows as he shifted from foot to foot uncomfortably.

He was obviously doing this for the same reason I was: retaliation. Alice was mad to dump him for Vaughn.

"All evidence points to that being the case," I blabbed, releasing a nervous chuckle. "I'm grand, really. This is...lovely. I mean, not your penis." Penises were not lovely, were they? "Not that I'm saying that your penis is *not* lovely. It's just. Oh...never mind."

"Yup. A virgin," Vaughn said from beside me, victorious satisfaction laced in his voice.

He was laughing, just like he had when he'd caught my eyelids moving the night It Happened. Lava boiled in the pit of my stomach, and with newly found rage, I dropped to my knees and looked at Vaughn.

Alice quickly mimicked my movements, like it was a competition, getting down on her knees and trying to yank at Vaughn's black briefs. He snatched her hand and kept them in place, not letting her pull them down, his eyes on mine.

I curled my fingers around the edge of Jason's briefs and pulled them down. I wasn't going to admit my virginity here, in this room, for Vaughn to laugh at me for eternity.

Jason's penis sprung out, purple and angry, just inches from my face. I sucked in a shocked breath and reminded myself about the ghosts in Carlisle Castle. If I could handle sleeping in a haunted place all alone in a room, surely I could handle a penis, and not even a disproportionately huge one.

"Len…" Vaughn's voice trailed off. For the first time, he didn't sound so darkly amused by me and my antics.

I grabbed Jason's penis, my entire body shaking with anger and adrenaline. I wanted to do this, to piss Vaughn off beyond repair. To hurt him. To hurt *me*. I leaned forward, screwing my eyes shut and thinking good thoughts…

Home.

Far away from here.

Home.

Chips with vinegar and ice-cold cider.

Home.

Running wildly in the fields behind my house, letting the grass slap my ankles.

Home.

Working in the studio again.

Home.

Making beautiful things out of ugly things.

Home.

Kissing boys. The right boys. Boys who don't make me feel like dying.

Home. Home. Home.

"Fuck!"

I felt myself jerked by the collar of my Metallica shirt to the other side of the room. Vaughn was now standing between me and

Jason, as a buffer, while I was still on the floor. He pointed back at me, facing Jason.

"What is wrong with you, you pile of oxygen-wasting shit? You could *see* she didn't want it."

"Is this a joke? You just propositioned my girlfriend in front of me!" Jason shrieked, his face bright red and glistening with cold sweat.

"Your girlfriend is *not* a virgin," Vaughn yelled.

"And that makes it cool for you to treat her like a cum-bag? Don't spin this on me, Spencer. There's only one twisted mother-fucker in this room, and it's the guy who just told my girl she should suck him off in front of his crush to make a point."

Vaughn threw his head back and laughed while Jason tucked his half-mast penis back into his briefs, pulling up his trousers. With every second that he became more dressed, I felt my heartbeat calming down.

Vaughn mumbled the word *crush* like the idea was crazy. I was going to kick him in the bollocks. I even had a good angle from my spot on the floor.

"Get the fuck out of here and don't come near her again. Tell your douchebag, debate-club friends to do the same. They get near Lenora Astalis, they die. Everyone knows she is my property. And take *her* with you." Vaughn shoved Alice in Jason's direction, his face expressionless, and pushed them both out. He slammed the door shut just as the bell rang. I scrambled to my feet, lifting my chin. It was musky and entirely too small in here. I wanted to get out.

Most of all, I didn't want to look at Vaughn's face after he'd seen me mortified by a human penis like it was a three-headed monster.

"Your property?" I growled. "Screw you, Spencer. I'd Airbnb myself to sex-diseased gang members before letting you cop a feel."

"Shut up," he snapped, turning his back to me again and bracing himself on the desk, clutching its edges with his fingers. He couldn't even look at me, he was so angry.

Just as well. I was done with him too.

"I have lab." I started for the door.

He grabbed my wrist, turning me to him. I looked up, expecting him to appear smug. Triumphant. Happy. Vaughn received blowjobs from anyone with a pulse in this part of the state, and I'd never touched a penis in my life. Today just confirmed that.

How fantastic.

To my surprise, his face was devoid of any emotion—the usual cold, unreadable air I couldn't crack. A blank canvas.

I guess he wasn't so mocking when we were alone. Just quietly cruel.

"You skipped a grade," he said.

What?

I scowled, hoping my cheeks and ears weren't as red as they felt.

"When?" he pressed.

"Ninth to tenth."

"Why?"

I'd lost my mother and shut the world down. I focused on studying and making art and staring at my bedroom ceiling, perched in my bed, listening to "Last Night I Dreamt" by the Smiths on loop, smoking nasty clove cigarette butts I'd found behind the rosebushes of Carlisle Prep.

I'd decided falling in love was pointless. We all die in the end. I'd even told Papa so—that I wanted to marry my art, like he did after Mum. Art never leaves. It never dies. It never ceases to wake up one morning.

Ars Longa, Vita Brevis.

Art is long, life is short. I tattooed it on my inner thigh the moment I turned seventeen—somewhere private and intimate, to remind myself all I wanted to give birth to was more beautiful, lifeless things.

"Some of us have goals that don't include catching STDs and getting high. I work hard for what I want."

"You stayed in England when your dad and sister moved here. Why?"

Because of you.

But that was only partly true. Going away felt like leaving Mum behind.

I said nothing.

"What made you come here? Why now?"

Papa had twisted my arm. Besides, loneliness had nibbled at my insides, like cancer. I'd put on war paint, hoping it'd be enough to keep Vaughn away. As it turned out, he took this as an invitation to battle and geared up for combat.

"What about boyfriends? Girlfriends? Social life?" His fingers around my wrist tightened into a bruising grip.

I wanted to cry. Not because he was hurting me, but because I *liked* it. I liked that he wasn't treating me with kid gloves because I'd lost my mother. I liked that he was experienced and unfazed by sex. I liked that he was stunning, cold, and promising like Christmas morning, and I had his undivided attention, even if it was the wrong kind of attention. And I was absolutely horrified to find out a part of me wanted him to bend my wrist harder until the dull pain became a sharp one.

I shook my head. My personal life was none of his business.

"No social life." He tsked. "Fine. How's the internship project going? What are you handing over?"

Why did he care? He'd just invited me to see someone sucking his cock. I looked the opposite way, at the wall, ignoring him. The less I responded, the more he'd grow tired and bored of me.

"I started working on mine yesterday," he informed me. "The composition was a bitch to figure out."

Was he making small talk?

"There's no way you'll be able to turn it in on time," I said.

We had to hand in our submissions for the internship fairly soon. My project was done. I just had some fine-tuning to do.

He shrugged.

My heart began to race. This was good. This meant he was behind, and I had more of a chance to snag the spot.

I swallowed, trying to hide my glee.

"Don't worry, even quarter-finished, your father will choose my project over yours any day."

I said nothing to that, so he continued.

"You know…" His cocky smirk reappeared just when I thought I was saved from it, and my blood boiled in my veins again, my eyes hooding with lust and irritation. "What I told you behind that fountain when we were kids still applies."

He leaned against the desk, jerking me into his long, hard body. I was flush against him now, and he felt like granite against my soft limbs.

"I could kiss you, and you'd still let me. Because you're still good, and I'm still bad. Nothing has changed. We're still the same kids. Our game is just more dangerous now."

And my mother is no longer alive to warn me off sugar or boys like you, I thought bitterly.

"I thought you weren't dealing our cards just yet." I arched an eyebrow.

"I changed my mind. One little game won't hurt. Me, anyway."

"Test it, then," I hissed. I wanted to make my first chip in him, so when he came to break me, I'd know where to aim.

He stared at me for a moment, his gaze dipping from mine to my lip ring. He leaned down, almost in slow motion, going in for the kiss. I couldn't believe what I was seeing. What he was *doing*. The boy who hated me brought his lips to mine. But there was nothing romantic about it.

It was a dare. A bet. Another challenge.

A power play.

When our lips touched, a shiver skated down my spine like a lit match. He traced his lips along the seam of mine patiently, his hot breath fanning my mouth. My heart accelerated to a dangerous speed, fireflies bursting forth as though escaping a mason jar. Kissing him was like standing on the edge of a cliff. Nice view but you knew it was deadly. Still, a stupid, irrational, dangerously alive part of you wanted to hurl yourself down to meet your own demise.

I felt his lips on more than just my lips.

I felt them in my fingertips, all the way down to my toes.

I felt them when my skin broke into goose bumps.

He was actually doing it. Kissing me. The minute his mouth locked in on mine, I opened up and clamped my teeth around his lower lip, not stopping until I dug so hard, I could feel my teeth slamming against each other. Warm blood filled my mouth. He didn't retreat, and I didn't let go. I dug harder with my teeth as his hand moved between us, his thumb slipping into my lip piercing, tugging at it tauntingly, hurting me back.

He smiled into our kiss. He liked it, I realized. Me hurting him. Making him bleed.

It was only when he was about to yank the ring out of my lip that I finally pulled back. He dropped his hand completely.

So this was the game, I thought. *I hurt him, and he hurt me back, but only as much as I could tolerate.*

I ran my tongue along my teeth, savoring his warm, salty blood. When I looked at him again, he looked incredibly mortal all of a sudden. Boyish even. With a red slash of blood smeared over his mouth, waiting for me to say something.

To acknowledge he wasn't the only screwed-up person in the room.

"You were wrong. I didn't want you to kiss me." I licked the corner of my lips, mocking him.

He smirked, leaning down and capturing the tip of my ear with his teeth, whispering. "You wanted it, you enjoyed it, and next time I touch you, Good Girl, I'm not only going to dirty you up. I'm going to make you filthy, like me."

Three things happened simultaneously from that day onward:

1. Vaughn began to monitor my interactions at school, especially with the lads. Guys stopped acknowledging my presence completely, in all grades and statuses, other than Knight and Hunter, who weren't scared of their lunatic mate. Everyone else caught word that Lenny Astalis was Vaughn's unwilling possession, and even though I had no interest in any of them, I still thought they were cowards for listening to Vaughn. Of course, I was the worst type of property—the neglected kind. Vaughn went even further out of his way to make sure people knew I was nothing to him. There was a brief rumor about my catching chlamydia from a Brazilian male model I'd allegedly had sex with over the summer, but it died quickly when Vaughn said no one was desperate enough to fuck me.

2. The girls, who all heard different versions of what happened in the janitor's room (exclusively from Alice and Arabella) and knew now without a shadow of a doubt that Vaughn had taken an unlikely interest in me, went from disliking me to actively despising me. Poppy often had to skip some of her afterschool activities just to see me home and make sure no one was following or harassing me. Arabella and Alice continued to call me Vampire Girl because of my attire and fondness for all things black, and they nagged me about Vaughn whenever they came to visit Poppy. Their questions were met with silence.

3. Vaughn began to show up at my house nearly every day to work on his mysterious project with my father.

Papa had taken a liking to Vaughn when he'd first witnessed his artistic greatness at summer session, and now that Vaughn had expressed interest in working closely with him, I guess Papa felt flattered. Even though Vaughn wasn't aware of the fact that I was too starstruck to talk to my own father about my art, he knew he was hurting me by coming here. Every time I opened the door and he was on the other side with his sculpting equipment, he gave me a lopsided grin that reminded me he'd kissed me not too long ago, that no matter how disgusting I found him, I'd once had his blood in my mouth.

His bottom lip was still bruised from my bite.

"Given up on that internship yet?" he'd ask.

"In your dreams," I'd answer, and he'd laugh good-naturedly and shake his head, brushing past me.

CHAPTER FOUR
LENORA

On the day Knight broke up with Poppy, I sat in her room, stroking her hair.

The boy who'd warned guys off of her because he was so worried for her precious heart ended up stomping all over it like it was a dance floor.

I kept busy trying to keep my sister from flinging herself off our roof.

The rumor that Poppy had been prematurely disposed of for a college girl spread like wildfire in a hayfield at All Saints High. Her locker had been graffitied, and when she'd opened it today, she found a real human turd on top of her books with a Post-it Note:

Dumped!

Knight had been nowhere in sight today, and Poppy had sworn off going back to school for the remainder of the year. I hugged and consoled her all evening. Poppy rightfully couldn't trust her so-called best friends, Alice and Arabella, who had been the first to spread the gossip of her breakup down the corridors of the school.

The queen bees of All Saints had turned against my sister now that she was no longer under the protection of *the* Knight Cole.

The year had been crappy with a side of shite to me, but Poppy actually liked it here before the whole Knight debacle. I'd made no friends, gone on no dates, and collected no memories. In a lot of ways, it felt like a long, excruciating night, with no dreams or even nightmares to occupy my mind—a big, fat nothing of staring at the ceiling that made me wonder if I really even existed.

At least we were nearing graduation. I still hadn't applied to any colleges, in Europe or elsewhere, praying for that internship. Wherever Vaughn went, even if it was to England with me, I'd be in my home field. He wouldn't have so much power there. Anyway, he still wasn't done with his piece, and who knows what he'd actually sent them when the internship application was due. It had been a month now. But I had bigger fish to fry.

Knight wasn't a bad person, but as a boyfriend, he was rubbish, and I thought Poppy deserved a lot more than what he'd offered her.

"Let it all go." I stroked Poppy's light hair, kissing the crown of her head while she nestled in my arms on her bed. She had a canopy-style princess bed, all baby pink and white, and a vanity desk the size of my entire room. I didn't care about those sorts of things, but Poppy did.

I didn't fault her for that. We were who we were. She had to take care of me at school because I got into trouble all the time.

Poppy blew her nose into the hem of my kilt, and I let her.

"He is such an arsehole!" she exclaimed, bursting out in a fresh bout of tears.

"A world-class one." I nodded, rallying behind her statement. "He should be internationally recognized for the level of arsehole-ness he exhibits."

"But he's so gorgeous."

"Sure, if you're into that Shawn-Mendes-meets-Chase-Crawford look. But there are a lot of gorgeous guys, and you deserve one who will recognize just how special you are." I gently removed the hair that stuck to her damp cheek, tucking it behind her ear.

Poppy sat up, patting her eyes with a tattered tissue.

"Am I, though?" She narrowed her puffy eyes at me.

I plucked some fresh tissues from her nightstand and handed them to her, along with a bottle of water.

"Are you what?" I asked.

"Special. *You* are special, Lenny. With your art and quirky attitude and the way you pretend not to care when gorgeous, rich guys like Vaughn Spencer make you a walking target. But I'm not like that. I'm not talented or strong or particularly interesting. I don't have any special looks or clothes or abilities. I'm not even book smart." She sniffled, eyeing me with a suspicious frown now, like it was my fault she chose to wear mainstream, high-end brands and put highlights in her hair and have normal, popular "friends."

"You can be talented and completely horrible," I said cautiously, thinking of Vaughn. "And you can also have not even one artistic bone in your body and still be the rarest thing in the universe. It's in your actions. It's your soul. You are special, Poppy, because you make people feel good. No one can take that away from you."

She sank into my arms, and we sat there for what seemed like forever, hugging and rocking back and forth, relishing the bitter-sweet agony of loving a boy who didn't love her back—not that I knew anything about that. Heartbreak was a mystical, double-edged sword from where I was standing. And I had no desire to experience the full range of emotions in a car crash of feelings. Not *ever* going there.

That day in the janitor's closet had rattled me. Not that I'd found Jason's...*member* appealing, but there was a thrill there. If I was being honest with myself, the thrill had more to do with biting Vaughn's lip and watching as he licked his own blood with a little smirk and less to do with Jason. I liked that Vaughn had pulled me away from Alice's boyfriend, that he was possessive of me. And even though I'd heard of his antics since then—disappearing with girls into rooms during parties I wasn't invited to—I also knew he wondered.

He wondered who I was seeing.

Who I was with and what I was doing with them.

I fed his curiosity and played his mind games.

I was always on my phone at school. I texted Rafferty, my best friend from Carlisle Prep, and smiled at the phone. I put a hand to my cheek and pretended to blush.

On nights I knew Vaughn would show up at my house—because my father was already in his studio, preparing his tools—I'd go out, even if just for a drive, and come back with my hair messy and my black lipstick purposely smeared.

I drove him crazy because he was driving *me* insane. I wanted to fight him, to hurt him for what he was doing to me. Bite him. Taste him. Feel him.

I often snuck into the house as he was leaving, tired and dirty, his hair a disheveled mess. He would climb into his beat-up truck and frown at me silently, as if trying to squeeze answers out of me telepathically.

"Lenora?"

I heard a soft knock on Poppy's door. Dad must've heard my voice coming from this room.

"Come in, Papa." Poppy quickly wiped the remainder of her tears with the tissue I'd given her and straightened her back, plastering a rather creepy smile on her face. She never wanted to upset our father. One of the many sacrifices she'd made since we'd lost Mum. Poppy was the epitome of a considerate daughter, while I wore morbid clothes and bit boys who pissed me off.

My father stood in the doorway, his long, gray, curly hair spiraling atop his head like an eccentric Elton John hat, his beard almost reaching his round Buddha belly. Papa looked like a Harry Potter character—a soft-hearted wizard professor who seemed big and intimidating but wouldn't hurt a fly. He loved Mum and us, I knew, but I always had the distinct feeling we came right after his art.

Mum hadn't wanted him to open Carlisle Prep—he still had.

Mum would have killed him if she were alive to see that he'd ripped us from England to America for his project. He couldn't resist a good challenge.

Papa knew I never wanted a life outside art, and he never pushed me for more—not to date boys, not to make friends who weren't Rafferty, not to live life.

The list went on, naturally.

"What are you girls up to?" He glanced between us with an apologetic smile. That was the sort of relationship we had with Papa. A bit too formal for my liking.

Again, he *cared*—didn't miss one parent-teacher conference and always made sure we were provided for and did something fantastic over the summer. He planned elaborate trips—admiring the wild architecture of Valencia, museums in Hong Kong, galleries in Florence, the pyramids of Egypt. Being a father, however, did not come as naturally to him as being an artist.

It was the Vaughns of the world he found a common language with.

"Oh, nothing much. Just gossiping. How are you, Papa?" Poppy singsonged, springing to her feet and smoothing her pajamas. "You must be starving. Shall I put some leftover lasagna in the microwave for you?"

I tried not to stare at her too bewilderedly. I wondered what it felt like to cut your feelings off with scissors, like a broken marionette. In trying to be so strong, she weakened herself. I hated to see her hurting.

"That'd be grand, Pop. Cheers. Lenny, may I have a word with you?" He reached his giant, cracked palm in my direction.

I took it and silently stood up.

It was unlike Papa to initiate a serious conversation. Had Vaughn told him something? Did he snitch on me? Tell him I was seeing boys? Not that Papa would care. If anything, he would encourage it.

What the hell was it?

"In the studio." Papa tugged my hand, leading me to the attic, where he had a small studio—in addition to the one in our backyard where he kept some of his unfinished work. The attic was more intimate.

I followed him, racking my brain for what was to come. My father and I chatted all the time during dinners and when we were watching the telly. We talked about the weather and school and Poppy's busy schedule and his work. The only thing we didn't talk about was *me*.

Even when I'd given him my final piece for the internship assignment last month—a human-sized skull made solely from vintage tin cans—I'd quickly averted the conversation to something else, careful not to catch any disappointment or boredom he might be feeling toward my art.

I was expecting the results about that any day now, but in the form of a formal letter. I knew better than to expect my father to bend the rules and break the news to me in person.

We climbed up the narrow, spiraling stairs to the attic. The white wooden floor creaked under our weight as we entered the roof-shaped loft. The aroma of shaved stone, the coldness of the marble and granite giants, and clouds of dust did nothing to disguise the unique scent of Vaughn Spencer that immediately crawled into my nostrils—delicious, formidable, and full of danger. I tried to ignore it—and the shiver it brought along.

He had been here tonight. I had heard their voices drifting through the open window of the attic only ten minutes ago.

"Gentle with the chisel, now, lad. Do not cock this one up. It's too precious for both of us."

"Put down the power drill. Slow strokes. Love this stone like it's a person."

"Let's call it a day. You've been battling this piece all night. You are not in sync with it. You are at war."

Vaughn was struggling with the piece, and I wasn't at all sure he'd submitted any other project for the internship. That gave me hope. Maybe I did have a chance. At least I'd handed in my piece in a timely manner.

"Sit down," Papa instructed with a tired groan, pointing at a huge, untouched stone in the corner of the room.

I brushed away *Human Anatomy for Artists* by Eliot Goldfinger, which sat atop it, and did as I was told, crossing my legs at the ankles. I ignored the huge horizontal piece covered by a large, white sheet standing in the corner of the studio. I knew how intimate an artist's relationship was with his work. It was like being pregnant, knowing the baby inside you was growing each day—more cells, longer limbs, more defined facial features.

I also knew that was Vaughn's piece, and I was not supposed to see it.

"You are going to receive a letter from the board, but I thought this warranted a more personal conversation. Let me start by saying that your assemblage piece was phenomenal. The way you worked the tin, the little escape wheels for eyes, the detail—it was fantastically executed. It evoked many emotions in all three of us. Your uncle Harry called you a genius, and Alma said yours was by far her favorite. I've never been prouder to call you my daughter."

My breath fluttered in my lungs, and I tried to keep my smile at bay. It was happening. I was getting the internship. I'd already decided what I wanted to show at Tate Modern. I had it all planned. I needed to sketch it first, but the bones were there. It had come to me in my sleep, the night I bit Vaughn.

"Thank you. I—"

"Lenny, you know I love you, right?" Papa crooned, his head falling into his huge, open palms all of a sudden.

Uh-oh.

"Yeah. Of course," I faltered.

"Do you really, though?" he asked from between the cracks of his fingers, peeking through them like a little boy.

Suddenly, I was pissed at him. Because he wasn't a little boy. He was a grown-up man. And he was taking the easy way out, playing on my emotions.

"You sound like you're sending me off to a boarding school on the other side of the world. A bit late for that, Papa." I kept my tone light, clearing my throat.

Then it hit me. My stupid joke turned into a brutal reality.

No. No, no, no.

Papa dropped his hands from his face and averted his gaze to the floor. When I said nothing, he started pacing the room, back and forth, his hands knotted behind his back. He stopped after a few seconds, as if deciding what course of action he wanted to take, and pivoted toward me, leaning down and putting his heavy hands on my shoulders. He caught my gaze, the intensity radiating through his eyes almost knocking me down.

"You're enough," he said.

"Of course," I managed, feeling the walls of the tiny studio closing in on me.

This wasn't happening. God, please. I'd worked so hard. This was all I'd ever wanted—to have my work exhibited at Tate Modern. I didn't enjoy sordid relationships and midnight blowjobs at rich kids' pool parties or flirt with drugs, fights, and the wrong side of the law. My parents weren't Californian royalty. I didn't have football friends and popularity and the entire bloody world at my feet.

All I'd ever asked for was this internship.

"You are. And one day, you will see that I mean this, but, Lenny... you didn't get the internship."

I closed my eyes and took a shaky breath, refusing to let the tears fall. I wanted to believe him. But if I were the best, I'd have gotten the internship. We both knew that.

"Vaughn Spencer?" I heard myself asking. I didn't dare breathe. I knew if I twitched or even moved a finger, I would go berserk and crash, break, and destroy everything in sight—knock over the statue

Vaughn was working on, rip the walls down, and jump headfirst into the pool, praying to hit the bottom and die.

I'd sat back and let Vaughn do this—worm his way into my father's good graces, right here in Todos Santos. I'd let him into my kingdom, into my family, into my *house*, every single day, and watched as he stole the only thing I cared about night after night. Because I stupidly thought my work would speak for itself, that he couldn't cheat his way into the gig.

I was exactly the naive little idiot he saw me to be.

"Yes," my father confirmed behind the fog of my red anger.

I popped my eyes open and darted up from the stone.

"His project is not even finished! He told me himself!" I seethed.

I never raised my voice to my father. Or anyone else, for that matter. Right now, my cool was slipping through my fingers like water.

My father stood across from me, his arms open as if he was surrendering. "Yet it still appears a cut above the rest, though it is not half-finished."

"Not even half-finished?!" I exclaimed wildly, throwing my arms in the air. "Is that even allowed? Is it not against your rules and regulations or whatever? Maybe I should've just presented you with a fucking can of Heinz."

I was grasping at straws. The board of Carlisle Prep, and the internship judges, consisted of the three founders of the school—my father; his cousin he'd grown up with, painter Harry Fairhurst; and Lady Alma Everett-Hodkins, a former chief curator at the Guggenheim. If they'd decided to choose Vaughn, there was nothing I could do about it. I was Don Quixote, fighting windmills, knowing they'd continue turning no matter how much I wiggled my imaginary sword at them.

"Lenny, his is not a good piece." Papa closed his eyes, his face marred with pain. "It is an astonishingly brilliant one, and if you saw it, you'd agree."

"Great idea. Why don't you show me this quarter-finished bullshit so I can judge for myself." I kicked a block of modeling clay, sending it spinning across the floor until it bumped against the wall. "Show me what's so brilliant about a general fucking shape of a sculpture without the faintest detail. A shrimp in the uterus, without eyes, nose, and lips. Show me how much better he is than me."

We both stood there for a beat before I darted toward the covered statue, intending to rip the sheet from it and see for myself. Dad snatched my hand as soon as I reached it.

I threw my head back, laughing bitterly. *"Of course."*

"That's enough, Lenora."

"I bet it sucks. I bet you only chose him because he's a bloody Spencer." I turned around, smiling at him.

Emilia LeBlanc-Spencer, an artist herself, had poured a lot of millions into Carlisle Prep over the years. She was apparently helplessly in love with Harry Fairhurst's paintings and had a few of them in her mansion.

I knew it wasn't a wise thing to do. My father did not take well to thoughtless, vindictive behavior. But my filters had gone MIA, along with my sanity, it seemed.

"You're an Astalis." His nostrils flared, and he slammed his fist against his chest. "My own blood."

"Your own blood is apparently not good enough." I shrugged.

Suddenly, I was too tired to even go back to my room. Fighting him was useless. Nothing mattered anymore. Vaughn had won the final round and knocked me out of the race. My only mistake was to be surprised. I'd actually thought he couldn't get the internship with an unfinished job.

But of course, Vaughn at his worst was still better than me at my best.

The bad boy of sculpting. Donatello and Michelangelo's lovechild, with a dash of Damien Hirst and Banksy thrown in for good, rebellious measure.

"Well, if you'll excuse me, I must go apply for approximately five hundred internships, now that my plans for next six months are six feet under, along with my pride." I tasted the bitterness of the words on my tongue.

As I started for the stairway, Papa grabbed my arm. I turned around, shaking him off.

"Leave me alone," I groaned, not daring to blink and let my traitorous tears loose.

"Lenny," he begged. "Please listen to me. You were neck and neck. There were five hundred and twenty-seven applicants, and other than Rafferty Pope, you were the final two."

He was only making it worse. It wasn't fair to be mad at him for not getting the internship. But it was fair to be mad because he'd chosen someone who didn't even bother finishing his statue. That's the part that hurt the most.

"Got it. I almost made it. Anything else?"

"I think you should be his assistant for those six months, since you are not interested in attending university. This could bump you up the other internships' lists. It was my idea, and Vaughn said he'd love to have you help hi—"

"*Help!*" I barked out the word. "I'm not going to help him. I'm not going to assist him. I'm not going to work with him, *for* him, *under* him, or even *above* him. I want nothing to do with *him*."

"It's your pride talking now." Papa fingered his beard, contemplating my reaction. "I want to speak to my daughter—my bright, talented daughter—not to her wounded ego. It's a golden opportunity. Don't let it go to waste."

"I'm not—" I started.

"*Please.*" He scooped my hands in his, squeezing them like he was trying to drain the defiance out of me.

We had the same blue eyes—dark, big, exploring—with the same golden rings around them. Everything else, Poppy and I took from Mum. The pint-sized figure, fair hair, and the splotchy, pasty skin.

"It could open so many doors for you, working as an assistant intern at Carlisle Prep. It is a solid, paid gig. You will get to work alongside me, Harry, Alma, and so many other great artists. You will get a salary, a room with a drafting table and all the equipment, and a fantastic start to your portfolio. I've been to high school once too, Lenora. Believe it or not, I know boys like Vaughn can be trying."

"Climbing a volcano is trying," I interjected. "Working alongside Vaughn Spencer is downright impossible."

"Yes, and still. Would you have turned down this internship for a boy you'd met and fallen in love with here in America?"

I stared at him with wild shock. First of all, he knew damn well I wasn't in the business of falling in love. I'd been very vocal about it since Mum had died and I watched him deteriorate emotionally to the point that he was only half-human now. Second, I would never pass up an opportunity for a guy.

"Of course not."

"Then why would you give up a position that could make or break your career for a boy you fell in *hate* with?" He clicked his teeth, a triumphant smile on his face.

Ugh. He was right.

He was right, and I wished I could take the merits of his argument and shove them up Vaughn's arse.

Taking the assistant job was a blow to my ego but still a win for the rest of me. Another six months of Vaughn playing his silly mind games wasn't going to kill me. For all his power plays, Vaughn had never physically hurt me.

Yet, anyway.

In England, though, he'd be a no one, just like me. No, worse than me. Because I still had the prestige of being an Carlisle Prep almost-alum—I'd only studied my last year of high school in California—and my father owned the bloody school.

Plus, Pope would be there, working alongside me. Putting Vaughn's so-called genius work to shame.

The rules would be different.

I'd fight him harder.

He is just a boy.

Not a god, a boy.

And you're not the same girl trembling under her mother's quilt.

You made him bleed, and he did, human that he is.

Now. Now you can make him break.

"I'll think about it." I massaged my temples. I'd completely forgotten about my sister, who was probably filling a fresh bucket of tears downstairs. I'd selfishly dwelled on my own drama and forgotten all about her heartbreak.

"That's all I'm asking." Papa squeezed my shoulders.

I went straight to Poppy's room, but she wasn't there. I paused, hearing her and Papa chatting and eating in the kitchen downstairs. It sounded like a pleasant conversation about the college she'd applied and gotten in to back home—the London School of Economics. She sounded excited and hopeful. I just hoped she wasn't faking it, that she really was happy.

Grabbing a Polaroid photo of Knight from her nightstand, I took a Sharpie and quickly drew a ball sack over his chiseled, dimpled chin, peppered with wrinkles and hair, added an elaborate mustache, and gave him a unibrow, signing the picture and writing under his face:

Stay away from the heater, Cole. Plastic melts.

I slid it under her pillow and went into my room, inching toward my window, planning to close the shutters and curl in bed with "I Started Something I Couldn't Finish" playing in my earbuds and a good fantasy book. Then I noticed Vaughn's truck parked below my window.

What is he still doing here?

He flashed his lights twice, causing me to squint and lift my hand to block the light. Feeling the rush of anger pouring back into my stomach, I slid into my boots and ran downstairs, flinging the front door open, about to congratulate him on the internship with spit to the face. I never made it past the threshold.

I skated over something slick and rancid. It smelled like all the armpits in the neighborhood had been lit on fire, but I didn't have the chance to contemplate that as I dove headfirst into a white plastic bag.

He'd left a rotten pile of rubbish at my door, and I fell right into it. Slumped on the bag of trash, I wiped a yellow Post-it Note from my cheek, scowling as I read it.

For your future project.—V

It was all the invitation I needed to make Vaughn's life the hell he'd made mine.

He thought he'd won the war.

But the internship was just the battle.

He was going to raise the white flag.

Right before I burned it.

CHAPTER FIVE
VAUGHN

The quietest man in the room is also the deadliest.

I learned that from a young age observing my father. People milled around him like homeless puppies, tongues flapping, eager to please. I became a man of few words as well. Not a fucking challenge, if I may say so myself. Words meant nothing to me. They had no shape or weight or price. You couldn't mold them in your hands, measure them on a scale, put a chisel to them, carve them to perfection. On my list of ways to express myself, sculpting was number one, fucking someone's mouth was number two, and talking sat comfortably somewhere at the bottom, between smoke signals and tin cans with a string between them.

My dad wasn't big on words, no, but his actions spoke volumes. He crushed his business opponents with an iron fist, without a blink or a worry.

He'd *showed* my mother he loved her a million times—by planting a pink cherry-blossom garden in the backyard.

By tattooing her name over his heart.

By fixing her with a look that said, *I'm yours.*

The less you said, the more you were feared. The simplest trick in the book, yet for some reason, men were hell-bent on running their mouths to prove something.

I had nothing to prove.

I'd shown Edgar Astalis a work that was maybe twenty-percent done, submitted it to the board of Carlisle Prep, and bagged the internship without breaking a sweat.

It was embarrassingly easy. Pathetically so. Yes, I manipulated the board. Especially Edgar, who had a dog in this fight, and Harry, who owed me a solid. And yes, if Lenora was ever to find out, she'd kill me, her father, and her uncle.

Then again, I would beat her to it, just as I had with the internship.

Everyone on the board had agreed I needed the full six months of the internship to complete something as complex as this sculpture.

I had time.

I had a plan.

I was ready to put things in motion and finally savor the sweet, poignant taste of fresh blood.

And it looked like I was also going to have a stubborn, feisty assistant to put up with my shit—one I could keep an eye on, to make sure my secret was intact.

Taunting her with a pile of garbage was not my finest moment, but the message had hit home.

Mercy was not on the menu.

She would fight for her place next to me. Always.

After Edgar broke the news to his baby daughter, I drove around her block, playing the CDs I'd shamelessly taken from her room when she wasn't there one day—Kinky Machine, The Stone Roses.

A couple hours later, I parked my banged-up truck next to my motorcycle—both purchased with my own money after summers of hard work in galleries—and noticed the orange glow of the fireplace in our living room through the floor-to-ceiling windows. I ran my hand over my dusty hair and cursed under my breath.

We had company.

I *hated* company.

Striding toward the entrance, I saw a shadow loitering in

the rosebushes. The leaves danced above the sunbaked ground. I crouched down and whistled low.

Empedolces emerged from the rosebushes, strutting his ass like a Kardashian in my direction. I'd named my blind black cat after the Greek philosopher who discovered the world was a sphere. This cat, like the philosopher, thought himself to be God. He had a fierce sense of entitlement and demanded to be stroked at least an hour a day—a wish that, for a reason beyond my grasp, my sorry ass granted him.

It was by far the most human thing I ever did, being pussy-whipped by a literal pussy. Emp brushed past my dirty boot. I picked him up, rubbing the spot behind his ear. He purred like a tractor.

"Are you sure it's a good idea for your blind ass to roam outside? These hills are full of coyotes." Kicking the door open, I walked into the house with him in my arms. I heard the sweet laughter of my mother, my father's deep chuckle, and a gruff male voice with an English accent I instantly recognized.

A toxic smile spread on my lips.

Time to rock 'n' roll, motherfucker.

Glasses clanked, utensils cluttered, and soft classical music seeped from the dining room. I put Emp down in the kitchen, dumped a packet full of wet food into his bowl, and advanced into the dining area, my boots thudding against the marbled floor. When I appeared at the doorway, everyone stopped eating. Harry was the first to dab the corner of his mouth with a napkin.

He stood, opening his arms with a shit-eating smirk. "I believe congratulations are in order for my favorite prodigy." He gave me a little bow.

Expressionless, I walked into the room, eating the distance between us. He went in for a hug, but I slid my palm into his and squeezed hard enough to hear his delicate painter bones cracking.

He extracted his palm from mine and massaged it lightly.

Mom and Dad stood up. I kissed Mom's forehead. Dad clapped my back.

"Harry was in town visiting Edgar and his nieces," Mom explained. "I thought it'd be nice to invite him for dinner. I just bought another piece from him. I'm planning to put it right in front of your room. Isn't it exciting?" She turned to grin at him.

"I can hardly fucking contain myself," I said dryly.

Considered the most critically acclaimed expressionist painter in modern art today, Harry Fairhurst usually sold his paintings for $1.2 million a pop. Not a bad gig, considering his half-assed day job as a board member and professor at Carlisle Prep. Mom, of course, would hang anything he made, including his turds, for everyone to view and admire. His paintings were all over our house: the foyer, my parents' bedroom, the dining area, the two living rooms, and even the basement. She'd gifted some of his paintings too.

I couldn't escape the fucker, no matter my continent. His art chased me like a rotten fart.

"It's a breathtaking piece, Vaughn. I can't wait for you to see it." Harry exhibited the modesty and humility of a newly moneyed rapper. If he could have physically sucked his own cock, his mouth would always be full.

"That's exactly what this house needs, more Harry Fairhurst paintings—oh, and rooms." I yawned, checking the time on my phone. We had eighteen rooms. Less than half were occupied. Emp loitered at my feet, giving Harry the stink eye. I picked him up again, scratching his neck.

"I'm off to the shower."

"Have you eaten? I thought you'd at least like to join us in the drawing room for some port?" Mom cocked her head and smiled, every nerve in her face full of hope. "Just the one, you know."

I loved my mother and father.

They were good parents. Involved, on top of their shit, supporting me ruthlessly with everything I did or pursued. My mother didn't even mind that I wasn't *normal*. She took it in a stride, probably because she was used to my father, Lord McCuntson himself.

Me and Dad, we had a lot in common.

We both hated the world.

We both watched life through death-tinted glasses.

But sometimes we pretended to be different for her sake. Like, right now, I knew my dad would have preferred to stab his own crotch with training scissors than entertain the flamboyant, self-centered Fairhurst. Love made you do fucked-up shit.

I was glad I'd never catch it.

"*One* port," I stressed.

Dad slapped my back again, his form of saying thank you, and we all settled by the fire, pretending it wasn't fucking California and downright stupid to put fire to anything that wasn't a joint or Alice's and Arabella's retina-insulting wardrobes. Harry sat back and pressed the tips of his fingers to one another, staring at me, the orange glow of the flame casting his face like a crescent.

Half-angel, half-devil.

Mostly devil, like the rest of the world.

With his sandy hair slicked back, tall frame, and greyhound-lean physique, he looked like an asshole salesman—the kind of man you wouldn't trust with a toilet paper roll. I eyed the fire, ignoring Graham, our servant, who came in with a silver tray and gave each of us port.

"Thank you, Graham. Please take the rest of the night off. I'll do the dishes." Mom squeezed his arm with a warm smile.

Always such a softie for the help, this one.

Awkward silence stretched among us. I put the port to my lips but didn't drink.

"How's the single life treating you, Harry?" Mom broke the tension with small talk.

He'd married a Croatian male model three years ago, but the marriage went down the shitter after he cheated on Harry, took half his shit, and ran off with a backup dancer for a pop star.

Harry's head snapped in Mom's direction.

"Oh, you know. Playing the field."

"Hopefully with a prenup intact this time," I muttered.

Dad snorted. We shared smirks behind our port glasses.

"Vaughn," Mom scoffed.

"You weren't supposed to hear that."

"You weren't supposed to *say* that."

Dad gave up on taking any interest in the conversation and began openly answering emails on his phone.

Harry tapped his finger on his knee and toyed with his tie. "Lenora is devastated she didn't get the internship."

I smirked into my drink. I wondered how she hadn't connected the dots yet—why she hadn't gotten in, why I did. She didn't strike me as completely stupid. Perhaps a little slow.

And a lot annoying.

"Heard from her father just before I came here. Positively crushed, that one. I do hope she'll take the role as your assistant," Harry continued.

My eyes snapped up. "She'd be stupid not to," I fired out, the first real words I'd spoken to him.

His chest caved visibly under his crisp, powder-blue dress shirt. He looked relieved, as if he'd been waiting for some sort of participation from me to prove a point to my parents—that we were on good terms.

"She is a proud girl."

"Pride is just a synonym for *stupid*. It leaves room for error," I retorted.

"We all make mistakes," he said.

I smiled politely. "Speak for yourself."

There was a beat of silence before he continued.

"She thought she deserved the place. And in Alma's opinion, she did." Fairhurst sat back and glared at me.

Was he trying to rile me up? Privately, and only to myself, I could admit that Lenora wasn't, in fact, completely talentless. Her art was a little psychotic, which obviously spoke to my unbalanced self. Lots of skulls, monsters, dragons, babies crawling on spiders' legs, and dead horses were created under her small hands. Her mind was a fascinating place if you didn't consider one thing she kept there—a particular memory of me—that I wanted to erase.

"Who the fuck cares? Edgar and you disagreed." I yawned.

Both Edgar and Harry had a reason to give me the internship. It had nothing to do with my prodigious talent.

I pitied Lenora in a sense. She didn't lack talent, skill, or discipline. What she lacked was balls, lies, and a cunning mind.

"Correct." Harry stroked his chin. He would have chosen her if he could.

Edgar too.

"Discussing who *didn't* get the internship and revealing her reaction to her opponent is a waste both of time and manners," my father said pointedly, crossing his legs on his imperial recliner, putting his phone aside.

"I'm sorry. That must've sounded inappropriate. Lenora is my niece, and I care about her dearly." Harry looked over to my father.

"Raw meat. Don't dangle it in the boy's direction and expect him not to feast on it."

"I'm not a boy," I snapped.

"Stop acting like one, then," my father deadpanned.

I knew what that was about. The parties. The blowjobs. The aftermath.

The servants talked, and I didn't think there was any doubt that I was a loose fucking cannon in a very dangerous, fully operating machine.

"My life's none of your business." I felt my nostrils flaring, my fingernails clawing at my recliner.

"What an incredibly mindless thing to say. You are my son. Your life is nothing but my business." My father's voice was neutral, factual, and dispassionate.

Mom patted Dad's hand. "Time to tone it down."

He took her hand and kissed the back of it, dropping the subject.

We entertained Harry for another twenty minutes before he fucked off. I could tell he wanted me to escort him to the door, along with my mother, but I had other plans, like, I don't know, digging my tonsils out of my throat with a kitchen knife. It was bad enough I'd have to suffer his existence up close for six months.

A few minutes after the door shut behind Fairhurst, Mom appeared at my bedroom door, hugging its frame and looking at me in a certain way. Though I lived in an existential vacuum and viewed girls' mouths as a free parking space for my dick, Mom sure knew how to butter me up with just a glance.

I was glad no girl would ever measure up to her. It made life simpler.

"Take a picture. It'll last longer."

Fairhurst had put me in a crap-ass mood. I wasn't sure if it was his sheer existence, the fact that he'd said Lenora might not take the assistant intern role, or both. I was lying on my bed, staring at the ceiling, wondering why I'd stolen the vintage CDs I saw on her desk one night when she wasn't home and Edgar had taken a shower.

Only I *knew* why. They were right there for the fucking taking.

Blur. The Cure. Joy Division.

My truck was older than the queen and had a CD player. It made sense. Plus, served Lenora right for being a weirdo who still used a Discman.

I just didn't find her taste appalling, and that bothered me. I'd also downloaded all the movies on her iPad—*Shaun of the Dead*, *A Clockwork Orange*, *Monty Python and the Holy Grail*, and, unfortunately, *Atonement*, which turned out to be such a chick flick that even Keira Knightley getting nailed against a library shelf couldn't save it for me.

But just because her taste wasn't awful didn't mean the rest of her was bearable.

"You were acting strange out there." Mom pushed off the doorframe and walked inside, taking a seat at the edge of my bed. I toed my army boots off, grabbing a bottle of water from my nightstand and squeezing it into my mouth.

"News flash, Mother, I am the strangest asshole alive."

"Top two." She scrunched her nose on a smile, reminding me that Dad took first place. "So, what's the deal? Do you not like Fairhurst? I thought you've always gotten along."

I felt the muscle in my jaw twitching but smiled to ease it away. The painting she'd hung in front of my room in record time—not even *hours* after she purchased it—made me want to burn down the motherfucking house.

"What's not to like about him? He's a fine artist and a well-connected son of a bitch. I can't wait to get his input on my piece."

"What's your piece about?" she asked.

I shook my head. She was pretty rad for a mom, but sharing was not in my nature. "Nice try."

"You're too complicated for your own good." She sighed.

"Easy when you're surrounded by teenyboppers and simpleton jocks."

She scanned my face, trying to read me, before nodding and adding something about how she'd arranged for my piece to be sent from Edgar's house to England next month, so I could continue working on it.

They deserved more than the ungrateful, moody bastard I'd turned out to be.

Two things a man can't choose that define him: family and height.

Mom and I talked shop, mainly about her gallery, and it was only when she was completely sure I was happy (as much as an ass face like me could be) that she finally retired to her bedroom.

"Close the door after you," I demanded, unnecessarily snappy.

She did, shaking her head and smiling at my antics. Nothing disarmed an asshole more than a person who didn't take them seriously.

"Sweet dreams, my love."

"Whatever."

"Love you."

I looked the other way. *This shit again.* "You too."

I could hear her laughter carrying down the hallway laden with stupid paintings.

Restless, I picked up my phone and scrolled through my text messages.

Knight: I'm having THE talk with Luna today. Wish me luck.

Good luck trying to get your man card back, you ball-less sack of emotions.

Stacee: You awake? ;)

Not for you, Stacee, you slut-shaming, gay-bullying, diet-personality Barbie, whose only unique characteristic is that your parents were illiterate enough to fuck up your generic name.

Hunter: On a scale of one to ten, when one is yawn, why-are-we-even-discussing-this and ten is I-will-fucking-dip-you-in-cold-fire-then-feed-you-to-my-blind-cat, how angry would you be if I told you I namedropped you to fuck the Lenke twins? (P.S. at the same time, if it makes a difference)

Minus thirteen, and their name is Lemke. At least that's what their matching lower-back tattoos said when they licked my balls at the same time. (P.S. it doesn't)

Arabella: You awake?

No, idiot. I'm asleep at seven pm, the time you sent me this message. I'm eighty like that.

Alice: Soooo, it's official now. Jason and I broke up. Drinks
at mine?

Only if it's cyanide, and you're the one doing all the drinking.

I had no idea what made me think I'd find a text from Lenora.
We never exchanged numbers.

Or words.

Or fucking glances for that matter.

We weren't exactly on good terms. Then again, it was unlike her
not to fight back when I pushed her. And this time, I'd shoved her
out of the fucking picture and into another time zone. Why was she
keeping silent?

Are you up to something bad, Good Girl?

I tossed my phone across my nightstand and squeezed my eyes
shut. My room was my kingdom. All black, not a drop of color except
for the occasional white or gray, and yet I felt so trapped inside. I
wondered if that was going to change when I moved to England.

Negatory, ass face.

I'd always felt trapped. Even in the wild.

I'd traveled all across the globe, spending entire summers in
France, Italy, Australia, the UK, and Spain. And my damn demons
always tagged along, like they were chained to my ankle, their shack-
les noisy in my ears.

I was going to slay them this summer, though.

I even knew which weapon I would use to cut the link between us.

A sword I'd be making from scratch.

CHAPTER SIX
LENORA

The following weekend, Poppy dragged me to one of Arabella's pool parties.

Showing up uninvited was my idea of hell. But Poppy used the cheapest trick in the book: the heartbreak excuse. True, Knight wasn't going to be there—he had family matters to take care of—but she didn't want to face Arabella, Alice, Stacee, and the rest by herself.

So I tagged along, praying the entire drive there that Vaughn wasn't going to show up and use his cock as a party trick. I was tired of fighting him, of shooting him mean comebacks, of standing my ground.

Oh, and also, I'd sort of retaliated by pouring superglue into his locker. It was childish and silly, but in my defense:

1. He started it, using actual garbage.
2. Not many things in the world made me smile like watching *the* Vaughn Spencer trying to unglue his chem book from the bottom of his locker before putting a dent in the neighboring locker with a vicious kick.

We walked into Arabella's Spanish villa, located in the gated community of El Dorado, already wearing our swimsuits.

Poppy had opted for a coral-pink bikini under her white beach dress, while I had on a black, studded one-piece and ripped jean shorts.

"You're So Last Summer" by Taking Back Sunday blasted from the sick surround-sound system. People cannonballed into the Olympic-size pool and did shots from bikini cleavage. Arabella, Alice, Stacee, and a guy named Soren were sitting in a circle outside, drinking pink champagne from colorful sand buckets.

Arabella sneered as soon as she looked up and caught sight of me.

"I thought your kind can only enter when invited?" She arched a microbladed eyebrow, comparing me to a vampire.

"That's just a rumor. We're actually perfectly able to barge into your house unannounced and drink your blood like it's happy hour." I helped myself to one of the buckets, pretending to take a sip. I wasn't so dumb as to actually drink their alcohol.

"All we can hope is for you to burn under the sun, then. It's not like anyone is going to miss you." Arabella batted her lashes, unwrapping a popsicle and sucking on it with the enthusiasm of a porn star.

This earned her a chuckle from everyone around.

I bit my tongue. I couldn't exactly compliment her on her literary knowledge about vampires, which she'd probably learned from *Twilight* (the movie, not, God forbid, the book) and only because Robert Pattinson was, like, "*super-freaking-hot.*" It was her house.

"Be nice," Poppy sighed at Arabella, plopping on a lounger next to them.

"Sorry, dude, but you don't get to tell us what to do now that Knight Cole is no longer banging you." Alice started braiding Poppy's hair, while Soren checked out my sister's generous rack.

I made myself comfortable on the end of the lounger next to my sister, blocking out the gossip about the cheer squad and texting with Pope.

Lenny: At a pool party with Poppy and I hate everything about this place. Only a couple more months till I'm back.

Pope: You're missed.

Lenny: I'm going to be in a sour mood working for Vaughn Spencer. He put the twat in the word twat.

Pope: So...basically, he is a twat?

Lenny: Precisely. You get me on another level, Raff.

Pope: I won't let him be a twat to you while I'm there. Now please tell me there's a token villain cheerleader and at least two nominal sidekicks at the party, plus a one-dimensional meathead who is their soldier.

I looked up, catching a glimpse of Arabella yelling at Alice and Stacee for blocking the sun, while Soren stared at all of them, tongue lolling out of his horn-dog mouth.

Lenny: Yup. And I'm the awkward girl they compare to a vampire.

Pope: Can't wait for Freddie Prinze Jr. to finally notice that underneath the glasses and the awkwardness, you're all that.

Pope: He'll whisk you off to the sunset.

Pope: Slap a close-mouthed, PG-13 kiss on your lips.

Pope: Sometimes when you open up to people, you let the bad in with the good.

I rolled my eyes, feeling a goofy grin stretching across my lips.

Lenny: I feel like that was an actual quote from the movie.

Pope: Don't be so scandalized. Took me three seconds to Google that shit.

Lenny: Turning goth was a mistake. Should've practiced my cheer moves.

Pope: You're no dancing puppet, Lenora Astalis. You're an innovative artist through and through, and fuck the fakers. <3

A herd of guys swaggered by. They stopped and saluted Alice and Arabella, their fists curled around cans of Bud Light. "America without her soldiers would be like God without his angels. We salute you veterans for your invaluable contribution to our society."

The hell?

The confusion must've shown on my face because Arabella flicked her dark extensions over her shoulder and scowled.

"Your sister doesn't even know what's up. Jesus, Poppy, can she be any lamer?"

Poppy turned to me, hitching up a shoulder. "There's a system. Every time a girl at All Saints High hooks up with seven guys or more from any of the sports teams, she gets veteran status. Veterans are saluted at parties. They also get free drinks and dibs on new guys."

"That is literally the stupidest thing in the world," I said, trying to recover from the amount of inanity crammed into a one-paragraph explanation.

"Ever looked in the mirror?" Soren deadpanned, tilting his Ray-Bans down and giving me a degrading once-over.

"Vampires can't be seen in the mirror, eejit." I tapped the Kindle app on my phone, getting ready to read. "But before you spoil it for me, I know, I know. I look like a cross between Drusilla from *Buffy the Vampire Slayer*, Edward Cullen, and a bottle of lube. Very funny."

The afternoon snailed by. No one paid attention to me, but that meant the girls weren't actively in bully mode. I drank bottled beer I opened myself and read a book. In between, I provided Pope with a live feed of what was happening. I wished I could see him as boyfriend material, but after growing up with him, he felt more like a stepbrother. When the party began to die down, most people retired to Arabella's living room. (Her parents were on a mysterious vacation in Europe, and her sister, according to the rumors, basically lived at her nanny's house.)

Arabella ordered pizza, and everyone napped on the couches and floors, sunburned and drunk. I stayed outside and enjoyed the breeze, watched the sun descending into the ocean like an elusive temptress teasing her lover.

I was sitting on the edge of a swing, hidden by palm trees, away from the pool, when I heard low voices behind me.

"…an outsider. You really thought you could date Knight Cole with little to no consequences? He never had a girlfriend. Then you showed up and just took him. You think people don't talk? That they don't hate you for it?" Alice accused in a nasal voice, slurring. The words dragged, twisting in her mouth. "Arabella almost had sex with him before senior year, you know. At Vaughn's house party. You ruined her progress."

Progress? Christ. As a feminist, hearing that word in Alice's mouth made me want to slap her with a lawsuit.

"I…I…" my sister stuttered behind the palm trees.

Poppy had also had a few drinks. I didn't nag her about it because I was here to look after her and I understood she needed to unwind after the shitty few weeks she'd had.

"I didn't know there were codes and such. He was fit and single, so I went for him. I never imagined it'd offend anyone." She sounded weak, apologetic.

I felt my nostrils flaring, but I didn't move from my hidden spot on the swing.

Fight back, Poppy.

"Well, you did. God, you're almost as stupid as your freakshow of a sister." Arabella chuckled. "Payback's a bitch, girl."

"Payback?" Poppy mumbled, her voice sobering at once. "What are you talking about?"

"We know your sister has something going on with Vaughn Spencer."

I could practically envision the disapproving glower on Arabella's face.

"Call her now and force her to tell us what's up. Are they screwing or what?"

"*What?*" Poppy snorted. "Have you even met my sister? You can't get her to do anything, much less talk about Spencer."

"*Make* her," Soren said, the threat thick in his voice.

"No! I will do no such thing. She's her own person. And a bloody stubborn one at that."

"Oh, you will," Arabella whispered with conviction. "Unless you want to be punished. See, there's a hierarchy in this town. Anywhere, really. Even in your gray little kingdom, right? And here, Alice and I have birthright to Knight and Vaughn. We went to kindergarten with them. Now Knight is out of the race. Luna Rexroth has him, and honestly, he's too far gone for her, so there isn't much point in making an effort. But Vaughn is still fair game, and you and your sister are newbies. You screwed up, and now you're going to *pay* up."

Poppy said nothing.

"We promise not to touch her lily ass if she tells us whether she's bangin' Vaughn or not."

I'd gladly confirm to anyone else that I'd shag a hedgehog before touching Vaughn Spencer. Unfortunately, I didn't want to give them the satisfaction of knowing the truth. They obviously wanted to hear that, and apparently, my lily arse was also a vindictive one.

"No," Poppy said with conviction that filled my heart with joy. My sister was not faultless, but she was loyal to a fault. "You can't mess with my sister. I won't allow it."

"Well, well, well," Soren drawled, amusement dancing in his voice. "If we don't have your little lapdog to keep us entertained, I guess that leaves *you* as the main show."

I heard a huge splash, and the hiss of bubbles surfacing above water. I darted up from the swing, rounding the palm trees and running toward the pool. I found Soren crouching down at the edge, holding Poppy's head underwater. Her arms flung wildly, trying to claw at his hand. She was desperate for air.

I was going to kill him. That much I was sure of.

Soren jerked Poppy back up by her hair. She gasped, water dripping down her blue face.

"Is she fucking Vaughn?" Arabella growled in my sister's ear, baring her teeth.

"Eat shit!" Poppy screamed.

Arabella gave Soren a little nod. He shoved Poppy's head back into the pool. Bubbles gathered around my sister's head, like a crown.

"Maybe this'll refresh her memory," Arabella purred, perching her butt on the edge of the pool, lazily braiding her long, dark hair. I grabbed a telescoping pole, advanced toward Soren from behind, and flung the pole at his head like a sword. He fell onto the grass like a toy soldier. His wail rose from the green blades.

"Jesus fuck. The crazy bitch really did it this time!" Alice slapped her thigh.

She didn't help Soren, though. She simply stood there, glaring at me. Ignoring her, I rushed to the pool and pulled Poppy up, hooking my hands under her arms. I dragged her to the grass next to a groaning Soren and turned her on all fours, slapping her back.

She coughed out spurts of water, crying and wheezing. Once Poppy turned around and sat on the grass, I spun on my heel, eager to deal with her so-called friends.

"What's wrong with you?" I shoved Arabella's shoulder.

When Alice stepped to her rescue, I slapped Arabella so hard, she stumbled before falling on her ass. An audience of curious party-goers was forming around us. I didn't care.

They'd taken it way too far. Their words, I could deal with. But nobody touched my family and got away with it. Nobody.

"You only have yourself to blame, Vampirina. You were the one eager to open your legs to Todos Santos's royalty without figuring out who called dibs on them first." Alice pushed me, poking my chest with her finger accusingly.

I threw my head back and laughed. "It happened because you girls can't see that sucking people's cocks publicly is not the same as dating them. Vaughn and Knight will never be yours. Not because of

Poppy or me or Luna Rexroth. They won't be yours because you're rotten and unworthy of the air you breathe!"

I found a semi-friendly face at the party—Hunter, of all people—and he helped me carry Poppy back to my car. I buckled her up, got her home, hurled her into the shower, and nursed her back to health for the rest of the weekend.

Poppy never spoke to Arabella, Alice, Stacee, or Soren again.

She no longer cried about Knight or about moving back to the UK.

She was done with All Saints High and waiting to go home—just like me.

I kept my profile lower than the Dead Sea for the remainder of senior year—even when word got out that Vaughn had decided to take Arabella to Indiana and parade her in front of everyone at Daria Followhill's wedding proposal. The invitation came out of the blue, but it garnered a lot of rumors about them being an item.

Afterward, I overheard Alice whispering to Stacee that Arabella had tried to kiss Vaughn during that trip, and he almost broke her nose fighting her off.

Why he took her with him across the country was a mystery I was going to have to live with. Did he really hate me so much that he was willing to bear the presence of my enemy just to prove a point?

Anyway, Papa was right. I needed to take the assistant job, suck it up, and move on with my life.

I'd been resilient and unaffected, even when Vaughn spent the weeks after his internship announcement looking for every reason under the sun to smirk at me tauntingly, trying to rile me up. I always knew when he was in the same room with me, even if I had my back to him, because it felt like clouds rolling in, bringing thunderstorms. He'd yet to offer me the assistant's position officially, and so I'd yet to accept.

In the meantime, Vaughn had decided to burn the days until

graduation by spiraling out of control. It was as if getting what he wanted—the internship—had destroyed whatever was left of his joy, instead of giving him something to look forward to. He seemed utterly miserable, even more than his usual morbid self, and he'd started skipping school for three and four days at a time, perhaps giving up on his high school diploma altogether.

One day I caught a glimpse of his father prowling the corridor of All Saints High like a demon. Clad in a sleek, black suit and a scowl that made no room for error, the man left no doubt that Vaughn was his flesh and blood. His gaze could wound you from across the hall, and heat spread across my cheeks when I remembered how I'd told Vaughn I was going to call the police on him and he'd said his father owned everyone in this town.

It wasn't a figure of speech, I'd later realized.

The principal had invited Vaughn's parents for a discussion, but when Baron Spencer left the premises an hour later, a triumphant smile on his face, I didn't think he was the one who'd gotten the third degree.

It made me so frustrated, I bit my cheek until warm, salty blood swirled inside my mouth. Vaughn did nothing to earn the unabashed love and support his parents offered him.

When Vaughn *did* attend school, he looked like he'd been dragged through every section of hell—bruised, beaten, with cut lips and black eyes. I'd heard he'd gotten into plenty of fights, and his face confirmed that. His cuts opened if he spoke or moved the wrong way.

He'd stopped talking to people, attending parties, and according to his friends, responding to text messages and phone calls. There were no more rumors about him getting blowies on school grounds or elsewhere, and the only people he seemed to still be communicating with were Knight Cole and Hunter Fitzpatrick.

I wanted to ask him if he was planning to offer me the assistant position anytime soon—or at all. Just because Papa said he'd discussed it with Vaughn didn't mean he would follow through with the plan. But my pride, mixed with the fact that I really didn't want to draw his attention to me when he seemed to have finally forgotten about my existence, held me back from asking.

All that changed the last week of school.

I came home after classes with the intention of swimming, then trying to work on the sketch for my next piece, which just wouldn't come. It drove me nuts that I couldn't nail down the way I wanted the assemblage to look. I was beginning to suspect Vaughn had not only messed with my head but also with my creativity.

I dropped my backpack by the stairway, kicking the door shut behind me and double locking it for good measure. I wanted to swim naked—not because of the stupid tan lines, as Vaughn said—but because I'd read somewhere that swimming naked reminded people what it felt like to be in the womb, and I desperately longed to feel that, a sort of connection with Mum.

I tugged at my shirt, advancing toward the glass doors, when I heard it.

Drip.

Drip.

Drip.

I spun sharply. The leak came from upstairs. Broken faucet? Bollocks. There went my afternoon. I'd be glaring at the back of a frustrated, grunting plumber.

I took the stairs and stopped dead when my boot slipped over the marbled surface. I looked down. *Blood.* There were drops of blood trickling down from the second floor.

Shit.

"Papa?" I called, gripping the bannisters so I wouldn't slip again, taking the stairs two at a time. "Are you all right?"

It wasn't just drops. The stairs were smeared with blood, with traces of bloodied fingertips crawling up the white granite, like in a horror movie. It occurred to me that maybe I should call the police, but I was too panicked with the prospect that something had happened to Dad or Poppy.

I climbed up to the second floor and realized the blood prints led to the bathroom closest to my room. I flung the door open and immediately had to suck in a breath. The entire expanse of crème ceramic was painted red. Nearly every inch of it. Vaughn Spencer was sprawled in my bathtub, clothed in a black V-neck shirt and black skinny jeans, dangling one army boot over the edge and smoking a joint. He bobbed his head back and forth, his face covered in cuts— like he'd just fought a rabid house cat—and that's when I realized he was listening to my CD player. I yanked the earbuds from his ears, my heart beating so fast and wild I felt nauseous with adrenaline.

"Spencer!" I cried.

He looked up, finished the remainder of his joint, and tossed it to the floor. The blood killed the ember with a vicious hiss. Vaughn exhaled a ribbon of twisted smoke into my face, slow and deliberate, forever a connoisseur of cruelty.

"Lenora."

"Forgive me for being so dense, but could you please enlighten me as to what are you doing in my bathtub bleeding to death?" I exhaled slowly, shaking with anger and, yes, fear too. His dark shirt was soaked with blood, reminding me that he was human after all. Something worse than the scratches on his face lay under there.

He needed to go to hospital. Immediately. I yanked my phone out of my leather jacket's pocket, but he shook his head.

"Stitch me up, Buttercup."

"What?"

"I've seen your *Tree in Fall* piece. You know your way around a needle."

My *Tree in Fall* assemblage was a lone tree I'd found in a Hampstead Heath park. It had been completely naked of leaves. It looked cold. I'd stitched a garment on it from scratch, then hung clothing items, like leaves, on its thin, bare branches. By the time I was done, the tree looked a bit like a ghost. I loved that it went from looking weak and helpless to fearsome and goth-like.

I wondered how Vaughn had seen it, since I'd only posted it on my Instagram, and he didn't have any social media accounts. But now wasn't the time to ponder this question.

At any rate, Vaughn was right. Mum had taught me how to sew, stitch, and crochet.

That didn't mean I was going to play the role of his devoted nurse, though.

I started dialing. Screw him. I wasn't helping him beyond what the law required: tossing his ass in an ambulance.

"I wouldn't do that if I were you," he said calmly.

I stopped, looked up, waiting for the other shoe to drop.

The first words we'd spoken to each other in weeks, and he was already getting on my nerves. Vaughn Spencer had the uncanny ability to make me feel twisty, like if he didn't touch me with his icy fingers, I'd burn. But I was also repelled by his behavior.

"I came here to offer you the assistant's job, and I just might withdraw it if you're already being such a bad sport," he drawled.

Wanker.

He'd left me hanging for weeks, and in that time I'd come to terms with my bitter loss to him. I found myself waiting to be approached. His plan had worked. Now he dangled it in my face, asking favors in return.

Don't make decisions with your ego. My father's voice pierced the red fog of my fury.

"I don't want to be your anything," I croaked.

It was the naked truth *and* most terrible lie I'd ever told anyone. I didn't want to explore what I thought or felt toward Vaughn. I wanted to serve him a nice dose of pain, as he had me.

"Liar," he said.

"Congrats on using your last name to get the gig."

It wasn't the right time for small talk, but if Vaughn dropped dead in my bathroom, the only part I'd hate about it would be testifying to the police and the paperwork that came with it. Anyway, he didn't seem terribly bothered by his state, either.

"Eh, jealousy. Bitterness's oldest companion. It's not easy being a genius, let me tell ya. One is the loneliest number."

"There are literally two of you, Mr. Shit-for-brains. Rafferty Pope got the internship too. In fact, I could be *his* assistant."

God. Why hadn't I thought about that earlier? Maybe it was too difficult to swallow being my best friend's assistant when we'd supposed to intern together, side by side. But this made perfect sense. I could just text Pope and get it sorted. A Vaughn-free future was a phone call away.

Vaughn smacked his lips.

"The position for Rafferty Pope's assistant has been filled, I'm afraid."

"Says who?" I scowled.

"I saw to it myself. Now, about your first assignment…" His eyes sliced back to his bloody shirt.

"No. If you die, I'll get your internship."

"If I die, I'll haunt your ass so good, you'll be praying ghost-busters are real," he deadpanned.

"You've been skipping school and getting into fights. Why?"

"Your face disgusts me so much, I couldn't risk running into you." He ran his icy-blue eyes over my body. "And here I am. Irony's a bitch."

Disgusted or rattled? I thought, slightly pleased. Because if avoiding me was the reason he'd stopped showing up at school, that meant I'd gotten to him. I flustered him as much as he did me.

I groaned. "Let me see the wound."

He raised his shirt, exposing bronzed abs and a muscular V. He had a perfect six-pack bulging out of his lean stomach, a narrow waist, and a dusting of dark hair arrowing south of his belly button. A gash sliced through the smooth skin across his side, just above the V. It looked nasty. Like someone had tried to cut him in half.

"Bloody hell," I muttered.

"Correct, for a fucking change." He yawned, flicking a gray flake of ash from his knee. He dropped his shirt, eyeing me with mild, amused interest.

"Well?" He raised an eyebrow. "This bitch is not going to stitch itself up. You may want to offer me some alcohol. Not just to clean the area but to make sure I don't yank your hair out when you close me up."

"Just to make sure we have an understanding—I'm not doing this because of the assistant job or because I'm afraid of you like the rest of our pathetic classmates. I'm doing it because I truly believe you're stupid enough not to go straight to the emergency room, and I don't want your death on my conscience."

With that, I got to work. I went downstairs, bringing back a bottle of whiskey—the cheapest I could find—and my sewing kit. When I got back upstairs, Vaughn was listening to my CD player again. I yanked it from his hands, this time placing it on the counter across from the bathtub, where he couldn't reach it.

My eyes narrowed. "Stop touching my things."

"Better get used to it, Len. I'll be touching a lot of your shit when we work together next year."

I ignored his use of *Len*, which I hadn't heard from him before, and tried to kill the butterflies in my stomach as I took a pair of scissors from the sewing kit and lowered myself on one knee, cutting the front of his shirt vertically.

"I didn't accept your offer yet." I kept my eyes on the damp, bloodied fabric that soaked my fingertips.

"Don't embarrass yourself. The only reason you don't let my ass die in your bathtub is because you want this position."

I wish that were the case.

When his shirt was a pile of fabric beneath him, I plucked my black towel from the hanger above my head and soaked it in whiskey, bringing it to his side.

"Aren't you going to ask how it happened?" He stared at my face as I worked, not even wincing when I put the alcohol directly to his open wound.

He was particularly chatty today, in a good mood—better than he'd been in weeks. I wondered if fighting was a defense mechanism.

If physical pain took away from the mental decay that was nibbling at him every hour of the day.

"No," I said simply. What if he'd committed a horrible crime? I didn't want to be involved.

His glacier eyes skimmed my face. "They say you slapped Arabella at her pool party."

"*They* need a hobby or a bloody pet," I said dryly, half-glad the rumor had spread fast and caused an uproar, "if that's what they're talking about. I'm not opposed to slapping her again if she tries to mess with my sister, so you can pass the message along to your little girlfriend."

I loathed myself for inadvertently admitting I knew he'd taken her to Indiana. It was clear they weren't together, but that apparently didn't stop me from wanting to hear a denial straight from him.

"You hate her," he said instead.

"Thanks, Captain Obvious. I wish your superpowers included not getting stabbed and crawling into my house uninvited." I continued cleaning his wound.

He ran his long finger along the edge of the bathtub between us slowly.

"You know about Indiana."

I said nothing, but my heart jumped in my chest as I tossed the black towel to the floor.

"My parents called her Mystery Girl because it was a mystery why I brought her." His eyes clung to my face, gauging me for a reaction. He wanted me to ask him why.

Over my dead body, boy.

I cleared my throat. "I honestly can't think of a better match."
Silence.

"What's your favorite band?" He changed the subject. He was doing it again—making small talk in the midst of an awkward, violent, insane situation.

I shook my head, plucking out a needle and a thread. I chose green because I wanted it to stand out. I wanted him to look down at it and remember me in the following weeks. And I didn't even know why.

"It might leave a scar." I looked up at him, arching an eyebrow.

He stared at me with a desolate look, dark and feral, but somehow full of hurt and shame too. There was something behind those arctic icebergs that begged to be thawed, I swear.

"Good. I might remember your insignificant existence in a couple years."

I faltered. "Pass me your lighter."

I needed to heat the needle to make sure I wasn't going to saddle him with a bacterial infection from hell. Not that he didn't deserve it.

He elevated his groin and fished out his Zippo, throwing it into my hands. I ran the flame along the needle, back and forth.

Vaughn stared at my face with an odd concentration that made me blush, despite my best efforts.

"The Smiths, right?" he asked.

God. What did he want from me?

I put the needle to his skin, taking a deep breath. Even though he'd bled a lot and probably needed a bottle of water more than he did whiskey, the wound didn't look too deep upon closer inspection. He was right. I *could* stitch it, but I wasn't going to do a bang-up job. My hands were clammy and my fingers shook, but I needed to close his wound.

"Most of your CDs are the Smiths." He snatched the bottle of whiskey from the edge of the bathtub and took a swig.

It was the first time I'd seen Vaughn drink—not just alcohol but at all. Which was bizarre.

I didn't answer, sliding the needle to the base of his wound. He hissed but stared directly at what I was doing, our heads touching as we focused on my hand movement. When the needle pierced his skin that first time, coming out of the other side, I let out a ragged exhale of relief. I hadn't breathed for a few seconds.

Mortal after all. Flesh and blood and insecurities and secrets.

I moved the needle again, whip-stitching the wound in careful strokes, convincing myself the blood wasn't real and the entire moment was a nightmare I was going to wake up from. It helped me keep my cool.

How Vaughn put me in these situations, I had no idea. But I had noticed the pattern. It was always him who came to me. He dropped trouble at my doorstep like dead mice, untamed cat that he was. And, silly girl that *I* was, I always opened the door and let him in.

Vaughn took another mouthful of whiskey.

"What do you do all day? You don't have any friends." He eyed me, his voice more bored than venomous.

Homework. Art.

"You don't fuck anyone either. Don't try to lie to me. I have eyes and ears everywhere. You just drive around by yourself like a failed Uber driver."

And there it was. The malice.

He groaned when I dug the needle in without my usual gentleness. I didn't appreciate his line of questions. When he realized I'd hurt him on purpose, he smirked.

"Hold on to that virginity, baby girl. Prince Charming is just a fantasy book and a vibrator away."

"Fuck you, Vaughn," I snarled.

"I'm starting to consider it. You'll be my pro bono case. Not full-on fucking, but feeling your lip ring on my cock no longer makes me want to vomit."

"Well, it makes *me* want to vomit, so that's still firmly off the table."

I dug the needle harder again, and he laughed, drinking some more and placing the bottle back on the granite surface. It slid and almost slipped from his hand. He caught it at the last minute.

"Wanna know something?" He glanced into the bottom of the whiskey bottle.

No.

"You're pretty."

I stilled, the needle hovering in the air over his skin. I wished he hadn't said that. Because if he hadn't, I wouldn't have to live with the shame of my heart nearly bursting with sweet, smoky ache. My breath hitched, and I had to swallow and refocus my gaze on his wound.

He's drunk and in a tremendous amount of pain. He doesn't mean it.

"It's a slow-burn kind of beauty. The more I look at you, the more it sneaks up on me. You remind me of Robin Wright in *The Princess Bride*—the kind of pure, wide-eyed innocence no amount of black shit and piercings can tarnish. But that's not why I don't hate you." He shook his head, his eyes trained on the side of my face as I stitched him. "Everyone in this town is fucking pathetic—slaves to materialistic bullshit and ticking the predictable boxes of school, college, football, cheerleading, jogging, fucking, falling in love, getting a job, blah blah blah. Money is cheap, dirty, and boring. Everything is a popularity contest, and you're out of the rat race. I guess..." He threw his head back with a sigh, staring at my ceiling. "You're real. Maybe that's why, sometimes, even when you're not around, it feels like you are."

I feel that way too.

Vaughn was always here, even when he wasn't. I could feel him from miles away. I recognized his scent, his touch, the air he brought into the room when he entered. I could spot his dark soul in a carnival teeming with colors and smells. For better or worse, he was the most unique guy I'd ever come across.

I continued stitching him up silently, his gaze caressing my cheek.

"Hunter said he was gonna make a pass at you."

I licked my lips, tugging at the thread before sliding the needle into his skin again.

"I put him in his place," he finished.

I poked his skin with my finger lightly, pinching it back together. This was where I was supposed to tell him he was delusional—I was *not* his—but I decided to listen to the entire story before I bit his head off.

"We were at his house. He was drunk. He thought I was kidding when I said I'd fuck him up if he tried to mess with you. I beat him up so bad, he came after me with a steak knife. He was supposed to miss. But that's the thing about shitty aims—when they want to miss, they don't." He laughed without a care in the world. Like he hadn't just lost a gallon of blood.

I paused, moving my gaze from his wound to his face.

He got stabbed because of me?

"Is this a joke?" I frowned.

"Do I look like the joking type?" He cocked his head, looking at me like I was an idiot. "You made this mess. Only fair that you clean it up."

My eyes widened, a fresh dose of rage coursing through my bloodstream.

"We are not together," I said, dumbfounded. "Never will be. You're an asshole."

"If you think that has anything to do with my controlling your every move, you obviously haven't been paying attention."

I thought about the public blowjobs I'd heard about until not too long ago, the internship he'd snatched from me, what I'd seen in the darkroom all those years ago.

His threats.

His cruelness.

His taunts.

I stabbed him with the needle, shoving it deep into his healthy skin, twisting it to make my point. He groaned, pinching his eyebrows together, but he didn't retreat.

"Push me, Vaughn, and I'll push harder. I'm not the same girl you threatened in Carlisle Castle. This time, I will hurt you back."

He snatched my jaw, jerking my face close to his. The needle slipped from my fingers, clinking in the bathtub beneath him. Our breaths mingled, hot and heavy and full of thick lust—the metallic scent of his blood and sweetness of my breath, sugared from a watermelon slushie I'd inhaled before coming home.

"Don't pretend my blood doesn't turn you on. You sucked good and hard on it, and my cock will be next."

"In your drea—"

It all happened so fast, the way our lips crashed together like fire and ice. Euphoric pleasure exploded between my legs, heat spreading in my lower belly like lava as his lips opened on mine and his tongue slid into my mouth. I grumbled when our tongues touched because I didn't expect him to be so soft, so delicious.

My knees sank to the floor. Vaughn took my face in his hands and kissed me more roughly, biting the corner of my lips, pushing his nose against mine, devouring me with the same desperation I felt for him. I imagined it looked like he was trying to eat my whole face, and though it probably looked awkward, it felt perfect.

I was the willing, stupid prey.

I whimpered when he broke the kiss all of a sudden. He lurched back, like I'd bitten him. The look on his face was priceless—as if he'd just woken up and discovered me in bed with him. Like *I* was the one who kissed *him*, who invaded his universe repeatedly.

"Fuck." His chest rose and fell with heavy pants, his eyes dropping to my mouth again.

It was the first time I'd ever seen him out of control.

"Not in this lifetime, Spencer." I cleared my throat, trying to pick up the slippery needle from the bathtub with shaking fingers. I snapped the thread. I was done stitching him. "I'm going to clean the wound up now. Hold still."

"Shut me down next time." He took the whiskey bottle and gulped the rest of its contents in one go. His lips were puffy and bruised, and I realized we'd been kissing for a few minutes. I wondered if I looked like I'd been kissed too.

"No. *You* make sure there won't be a next time," I whispered hotly, licking my lips. "Not sure you've noticed, but it's the twenty-first century. Men are responsible for their own actions. Or are you one of the so-why-did-she-wear-this chauvinist brigade?"

"Turning me off with your clothes seems like a lifelong goal of yours, so no trouble in that department," he scoffed, taking a fractured breath as I dug the needle deep into his skin again in retaliation. I was done mending him.

He captured my wrist in his hand, squeezing lightly to make me look at him. I did.

"I don't want to like you, Lenora. I want to ruin you."

"Then do it already!" I broke free from his hold and threw my hands in the air, exasperated. "Why don't you put me out of my misery and just finish the fucking job if you're so high-and-mighty?"

He had plenty of opportunity, power, and the means to get Poppy and me kicked out of school. Yet he never did. He never went the extra mile, always skating on the outskirts of making my life uncomfortable, though not unbearable.

"The former interferes with the latter." His mouth twisted in revulsion as he turned to look at the wall.

My jaw almost dropped to the floor. Was he saying he *liked* me?

He turned his head back to me, a slow smile spreading across his lips.

"Oh, shit. Look at you. You bought it." He shook his head, laughing. "Wrap it up, GG. I have somewhere to be."

I went downstairs, got a bottle of water, and came back up, handing it to him.

"Next time someone busts you open, do yourself a favor and go straight to the hospital. Now drink this and then clean up your mess. All of it. Every drop of blood," I said as coldly as I possibly could. "Friendly reminder: I may be your assistant one day, Vaughn, but I will never be your bloody servant."

CHAPTER SEVEN
VAUGHN

I came to school every day for the rest of that week.

And on the last day of school, I really fucked it up with Len Lenora. *(She is not your fucking girlfriend, ass face.)* The air was swollen with mischief and ninety-five degrees. Humidity level: two fucking thousand.

That was SoCal for you. Palm-tree-lined hell.

Everyone was wearing bikinis and swim shorts under their miserable excuses for clothes. Guys skidded on the damp floors, shooting water guns and chasing each other in the hallways, making it difficult to believe they were the sperm that won. Someone had sprayed black paint over the mirrors in the girls' bathrooms, resulting in hysterical teenyboppers who couldn't get ready for the traditional school's-out selfie. And someone else had too much free time because helium balloons sailed idly across the ceiling, nasty rumors written on them in Sharpie.

Alice Hamlin sucked Vaughn Spencer off in front of her boyfriend.

Hunter Fitzpatrick gave the Lemke twins crabs.

Knight Cole is a virgin.

Lenora Astalis is a creeper.

Re—the. Fuck—wind.

Even though I hadn't spoken to her since I chivalrously bled all over her bathroom and hoovered her face into my mouth, I wasn't down with the idea that some asshole who wasn't me was going to ruin her last day of school. I still remembered how she tasted—like the black roses in Carlisle's courtyard would. Delicious, sweet, and fresh, like raindrops on petals.

Like raindrops on petals? Get the fuck out, and take the vagina you grew with you.

I plucked my Swiss Army knife out of my boot and hurled it at the balloon. It burst noisily, the sound making people in the hallway yelp and jump. The rubber fell at my feet. I picked it up and walked the length of the hall, tucking my knife back into the side of my boot and fingering the material.

"Who's responsible for this piece of fine art?" I wondered conversationally, looking around as people glued their backs to the lockers.

Some students aimed their phones at my face, recording my unexpected outburst, but no one spoke.

I stopped in the middle of the hallway, sneering. "Well, then, if no one speaks up, I guess it's time to rate each blowjob I've been given from freshman year till now. Ya know, for old time's sake. Fair warning: some of you have *failed.*"

I took a black Sharpie from my back pocket, uncapping it with my teeth. I put the pen to a locker and started writing Stacee's name over it when a voice behind me shrieked.

"*Bruh!* It was just a fucking joke. Chillax."

Soren Kayden.

If the dictionary had pictures—which, for people like Soren, maybe it should—his blond-bearded, stoner-surfer face would be featured under the word *douchebag*, complete with his dumb, what-day-is-it-today? expression (*Thursday, assclown*).

He dealt Oxy and Vicodin so he could feed his gambling addiction and was shadier than a three-dollar bill. He'd once tried to fondle my selective-mute friend, Luna, hoping she wouldn't tell anyone. Spoiler alert: she did. A week later, he had two implants for teeth because Knight had knocked them out, and I decorated the rest of him with shiners and a forehead scar in the shape of a dick.

I spun, shoving him against the opposite wall of lockers and snapping the torn rubber in his face. He flinched, squeezing his eyes shut and rubbing at the red spot on his cheek.

"Ouch! What the fuck!"

"The fuck is you're a piece of rotten shit." I stepped on his toes, shifting all my weight onto them, so angry I could kill him.

I shouldn't have come. Cutting a bitch was already on the menu because I was on edge about the move to England. Soren was just an easy excuse. I wasn't Lenora's savior. I wasn't even her fucking friend. I cared about her ass a little less than I cared about Uncle Dean's ingrown toenail. If anything, she was corrupted by soft living. Getting pushed around a little was just what the doctor ordered.

By *me*.

Not anyone else.

Only. Ever. Fucking. Me.

"Throw down at three o'clock!" someone hollered, cupping his mouth.

Knight and Hunter showed up behind me. Soren's surfer friends rushed in too, but they stood on the sidelines, too pussy to come at me or my crowd.

"It was a joke!" Soren cried, throwing his arms up defensively.

Arabella hurried to his rescue, blazing toward us in her nine-inch heels and planting a hand on his shoulder. The entire school gathered around us in a circle, glaring.

"Oh, come on, Spence. Since when do you get butt-hurt over harmless fun? All the rumors on the balloons are true, anyway."

They weren't.

Alice never sucked me off in front of her ex-boyfriend, Jason.

The Lemke twins gave Hunter crabs, not vice versa (file under shit I really need to throw into the recycling bin of my brain).

And Lenora Astalis was a lot of things. She was not a creeper, though.

Speaking of, Good Girl peeked out in the sea of faces, staring back at us. She wore her hair up in a ponytail, her eyeliner extra thick today. Combat boots like mine, and black skinny jeans with a Stone Roses T-shirt. She looked only mildly interested in the scene, yanking her huge earbuds out of her ears and tucking her Discman into the waistband of her jeans.

Arabella followed my line of sight and plastered a poisonous smile on her pink lips.

"*Creeper* at three o'clock. What's up, Good Girl? Is this a figment of my imagination, or did you suck Vaughn off and get a perfect ten, so now he's your knight in Walmart armor?"

Len's eyes widened and sliced to mine. She thought I'd told people about our kiss. Maybe worse. Arabella called her Good Girl, but that was a fluke. Truth was, I hadn't told anyone about her nickname or kissing her. Twice. I would erase both kisses from my memory if I could.

Lenora pretended to laugh. "Don't flatter yourself. You don't have brains, much less imagination, Arabella."

"That's not a denial." Arabella popped her finger in her mouth, sucking suggestively.

"You want an official statement?" Len rolled her eyes, folding her arms over her chest. "Fine. I'd never kiss Vaughn Spencer, let alone do anything more with him. I'd rather die than touch him. Happy?"

A dispassionate smirk played on my lips. "Feeling's mutual, Astalis."

"Ouch, Spence. That means you defended her pasty ass for nothing. She doesn't even want you," Arabella taunted.

Anyone with half a brain could tell from a hundred-mile radius that she was trying to rile me up. That, in itself, didn't bother me. It was Lenora's words that pissed me off.

I'd never.

I'd rather die.

Fuck. You.

"*Defend?*" A smirk curled in the corner of my mouth. "I didn't defend anyone. The mean-girl bullshit just gets old. And boring."

"I-I'm not a girl," Soren pointed out, stuttering.

I threw him a disinterested glance. "But you *are* a pussy."

"Liars. Both of you." Arabella stretched like a kitten, trying to be sexy.

Soren looked between me and Lenny. They were right. If I had a penny for every time I stood up for someone who'd been bullied at school, I wouldn't be able to afford a fucking used piece of gum.

So why her? She was the only girl at school *not* to give me mad respect.

"Oh shit, man. I didn't know she was your girlfriend." Soren cupped his mouth, his eyes glittering.

He thought she was my weakness. My Achilles' heel. He thought *wrong.*

"She is not my girlfriend." I yawned.

But Lenora had the poker face of a tablecloth. She was scarlet red and had her fists curled beside her body. Everything about her screamed *rattled.*

"I hate him," she said, losing her footing.

It was annoying but not unwarranted. I took her internship, manipulated her dad, bled all over her bathroom, and threw garbage at her door. It was only a matter of time until she snapped.

"Why would I ever want to be with someone like him?" Lenora shook her head, oblivious to the audience around us. "I despise him in every single way. He is a monster. A cruel bully. A fuckup."

Monster.

Cruel bully.

Fuckup.

I swallowed but grinned, cocking my head at Arabella.

See? my humorless smile said. *No love lost here.*

"Hmm. Still unconvinced. Prove it." Arabella jutted one hip out, pushing her breasts in my direction, even though we were standing a few feet apart.

"You act like I give a fuck what people think. That is very unbecoming for someone who is not a complete idiot. You know what the word *unbecoming* means, right, Arabella? And *idiot?* I'm sure you're familiar that word too."

Arabella blushed under her five coatings of makeup and insecurities but didn't break character. She knew how to fake it—unlike Lenora, who was too real for her own good.

"Why don't I suck your cock in front of Emma Watson's goth twin? Let's see if you caught feelings. It's been long overdue anyway. You *did* take me on a family vacation, did you not?"

Fucking Indiana.

Everyone in my family was on my case after that. Nobody bought our relationship. They all wondered who I was trying to piss off.

Myself, I wanted to scream. *I deserve a piece of shit like Arabella, so that's who I invited.*

Arabella's lifelong goal was sucking my cock. She put more effort into her cause than most researchers working to cure cancer. Unfortunately, her sheer desire to please me made her a boner slaughterer of the highest degree. I'd get turned on by a baboon trying to lick its own armpit before considering dipping my dick into her mouth.

But Arabella didn't only want to suck me off. She also wanted to hurt Lenora, who never bowed down to her Queen Bee status and had slapped her at her own party.

I happened to have a dog in this fight too.

Good Girl thought she was too good for me. Maybe she was

right, but it was time to teach her a lesson. I was going to take every single thing she loved and cared about. Not because she interested me, of course, but because she was a means to an end. A way to get what I wanted.

Both kisses had been mistakes.

The first one, in the janitor's room, was to calm her the fuck down and prove a point—that I could have her if I wanted her.

The second one was human error.

I was drunk, busted up like a piñata, and she was there, piecing me back together. Literally. Not metaphorically. I refused to grow a vagina like Knight, who was a total fucking goner for Luna, the girl next (to his) door.

I wasn't going to make a third mistake, and the sooner Lenora knew that, the less chance I'd have to gain another pathetic stalker.

Plus, it fucked me up to think I hadn't gone all the way with Alice in the janitor's room. I always went all the way, and Lenora couldn't continue screwing shit up for me.

"Spen-cer! Spen-cer! Spen-cer! Spen-cer!" People threw their balled fists in the air, chanting in the circle formed around us.

It was nine o'clock in the morning and way too goddamn early for anything that wasn't coffee or a bullet to the head. But Arabella wanted to suck me off, and everybody wanted to see it.

I glanced at Good Girl. Her eyes glittered with rage. She'd never witnessed me getting a blowjob. *Yet.*

Her eyes said, *Don't you dare.*

Mine answered, *Fuck off.*

Students cupped their mouths, barking, howling, snickering between them. It was one last hurrah before I pissed off from this town for good. Why not?

I pushed the tip of my boot toward Arabella.

"Kiss it first."

This was where it was supposed to end. I didn't think she'd do it. Arabella had a reputation to uphold. But I'd underestimated how far she would go to hurt Lenora. She strutted her way to me on her studded heels, stopping when we were toe-to-toe. She sank to her knees, placing her glossy lips on the tip of my muddied boot.

Everybody took pictures of that shit. I looked between Lenora and Arabella. There was a story behind this, more than just this BJ. This wasn't about riding someone's dick. No. This was personal. *Revenge.*

What did Lenora do to Arabella?

I glanced at Astalis with a smirk. Her expression made me want to throw up, but she said nothing.

Step forward and end this, my eyes challenged her.

She looked like fire, radiating heat from across the room with her gaze alone.

But she didn't move an inch. She just watched and let it happen.

Arabella looked up, grinning at me in triumph.

"Unzip, Spence." She put her hand to my crotch.

I swatted it away. "If I don't come, you won't be able to show your face in this town again," I warned.

Why the fuck did Lenora pretend to care? She said she'd never be with me and meant it. But now she looked like she'd kill me if I went through with it. Which, naturally, made me want to do it even more.

"Daddy bought my way into a fancy school already. After that, I'm probably headed to Miami. Cali is so basic these days."

Everybody laughed. Everybody other than one girl.

"Soren, Hunter, guard for teachers." Knight sighed, rubbing his eyes tiredly. He always had my back. He shot me a glance, shaking his head. "You're such an asshole, V. I'm just waiting for a bitch to bring you down. Hopefully she'll stab your ass as a part of the process."

"Don't threaten me with a good time, Cole." I smirked.

When Arabella's lips touched my dick, I realized it was real, and it was happening. Fortunately, my cock was hard from the prospect of moving something in the little English Rose's chest. Her defiance infuriated me. Her rejection angered me. And I still wanted to fuck her up a little before we moved to England, make sure she was sufficiently mortified.

I looked at Lenora with my most unaffected expression, locking eyes with her as Arabella's head bobbed back and forth at my waist for everyone to see and laugh at.

She stared right back at me. But this time, her face said something else. *War.*

I heard Arabella sucking and moaning around my shaft and hardened more as I stared at Lenora, imagining it was her lips on me.

Submitting.

Cowering.

Raising the white flag.

There was noise around us. So much noise. Yet somehow, I could hear her silence clearly. Loudly. The way she digested everything.

"Push me, Vaughn, and I'll push harder. I'm not the same girl you threatened in Carlisle Castle," she'd warned after she stitched me up. I believed her.

"Do your worst," I said out loud, looking straight at her, ignoring Arabella as she tried her hardest to get me to come. I couldn't even feel her.

Lenora smiled, but the fire in her eyes was out.

This was the one war England was not going to win.

CHAPTER EIGHT
LENORA

That night, I dreamed I was a warrior in a fae world.

In the dream, I had a spiked sword and a huntsman's raven cape and gauntlets. My natural blond hair danced in the wind like snakes. We were in a magical forest, of all places. The kind where orange and yellow sunrays seep past green branches and butterflies roam free.

Vaughn and Arabella were my captives, trapped in ivy against a thick tree trunk, their hands laced together.

I pierced the sword through Vaughn's heart first, watched as blood poured from his mouth as he struggled for his last breath, his face still cold and defiant. Next was Arabella. I stabbed her numerous times in the chest. She laughed and laughed and laughed, and I just kept stabbing her.

"Die!" I yelled. "Why won't you die?" Warm tears stung my cheeks.

But Arabella refused to die. She broke off the ivy chains and advanced on me, zombielike, leaving a dead Vaughn chained to the trunk. She grabbed my shoulders and shook me.

"Lenny!" she screamed.

"Lenny! Lenny! Lenny!"

My eyes popped open, and I darted up in bed, panting. Poppy sat on the edge of my mattress, staring at me with a mixture of horror and pity. She was wearing one of her little satin pajama sets.

She frowned, running her thumb under my eye. "You were crying in your sleep."

I shifted uncomfortably, coughing. My throat felt groggy, my entire body foreign to me, like I was trapped inside it. So much for the new me. I sucked—not as hard as Arabella, granted, but I still did. All it took was one shove from Vaughn, and I was distraught.

The jolt of jealousy I'd felt when Arabella sucked Vaughn off earlier today had shocked me into submission. I felt helpless, weak, and nauseatingly miserable. My fever spiked every time I thought about them touching each other. And I thought about it all the time.

There was something I hadn't told anyone. Not even Poppy.

An altercation involving Alice, Arabella, and Soren shortly after the pool incident with Poppy. In fact, the day after Arabella and Vaughn came back from Indiana.

It happened after PE class, in the girl's locker room—the whole cliché, American high school nightmare wrapped in a barbwire bow. I changed my clothes next to my locker, somehow squirming out of my sports bra and shorts after putting on a black dress. It was extremely uncomfortable, but it beat being seen naked for even half a second by miles. I didn't trust people not to barge in and take pictures. I knew I was a target, and I refused to give anyone in this school more ammo than they already had.

I was in the middle of closing my locker when someone else did it for me.

A hand shot from behind my back, slamming the metal door shut. It flew from impact, crashing against my face. My nose went numb before the burning sensation took over, and I felt warm blood dripping from one of my nostrils. I blinked, too stunned to understand what was going on.

"Hello, Drusilla," Alice drawled.

Ever since the janitor room incident, she'd alternated between this and Vampirina. Everyone seemed to adopt the nicknames. Not that I cared. Better to be Drusilla than the airhead extra whose only role in the show is to parade her tits and blurt stupid one-liners for comic relief.

I turned around, refusing to cower, wince, or pinch my nose to stop the bleeding.

Arabella and Soren were standing behind her, their arms folded over their chests, grinning.

"So, I was wondering…" Alice tapped her lips, frowning. "What is it about you that interests Spencer so much? You're ugly. You wear basic-ass clothes. Your accent is a boner-killer, and now your sister is a goddamn reject, just like you."

"Also, you're ugly. I know she already said that, but I feel like it's worth repeating." Arabella shrugged.

Soren burst out laughing.

I let out a very provocative yawn, ignoring the blood that crawled from my nose and mouth.

"Sophisticated," I pointed out.

Alice shoved me against my locker, hard.

"I don't need to be sophisticated. I'm pretty."

There were so many things wrong with what she said, but starting to list them seemed counterproductive.

"I would love to know what he sees in you." Arabella stepped forward, grabbing my jaw and angling it side to side, like she was examining a frightened animal.

I slapped her hand away.

Alice and Soren jumped in, each of them holding one of my wrists against the lockers behind me. People were long gone—the misfortune of always having to be the last to get dressed so I didn't get harassed—and I knew I was all theirs. There was a football practice going on outside, and even if I screamed, no one would hear me. The boys and coach were yelling and laughing far too loud.

I resisted Soren and Alice, trying to unchain myself from their grip.

Arabella crashed her open palm against the locker behind me with a warning thud. I didn't even twitch.

"Are you fucking him?" She narrowed her eyes, growling.

I wasn't going to answer her. Screw that. Giving her what she wanted was letting her win. Let her think I screwed Vaughn into oblivion.

"None of your business."

"Are you guys, like, friends?"

God no. He just kissed me twice and made me fantasize about sucking his blood.

A throaty laugh escaped me. "If you like him so much, you shouldn't have sucked his best mate off." I'd heard the rumor that she was with Knight before senior year started.

Arabella pinched my nose hard, squeezing more blood out of it. She released it when I started coughing. My eyes watered, but I held back the tears.

"Look at her, Bella. She's shitting her pants."

"I think the nasty smell is coming from your mouth." My voice rang unsteady, even to my own ears.

"Maybe she's just his little bitch. Is that it?" Alice pondered, ignoring my jab. "His errand puppy. Another one of his soldiers."

"Maybe he gives her attention because she knows his secret," Soren chipped in. "I'm telling you, dude, something made him the way he is. He's too fucked up to be normal. He ain't like us."

I choked on my saliva. I couldn't believe they smelled the secret from so many miles away. Not that what I'd seen back there was all that scandalous, but Vaughn hadn't wanted me to see it. That much was clear.

A lightbulb flashed behind Arabella's eyes, and she grinned.

"Vaughn Spencer has a secret, and you're going to tell us what it is," she whispered, her voice laced with threat.

"Go wank a cactus," I muttered.

The slap came out of nowhere. It rang in my ears before the sting spread across my cheek. I couldn't believe it was happening to me. I'd never been hit before. Ever. Maybe that's why I reacted the way I did.

I spat in Arabella's face.

I saw the way her features twisted, morphing from calm to horrified and finally disgusted. She raised the back of her hand, and I thought she was going to smack me again, but all she did was wipe my saliva from her cheek and the corner of her mouth, rubbing the leftovers on my dress.

"Hold the bitch down," she commanded Soren and Alice.

Within seconds, I was lying with my stomach flat against cold tiles that smelled of bleach and feet. I resisted, squirming back and forth as Soren seized my legs. Alice pinned my wrists. I swallowed back tears and barely grunted when I felt Arabella's heel digging into the base of my spine. *Christ.*

"Now, Drusilla, I'm going to give you one more chance, even though you behaved like an animal and spat in my face. Before I make sure you never walk again, tell me: what's Vaughn Spencer's secret?"

I screamed with the rest of my power, letting out steam, without actually producing any words. Somehow, even though I didn't even remotely like Vaughn, it hadn't occurred to me to compromise his secret. Not even once.

The taste of the blood from my nose mingled with my saliva, and I coughed, feeling her heel digging deeper into my lower back. It pierced my skin and pressed against my bones. A door slammed shut in the distance, the thud carrying into the locker room.

"Someone's coming, hurry up." Soren slapped my unruly legs back into place when I tried to kick his face. Arabella stepped over me, her entire weight shifting onto my back.

The last thing I remember before I fainted was screaming so loud the walls rattled. When I woke up afterwards, a few junior girls helped me to my feet. I was fully clothed, so they didn't see my back, but the blue and purple marks stayed for two months.

Now, Poppy was giving me a long sideways look, demanding to know why I was so upset.

"Why were you crying? Why were you yelling at someone to die? What's going on, Lenny?"

There was no point in telling her. The school year was officially over. By next week, I'd be on the plane, picking up where I'd left off at home.

Carlisle Castle.

Art.

Pope.

There was going to be an entire ocean between Arabella, Soren, Alice, and me. Vaughn would be there, true, but he'd never hurt me physically. He just liked to taunt me with his venomous kisses and mind games. I could handle him.

I shook my head. "I just had a bad dream, that's all. You know how I miss Mum extra hard every time we go through a change in life. I'm thinking about what's next. Moving back is going to be weird without her there."

It wasn't even a complete lie. I did miss Mum like hell. But I was delighted to go back home. Poppy scanned my face intently before sliding under my duvet beside me, scooting her butt next to mine.

"Oh, I know, Lenny-loo." She wrapped an arm around my shoulders and kissed my temple.

Poppy had been there for me since Mum passed away. That's why I was never going to fully forgive Knight for breaking her heart, even though the writing was on the wall.

"But I'll be attending the London School of Economics, just a few short hours away from Carlisle," she reminded me. "I'll check on you all the time. I promise."

I believed her.

She wiggled and took something from the back pocket of her pj's. A Hershey's Kiss. Unwrapping it, she popped it into my mouth.

"Here. I was going to indulge a little, but you seem to need it more than I do. Chocolate has always soothed you, since you were a kid. Now go to sleep, and have sweet dreams, all right? I promise you, life will be sweet from now on." She kissed my temple again, brushing my hair away from my forehead.

The nightmare didn't come back.

The next day, I woke up to a basket full of assorted chocolate on my nightstand.

Poppy.

I bought a hair dye remover and washed my hair, gradually bringing it back to its natural sunshine color. I dumped the lip ring and the septum piercing in the bathroom bin. There was no more need to pretend.

I was who I was, and I was going to be enough.

———

Graduation came and went in a blur of flying hats, silky robes, and wholesome family pictures everybody faked their smiles through. The night before we flew back to England, Poppy threw a goodbye party and invited all of her old mates, even the assholes.

Even Arabella, Alice, and Soren.

I couldn't dispute it. She had no idea what they'd done to me and had no clue I was so shaken by Arabella and Vaughn's public blowjob. Besides, Poppy wanted to erase the aftertaste of the last pool party we'd been to—the one where they'd almost killed her.

The house was naked of furniture at this point. Everything was packed, wrapped, and shipped back to England. It was a bare, open, cold space with loads of alcohol and snacks on the kitchen counter.

Poppy had asked me several times if I was okay with her throwing a party.

I'd said yes. And I wasn't lying. Even though I knew damn well I was going to be locked somewhere for a few hours, feeling like a reject, I didn't want to ruin it for my sister. I had it all planned out.

I spent the time in the attic, in Papa's studio—now an empty space, with the vacant shape of Vaughn's sculpture in the center of it, adorned by a thick layer of stone dust.

No one could get into the studio without the key, and I locked myself in from the inside, stocking up on water bottles and a party mix chocolate bag Poppy had left on my nightstand earlier that day. I slipped the key onto a shoestring and made a bracelet out of it, tying it around my wrist so I wouldn't lose it.

The echo of the music downstairs rattled the attic's walls and floor, but I had my headphones on, bobbing my head to "Handsome Devil" by the Smiths and sketching on my pad, sitting on the floor with my back against the wall.

I took a bite of a chocolate-peanut pretzel and clapped my tongue against the roof of my mouth, savoring the taste of the cocoa and salt dissolving. I made a mental note to thank Poppy for leaving me a pack of sweets every single night since The Nightmare, the night Vaughn and Arabella had provided me with a horror show.

She was religious about it, which made me feel incredibly loved.

Flipping a page in the sketchbook, I drew the general shape of a head, then gave it an elaborate crown of thorns. My mind began to reel as I thought about all the possibilities. I could find thorns in all the rosebushes in Carlisle Castle and make a crown out of them. A real one.

I could shape the head with clay—no, tin. Dirty, rusty metal. Carve the curves of the face with a dremel.

A shriek from outside pierced the music coming from my headphones. I pulled them down to my shoulders and put the sketchbook aside, standing up and walking toward the window. My investment levels in what happened were low. Really, I only wanted to check to see that Poppy was okay.

I didn't even wonder if Vaughn had come to the party. Not even once. It seemed like he wouldn't. He'd been pretty much MIA for months but had stopped attending parties altogether after our kiss in my bath—the height of his insanity, I suppose.

I watched the people in the pool.

It was completely dark at eleven at night, with glow sticks floating in the water, as well as glowing balloons and floats in the shape of bacon, onion rings, swans, and glowing hearts. Girls in bikinis splashed each other. Some were sitting on guys' shoulders, playing chicken fight.

And then there was Vaughn, my eyes drawn to him like a magnet. He was perched on one of the sunbeds outside the pool, completely clothed, engrossed in a conversation with Knight and Hunter. Knight was shirtless, a ball cap atop his hair without him actually wearing it, and the seahorse tattoo on his spine drew attention to his ripped, muscular back.

Guess Knight and Poppy got over their weirdness, then, if he was here. Because Knight was definitely committed to Luna Rexroth at this point, one hundred percent.

"What was that scream?" Poppy burst through the glass doors from the kitchen with a pitcher in her hand, clad in a tiny bikini, her bra like two light pink seashells.

Hunter looked up from his conversation with Knight and Vaughn, explaining evenly, "Arabella, Alice, and Stacee played cock fight. It's like chicken fight, but whoever makes a guy come first by sucking his cock underwater gets the prize."

"That sounds utterly terrible," my sister gasped. "What was the prize?"

"Vaughn." Knight and Hunter laughed in unison.

My heart lodged in my throat. Not this again. I took a step back from the window, not wanting to see any more of it, just as Vaughn stood up and cut through the throng. The crowd parted for him. Of course it did.

"That's not why I came here," he said.

"Why *did* you come here?" Hunter wondered aloud. "You're being a miserable piece of shit."

Vaughn looked around but said nothing.

"Come on." Arabella hopped out of the pool.

My pool, that I swam naked in. I tried not to think about that.

"Don't be such a party pooper, Vaughn. One last hurrah before we all say goodbye. I'm winning!" She laughed.

Alice was at her heels like a puppy. They both had thong bikinis. Alice's was bright yellow, and Arabella's was orange and looked lovely against her tan skin. I hated that they were attractive. They made it difficult to believe in karma, because if karma really went after the bad people, how come they had everything (including both parents)?

Hunter and Knight stood up too. Knight retired into the house, putting his phone to his ear, and Hunter frowned in Soren's direction on the other side of the pool. I followed his steps toward him with my eyes. Soren was sitting on a lounger next to a nearly passed-out girl who used to take calc with me—Bianca. Quiet, quite nerdy, always wanting to fit in. She was obviously drunk. It looked like Soren was making a move on her, and Hunter didn't like it.

Vaughn ignored both Alice and Arabella and got ready to leave. This time, Alice was the one who grabbed his arm. Even I knew that was a mistake. Vaughn didn't like to be touched. He stopped on impact, narrowing his eyes at her.

"I broke up with Jason for you." She thrust her body against his.

"I'd break up with Jason for a rock, so no great loss there. 'Sides, no one asked you to."

"You asked me for a blowjob." She stomped her foot.

"Could've said no. Or is that word not in your vocabulary?"

"You're an asshole, Spence."

"Smelled many to recognize one? Any other mind-blowing revelations?"

"Yeah, actually, your little friend, Drusilla, told us your secret. It is quite the scandalous secret, Spence."

The floor quaked beneath my feet, and I gripped the windowsill, trying to regain my balance.

She's lying.

My teeth slammed together in anger, my fingers itching to fling open the window and call her out on the lie. I could see the shift in Vaughn's face, even from where I was standing, the telling way his jaw ticked, just one time, his entire face remaining calm.

"Lenora is a liar," he said.

I closed my eyes and exhaled raggedly.

I didn't tell them anything, you eejit.

On the other side of the pool, Hunter and Soren's exchange of words was getting out of control. Poppy rushed to them, trying to remedy the situation and figure out what was going on. Knight got back to poolside, and as soon as he saw Hunter and Soren, he hurried to them too. My eyes ping-ponged back to Arabella, Alice, and Vaughn.

"She said that's why she doesn't want you." Arabella continued with her bullshit. "That you're too much of a freak, even for her."

God. She was lying to him, and he was eating it up.

"I don't care if she wants me or not," Vaughn said drily, but he didn't make a move to leave. Something was rooting him in place, and he took the verbal beating. He *wanted* to hear this, I realized with horror, to believe I'd done this to him.

"She said she'd tell everyone." It was Alice's turn to strike.

I'd just shoved the window open, planning to set the record straight, when two things happened simultaneously:

1. My shoelace bracelet, and the key attached to it, flew off and fell straight onto the deck by the pool, where someone kicked it into the water while passing by, leaving me locked in the attic.
2. Hunter threw a punch at Soren's face.

Soren stumbled and fell into the pool, making a huge splash that had people whining and shrieking. A police siren wailed down the road. Someone had called the cops—probably because the music had been blasting for hours and way past an appropriate bedtime. Girls screamed, and guys pushed each other to get to the door. Knight jumped into the pool to drag Soren out. The sirens grew louder and closer, and I cursed under my breath. I was locked in my attic.

Vaughn, Alice, and Arabella still stood in the same spot, though. Like nothing could pierce their bubble of anger and deceit.

"Vaughn!" I finally remembered the reason I'd opened the window in the first place. He looked up, his frown smoothing into boyish surprise when he saw my face. "They're lying."

"We're not," Arabella snapped.

"She told us in the locker room weeks ago. Spilled it all out," Alice added.

He just stared at me, unmoving, like a sculpture—an angry god, a heartless prince. People were running around everywhere. Yelling. Screaming. Pulling their friends by their sleeves. I didn't know for sure but guessed there were drugs at the party. Poppy would never touch them, but that didn't mean people hadn't brought them. It was beyond her control.

I scanned the pool area. Joints, lines of crushed pills and powders, bongs, pills in bags, and more laid around everywhere. Anyone caught inside could very well kiss their college dreams goodbye.

"Get down here right now," Vaughn barked at me. He sounded impatient but not impersonal. I don't think he realized that.

I shook my head. "I can't. I'm locked upstairs. The key dropped into the pool," I explained, just as the lights went out.

Poppy probably wanted to do some damage control on her way out, make it look like there hadn't been a party.

Arabella sashayed toward a fire lamp standing on the wooden table by the loungers, making a show of running her finger around its edges, taking her time.

"Since you two are all secretive, and since this is getting on my nerves, I guess there's only one way to find out if Vaughn really does like you, Drusilla. Oh, you thought changing your hair color was going to help cover your fugly face?" She looked up, scanning my recently restored hair. "So *dead* wrong."

With a flick of her wrist, she knocked the lamp to the ground. The glass shattered, and the fire inside licked the at table, spreading fast.

The alcohol.

Everything was soaked with alcohol. Arabella jogged toward Alice, tugging at her bikini string.

"Come on. Let fucked-up Romeo save his creepy Juliet. Oh, and, Vaughn…" She looked back, smiling. "Thanks for all the help getting what I wanted. No hard feelings, right?" She winked.

I watched as the girls ran for safety as the fire spread across my backyard. The sound of the music died, replaced by wheels screeching to a stop as the police arrived. I closed my eyes and shook my head.

It was done. I knew it. There was no way for me to get out of here. Papa was still at work, off at the gallery. Everyone else had left.

"Jump," Vaughn snarled.

I shook my head. I no longer cared about being caught inside a house full of drugs. I cared about surviving. Vaughn glanced at the pool, looked up again, and frowned. He was calculating something. Then it occurred to me.

He believed them.

He thought I'd told them his secret.

He wasn't going to help me.

I swallowed hard.

Don't beg.

Fear creeped in on me, coating every inch of my body with cold sweat, but I still couldn't find it in me to plead with him to save me.

And he wasn't going to. He was going to let me burn for what he thought I'd done to him.

I took a step from the window, turned around, and tried kicking the door open.

I clawed at the wood, feeling my nails chipping, and knew I

had absolutely no shot at getting out of this room on my own. How had I been so stupid? Why did I fling my arm out, trying to talk to Vaughn, a guy who'd made it clear he wanted to hurt me? What the hell was wrong with me?

I grabbed the doorknob and pulled at it, propping one leg against the wall and using all of my strength. I was too shocked and full of adrenaline to cry. Then I heard something behind me. When I turned around, I saw the window was smashed, completely broken, and Vaughn was crawling inside. He'd climbed onto the roof, probably after calculating that it'd take him too much time to find the key underwater in the dark. Tiny pieces of glass clung to his shirt and flesh like fangirls. His left bicep had a tiny open wound. I'd never met a god who bled so often.

Wordlessly, he turned around and started kicking out the remainder of the window glass so we wouldn't get cut on our way down. The fire was gaining speed and body. I saw the tips of orange flames dancing at my eye level on the second floor.

More sirens—this time firefighters—rung in the air, deafening me. The sound of heavy wood splitting suggested the front door had been kicked in. The cops were downstairs.

"Won't they see us?" I asked.

He didn't turn around to look at me. Just nudged the last piece of glass aside to make the window a perfectly glassless hole.

"I'm going down first, and then you'll jump into my arms."

"You can't catch me," I told his back.

Vaughn was bigger than me, but he wasn't the Hulk. Jumping into the pool made more sense, although I'd have to take a leap and hope not to hit the deck. Bloody hell, hoping to be saved at the last minute by a flying unicorn was more likely.

He turned around to me, seething. "You do it my way, or you burn to death. I really don't care. This is a one-minute offer. I'm not fucking up my life to save yours, Good Girl."

Vaughn slipped out the window without glancing back at me. I realized it was still more than I could have hoped for. Everybody else had run away. Poppy probably forgot I was even in the house.

I ran to the window and watched Vaughn climbing down the roof, then taking a leap to the patio. He walked backward, watching me with his calm, dead eyes, and waited for me to jump. I held the window frame, shaking all over. There was not even one bone in my body that wanted to do this. I tried to tell myself he was going to catch me, that he wasn't just saying that to let me die. He wouldn't go through the effort of climbing up just to watch me plunge to my death.

"I didn't tell them your secret." My fingers dug into the wood of the window frame, the splinters cutting through my skin like little blades. The police officers were raiding the second floor, I could tell. I could hear them. They were going to find the attic and then me. "Tell me you believe me, and I'll jump."

"What difference does it make?" He bared his fangs, staring at me with forced boredom.

The fire spread, licking at the grass and approaching us with surprising speed, though he didn't seem to mind at all. We were already dangerously close to getting caught.

"Because it's the truth," I screamed.

Our eyes met in the dark and held for a moment.

"I don't believe you, but I'll still catch you," he said. "I will always catch you, the fucking dumbass that I am."

"What do you mean?"

"You soften me."

"Why?"

"Because I don't want to fucking kill you! You're too fun to fuck with. Now get. The. Hell. Down."

I jumped with my eyes shut, not expecting it to work, but Vaughn defied gravity and somehow caught me while still managing not to fall back. It was like my bum knew exactly how to land in his palm, my back braced against his other hand. In one smooth, continuous movement, he ran to the back of my house, ignoring the fire at his feet, keeping me closely pressed to his chest.

He shoved me behind the bushes, then joined me, taking shelter and hiding. The cold, moist earth was a welcome relief from the dancing flames, and I shuddered with pleasure as I took a clean breath—just in time for the firefighters to start yelling among themselves and turning on their hoses.

We watched them from behind the grand bushes.

We're safe, I thought. *He saved me.*

Yet I couldn't thank him. Not after what he did with Arabella. Not after he called me a liar. Not after he'd humiliated me so many times in front of the people I hated.

I'd dreamed of piercing his heart with a spiked sword, and this act of kindness, of heroism, only made things worse somehow.

"Why did you even care? You said your father owns the police."

"I'd walk away unscathed. You, on the other hand…" He trailed off, watching the firemen roam my backyard.

"And you care because…?"

He turned around to look at me. "I'm not done fucking with you."

I wish you wouldn't come to England.

For a moment I didn't realize I'd said it out loud, that it had slipped past my lips, bitter and full of menace. I had a violent need to hurt him back. To get even. Then to save him too. To be his equal. A god and a mortal, defying all odds.

"Wait till I get there, GG. You'll wish I were dead."

CHAPTER NINE
LENORA

No one mentioned the party after what happened.

Not the next day, when Papa, Poppy, and I boarded the plane to Heathrow, or the days that followed, when everyone settled back in England—Dad and I at Carlisle Castle, which was empty due to summer break (summer session hadn't started yet), and Poppy at our Hampstead Heath house.

Poppy naturally presumed I'd escaped the attic on my own—she didn't know I dropped the key—and I didn't correct her assumption. When Papa questioned us about what happened that night, we were both adamant that a lit cigarette had caught the bushes on fire, and we'd called the firefighters.

Naturally, the Todos Santos police came to investigate too. And when they'd concluded, they backed this version of events. All they needed was one tilt of the head from Vaughn Spencer. He wasn't joking—his family really did rule the bloody town.

I wasn't mad at Poppy. She had no way of knowing I was trapped. I didn't have my phone with me, and when I dropped my key, there was so much commotion and noise in the backyard, she surely missed it. But there was one persistent part of me that wondered why she hadn't looked for me—at least checked.

Even though I was in Berkshire and she was in London, Poppy still sent me a fresh basket of something sweet every day. Sometimes a courier knocked on my dorm door. Sometimes Papa left it on the threshold of my room. Sometimes it simply showed up on my nightstand in the morning. It was her silent way of saying she'd cocked up, she knew it, and it wasn't going to happen again.

Apology accepted, Sis.

My abbreviated summer came and went in a colorful, sticky blur. Pope was yachting in the Seychelles with his parents and two older sisters. I very much doubted he spent the time preparing for his internship. I didn't know what Vaughn was up to, but I was sure it involved some sort of satanic rituals, knife play, and torturing babies.

Me, I was holed up in my new room in Carlisle Castle on the staff and interns' floor, devouring book after book, greeting Papa in the hallways occasionally, and planning for my next assemblage. The new room had been furnished and decorated with the things Papa had found in my old room, the things I had purchased with Mum when I was twelve: the *Nightmare Before Christmas* sheets and pillows from our visit to Stratford, the Cure posters we got in Camden Town, photos of my portfolio—yellowed and dated, curling at the edges—stapled to the walls. Even Mum's flowery quilt was still there, and when I inhaled into it really deeply, squeezing my eyes shut, I swore the faint scent of her clean perfume and sweet self wafted into my nostrils.

My things in my room hadn't changed one bit from the last time I was here, yet it didn't feel like mine anymore.

The year in Todos Santos had changed me. Everything looked silly and juvenile through the same eyes that had watched a house burning, an angry boy being pleasured in front of the entire school, and my sister's heart shattering on the hallway floor of All Saints High in front of the "It" crowd. I couldn't help but look at my room through Vaughn's icicle eyes, and what I saw embarrassed me.

I didn't even know why but still couldn't bear to make any changes.

It wasn't like it mattered. It wasn't like I was planning on inviting him over. In fact, I'd filed a request to change the lock on my room because most locks were too easy to pick, and I didn't want to take any chances where it came to Vaughn Spencer.

———————

Two weeks after my return to Carlisle Prep, I sat in my room, working on my next assemblage. I'd started from the prop—the crown—because I figured it would take me the longest. The pinnacle of thorns was almost done, elaborate and heavy, coiling up like a gigantic crest. Thorns, like Vaughn, were difficult to work with— spiky yet delicate. They broke so easily but made me bleed so often. I'd never worked with such an evasive material before.

A spike pricked my thumb just as a knock came on my door. I sucked the blood from my flesh, spinning around in my chair and bracing my elbows over the drafting table behind me.

"Come in," I said.

I thought it'd be Papa. School didn't start until next week, and the interns weren't supposed to be here before the following Saturday.

When the door opened, the pliers in my hand dropped.

Rafferty Pope stood in the hallway, his golden mane a mass of curls, highlighted by the sun, his piercing green eyes shining all the way across the room. He was taller and broader than I remembered, with a youthful, deep brown tan and dimples that kissed his cheekbones. He looked...

Handsome? Stunning? Glorious?

All those titles couldn't do him justice, and still, Pope stirred nothing in me—except an ecstatic rush of platonic love. He took a step into my room, his balled hands shoved into white polo pants that only further highlighted his tan.

"Lenora Astalis, misery treats you well. You look fit." He stopped a foot from me, quirking his head sideways with a smile.

"Rafferty Pope, happiness treats you well. You look brilliant yourself." I moved to stand toe-to-toe with him.

The boy who'd gone ghost-hunting with me when we were kids in the castle. Who'd explored hidden paths and unearthed secret doors with me. We shared history, entwined interests, and a deep respect for each other.

Our arms found one another, and we hugged long and hard. He still smelled of the ocean, the sun, and foreign spices that made my mouth water. Pope ruffled my hair in an older-brother gesture.

"Sorry you didn't get the internship. You bloody deserved it, Lenny."

I didn't say anything. It didn't matter. We pulled away. I frowned at him, our fingertips still hovering over one another, not quite ready to fully let go.

"What are you doing here so early, Raff?"

"Oh." He ran his hand through his hair, chuckling awkwardly. "I thought I'd get a head start on my piece. It's a bit complex, and I heard Spencer is already bollocks deep in his project. You know I'm a competitive prick. I can't believe they let him continue working on the piece he auditioned with." His mouth curled in dissatisfaction.

"I do," I scoffed, stepping away from him. The mere mention of Vaughn ruined my mood. "Vaughn Spencer can get away with anything. Even murder."

There was a beat of loaded silence as my words soaked into the walls, as if inking themselves into my room, settling as a universal truth.

"I better go see Ms. Hawthorne about my room." Pope jerked his thumb behind his shoulder.

Was he as nervous about Vaughn as I was?

"Sure. Duh." I rolled my eyes with a smile. "Well, good to see you. Maybe we can grab a bite downtown after you're done settling? Kebab and Irn-Bru?"

It had been a tradition for us in prep school.

Each weekend, Pope and I would march an hour into the nearest town to get kebab and chips in vinegar from a little tourist shack by the Thames. We'd never determined whether the food was divine because we were used to the organic, sugar-free cafeteria food at

Carlisle Prep or because the hour journey each way in the rain, snow, or baking heat unclogged our appetite and led us to devour the food when we got there.

"Ah, the feast of warriors and nectar of gods." He offered a theatrical bow on his way out, tipping an imaginary hat. "Your wish is my command, milady."

"Nerd," I scoffed.

"Drusilla," he teased, his smile radiating just enough heat to make my childish room seem more bearable.

After Pope left, I sank back to my chair in front of the drafting table and shook my head on a chuckle as I bent down to pick up the pliers. When I glanced at them, I realized my thumb was still bleeding. Too lazy to make the trip across the castle to ask our secretary, Ms. Hawthorne, for the first-aid kit for just a Band-Aid, I sucked the remainder of the blood into my mouth.

I threw my head back, closing my eyes.

His blood.

Why was I so thirsty for his blood? Why couldn't I stop thinking about it? Despite what Arabella had said, I wasn't a vampire. I wasn't into blood play. At least, I didn't think I was. Yet there was something about Vaughn Spencer I wanted to break.

I had a fierce need to peel down his flesh and see what was underneath. Unveil all his secrets.

I dropped my eyes shut, shook my head, and smeared my blood across the crown of thorns.

There is so much beauty in the darkness. It's just harder to find.

―――――――――

As Pope and I spent time together over the next week, I got a lot better at pushing Vaughn out of my thoughts. He barely occupied my mind anymore. I gained confidence with each passing day, convincing myself I'd be able to assist him with his mysterious piece *and* still work on mine.

I'd survive his cruel words, his annoying tendency to burst into my life with garbage and blood and taunts. And for all I cared, he could parade his blowjob partners around all day long. The vast majority of students at Carlisle Prep weren't of legal age yet, and I doubted he was dumb enough to try any funny business with them.

Pope and I worked all day from dawn till sunset—he on his piece and me on mine—eating biscuits and drinking sweetened tea during lunch breaks. Pope worked on a magnificent, floor-to-ceiling painting on canvas. He was attempting to paint a futuristic, postapocalyptic London—dark, edgy, and extra gray. For now he was setting the general tones and coloring on the canvas. For this moment in time, the castle felt like our playground, as it was completely empty, aside from a handful of staff and my father, who was holed up in his office. At dinnertime, Raff and I walked to the nearest town for fish and chips and came back full, satisfied, and slightly drunk on ice-cold lager. Poppy still sent me sweets, and sometimes Pope and I dropped chocolate buttons into our morning coffees and devoured them before we started the day.

On Friday, summer session students began to trickle into the castle. Saturday, they were going to pour through the hallways in a rush of squeaks and giggles, getting ready for classes on Monday. Raff and I avoided the entire commotion by borrowing Papa's boat and sailing it on the Thames all weekend while getting drunk on cheap wine. The sun shone so bright, its rays sank past my skin. My freckles came out, and my hair became golden and softer. The little crinkles beside my eyes reappeared too, which meant I was finally smiling again.

On Sunday, we anchored the boat by a little hill and had a picnic. Pope was juggling fruit. "Catch!" he'd command when I least expected it, throwing grapes and apricots into my mouth. He was always in a good mood, goofy and sweet-tempered—so different from the tortured, scowling artists I'd grown up around. Only I knew better than to think there wasn't darkness hiding behind his ultra-bright smile.

"How's your sister doing?" he asked out of nowhere, after we'd both decided to dip our feet in the freezing water.

I had absolutely no doubt Raff had zero interest in Poppy. Growing up with him, I knew his style. Neither I nor Poppy was it. He liked the sweet but psycho ones. Emphasis on the latter. Every girl he'd dated at Carlisle Prep had ended up dropping out due to poor grades, suspension, or expulsion. Whether drug use, body dysmorphia, or cutting and severe depression, they always had a reason to disappear.

Normal bored him to death, and I knew even my slightly goth self was too sweet for more than friendship. Probably the extra-strength All Saints version—with the dyed hair and extra-weird clothes—would've still been too vanilla. To him, Poppy was a prudish angel.

"She's fine. She quite liked California," I said carefully, thinking about her time before the breakup with Knight. "But I think she's happy to be back in the UK."

"Poppy fits right in with the California girls." Raff popped a grape into his mouth.

I shrugged off his comment.

"And Vaughn Spencer? What terms are the two of you on right now?"

I wanted to laugh because *who knew?* Last I saw him, he'd saved me from a fire before promising to give me hell. No one knew what Vaughn was thinking, including, I suspected, Vaughn himself. God knew I'd stopped trying to figure him out.

"Doesn't matter." I drew circles in the water with the tip of my toe. "I want to stay here. I want to work with Harry, Papa, and Alma. With *you.* If that means tolerating the bastard for six months, so be it. He's not the king of the school anymore. And if he tries to hurt me, I'll make sure he stands corrected."

Pope grinned.

"What?" I frowned.

"Bastard toughened you up," he observed, standing up and shaking his wet feet in my face.

I tried to punch his thigh, but he took the hand I sent his way and pulled me up. I didn't want to go back to Carlisle. The hallways were going to be jammed with students, the toilets forever clogged, and I'd have to go back to wearing flip-flops to the shower to avoid fungus. I was going to miss the quiet and seclusion of having Papa and Rafferty to myself.

"*I* toughened myself up. The so-called bastard had nothing to do with it," I hissed.

"So feisty for a Virgo," Raff replied, reminding me he was little brother to two horoscope-enthusiasts. "Which reminds me, your birthday is coming up. Anything special I can give you?"

I had something in mind, but now wasn't the time to ask for it. The idea was so crazy, I knew he'd be into it. Although it wasn't the sort of thing one usually asks from a childhood mate. Then again, Raff and I were both quite abnormal, and he never shied away from bizarre things.

"Yes, actually, but you'll have to keep your mind open."

"My mind is nothing but open. An artist with a closed mind is like a builder without a hammer." He winked.

We gathered our things and hopped on the boat. As we sailed our way back to the castle, it began to drizzle, the first rain of the season. Summer was coming to an end, and with it, my few weeks of uninterrupted bliss. Come Monday, everything was going to change.

I wasn't ready, yet at the same time, I felt ripe for something I couldn't describe, bursting at the seams. The air was thick with possibility. I hadn't told anyone what I was working on. I wanted to help Vaughn deliver his piece to Tate Modern, then reveal mine to private galleries in hopes of snagging a good internship.

Something occurred to me while Raff was anchoring the boat and helping me hop onto the grass. I threw my backpack over my shoulder and frowned at him.

"You know, I never bothered to ask who you chose for your assistant."

It made sense that he would've asked me the minute we learned I didn't get in, but he never did. I hadn't brought it up because the subject of the internship was so sore, so sensitive for me. For a while there, I'd barely agreed to talk about it at all.

Raff smiled his cocksure grin and gave me the answer that shook the earth beneath my feet. "Oh, no one I know. She wrote me a heartbreaking letter about how much she wanted to get in, and frankly, it helped that her father invested eight hundred thousand quid in the exhibition I have planned for next summer. Her name is Arabella Garofalo. Actually, she's from California too. Perhaps she could be your friend."

Fat chance.

And though this was yet another cruel turn of events, I couldn't really muster much surprise. I made some excuse to Raff and left immediately, the blood draining from my face as rage filled my heart.

Fat chance with a side of making me borderline suicidal.

I didn't show up at the dining hall for the festive Sunday dinner, which marked the official beginning of both summer session and our internships.

The idea of Arabella sitting there next to Raff made me want to pull out every hair on my head, even without exploring the idea of seeing Vaughn again.

They were supposed to be here by now, but I had no intention of willingly seeing them.

I paced my room, fists clenched, my CD player tucked into the waistband of my sweatpants. Lit's lyrics reminded me I was my own worst enemy.

I passed out in my bed at some point, headphones still on. When or how, I don't know, but I was definitely sleeping until I felt a hand brushing my hair aside, a harsh, warm breath skating over my ear.

The headphones were pulled down gently, wrapping around my neck.

"I like you in this position, Good Girl—like a frightened dog curled into itself."

This time, I didn't pretend to sleep.

This time, I grabbed Vaughn's golden, almighty, so-talented-it-was-allegedly-insured left hand and twisted it, darting up to a sitting position. My eyes popped open, blinking and trying to find a slice of light in the otherwise dark room. In the half second it took me to adjust, Vaughn had pushed me back to the mattress, captured my wrists, and jammed them against the bed, his knee landing between my legs.

He growled in my face. "Never touch my hands again."

I laughed, then arched my back, trying to lift my pelvis and kick him, since my hands were firmly locked. He applied more of his weight to me, laughing darkly as his knee accidentally pressed against the sensitive nub between my legs. I wondered if he'd sat at Arabella's side at dinner. If they'd already made up after what happened at my house and charmed their way into Pope's good graces. I hadn't had the chance to warn Raff off Arabella. I'd needed to cool down before laying it out for him.

"How..." I trailed off, narrowing my eyes at him. "I changed the lock."

He shifted slightly, ending the friction between his knee and my groin, and I almost moaned. The pressure had felt good, and I did everything I could not to let my eyes roll and wiggle myself lower, so he'd touch my clit again.

"Haven't you learned anything? You can change your lock, your zip code, your hair, your wardrobe, your entire fucking *life*, and I'll still always find you. Touch your shit. Stake my claim."

"You are so bloody full of yourself."

"Bet you'd like to be full of me too."

"Keep telling yourself that while you hold me hostage underneath you. We both know I'll knee you in the bollocks and stab you in the heart if you let go."

I wished I were exaggerating, but after what he did with Arabella the last day of school, I wasn't. Even though he'd saved me, I hated him with all my heart after that humiliation, and I didn't even know why it bothered me so much.

"Don't confuse yourself for someone strong." He chuckled. "You will do nothing but suck my cock and cater to my every need this next semester, Good Girl. And fuck, do I intend to leave you with some nice memories and a few art tips."

"Drop dead."

"Soon, but not soon enough for you."

"Kiss me," I quipped, starting another mind game and trying to regain some of the power in our exchange.

His thick eyebrows dove into a scowl.

"Scared to catch feelings?" I smiled sweetly. "Don't worry, I won't beg for mo—"

He crashed his mouth down on mine like a storm, hungry and desperate and full of lust, and he grabbed my hair in his fist so I couldn't jerk back and deny him the kiss. His tongue slicked over mine, giving it a playful flick, a *been missing ya*.

I moaned into his mouth, and he released my wrists, cupping both my cheeks and deepening our kiss. I used one hand to rake my fingernails along his back over his shirt, trying to leave marks. A deep chuckle seeped from the back of his throat.

"Peace Sells" by Megadeth played distortedly in both our ears through the still-working CD player.

Vaughn and I hated each other, but our bodies didn't seem to share the sentiment.

What he failed to notice while threading his fingers through my hair, while devouring my tongue and conquering my mouth, was that

I slipped my free hand under my mattress, retrieving a little pocket knife. As his lips moved from mine to my neck, making me drunk and delirious with need, I put the dagger to his throat, the blade poking his flesh. His Adam's apple didn't even bob when the cold metal met it.

I felt his grin against my skin, his teeth running along my jawline, teasing me lazily.

"You gonna kill me, Good Girl?"

I poked the dagger harder against his throat, my pulse exploding like fireworks. I could feel his heartbeat against my chest, and it remained steady and slow. Maybe Vaughn really was a psychopath. I'd never met someone so cool and unaffected in my life.

"Yes, if you don't quit taunting me. We're going to play by my rules on my home field."

"Wanna bet?"

"You hooked Arabella up with the assistant job. You even got her daddy to shell out some money to make it happen. Why? You hate her."

"I hate you more."

"Again—*why*? I haven't done anything to you. I kept your secret." *Your stupid, meaningless secret*, I wanted to add.

"You were a little pushover mouse, which turned me off. Now you're a mouthy little shithead. That version of you pisses me off too. But I don't think you're capable of digging this knife in, sweetheart."

"Don't try me," I warned with a shaky voice.

I'd never hurt anyone before, but I knew Vaughn could bring me there. He always made me do crazy things. I'd stitched him up. Stabbing him seemed like coming full circle.

You need a bitch to bring you down. I hope she'll stab you while she's at it, Knight had said to Vaughn on the last day of school.

He wasn't wrong.

Vaughn finally detached his lips from me, elevating his head just enough to look me in the eye in the dark. He was so heart-stoppingly beautiful, I couldn't breathe.

"That's exactly what I'm doing. I told you to do your worst. *Play along,*" he enunciated.

Lord. He practically invited me to hurt him. And I was going to do it. I rearranged the angle of the blade away from his Adam's apple, picking a place where I couldn't see or feel the bulge of a vein. When he stayed silent and still, I poked. I didn't stop until a trail of thin blood began to run down into his black shirt, like a tiny river. I held my breath, watching the cut in his throat, mesmerized.

Before I knew what was happening, Vaughn had snatched the knife from my hand and pointed it to my neck, smiling politely.

"My turn. Now suck on it good. I know how much you like my blood. Arabella and Alice don't call you Drusilla for nothing."

I swallowed hard but made no move toward his wound.

He was right, of course.

Drawing and sucking his blood turned me on, and that mortified me.

I knew I was going to get off on it, and I didn't want to give him the satisfaction.

"Nah. I think I'll wait to see who cuts deeper," I heard myself say.

I couldn't believe those words had left my mouth. I was obviously drunk on our kiss. I didn't want him to cut me. And I had no doubt he would. He was Vaughn bloody Spencer, for goodness' sake.

Literally Vaughn bloody Spencer. And it was all my doing.

He poked the blade a little into my flesh but stopped before it even hurt. "Fuck, you're crazy," he laughed, his eyes lighting up as if the revelation relieved him.

He now had a partner in crime. I didn't say anything. Just waited for him to return the favor, so to speak. Then I felt something I hadn't felt either of the first two times he'd kissed me.

His erection pressing against my stomach.

I was terrified and elated all at once. My heart jerked everywhere in my chest without a rhythm or particular pace.

I'd seen him hard before, kind of, when Arabella sucked him off, although he never *did* come. He was the least horny bloke I'd ever met. Vaughn's eyebrows pinched together, and both our gazes skated down to the point where our bodies met, his groin against my belly button.

My heart. My wild, desolate heart couldn't take all the adrenaline. My body, however, was coming alive in a way I'd never experienced before. Blooming, warming up, and begging for permission to grind against him.

"That," he said, still pointing a knife to my neck, "never happened before. I usually...control them. Sorry."

Did he just apologize for getting hard when we were pressed against each other? I wanted to laugh but bit down my smile.

"You're fine."

"Unfortunately, so are you." He looked back at me, a faraway, slightly shocked expression on his marble face.

"That sounds dangerously close to a compliment." I couldn't help but grin. Vaughn never said anything about how girls looked. He was perpetually immune.

"Suck my blood," he said wryly, changing the subject.

"Will you stab me if I don't?"

"Your neck is too pretty to slit. I could cut other things, though." He ran the knife down to the center of my shirt, poking the hem.

My eyes flared, but I pretended to keep my cool. He tugged at the fabric, ripping my shirt open in the middle. My breasts were bare in front of him now, my nipples erect and pointing expectantly at his face.

Touch us. Bite us. Hell, put a ring on us.

Everything was swollen, with sex in the air. What was up with my idiotic body? This person and I hated each other. Tomorrow morning, we wouldn't say hi in the hall.

"Suck. My. Blood," he repeated, hovering over me. A drop of said blood fell directly to my mouth. I refused to taste it, pressing my lips together.

His hand moved between us, about to cut off my jammies. The knife trailed along the slit of my pussy through the fabric, and I shivered all over. I snatched his wrist.

"*Christ*," I snapped.

I jerked him by the hem of his shirt, hungrily sucking on his blood. I didn't know what it was about it that drove me mad—the fact that it was hot, metallic, and sweet against his cold, stony features or the idea that I'd done this to him. I'd hurt the guy who managed to destroy everyone and everything in his way. I felt wetness pooling between my legs and found myself rubbing against him without meaning to, sucking harder on his throat and moaning.

I wanted him to touch me, and I didn't care that I'd regret it tomorrow.

I wasn't doing it to make him feel good. I wanted him to make *me* feel good.

And tomorrow, when the reality of Arabella, Pope, Vaughn, and me inevitably crashed over my head, at least I'd have one good memory to cling to.

I took his hand and guided it between us, shoving it into my jammies with a lump in my throat as I continued suckling. His hand froze when it reached my waistline, refusing to dip farther. I frowned, peeking at his face. My lips felt puffy and sensitive.

"I want you to do this," I confirmed, in case he needed verbal consent.

He just stared at me, like I was a complete stranger. "I don't do that," he said after a beat, his voice thick and strange.

"You don't do *what?*"

His nostrils flared, the vein in his square jaw tightening in annoyance. "Any of that."

"Are you a virgin?" I joked, popping a brow.

He snorted in disgust, unplastering himself from me and standing up. It all happened so fast, I didn't have time to decipher his reaction. He rearranged his cock inside his black jeans, grabbing his phone and a joint from my nightstand. Obviously, the twat had made himself comfortable before he woke me up. *Again.*

Only this time, I hadn't pretended to sleep. No. I'd let him use me in my bed.

Yeah, you really showed him this time, Lenny.

Daft, daft girl.

Shame flooded me as reality trickled in.

I'd asked him to finger me.

And he said no.

I sat up, crossing my arms over my chest.

"If you come here again, I'll aim the knife at a vein, and I'll dig much deeper."

"More for you to suck on." He shrugged carelessly, lighting his joint and tightening the laces of his boots. He didn't even spare me a look.

"Or maybe I'll just kill you next time. No one's going to miss you. Maybe your mum," I mused, snapping my lips together.

"Doubtful." He spoke with the lit joint in his mouth, tucking his Zippo into his back pocket. "But if you kill me, I'll kill you too. So we can join the Tindall ghosts. Isn't your room the very place she killed her husband? Kinda fucked up, GG."

How did he know about the ghosts?

About my *room*?

He'd only been here for summer session. Once. And he hadn't talked to anyone.

My expression probably gave away my shock. He smiled his rare, patronizing grin that drove me to murder.

"Fairhurst ran his mouth about your daddy's little playground. You grew up here, but I know secret places you would never dream of finding yourself. If you play your cards right and prove to know how to suck a cock, I might show you some of them—just as long as you don't confuse this for a relationship or expect me to get you off. I don't get people off. Other people's pleasure turns *me* off."

He said the words so frankly, I almost thought he was joking. He advanced to the door, calm and serious.

"You expect me to make you come, yet you won't make me come?" I asked when he had his back to me, at the threshold to my room.

I couldn't wrap my head around why any girl would agree to that. Yet dozens of girls at All Saints High had. I'd witnessed it myself.

"Slow learner, but she's finally getting it."

He didn't bother stopping before he slammed my door shut.

CHAPTER TEN
VAUGHN

The next day, I managed to get rid of my parents, who had come along to help me settle in at Carlisle.

My dad went hunting with a bunch of his rich-ass buddies on the outskirts of wherever the fuck we were in Berkshire. Mom was busy furnishing my room and spending time with her GBFF (gay BFF), Fairhurst.

I started my morning at six o'clock with a jog to let off some steam. Discipline was going to be the key to surviving this bitch for six months, and I had plenty of it. After a quick shower, a coffee, and a smoke, I picked up the two keys to the cellar, where I kept my work in progress, and hit the studio. Apart from Edgar, I wasn't going to let anyone see it before it was done. That was the opposite of the point of having a prestigious internship, but fuck it, I didn't come here to learn.

I came here to avenge.

Getting into my studio was a tad harder than breaking into the Pentagon. I'd put an entire system in place to ensure complete privacy. To start with, the room used to be the castle's pantry—cold, dry, and underground—a perfect cave to keep marble and stone. There were two doors, and therefore two locks, so no one could see what I was working on.

And I was working goddamn hard to make sure mine was the best art piece.

I picked up a drill and began wrestling with the sculpture, stone dust gathering at my feet. Metric's "Help I'm Alive" blasted through my earbuds as I worked. The shape of the statue was starting to sharpen and take on three dimensions. I'd thought about this piece more than I liked to admit while I was fucking around in the Hamptons, playing normal with my extended family for a few weeks earlier this summer. I'd ended up sending it straight to England, because I couldn't stand to look at it and I knew there was a good chance people would be able to see it if I worked on it there.

I penciled reference marks and cut, carved, shaped, and polished the sculpture the entire day, knowing Lenora was probably somewhere upstairs, wandering aimlessly, trying to figure out where the fuck I was. She was free to do whatever she wanted with her mornings and afternoons. I wasn't going to use her services, unless her lips counted as service when they wrapped around my cock every night.

As long as I kept tabs on her, she was good to roam free and play with her garbage.

I tried to push last night from my thoughts—specifically the part where she'd pushed my hand into her jammies. I thought I'd handled it fine. Though she did suspect I was a virgin.

Fuck.

Did it matter how I handled it? She was a fucking no one. Why would I care?

Okay, Vagina McPussyson. Deal with this eternal question after you're done working.

At around six pm, I heard a knock on the outer cellar door. The way it was designed, there was a cobblestone stairway with a door at the top and another one when you reached the bottom of the stairs. Wiping the sweat and dust from my brow, I turned around and fished for the keys in my pocket. I didn't wear a protective suit, goggles, or a mask while sculpting. If my lungs were going to collapse at twenty-five from being filled with stone, weed, and tar, so be it.

I opened the first door, and when I reached the top of the stairs, I pressed an elbow against the second.

"Secret word?" I growled.

If it was Good Girl, who'd somehow found me, I was going to chain her to her bedpost and have her suck a gallon of my blood as punishment, watching as she squirmed in embarrassment as she did.

"Bugger off," I heard Edgar Astalis growl from the other side. The secret word we'd agreed on was *Michelangelo*, but *bugger off* seemed more fitting.

I'd told the old man he could monitor my work when we'd agreed I'd take this gig. Someone had to make sure I wasn't going to present a twelve-foot marble dick at Tate Modern six months from now.

I unlocked the second door, motioning for him to come downstairs.

When we stood in front of the sculpture, he frowned.

"I'd like to make one thing clear," he said, staring at the general shape I'd worked my ass off on all day.

"I know you made things difficult for Lenny in high school. And for the most part, I turned a blind eye to it because I believe it is our job to pave our own way in life. But if you try to hurt my daughter—or do it unintentionally, for that matter—I will make sure no gallery in Europe will ever work with you. Am I understood?"

"Perfectly." I shoved my fists into my pockets, all calm. I took his threat in stride—not necessarily because I didn't plan on hurting her, but because I wasn't counting on getting work as an artist. I sculpted because I liked doing it. I could work as a roofer and be perfectly content.

He shook his head.

"The heads are disproportionate. The composition feels wrong. You might have to start from scratch."

"Fuck that."

"Watch your language. And as I said—you might. This is not up to par with what I'm used to from you. You've put your skill into this, but where's the rest of you? You need to bleed your heart into this piece."

I don't have a heart. "Working on it," I said instead, ignoring the fact that he was right.

I'd gotten sloppy, not because I lacked the talent or technique but because staring at this statue was hard and doing it justice was damn near impossible. The air was thinner at the top. The more successful you were, the more suffocating the expectations for your work became—another reason why artists were depressed all around.

His eyes roved the sculpture. It felt like he was ripping my guts open, poking at my organs.

He shook his head. "Work harder. Connect with this piece," he rumbled, his voice as big as his body. "Professor Fairhurst is looking for you. He is upstairs. Oh, and, Vaughn?"

I turned to look at him, waiting for the other shoe to drop.

"You cock this sculpture up, you make me regret giving you this internship, and I assure you, Daddy Spencer is not going to save you this time."

It wasn't the first time someone had threatened that my last name wouldn't get me out of trouble.

But it was the first time I'd believed it.

I pushed Harry's office door open without knocking, leaning against its frame when I realized what I'd walked in on. He had a guy—a student, I bet—bent with his elbows pressed against the window-sill, pants down, his milky-white ass hanging in the air. Harry was inclined, ass on his desk, pants open, stroking himself and enjoying the view.

Bored, I took out my phone and checked the time, whistling the *Kill Bill* theme song.

"Bollocks." Harry groaned when he heard me, shoving his

half-saggy cock back into his pants unhurriedly, like I'd interrupted his meal or something.

The teenager at the window straightened his back and proceeded to fall on his ass with a surprised yelp.

I yawned. "Please. Not on my account. You look fucking cute together."

"Truly?" The young guy eyed me with huge, green eyes while standing up and fumbling for his jeans.

My name had been a big deal in this place due to my summer session shenanigans all those years ago, and a sour face like mine was hard to miss. He knew who I was.

"No," I said impassively, moseying in. "Now get the fuck out and close the door after you."

He did just that, still shimmying into his pants when he closed the door. I turned to Harry, who settled behind his desk and smoothed his dress shirt, pretending to have an ounce of decorum.

"Nice wheels," I commented, still standing.

"Pardon?"

"You're riding that, obviously." I jerked my thumb over my shoulder, toward the door.

"Oh, that." He waved a finger at the door, clearing his throat. "He's a senior. Turned eighteen two weeks ago. I haven't even touched him—"

"Trust me," I cut him off. "No part of me cares."

"Yes. Right. So…" He grabbed a huge file on his desk, flipping through it. He stopped what he was doing, scratching a pink ear, and looked up, opening his mouth before frowning. "Christ, what happened there?" He motioned to my neck. "Love bite?" He sniffed.

"Don't taint the special moment with a dirty word like *love*." I smiled mockingly. "Why am I here, Harry?"

"It's Lenny. I wanted to make sure you weren't too harsh with her."

No, he didn't. He gave zero shits about anyone but himself. I took my Zippo out of my back pocket and flicked it. I'd told Edgar what I needed to tell him to get the gig, and he'd told Harry, but no part of me even mildly sympathized with Lenny.

Harry sighed heavily. "We have a problem."

I glanced at the time again. I'd missed dinner, but I wasn't worried. My mother had stocked the mini-fridge in my room with sick shit.

"It's about your mother."

My eyes snapped up. "I'm listening."

"As you may know, she offered me a position to become a partner in her gallery in Los Angeles a few weeks ago. It is a very successful gallery, so it is with heavy regret that I will have to say no."

I blinked at him, steadfast. "Please tell me why this is my concern because I'm trying to weed out the fucks I need to give about this boring-ass story."

"The reason I cannot, in good conscience, become a partner in the gallery is purely legal." He sat back in his executive chair, a smug smile tugging at his lips. "Your mother, for lack of diplomatic wording, is a drug smuggler."

"Are you fucking high?" My eyebrows shot up.

I knew my mother. She was straighter than a ruler, never broke the law in her life. Aside from being the only saint in Todos Santos, she didn't need to smuggle drugs. As it was, she had more money than the Windsor family. She donated millions to charities every year just to get rid of the greens.

"I am when in Los Angeles—on the purest cocaine, courtesy of the hundreds of kilograms of coke trafficked into the United States under the canvas of the paintings sent to her in crates from all over the world. Quite a pity. Such a pillar of the community, doing something so shameful. Tell me, Vaughn, how many years in prison is it for hundreds of kilograms of cocaine? In California? I think we may be talking about fifty, sixty years in jail." He *tsked*, tapping his long, skinny fingers on his table. "Perhaps more, if they want to make an example out of her. Oh, the FBI and DA would be all over Emilia LeBlanc-Spencer. Not quite the low-hanging fruit, is she? A golden opportunity to cut the ties between the Spencers and the local police, who bow to your every whim. And your father has his fair share of enemies who would go to great lengths to see his beloved thrown in the can."

"Liar." I bared my teeth, slapping his desk with both my palms. But I knew he had something. Otherwise he wouldn't be so cocky.

He sighed, as if the situation saddened him. "There are pictures everywhere. Evidence for miles. Guess she is in business with the wrong people."

"*You.*" My eyes widened. "You hooked her up with suppliers."

He was the wrong person.

"Did I, now?" He clucked his tongue. "I don't suppose you can prove it?"

I couldn't, but it was the truth. He'd done this. Of course he had—made sure she ordered pieces that came with drugs without telling her and somehow made it untraceable to him. *God fucking dammit.*

"They'll know she has nothing to do with it." I shook my head.

"Is that a chance you're willing to take?" He arched a brow. He knew the answer to that question.

"What do you want?"

"*You,*" Fairhurst snapped. "Quiet. Obedient. And out of my bloody hair. When you came here, you thought you had leverage over me. You thought I chose you because I was scared of you. You darling, naughty boy, I chose you because I wanted to put an end to your scowling, scheming, and silly plans—to remind you I'm the one calling the shots. One wrong move, Spencer, and your mummy will find out the untimely answer to the question, Does she look good in stripes?" My mother's supposedly dear friend spread his arms melodramatically.

"I will kill you," I spat, my entire body humming with rage.

He stood, rounding the desk toward me with his hands behind his back.

"You think I haven't considered that? You're a wild card, like your father. That's why there's a file on my Dropbox ready to be sent to my good friends at the FBI if I'm found prematurely dead. You can't touch me, Spencer. At least..." He stopped, raking his eyes over me with a rancid smile. "Not the way you *want* to touch me."

I ground my teeth, feeling blood trickling from my cheek. I'd bitten myself without noticing. I needed to keep my shit together. Mom was the one sacrifice I wasn't willing to make in my quest to burn this place down.

"How?" I sneered. *How had he made this happen?*

He took another step forward, our chests almost bumping. I was taller and broader now—bigger, stronger, and corded with muscles that mostly didn't exist in his body.

"All those years ago, I saw who you really were, Vaughn. A heartless prince. A beautiful mummy. You lacked basic emotions: love, hate, compassion. I befriended your silly, naive mother to get ahead in the art world game. Your father? Now, he knew better than to trust me. Fortunately, he was pussy-whipped and easy to manipulate through your mother. If you came here with a vendetta, you may want to throw it out the window. Our secret is ours. You're going to play into my hands now, my darling child. Or I'll be the one ending *your* life."

CHAPTER ELEVEN
VAUGHN

"Come in."

I pushed open the door to my parents' cottage. Dad was standing in front of a window overlooking a lake, his hands tucked into the pockets of his hunting suit, frowning. Nothing was wrong. Scowling was his default expression. He only ever smiled when my mother was around.

"Busy?" I took a stab at small talk.

He turned to look at me, taking a seat on a recliner by the window and pouring cognac from a square crystal bottle into two snifters. God bless the UK, where it was legal for me to drink.

"Cut the pleasantries. It's not who we are."

He was right. We both hated mingling, but I was on edge. I took a seat in front of him, half-grateful Mom wasn't here. Then I remembered she might be with Harry, and my stomach twisted in disdain. I wasn't sure she was safe with him. Still, I was selfish enough not to tell my father what just happened with Fairhurst.

I was a pilgrim on a quest, and the demise of Harry Fairhurst was my own personal journey to redemption.

If I told my father everything, he'd deal with Harry himself, and where was the fun in that? I'd come to England for a reason. My own *Eat, Pray, Love.*

Kill, Prey, Lust.

"Nice hate bite." Dad motioned to his own neck but looked at mine. "Did she try to kill you?"

"Wouldn't put it past her."

He took a swig of his drink, arching a brow. "Knowing you, she probably had her reasons. Wrap it up, kid. Make your mother and me grandparents before retirement, and all hell will break loose. She'd want to help raise the baby."

"I don't want kids."

He placed his drink on the table, lacing his fingers together.

"You're too young to determine that at nineteen. Now's the time to practice. *With a condom.* Several, if need be. What's eating you, and how can I help?"

I sat back, blowing air. Dad always saw through me. Mom had a sixth sense about knowing what I needed when I needed it *before* I'd realized I needed it. But Baron Spencer? He *read* me like a vintage *Playboy* in a sperm-donation clinic's waiting room.

I frowned at the carpet. "Say someone else had something of yours you didn't want to come out. Like, a video or evidence of something you did. You knew what they had looked legit. No bullshit. They said they had it saved in their cloud, ready to be sent out if you make the wrong move..." I scanned his face, looking for traces of surprise or worry. There weren't any. "How would you go about retrieving this information, and how would you erase it from all their files and make sure they couldn't make duplicates?"

He said nothing for a beat. I wanted to punch the walls, then him, then myself. Grabbing my drink, I took a generous sip.

Dad finally opened his mouth. "Son, are you gay?"

I spat the cognac out, choking on the earthy liquid. Dad remained calm, crossing one leg over the other.

"Be frank. You know we don't care, and we'll support you no matter what. There's nothing wrong with being gay."

"There's nothing wrong with it, all right, but I'm *not* gay."

He blinked, saying nothing.

"Why the fuck would you think that?"

"You're not a huge fan of the other sex."

"I'm not a huge fan of the human race."

"Me either. But then there's your mother. I am a huge fucking fan of hers."

"*Don't* make a groupie sex joke," I warned sharply. "I like girls just fine."

Dad shook his head. "Not enough to bring them home."

"The back of my truck is just as comfy, and Mom's not there to offer cookies." I felt my jawline tensing.

His jaw ticked too. We looked too alike. Sometimes it felt like I'd gotten nothing from my mother, but that wasn't true. I got her artistic talent. Dad couldn't draw a straight line with a ruler and the moral support of a stadium.

"Are the public blowjobs your way of proving something?" He frowned.

What the fuck? I was running out of patience. Not to mention fucks. This was not why I came all the way from Carlisle Castle to the rectum of Berkshire on foot.

"Yeah. It's to prove I don't give a shit about reciprocating," I deadpanned. "Now can we move on with the program?"

"Watch it." He smirked, seeming pleased with my low tolerance for bullshit. "And yes. So someone has something on you."

On Mom. "Kinda."

"How bad is it?"

I thought about it for a moment. "Imagine the worst possible scenario, then keep going."

"Prison bad?"

I nodded. "In the double digits. But don't ask because I won't tell."

He flicked an eyebrow.

Don't ask, don't tell. "Fuck, Dad, I promise if I liked dick, you'd be the first to hear all about it. In unnecessary detail, just to make it awkward for both of us."

"I can make this go away." He uncrossed his legs, leaning forward to catch my gaze. "I run a clean shop, but when the need to get dirty arises, I have my ways. Give me their name. Address too, if you have it. But a name and a picture will do."

I shook my head. If he knew it was Harry, it'd blow my cover and kill my plans.

"I'm not here for a solution, just advice."

He scanned my face for a second, glowering. "You're telling me your liberty is on the line, and you think I won't see to this myself?"

"That's exactly what I'm saying."

"Grant me this indulgence, Son."

I noticed he didn't ask me what I'd done. It made my heart swell in my chest, and that made me goddamn uncomfortable.

I shook my head. "Sorry."

He took the snifter. Strangled it in his hand to the point of white knuckles. "I'll give you my guy's name. You can contact him yourself."

"You'll ask him to disclose the information." It was my turn to cross my legs.

"Damn straight I will. You are my son, and your trouble is my trouble."

"*Not* this trouble."

We both darted up at the same time, scowling at each other, hands curled into fists. His snifter smashed against the floor between us, still half-full. Our body language mirrored perfectly. Dad was the first to sit back down, taking a calming breath.

"Fine. He'll make it a priority. I'll see to that myself. But if shit gets out of hand, I expect you to tell me."

"I want your word." I remained standing, looking down at him. "That you won't try to find out who this person is."

He gave me a slight nod.

"In *writing*."

He smirked. "You want me to sign a binding contract, give you access to my fixer, pay for the entire dubious pleasure, yet ask no questions about the motherfucker?"

"Sharp as always, Pops."

"Well, I'll be damned." He laughed. "You *are* my son."

"Was there ever any doubt?"

Mom walked in as if on cue, clutching a brown bag with celery and carrots peeking out. Dad stood up. He kissed her lips and took the bag from her, placing it on the open-plan kitchen counter, and I wrapped my arms around her in a hug, kissing her forehead.

"If there was a doubt, there would be casualties." Dad began to unload her groceries.

They shared another kiss. Gross. I was ready for them to go back to America and leave me to deal with this mess without their Brady Bunch bullshit in the background.

"Vaughn!" Mom slipped out of her shoes, licking her thumb and rubbing it against my cheekbone to clean up a trace of stone dust like I was five. "I bumped into Harry when I filled your fridge at Carlisle. He said you missed dinner. Stay. I'm making a casserole."

"Not hungry," I said, checking the time on my phone. *Fuck.* It was already nine at night.

"Nonsense! It'll be quick." Mom rushed to the counter to wash her hands, getting ready to chop shit up.

"I'll give him a ride," Dad cut in. "Boy's got enough blisters on his hands. Maybe if his feet are not as banged up, he'll be able to score."

Mom laughed and swatted Dad's chest, and he pretended to bite her chin lightly. *Gross 2.0.* If they were going to hit first base in front of me, I'd be responsible for more than one body bag on this island.

Dad scooped up the keys to the Range Rover he was renting, and we headed to the door. The ten-minute drive was completely silent. When he parked in the graveled cul-de-sac of Carlisle Castle, he killed the engine and took his phone out of his pocket.

"Name's Troy Brennan. Lives in Boston, so there's a time differ-ence. He has the best IT people on retainer. But you'll have to give me twenty-four hours before you contact him. I need to brief him first." He slid his finger across the screen, and my phone popped with the contact name.

"Got it," I said.

"I'm telling your mother we're leaving tomorrow morning."

I blinked at him. They were supposed to stay for a week.

"You need to deal with this shit," he explained, "and the sooner you do it, the better."

"Appreciate it." I unbuckled my seat belt.

Dad put his hand on mine, stopping me. "Keep me posted."

"I will." I hesitated, frowning. "Aren't you going to ask what I did?"

Technically, I did nothing. It was allegedly Mom. But I was curious as to why Dad didn't poke. Did he not give a shit or just have no moral compass?

He shook his head. "Sadly, it wouldn't make any difference. I'd still save you from harm. But if you raped someone, if you hurt…" He closed his eyes, inhaling sharply. He shook his head. "I just want to look at you and see someone I'm proud of. Always."

I let out a breath. "I'd never do that," I said. "Touch someone like that. No. It's nothing violent or shit like that."

"Thank *fuck.*"

I opened the passenger door.

"One more thing." He clasped my wrist. There was a threat laced in his voice. "I promised not to poke, but if I *find out* who's doing this to you, they will be mine to deal with."

I stared at him long and hard. I didn't plan to leave any traces behind. I was not going to make a mistake. Dad was never going to find out. This was not my hill to die on.

I smirked. "Deal."

CHAPTER TWELVE
LENORA

"Mate, I've seen more signs of intelligence on a moldy sausage roll," Pope snorted, lying next to me in my bed in the dark, licking his fingers clean of chocolate smudges.

We were recounting our day and sharing the latest of the chocolate baskets Poppy had sent my way. This one had arrived this morning. I broke off a piece of chocolate, popping it into my mouth and savoring the sugar and saltiness of the pretzel balls inside it.

"That daft, huh?" I wiggled my brows.

I felt Pope shaking his head beside me. His hand was propped under his head. We stared at my ceiling like it was a drive-in theater.

"I don't know how you put up with her an entire year. This Arabella lass is actively stupid, like it's her patriotic duty. She doesn't even know how to mix paint. No. Actually, she can't even distinguish varnish from a cup of water. Should've let her drink it, frankly. That way I'd be given another assistant. How was your first day?"

Pope rubbed my shoulder.

Why couldn't I obsess over someone like him? Nice, decent, and at least outwardly sane? Why did I have to secretly salivate over Vaughn Spencer, who wanted me to suck his blood and cock but didn't want to reciprocate? The guy who'd vanished faster than an Agatha Christie character as soon as he'd arrived in this castle, and had me looking for him all day like a lovelorn puppy?

I was so mortified to tell Papa I couldn't find the intern I was assisting that I hadn't even asked him where he was. Instead, I asked Uncle Harry if he knew where Vaughn worked on his piece. He gave me a cryptic answer that ultimately suggested Vaughn's piece was not to be seen by anyone other than Papa.

"I couldn't find him," I admitted to Pope. "I looked in all the studios, in his room, and asked Harry and Alma. No one knows where he works." I shrugged, trying to downplay how badly that stung—especially after last night, when he'd refused to touch me where I craved him.

"What a wanker." Pope shook his head.

Not quite, I was tempted to correct him. *He wouldn't wank me.*

"Well, if you can't find him tomorrow, I could certainly use a hand."

"And someone with a brain," I volunteered. We both laughed.

Pope said Arabella had wandered out of his studio minutes after establishing she couldn't tell the difference between a brush and a canvas, looking for my father. He said she'd seemed frantic. Maybe she'd finally realized Vaughn wasn't going to be with her, even if she moved across the ocean for him.

"Pope," I said, my voice turning serious. "About my birthday present…I know what I want."

"Do tell."

So I did. I told him. It was one of the most embarrassing conversations I'd ever had. Fortunately it was dark, so he couldn't see my nuclear blush, and to my relief, he agreed. Part of me had thought he might laugh in my face and tell me to bugger off. But he was completely cool about it, said it wasn't going to be a problem. Then, to extinguish the awkwardness, he turned around and tickled my waist.

I laughed, pushing him to the corner of the mattress, against the wall, trying to tickle him back. We wrestled on top of my bed, and I was grateful that interns and assistants weren't under the tight supervision of the staff the way the students were, and I could sneak him in. We giggled breathlessly, and I managed to sneak my hand into his armpit, which caused him to jolt. (Pope was notoriously ticklish.) He climbed on top of me and straddled me to the futon, just the way Vaughn had the night before, my wrists locked beside my shoulders.

I twisted underneath him, panting with joy. "Sod off."

"Hmm, what you really mean is carry on, right?" Pope licked his lips, his eyes lighting up with mischief. "Because every sane man knows no means yes."

My stomach hurt from laughing. He was ridiculous. I pretended to fight him when, out of nowhere, Pope flew off the top of me, his back slamming against the opposite wall of my room. At first, he seemed to have been sucked by the air or an invisible monster, like in a movie.

I yelped, darting up in bed, but when a shadow loomed over Pope's figure like a dark demon, I knew exactly who the monster was.

"Touch her again, and you won't have hands to protect your ugly face with, legs to run from me, or a *tongue* to rat me out. We fucking clear on that, Rafferty Pope?" Vaughn's voice pierced the air like a snake's hiss.

Raff didn't even get the chance to answer before Vaughn's fist raised in the air, aimed at his face. I jumped on Vaughn, wrapping my legs around his waist from behind and jerking his curled fist back.

"You idiot!" I screamed, hitting Vaughn everywhere. Back. Shoulders. Head. "We were just taking a piss. He didn't try to hurt me!"

What was Vaughn doing here anyway? And since when did he care what happened to me?

He turned, and his eyes scared me. They were so much darker than their natural color, and full. Full of hatred and anger and...*fear?* I swear I saw something genuine behind them.

"You fucking him?" he spat.

"My sex life is none of your business," I said flatly, regaining my composure. He'd ghosted me the entire day and came back at night to do…what exactly? But the answer was obvious. *Me.* Or at least he wanted from me what he'd gotten from Arabella, Alice, and his harem of teenyboppers: complete submission and head.

He'd come to the wrong place.

He raised his voice. "Answer me!"

"Of course I'm having sex with Pope." I smiled sweetly as Pope stood up, eyeing Vaughn with fresh, new hatred. "Look at him, Vaughn. Pope is ten times more talented than you are, sane, *and* gorgeous. You taunted me about being a virgin our entire senior year, but you know what, Spencer?" I rose on my tiptoes, bringing my mouth to Vaughn's ear and dropping my voice so Raff couldn't hear us. "I think you're the one in need of a lesson or two. Standing there getting your dick sucked doesn't exactly require much skill, and I don't believe for one moment that you don't want to touch me. You just don't know *how*."

Shockingly, he took a step back. Then I saw his wild eyes, slightly out of focus, and knew I'd pushed him too far.

"Whatever you have going with him stops now," he announced. "You were my property at All Saints, and you're sure as fuck my possession here."

"Whoa…" Pope laughed behind Vaughn's back, causing both of us to turn toward him. He brushed the dust from his trousers. "Someone needs a Xanax, a drink, and a reality check. She's no one's property, mate. The 1800s came and went. Women get to decide these days. Radical, I know."

"Shut up," Vaughn snapped, turning back to me. "I'm staying here tonight."

I tried to swallow my hysterical laughter. And succeeded, for the most part.

"Out." I pointed at the door.

"Had a really shitty day, Good Girl, and I'm not in the mood for a fight. But if you pick one, you better know you're going to be on the losing end."

It was silly to consider his feelings, but even in the dark, Vaughn looked so tired and worn-out, I didn't want to be the one to break him completely. For some reason, even though I enjoyed drawing his blood, I realized I no longer craved his pain. And that worried me. A lot.

I exhaled, giving Pope a slight nod. "It's fine."

"You sure?" He frowned.

I stepped around Vaughn to hug Pope, realizing it was probably the first time he and Vaughn had met.

"Vaughn, Pope. Pope, Vaughn. Pope is my best friend. Vaughn is…" I trailed off, looking between the two guys standing in front of each other. "Vaughn is a cunt," I deadpanned.

"Arabella said you helped her fill out the application form I daftly accepted. Cheers for burdening me with a rubbish assistant who is barely literate." Pope extended his hand, and Vaughn examined it a moment before shaking it reluctantly.

"Touch Len again, and Arabella will be the least of your worries." Vaughn smiled politely, giving Pope's hand an unfriendly squeeze.

Pope whistled, arching an eyebrow. "*Len.*"

I swear Vaughn blushed, but it was too dark to tell.

"Run along now, *friend*," Vaughn admonished.

Once we were alone, he turned to me. I slipped back into bed, ignoring his presence. I was tired from roaming the castle all day trying to find him, and I didn't want to fight. I cracked open my fantasy book and perched it against the wall I was facing, as if I weren't in the pitch-dark. Behind me, Vaughn made a move to get into bed.

I held up a hand without even turning around. "Don't even think about it. I still have the knife. This time, I'll cut you where the sun don't shine."

"That would be the third mark you've left on me. At this point, you should know better than to think I'd care."

I'd noticed the purple hickey on his neck but had no idea what other scar he was referring to. I twisted my head to look over my shoulder, my curiosity getting the better of me. Vaughn lifted his shirt and showed me the scar from when I'd stitched him up in my bathtub. Apparently, I did a terrible job. I could still see the skin zigzagging shut like a wonky zipper. His flesh had healed around it. The mark was going to stay like that forever.

I turned my face back to the book, giving him my back. "I did you a favor."

"I wasn't complaining," he said lightly.

"Where've you been today?"

"Working."

"Why didn't you call me?"

"Because I don't need help."

"Why'd you offer me the role if you don't want me to help you?" I was still staring at the same page, unable to decipher a word without turning on my lamp.

Was I asking him about the internship or about everything else between us? One second he was interested—possessive, unbalanced, *rabid*—and the next he disregarded me completely.

"Because…" His voice grew nearer, and I knew he was above me, that he could touch me at any moment. The thought sent a shiver down my skin. "I wanted to keep an eye on your ass, and you wanted to be here. Look, I had a crappy day. I'm giving you free rein to work on your piece for six months. Don't worry about mine. It'll be ready in time, and it will be sick. Job offers will be coming out of our asses."

"You won't let anyone see it," I said.

"No."

"Not even my father?"

No answer. *Jesus.* I turned toward him, shutting the book with a thud. "He knew you weren't going to let me see it, and he still let me come here and waste six months of my life on you?"

Vaughn sat on the edge of my bed, regarding me with quiet curiosity. "You wanted to be here."

"As an intern."

"Should've specified."

"Oh, bugger off. I'm not a charity case."

"No one said you were," Vaughn ground out, losing his patience. "Look, you are getting the prestige without doing any of the work. I'm handling shit on my own, and I'll hook you up with an internship when we're done. I'm good for it, Good Girl."

I didn't know how or why, but something told me he wanted to touch me but wasn't sure how I'd react. His hands lay awkwardly in his lap. Vaughn was never awkward.

I threw my head on the pillow, exhaling as I studied my ceiling. "I should leave."

"Come off it, *Rub-in Wood*."

It was obviously a joke to him.

"You don't need me," I pointed out.

It was the truth, and it hurt. I didn't want the stupid assistant job to begin with, and now that I'd come to terms with it, it wasn't even available. My entire existence seemed pointless. Vaughn said nothing.

"I do." His voice came out of nowhere, surprising me. "I do need you, just not for my fucking piece." He bared his teeth, finally looking at me. "Happy?"

"How do you mean?" I sat up, rubbing my eyes.

He looked down to his lap, and after a brief silence, I followed his gaze. He was hard. We hadn't even touched. We didn't even *flirt*. But I guessed those things happened, right? He was nineteen. Boys that age were notorious for getting hard from anything, including shaved raccoons.

"This." He removed his hands from his lap, offering me a better view of his thick, throbbing erection behind his black sweatpants. "It doesn't happen to me. Well, it does, but only when I want it to, and it doesn't feel the same…as it does when I'm with you."

He grunted the entire sentence, like he was admitting a terrible crime. I licked my lips, swallowing a ball of something in my throat. Excitement? No. It was more than that. I felt…*triumph.*

"What are you saying?"

His gaze sliced straight to mine. He glowered. "What the fuck do you think I'm saying? You're hot, and I guess I want to fool around with you. I didn't use any fancy words, Good Girl. No need to crack open a dictionary."

There's the asshole again. But I knew he was frightened of the truth. For some reason, sex was a touchy subject for him. And maybe I was right. Maybe we were both virgins. I'd said it as a joke, but it made a lot of sense when I thought about it. I'd never seen him actually making out with a girl. I never saw him flirt or talk to anyone.

I'd never seen him kiss a girl.

Christ, I don't think I'd ever *heard* of him kissing one either.

I flung my legs out of the bed, moving to sit next to Vaughn, hip to hip. I asked my next question without meeting his eyes.

"Was I your first kiss?"

That would mean Vaughn's first kiss was at age eighteen, more or less. A prospect too ridiculous to be taken seriously. No guy gets blowjobs before *kissing*, surely.

He snorted, shaking his head. "Fuck off."

"Tell me."

"*No*, you weren't my first kiss," he snapped cruelly.

I said nothing. Maybe I got it wrong after all. There was a beat of silence before he opened his mouth again.

"You were the second one. I kissed Luna Rexroth at the pre-Christmas party at the Coles' last year to spite Knight, so he'd finally make a move."

My pulse kicked up again. He'd only kissed one girl in his entire life. Two, including me. And the first one didn't even count. It seemed not only unlikely but completely bonkers. Even *I* had kissed four guys. And I had no experience to speak of. Vaughn truly didn't want anything to do with girls if he was that reluctant to be with them. But why?

"Maybe I'm asexual," he said dispassionately.

I didn't think he was. The way we kissed...there was magic there. The wild, untamed lust of two hot, mortal bodies connecting, exploding, desperate to claw each other out of our skin and blend together into something intimate and the same.

The same.

That's why I couldn't resist Vaughn's kisses or when he laced his fingers in my hair or when he looked at me from across the room. When we touched, it felt like we were one entity, and that scared and thrilled me.

"I don't want to fuck you. I don't want to eat you out," Vaughn said gravely, his throat bobbing.

He seemed like he was on the brink of an epiphany tonight. What had happened to make him like this?

"But I want to kiss you. A lot. And everywhere. And..." He frowned, rolling his eyes with a sigh. "I guess I don't mind if you end up liking it when I do."

I burst out laughing.

He wasn't expecting that. His frown deepened, and he widened his eyes in annoyance. It seemed he couldn't understand why I was flattered and thoroughly entertained by the idea that he was attracted to me so much, he was willing to break many of his rules. He had to *come to terms* with making someone else feel good. Christ, with this lad, I needed to be careful. Moments like this made me like Vaughn as a person, see past the persona. Luckily, they were few and far between, and I truly was incapable of falling in love.

"It's not funny."

"It is. You're right, I shouldn't leave here. You're going to do the work for both of us, and I could use the time to work on my project. But as for kissing, I have a few inquiries before I make a decision regarding your offer."

"It wasn't an offer," he snapped, as if horrified that I might take this as a compliment.

I shrugged, pointing at the door, in case he'd forgotten his way out. He let out a heavy sigh. "Lay it on me."

"Will you be kissing other girls?" I grabbed my pillow and hugged it to my midriff. *Namely, Arabella.*

"No." He nearly shuddered, staring at me like I was mad. "Course not."

"Will you let them give you head?" I asked.

"Will *you* give me head?"

"No, not if you won't go down on me."

"Well, then, I guess, yeah. I'll get head elsewhere."

"Then we don't have a deal."

"Are you serious?" He pulled back to examine my face.

I shrugged. "I'm not asking for a ring, Vaughn. We both know this is going to be nothing more than fooling around, and I like making out with your sour arse. Now that I have nothing to do but work on my piece, I guess you could be a nice distraction until we get out of here. But I don't want anything to do with you if you continue sticking your willy in other girls' mouths."

"Fine," he spat, his lips thin with rage.

"Fine," I said breezily, and somehow—*somehow*—I realized I had managed to convince myself during this conversation that this was a brilliant idea.

That it was grand that Vaughn had given me all this spare time.

That it was lovely we were going to kiss and fondle and maybe even shag each other.

There was no chance on earth I was going to catch feels for Lucifer Junior. I didn't want to fall in love. To get married. To have children. That's why I'd tattooed Carlisle Prep's motto on my inner thigh.

I even managed to tell myself that Vaughn flexing his muscles in front of Pope wouldn't cause future problems, that I had both men under control.

In fact, the only bitter taste I couldn't shake off was Papa's betrayal. The way he'd hidden the truth about my internship from me. It felt like my father had compromised me to help my enemy, and I was furious with him.

Vaughn owed me nothing.

But my father? Oh, he did.

"And I mean, you could hurt me," Vaughn continued, clearing his throat. "I mean, blood and shit, if that's your jam."

I don't know why it saddened me so much that he offered me his pain as a token for our deal. I liked hurting him when he was hurting *me*. I wasn't a connoisseur of pain, like him.

"I don't want that." The timbre of my voice reminded me of padding on tiptoes.

"Okay."

"Now that we've got that out of the way." I slapped my thighs, desperate to push the rage and disappointment with my father out of my consciousness. "Remember your first kiss with Luna?"

"Vaguely…" The ruby in his cheeks flared again. He wouldn't look at me.

Oh, Vaughn.

"I want you to erase it from your memory." I stood up, stepping between his legs and draping my arms around his neck. Slowly, I sank down, my knees straddling his waist. His breath hitched. Mine stopped completely. The air seemed thick and moist again. I settled on his hard-on, feeling the thick bulge pressed against my center.

"And all the ones with me that followed. This is your first kiss." My lips fluttered over his as I spoke.

"Len." My nickname dropped from his mouth into mine, hot and desperate.

His eyelids slid shut, despite his best efforts to stay in control.

But not mine. I stared at him as I kissed him, with eyes wide-open.

There was nothing more beautiful than watching Vaughn Spencer let go.

CHAPTER THIRTEEN
VAUGHN

There.

I fucking did it.

I kissed a girl, and I liked it.

A whole fucking lot.

It wasn't the first time I'd kissed Lenora Astalis. But now we had an arrangement, and I was going to milk the shit out of it until I finished this damn internship. I was going to kiss her, fuck her eventually, then get out of Carlisle Castle a normal person, sexually.

Maybe.

Fine, probably not.

After the conversation with Dad where he'd asked if I was gay, I knew I had to take a proactive step toward dipping my cock in more than one hole. People had started to notice, and I didn't like that.

I spent the next couple weeks working from seven in the morning till nine at night. The sculpture was shaping up nicely. The heads were proportioned now, and I'd carved the faces in detail, down to the very last vein, crinkle, and freckle. Getting each individual hair right was going to take weeks, though. Having Lenora around in the studio would probably cut the time it took me to get shit done in half, but I didn't want her help.

It looked good, though—the sculpture. Edgar had come to check on the piece a few times, muttering profanity all the way from the first door to the second about the fungal smell and creepy atmosphere. But he said my soul poured out of the sculpture.

"Keep this up, and you got yourself an easy sell. *If* you could sell it. As it happens, it is going to be Carlisle Prep's property. Forever."

Bet he wouldn't be so smug if he knew that after I worked on my piece, I ran to my second shift: making his daughter, my *other* piece, moan my name every night.

The good thing about my working hours was I managed to avoid human interaction almost entirely. I woke up every morning at five thirty, jogged, took a shower, went through my emails with my coffee—answering Dad, Mom, and Troy Brennan, aka the Fixer, who'd started working on the Harry Fairhurst case—then locked myself in the cellar before classes started at eight. By the time I finished working at nine, people were already in their dorms. The dining hall was closed, and other than random punks who bowed down in my presence and the occasional dry-humping couple, I didn't see a fucking face.

Not even Arabella's.

Definitely not Rafferty Pope's.

And, thank fuck, not Harry's either.

I was sure he kept his guard up despite my lack of presence in his life. He'd gone as far as framing my mother to make sure I wouldn't retaliate, so I knew he wasn't the dumbass I'd pegged him to be. However, just because I was silent about it, didn't mean I wasn't working on taking him down.

Then there were the nights with Good Girl.

After a shower and an entire buttered loaf of bread and ham, I'd slip into her room and kiss her mouth.

And neck.

And eyes.

And hair.

I was ready for more—tasting her tits, maybe. I hadn't touched them yet, but I'd been thinking about them since that day she got out of the pool naked.

Len made me rock hard, and that was both an unwelcome distraction and a relief. Each night, after hours of first base, I'd crawl back to my room, dizzy because all my blood was in my cock, and beat one off before passing out in bed. I came *buckets*. I hadn't come often before my arrangement with Good Girl, and never this much. I'm talking enough to fill a carton of milk. I had to Google that shit to see that it was normal.

For some reason, Lenora seemed perfectly content to kick me out as soon as we were done. Neither of us wanted anything more, so I wasn't exactly fucking begging for spooning. She didn't strike me as clingy or possessive, and I dug that.

I even started feeling a little sorry for hijacking her internship.

Okay, not really.

My streak of not seeing people in a castle full of fucking people ended on my sixth week at Carlisle Prep. It was ten past seven in the morning, and I strode down the fourth-floor hallway where all the interns, assistants, and staff resided.

Basically, all the assholes of legal age who could fraternize with each other without getting their asses thrown in jail.

That's when I saw Arabella slipping out of a room.

Edgar's room.

She closed the door with a soft click, tucked her chin down, and shook her head. She looked like shit—tired, emotional, crying. When she looked up and spotted me, a slow, bitchy grin spread on her face.

She wiped her cheeks clean of tears.

"Thought you'd look for me, Spence." She popped one hip out, parking her hand on her waist. She wore... What the fuck was it that she wore? Some sort of red, lacy nightgown with a matching robe. She'd clearly paid the sculptor a social call. On her back, most likely.

I continued advancing toward Len's room, ignoring her. She followed me, chasing my steps like the desperate chihuahua she was. Good thing I didn't have any loyalties to Lenora. Breaking the news that her fiftysomething pops was porking a teenager would make for awkward foreplay conversation.

Not that we had any, thank fuck.

Although, I couldn't be completely sure I *wasn't* going to tell her either. Who the fuck knew what was going to come out of my mouth when I met her again? Sometimes I wanted to ruin her, sometimes save her, and most times I was indifferent to her existence, save for what her stupid body made me feel.

"Did I tell you all my clothes got stolen and burned last week?" Arabella called after me. "I had to walk around in an actual uniform until my parents shipped me some clothes."

I knew. I was the one responsible for it. Arabella seemed to have completely forgotten that the last time I saw her, she'd set Lenora's house on fire and left me to save her. I thought it'd be a nice way to say hello without actually seeing her face.

"Damn shame." I moved deliberately fast to make it hard for her to keep up. "Then again, most of the time you're out of your clothes and on your knees, so I bet no one will notice."

"You're so funny." She swatted my shoulder, shadowing me, still. "Where's your room?" she panted.

She'd been crying just a second ago but now looked like a ball of fucking sunshine. I hated soulless, preppy, hedge fund girls. I passed Len's room and headed toward mine. I didn't want Arabella anywhere near my business.

"It's room stop-being-so-desperate," I quipped.

"I haven't seen you around, and we live on the same floor."

I passed my room too, reached the wide stairs, rounded them, and went down the other stairway, toward the second floor. She followed.

"I'm working," I said finally.

"Well, I'm not." She burst out laughing. "Poor Raphael, or whatever his name is. Vampire Girl helps him sometimes, but honestly, he's lonelier than a virgin in a Panic! At the Disco concert. I go downtown every day in search of cute clothes and, like, a life. There are zero malls in this area. Total bore."

So Lenora was still hanging out with fuckface. I made a mental note to remind both of them to keep their hands to themselves. My pulse began to drum against my throat.

Best friends since childhood, my ass. I'd seen how it ended between Knight and Luna. Spoiler: They weren't very platonic since she'd started gurgling his cum on a daily basis.

I rounded the hallway, proceeding to the last stairway. Arabella could barely breathe, I moved so fast.

"C'mon, Spence. I'm lonely as hell."

"Leave, then."

She was the one who'd begged me to score her this gig when I dragged her ass to Indiana. I couldn't even remember why I'd complied—something to do with pissing Len off, and knowing I'd have a steady girl to suck my cock in a place full of minors. Didn't seem like such a bad deal at the time...

"I can't." She pouted, actually stomping her foot like a fucking three-year-old. "Something...*someone* is keeping me here."

"Then stay and shut the fuck up. Those are your two options."

"We used to be friends." She clung to my arm.

I shook her off. "Correction: we were friend*ly*—meaning I didn't actively hate you. But the road from there to liking you was still a mile long and a mile wide. Then, you set a house on fire and left me to rescue Drusilla. That homicide attempt put a little damper on our relationship."

I reached the first floor. Stopped. I wasn't going to go down to the cellar and reveal where I was working. Her chest rose and fell, and she shoved her rack in my face. Pushing her tits up, she knotted her arms around my shoulders and grinned. My dick was so soft I could've kneaded it like fucking dough.

"I'll make it good for you. Help you unwind. What do you say?"

That was an easy question.

"Fuck. No." I pushed her arms aside.

For some stupid-ass reason, the idea of Len walking by and seeing this pissed me off. Not that I gave a shit, but I didn't need the headache. And I really wasn't going to let Arabella suck me off again, so any second wasted in her presence was time I wasn't going to get back and could be used doing better things, like scratching my ass or staring at the wall.

"But I will throw you a bone."

"Really?" Her eyes lit up.

"Relax. I said a bone, not a boner. If you find it in yourself *not* to *bone* Edgar Astalis, I promise not to fuck your little sister's face when I'm back in Todos Santos."

I had no intention of returning. Permanently, anyway. But Arabella wasn't privy to that information, and there wasn't one motherfucker in Todos Santos who'd put it past me to let a minor suck my cock.

"My sister is barely seventeen, you sick schmuck!" She scowled.

I shrugged. "Legal next year. Perfect timing. I'd hate to do the *full house* thing, but your mom seems easy, and knowing your entire household had sucked me off would be a trip. Stay away from Daddy Astalis, and go find someone else to play schoolgirl with."

"You think I'm screwing Edgar Astalis?" There were tears in her eyes.

Maybe. Staring directly at her face seemed counterproductive. I wanted to eat today.

I curved an eyebrow. "Were you playing air hockey in there?"

"Jesus, you are pussy-whipped." She snorted. "She really got in your head, huh?"

"Who?"

"Drusilla."

Who the fuck thought it was a good idea to teach Arabella how to speak? I wanted to sue her nanny.

"You're high. Take a hike." I turned to leave. I stopped when I heard her voice, my back still to her.

"Yeah. The Astalises have this effect on people. Well, not Poppy. Poppy is a loser. But something about Drusilla and Edgar is irresistible, huh? They *change* people."

I smirked, turning around and getting in her face.

"No one and nothing will change me. Don't blame others for your lack of personality and the fact that your morals are looser than your pussy flaps. Now beat it, before your clothes aren't the only thing missing from your room by the end of today."

Arabella stared at me, dumbfounded. I bared my teeth and snapped my jaw. She took a step back, bumped into the stairway banister, turned around, and ran in the other direction.

Students began to pour out of the cafeteria into the hall, and all of them chanced a look at the half-naked, psychotic girl in lingerie running around. I turned and strolled to my cellar before more people could figure out what I was doing.

Change, my ass.

I was the same bastard. I just happened to be getting some ass now.

At lunchtime, I walked downtown to meet Uncle Jaime, Dad's best friend and my trust fund's trustee. My parents didn't want to handle that shit. Dad had worried Mom would grant me whatever I wished for, so he put his friend in charge. Jaime had flown all the way from Todos Santos to meet me, and it wasn't that his schedule was wide-open. He ran a hedge fund with Dad, Knight's dad, and Luna Rexroth's father. It's that I'd told him it was important.

This part was tricky because I needed to trust Jaime not to pass it forward. Luckily, he wasn't the snitching type.

We met at a local Gregg's. He ordered coffee, and I chose some type of weird pastry I had no plan to eat. I preferred eating alone somewhere quiet. I hated it when people witnessed me doing something so mundane.

"Yo." I bumped my shoulder into his, and he grabbed me by the back of the neck and jerked me into a hug.

"*Hello* is the word you were looking for, punk. *Hello*, godson."

We fell into our chairs. He had sandy-blond hair, not unlike Fairhurst but much friendlier features. His hair was buzzed close to the scalp, and he looked like California royalty, not some British douchebag who knew words no one knows the meaning of.

"Why am I here?" Jaime cut to the chase, taking a sip of his Americano.

"I need to break the piggy bank. Get access to my money," I said flatly.

He nearly sprayed his coffee all over me. I remained seated, wide-legged, my fists shoved deep into the pockets of my pilot jacket.

"Are you high?" he wondered aloud. "This is not half a stick we're talking about, son. It's the whole goddamn trunk and then some."

"If you knew what I needed it for, you wouldn't say that," I said calmly, my eyes on him the entire time.

He stared at me, rigid with rage. "*Try* me."

"First, you need to promise not to snitch to my parents."

Uncle Jaime said nothing, like I knew he would. I took a contract I'd drafted all by myself from my backpack and slid it across the round, plastic table between us.

"Vaughn—"

"They can't know." I cut into his words, handing him pen. I fucking love contracts. Paper scared the shit out of rich people, much more than a gun. "Just read it, sign it, and I'll tell you what's up."

A part of me was sure he was going to stand up, rip the contract to shreds, and throw it in my face. I released a breath when he actually signed it. Then he sat back and asked me what was up, and I told him about Harry blackmailing me about Mom.

I left out the other, really tiny part about killing him—semantics and shit.

"And this plan of yours, are we sure it's going to work?" He frowned.

"I'm not unsure." I smirked.

Uncle Jaime closed his eyes and took a deep breath. He wasn't happy. My trust fund wasn't anything to laugh at. Eight figures. The kind of shit most people would never even fantasize about having. And I needed every single penny.

"Am I going to regret this?" He rubbed at his cheekbone, his index finger hovering over the screen of his phone. To make this sort of transaction, you had to drag your ass to your actual banker, but Jaime *was* that banker, so he could do whatever the fuck he wanted.

I could feel the saliva pooling in my mouth.

Do it, old man. Release the fucking money.

"You're going to thank me by the time it's all over," I said calmly, standing and pretending I wasn't eager for him to just *transfer the money into my account.*

"I've done this dance before, son, and shit can go real bad real fast. Keep me posted?"

"Bet on it, Uncle Jaime," I lied.

I walked away without saying goodbye.

―――――

I got back to Carlisle Castle by foot. There were no buses to and from the castle, and I preferred it that way. It meant most students bailed or fucked off during the weekends, because the place was secluded and dead. And *that* meant fewer assholes to stand in my way.

It was an uphill journey, and I spent it sending the Fixer a long-ass encrypted email about my progress in the Fairhurst matter. I'd avoided the painter like the plague but wasn't necessarily happy about it. I wanted to put shit in motion, but not before Mom was completely out of the woods. Taunting him now would raise a red flag. I needed to play it smart.

After hitting the send button, I looked up. I was on the edge of downtown Carlisle Village, about to cross the street to a road bracketed by a thick wood, which led to the bridge that would take me to Carlisle Prep.

There was a little chocolaterie at the end of that road. The display window and doorframe were colored the same shade of frog green, and there were Christmas lights and little bullshit smiling china dolls dressed like medieval whores scattered among the confiseries biscuits, a tower of brownies, and fruit pastilles.

I stopped, staring at the candy. I didn't have much of a sweet tooth, but I knew someone who made her dentist very happy and very rich. Someone who'd appreciate a slice of that brownie very fucking much.

Someone whose pants I wanted to get into eventually.

I shook my head, glanced at the entry door, and crossed the street.

Don't change for a pussy.

CHAPTER FOURTEEN
LENORA

About the time I'd gotten used to seeing summer session students around, they left and the school year at Carlisle Prep started with a bang. I'd forgotten just how busy it got here—the hallways always teeming with people, chatter everywhere, shoulders brushing. And with the students, came the fall. The leaves turned yellow and orange and then fell from the trees completely, leaving them naked and exposed.

Like the leaves, a part of me wanted to jump ship. But I clung on, even when I felt crispy and brittle and curling at the edges, just like them.

In an odd juxtaposition, Pope spent weeks eagerly anticipating my birthday. I was pleased by this—particularly considering what I'd asked him for—but it was strange since the occasion had merited hardly a greeting card from anyone around me last year.

He seemed determined to erase that experience.

When the day finally arrived, I was awakened by my bedroom door, which flew open and slapped against the wall.

Pope barged in wearing a birthday hat, casually blowing a party whistle in my face.

"Happy birthday to you. Happy birthday to you. Happy birthday, dear Lenny," he sang, holding two full shot glasses and keeping a fancy liquor bottle tucked under his arm.

I squinted at the alarm clock on my nightstand. It wasn't even eight yet.

After a dramatic pause, he finished. "Ha-aaaa-ppy birthday to you."

He fell next to me on the mattress, handing me one of the shot glasses. We clicked them, mumbled cheers, and sent the stinging liquid down our throats.

"Mornin'," I greeted groggily, "in case someone forgot…"

"Is it really, though? Everything's relative, Lenny. Especially time. It's five o'clock somewhere." He poured himself another shot, motioning with the bottle to my empty glass.

I shook my head, sitting up. "In Sydney, actually. It's five o'clock there."

I was a bit of a nerd. I'd always been thirsty for information. It worked to my benefit for the most part. For instance, yesterday I'd worked on my piece and debated how to sculpt a shredded heart. I wanted it to pour out of the statue's chest, like lava slithering from an active volcano. Thankfully, I'd been hitting the daytime classes when I was bored to gather more inspiration, and I'd stumbled upon a papier-mâché technique Alma demonstrated in one of the senior classes. Paper was fragile, wrinkly, thin; I'd marched to the newsagent's across the bridge as soon as class was dismissed and purchased a stack of newspapers and glue.

The heart turned out deliciously dark. The paper exploded from the statue's muscular chest like fireworks, bursting with color and motion.

Rafferty elbowed my ribs, anchoring me back to the present. "How're we spending the day?"

"Working." I snorted. "You're pressed for time to finish your painting, and I've hit my stride too."

"Fuck my painting. It's not every day my best mate turns eighteen. Let's get pissed downtown."

"On a weekday?" I blinked at him. "Before noon?"

He snapped his fingers, pointing at me. "There's no better time than the present. Also, no queue at the bar."

"Also, no *bar*, because it's eight in the morning." I laughed.

He rolled his eyes, giving me a light shove. My head fell back to the pillow.

"All right." I pretended to sigh, feigning exasperation. "I guess we could go for a few pints and fish and chips. And…chocolate. Lots of chocolate."

"You need more chocolate like the royals need more skeletons in their closet." Pope jumped up to his feet, strolling to my drafting table and cocking his head. "Who's the admirer?"

"Huh?" I looked up, stretching in my bed.

There was a huge basket containing a mountain of individually wrapped brownies on the table and a white teddy bear with a red ribbon next to it. My mouth watered immediately.

"That would be Poppy." I swallowed the excess saliva, rubbing the sleep out of my eyes. "You know she sends me chocolate all the time. God knows you're good at demolishing it with me."

"Poppy sends you chocolate. These are brownies. Not the same. And this looks much more expensive," Pope commented, tugging the black satin strap that knotted the cellophane together around the basket. It fell open, and he helped himself to a piece of brownie, unwrapping one that had been tucked inside Harry Potter–themed paper.

I shook my head. "Still Poppy. I don't have any suitors. Crap, our family dog doesn't like me much." I shrugged.

Pope snorted. "You don't have a dog. Your sister's allergic. Anyway, this shit's good. Want some?"

"Let me brush my teeth first."

"Suppose you want your privacy."

"That would be nice." I smiled.

"And a bit rich, considering what you asked for, for your birthday." He wiggled his eyebrows.

I blushed instantly. He had a point.

"You can say no," I reminded him.

"I don't *want* to. It's a fun present to give."

"You'll have to come here every day."

"As opposed to now?" He laughed.

I curled my lips around my teeth, stifling a smile.

Pope took off, walking to the door. "Meet me at ten at the cul-de-sac, birthday girl."

My phone buzzed right after Rafferty closed the door. *Poppy*. She called to wish me a happy birthday. I thanked her for the present, and she waved it off and said it was nothing.

"How're things over there?" she poked, munching on a granola bar on the other end of the line. Since she'd started studying in London, she'd been hanging out with her new, fancy friends. Poppy loved socializing. Based on her tone alone, I knew things had worked out the way she'd planned. She had that shine to her voice, that extra I'm-happy timbre.

"Good," I lied. Sort of. "And there?"

"Fantastic. I'm having a blast. Papa said Arabella is Rafferty's internship assistant? How odd. Is she giving you trouble?"

"No," I answered honestly.

I hadn't mentioned anything about Arabella when Poppy and I chatted, partly because I hadn't had the chance to see her much. I occasionally saw her across the hall, but I didn't bother acknowledging her, or vice versa. She had been spending her weekends elsewhere and her weekdays holed up somewhere, and although I hadn't spoken to Vaughn about her, I trusted him when he said he wouldn't touch her. Which begged the question: What exactly was she doing at Carlisle Prep? She seemed to have no ties to the place. She wasn't an artist. Vaughn didn't want her. And she certainly hadn't worked half as hard at bullying me here as she had in Todos Santos.

Why is she here?

"What about Spencer? Killed anyone yet?"

"Shockingly, no." I fell back into bed, staring at my ceiling with a soft laugh.

I didn't want to admit I'd dreaded my birthday. Because I knew Vaughn better than to think he'd ever celebrate it, and it was likely Pope was going to whisk me off in the evening for an intimate, private dinner, which meant less kissing time with Vaughn. Papa, I suspected, would forget about it altogether, as he often did when it came to me.

"We get along," I explained. "For the most part."

"Don't forget his true colors," Poppy warned. "All of them are shades of black. He's the same guy who bullied you at school, dragged you into the janitor's room to look at him getting a blowjob, and then did it again on the last day of school."

I remembered those things all too well. I even had a retaliation plan in place.

"A-ny-way," she drawled, "have an amazing day, Lenny. Hug that teddy bear for me, yeah?" she teased when I failed to produce any more words about Vaughn. "All my love. Mwah. Cheerio."

I hung up the phone and slipped into my black skinny jeans, an Anti Social Social Club hoodie, and my Gladstone sneakers. I headed to my father's office before I lost the guts to do it.

I hadn't spoken to him in weeks—not since I found out he knew I'd be sitting around here doing nothing for six months and still recommended I accept the position. He and Vaughn had made me look like an idiot, and I was worried I'd lash out at him. But I figured if I didn't go talk to him, we weren't going to talk at all.

My legs grew heavy as rocks with each step I took toward his office. The air seemed to sear my lungs. I knew, logically, that I had every right to confront him. I needed to shake off the weird notion that my father was too important to deal with my problems and feelings. Wasn't that what I'd always done? Pushed myself out of the picture to make things easier for him?

That's okay, Papa, I'll stay here in Carlisle so you can focus on your job in America.

It's fine I didn't get the internship. I'd love to be Vaughn Spencer's assistant.

Oh, don't worry about me. I'll just marry my work so you don't have to carry the burden of any potential heartbreak or boy drama or, really, anything that might put you in the slightest discomfort.

Suddenly I realized I wasn't much different from Poppy. We'd both slid to the sidelines of our father's life to make sure he was comfortable. Poppy simply looked the part, with her cute cardigans and groomed looks, while I did it by wearing black lipstick.

By the time I stood in front of his office door, I was so riled up, fire licked at the walls of my stomach, rising to my throat. I curled my fist and raised it to the wood, about to knock, when the door flew open and out came Arabella.

She looked flustered, red, confused as she closed it behind her. She shouldered past me and ran down the hallway.

When she realized who she'd shoved aside, she stopped, turned around, and raised her open hand, signaling me not to talk.

She opened her mouth, about to say something nasty, no doubt, when Uncle Harry breezed into the hallway from his office on the opposite side of the floor, holding a thick batch of files under his arm. The showdown between us gave him pause, and he frowned.

"Ladies."

"Mr. Fairhurst." I nodded politely.

It didn't matter that I'd grown up in his lap and spent every Christmas and Easter at his Hertfordshire mansion. In school, I gave him the respect he deserved. Arabella, however, yawned provocatively, refusing his eye contact.

"Do we have a problem here?" He looked between us.

Arabella flashed him one of her Colgate smiles, which was faker than her lashes. "No problem at all."

He turned around and went about his day. I turned around to face her.

"What were you doing there?" I pointed at Papa's office.

It was one thing that he kept choosing Vaughn over me. But to consider he was so fond of Arabella that he mentored her in his office made me sick to my stomach.

Unless he called her in to tell her to pack her shit and leave.

But somehow, I knew it simply wasn't my luck to get rid of her. Blood ran hot in my veins. I wanted to lash out and yell at her.

"Oh, I think we both know what I was doing there." She cocked a defying eyebrow.

My eyes widened so much, I was surprised they didn't roll onto the floor. What was she insinuating exactly?

"If you have something to say, you better say it."

"I just did. You're so deep in denial, you just refused to listen."

"Break it down for me." I smiled cheerfully, ignoring her snark. "And use simple words. Romanian is my first language after all."

Vampire.

Though it had been her joke, the reference flew over her head like a kite. I could see it in the vacant, Barbie-doll expression plastered on her pretty face.

"I'm sleeping with your dad."

I stood there like an idiot, feeling my nostrils flaring. Self-pity consumed me, and the stupidest thought floated into my mind: *Why on my birthday?*

Why, indeed. Why did I find out about this on my birthday? Why here, in the place I'd grown up. Why my father, who I looked up to, put on a pedestal, and treated like a god? Was it a wonder I was so drawn to Vaughn Spencer? Maybe it was in my DNA to fall blindly for the ones I wasn't worthy of.

Arabella strutted toward me, picking up a lock of my blond hair and examining it between her fingers. "Jeez, Lenny, didn't your boyfriend, Vaughn, tell you he caught me slipping from your dad's *bedroom?*"

What?

I sucked in a breath but remained silent.

She shrugged, *hmmphing*. "Guess there's little talking on the agenda when his dick is in your mouth all night."

I was going to kill—no, *demolish* him.

My mind screamed on repeat: *Payback, payback, payback.*

But what I had planned for him wasn't nearly enough.

I swallowed, still weighing my next words. She pouted, her hand moving from my hair to the collar of my hoodie.

"I'm *so* sorry." She sighed melodramatically. "I was sure he'd give you the heads-up, at least. Guess you really are just another seasonal hole, honey."

"You're mad," I croaked, my voice too hoarse to be recognizable, "that he's not with you."

She scrunched her nose, like I'd said something gross.

"You think I wanted to come here because of Spencer? He's just a kid, and legit a sociopath. Now your dad, that's a different ball game. We're getting pretty serious, actually, so you might wanna try and be nicer to me. You know, for the future of your trust fund. I'm sure there's a lot of vampire shit you want to buy, not to mention all your stupid books. Wait, you wouldn't mind calling me *Mummy*, would you?" She mimicked a very bad English accent.

I lost it.

I simply lost it.

I grabbed the hem of her low-cut blouse, twisting it in my fist and smashing her against the wall opposite to my father's door. I got in her face, snarling.

"You're lying."

"Am I? Two sordid visits in forty-eight hours. Doesn't look too good."

"Arabella," I warned.

"Mummy to you." She laughed.

My hand flew from her collar to her neck, squeezing. I couldn't help myself. It scared me how little control I had over my emotions, my actions. I couldn't believe she'd said that word. *Mummy.* It was so sacred to me. What did she know about orphans? Both of her parents were alive. They'd bought her way here.

I realized Arabella hadn't stopped bullying me. She just played a different, more destructive game here.

Slept with Dad.

Sucked Vaughn off.

Tried to burn my house down.

Why? Why? Why?

I was a firm believer in the "bad person, good reason" approach. To be doing things like that, she had to have a motive. But I wasn't feeling sympathetic just now.

"Know what the best part is? I figured you out a long time ago. You pretend to be all tough and dark." Arabella pushed me back, and I almost crashed against Papa's office door. *Almost.* "But honestly? You're just your daddy's little puppet. You'll never confront him about me, about anything. You're scared shitless of him. Look how he screwed you over with that internship. I mean, *dayum.*" She shook her head, snorting. "I might be the one lying on my back getting dicked, but Daddy Astalis sure fucks you over—"

She didn't get the chance to complete the sentence. I grabbed her hair and dragged her down the hall, somewhere he wouldn't be able to hear through his door.

She wasn't wrong, but she was about to be.

I craved my father's approval and dreaded confronting him. But her revelation changed everything. He wasn't a martyr who'd sworn off women after Mum. He was a cradle snatcher, a perv who slept with teenagers.

God. No. Not you, Dad.

She protested with little whines, but by the time she started screaming, I'd shoved Arabella into Uncle Harry's office, which I knew was empty, and disposed of her on the floor. She was a bit bigger than me, but I was feisty and had enough adrenaline to kill three grown men.

Perched on the floor, her back to Harry's desk, Arabella laughed and laughed and laughed. There was a crazy zing with her eyes. And sadness. I could smell loss from across the room, and she'd experienced it.

"I can't get over how much people don't give a damn about you, girl. Your boyfriend didn't even tell you he caught me with your dad. He'd have probably stuck his dick in my mouth if my jaw wasn't busy pleasuring Papa Astalis. Your dad prefers your boyfriend to you. Your best friend, Pope, had to *beg* people to go to your surprise birthday party because nobody likes you…"

She trailed off, knowing exactly what she was doing, then pressed her fingers over her mouth, raising her eyebrows in false embarrassment.

"*Oops.* Silly me. Totally forgot it was supposed to be a secret. Pope asked me to come to your surprise party tonight. You sister's dragging her ass from London to bring the body count up. Everyone's gonna be there. I mean, all four people in your life. Including me," she cackled, getting to her feet.

I watched her every move, careful not to say or do anything that could put me in prison. I didn't trust myself with her. And I also knew Pope well enough to see why he'd invite her. He did have a weakness when it came to crazy lasses—even ones who'd hurt me, it seemed.

Arabella smoothed her skirt and swaggered to the door, making a show of yawning. "Anyway, I'm off to find something cute for tonight so I can upstage you."

Beat of silence. She ran her eyes over my figure. "*Not* that it would be a challenge. Tell your daddy you know about us, and I swear your life will be over. Catch ya later."

I leaned over Harry's desk, trying to regulate my breath.

I wanted to kill Dad.

Vaughn.

Arabella.

And I was about to be stuck in a room with all them tonight. Then I remembered I was supposed to meet Raff at ten. It was already half past.

But he just wanted to keep me busy until the evening. He was trying to be nice, while my older sister put things together. My fists curled again of their own accord, and I realized I was choking a piece of paper in my hand. I looked down and unwrinkled it, my heart hammering against my rib cage. I might have ruined an important document that belonged to Uncle Harry.

I looked down and read the words on the page, handwritten by my uncle:

To do list:

1. Gallery in Milan/call Karla
2. Rent/landlord/Chelsea flat
3. Check on VS (been quiet? Vindictive?)
4. Birthday present/Lenny
5. VS.

Vaughn Spencer.

Somehow I knew, clear as day, that he was talking about Vaughn.

It felt like pieces of a puzzle were falling together—but not into place. I couldn't get a clear picture of what was happening.

Arabella was here for a reason.

Vaughn too.

Neither of them was here because of art.

I slid the paper back on the desk, straightened my spine, and walked out the door just as my father came out of his office. He shut the door behind him, holding a paper bag with colorful things inside. When he noticed me, he shoved it back into his room, smiling apologetically.

No need to keep my party a secret. You already gave me one bloody surprise.

"Blimey, that's some coincidence. I was just about to head over to your room to wish you a happy birthday, Lenny."

That, after avoiding me for weeks. Yeah. Screw him. Without sparing him a look, I moved past him, my shoulder brushing his side as I advanced toward the stairway.

He called my name, confused, but all I could think about was Papa with his hands on Arabella.

Arabella's mouth around Vaughn's cock.

How they'd both chosen her over me—Papa knowing it'd break my heart that he romanced my schoolmate and Vaughn proving a stupid point with his stupid dick.

She was ruining every relationship I had with the men in my life.

And I was done sitting back and watching it happen.

CHAPTER FIFTEEN
VAUGHN

"They were supposed to be here almost two hours ago. I'm getting worried." Poppy poked out her lower lip, sitting at a black-mapped table in front of a tray of watermelon–Jolly Rancher–infused margaritas.

Fancy-ass drinks for the most unpretentious girl I'd ever met. Len was a vodka-straight-outta-the-bottle chick, and she was surrounded by extravagant people who didn't get her. Just like me.

Arabella plopped beside Poppy, drawing faces on a black balloon with a silver Sharpie, pouting.

"Could've taken the train to London and got some shopping done. What a dud."

"Zip it," Poppy barked, grabbing a margarita and downing it in one go.

Edgar scratched his beard, mulling the situation. He'd decorated the room all afternoon with Poppy. Saying he didn't look happy would be the understatement of the fucking millennium. I was surprised smoke didn't blow out of his ears.

The party was to take place in the second, smaller kitchen of the castle—the deserted one the staff never used. Poppy and Edgar had done a good job cleaning it up. There were black balloons everywhere, a *Happy Birthday Lenny* sign hanging in front of the door, and a crap ton of food and alcohol. I made it a point to be late, deliberately taking my sweet-ass time after I finished working, but even though I showed up an hour after the text said, Lenora still wasn't here.

"Did you try ringing her again?" Edgar frowned at his older daughter, running his paws through his wild silver hair.

"Every five minutes." Poppy stood up, plucking a second drink from the tray and raising it in mock salute before downing it on her way to the sink, where she disposed of the plastic cup. "Texted her loads too. Should we inform the police?"

"Inform them what? She's probably getting snogged under a tree by Rafferty Pope. That's who she left with this morning." A steel voice came from the door as Fairhurst strolled in, holding a boutique bag that looked in itself more expensive than some prime property in my neighborhood.

Good Girl's present, no doubt. I looked around. There was a small mountain of presents in the corner of the room.

Of fucking course.

"We know she's with Raff. That was the plan, but he would never whisk her off like that." Poppy shook her head.

"He'd better not," Edgar muttered under his breath, motioning for both Poppy and Arabella to come to him, perhaps to come up with a plan B.

Fairhurst grabbed two of the girly, pink margaritas and made his way toward me, propping a shoulder against the wall I was leaning on. He handed me one of the drinks, and I took it, keeping my eyes on the door.

"A quid for your thoughts?" he asked hoarsely.

Your taxidermied head hanging above my fireplace.

"You can't afford my thoughts," I deadpanned, swirling my drink in its cup.

"Don't be so sure. Everyone has a price."

"Spoken like a true whore. No wonder your career is going down the shitter."

"Always so thorny." He chuckled. "Truce?" He tipped his margarita in my periphery, his eyes clinging to the side of my face.

"Eat shit."

"Already am, every day we postpone our inevitable negotiation. May I present to you an opening offer?" he asked.

"What do you think you're bargaining on?"

I watched Edgar raising his voice to the girls, losing his shit. Good. I wanted him to be pissed enough to have Rafferty by the balls when they got back. I'd be happy to finish the job—and the douchebag.

"Vaughn?" Harry poked.

Right. Asshole was still here.

I had all my ducks in a row, not that he knew that. I knew exactly where he kept all the incriminating information about my mother, which meant that really, it was just a matter of breaking in and deleting it. He could've sent it to other people, but his email records didn't show any deleted items in need of recovery, which meant fucker had it saved on a cloud with an auto-email ready. Easy to delete without a trace.

Basic, asshole.

"My freedom," he said. Simply. Humbly.

"According to you, it was never in question." I finally turned around, wearing a cocky smirk I'd borrowed from my dad—the kind he used before crushing his opponents. "I'm just a fucking kid. Don't let a teenager cramp your style."

"You seem calm." He narrowed his eyes suspiciously.

"I am."

I *was* five minutes ago. Before it became apparent that Pope didn't give a fuck about my warning and Len might be *snogging* him.

It wasn't that I cared so much what Lenora Astalis did with her lips—both pairs. I had no sentiments toward her. But we had a deal, and I'd kept my end of it by not touching anyone else.

"The facts, such as they are, deem you dangerous and capable,

Vaughn, and I'd be daft to pretend otherwise. I think I may have been a bit harsh the first time we met here. I wanted you to get the full picture. Now that we both have leverage, I feel we could negotiate and walk away from this happily."

"Nobody leaves the negotiation table happy," I said.

The end game was never to be happy but to be smart. Plan ahead.

I *tsked*, shaking my head like he was a rookie. Harry took a step closer, giving me a *please* look. He smelled of desperation. My mouth watered for his blood. I could practically fucking *taste* it.

"This could go very right or very wrong. Time to reveal our cards, Spencer."

I opened my mouth just as the door burst open and in walked Pope, Len's arm thrown over his shoulder. Her feet shuffled along the floor, and she dragged like a rag doll. Her eyes were half-shut, out of focus. I could smell the alcohol on her breath from across the fucking room.

Called it. Vodka chick.

"Oy, we seem to have a bit of a problem here." Pope stopped by the table, trying to steady Good Girl on her feet. She collapsed into his arms, slithering down his body like smeared Jell-O. He held her upright, letting out a nervous chuckle and looking sideways.

She wasn't cute drunk.

She wasn't even sad drunk.

She was straight-to-ER-then-rehab plastered, and my mood turned from sour to murderous.

I stepped forward, leaving Harry hanging and brushing past Arabella, who was biting down a vicious grin, and Poppy, who'd slapped a hand to her mouth, giving Lady Macbeth a run for her money in the melodramatic department.

Edgar beat me to his daughter, holding her arms to keep her upright.

Shock filled every wrinkle of his face. Guess he wasn't used to his younger kid fucking up. For all the black shit she'd smeared on her face and worn, Lenora wasn't a bad kid. A straight-A student who never said a word when she'd been through hell her entire senior year. No boy trouble. No drugs or alcohol.

Perfect but not in a boring-ass way, like her sister.

She stumbled backward, squinting to try to bring him into focus. Her back hit the wall, and Rafferty and her dad both reached to help her. She swatted their hands away.

"Lenny, have you been drinking?" Edgar asked.

"Not as much as I should have, *Sherlock*."

Edgar glowered. Arabella giggled in the corner, covering her mirth with her manicured nails that hadn't seen a day of work. My eyes snapped from Len to Arabella, from Arabella to Edgar, then back to Len.

Fuck.

"She's been slipping shots when I wasn't looking, sir," Pope said, excusing himself of any responsibility.

Breaking his nose was going to be the height of my year. Maybe even decade.

"You're completely hammered." Edgar ignored Rafferty, barely restraining himself from shaking Lenora.

Everybody stood back. Even Pope took a step away from the shitshow unfolding in front of us. I stayed close. I wasn't in a trusting mood, especially where her father was concerned.

"Quite observant." Good Girl zigzagged her way to the head of the table and fell into a seat with a sigh.

She reached for a tower of triangle-cut BLTs, popping one into her mouth without chewing. She knocked over three plastic cups and a burning candle in the process. Poppy was quick to pick up the candle before it burned a hole through the tablecloth.

"Quite, quite observant. I guess that's one thing I didn't inherit from you." She dropped her head back and stared at the ceiling, her favorite thing to do.

I made a mental note to ask her why she was looking at ceilings all the damn time.

"What are you on about?" Edgar blinked, his stance still rigid. He stared at his daughter like she was mad.

And she was, I realized.

At *him*.

I glanced at Arabella, whose face was draining of color, even under her three pounds of foundation, blush, and bullshit fake smile.

"I'm talking about the fact that you're a pig." Len looked up and managed to somehow hold her father's gaze before her eyes rolled in their sockets involuntarily, crossing, then zoning out.

The room sucked in a collective breath.

I advanced toward her, yanking her up by the arm, and tugging her to the door. "Show's over. Come on."

She shook me off, slapping my hand away, hard. "Don't you dare touch me!" she screamed.

I turned around and glared at her. My teeth clenched in anger, and I took a deep breath before hissing, "Your ass needs a shower, water, and a loaf of bread. You're saying shit you won't be able to take back tomorrow. Unless you have a time machine handy, I'd strongly advise you let me handle this."

She thrust herself at me, and maybe if she hadn't been as drunk as an eighteenth-century sailor, people would've suspected we were banging, but she was so sloshed, I bet they chocked our familiarity up to sloppy drinking.

She whispered in my ear, "You knew and you didn't tell me. We're over, Spencer. Go find another unassuming girl to suck your blood and take your virginity. I won't touch it with a ten-foot pole."

My eyes flared in rage at her words. At my own stupidity.

Count to ten, I heard my mom's voice pleading in my head.

Then a hundred. Then a thousand. Do not react.

Good Girl turned around and stumbled through the door, but

the minute she rounded the hallway, I grabbed her arm and shoved her through a side door.

I slammed the door shut, hearing people outside looking for us. Since Harry had given me lengthy tours of this place when I was thirteen, I knew it by heart. This door was hidden under an alcove and looked like a part of the wooden wall. They'd never find us.

I cupped my hand over her mouth so she couldn't call for help and dragged her down the pantry stairs while she resisted, kicking her legs and trying to bite my palm. The scent of old food they used to keep here—sacks of potatoes, condiments, and canned food lingered in the air, though the place was completely empty. Mold was also a big player in the puke-de-toilette fragrance. Under the stairway, there was another hidden door. I took the Swiss Army knife out of my boot and jammed its edge into the lock, picking it with expertise and elbowing the door open. I pushed a still-kicking Len inside and closed the door behind us. It was the deepest shade of dark there was: pitch-black. She couldn't see anything.

I couldn't either, but I knew where we were. What was there.

"Where are we?"

She hiccupped, but her voice sounded considerably more sober and less pissed off. The sense of danger heightened her senses, maybe because we were officially underground, her family and friends were upstairs, and no one could hear her.

Maybe because they said this place was haunted, and they weren't wrong.

It was.

With my own fucking nightmares, for instance.

It was kind of rad knowing she was lying on the cold, damp stone bench and I was standing, hovering over her. It was my favorite position in any encounter, no matter with whom.

But it felt particularly good when it was Len because she was the only person who didn't cower, even when her body language said so. I'd never managed to get her on her knees for me, and fuck knows I tried.

I ignored her question. "What was that all about?"

"Oh, let's see. My father is shagging my nemesis—my *teenage* nemesis—and she threw it in my face this morning. Happy birthday to me! And she added that you knew about them and didn't tell me. Why?"

Because it wasn't my business.

Because hurting Len unnecessarily wasn't high on my to-do list.

Because I didn't get the fucking chance to.

That was the worst part. She was fucking mad at me for not doing something before I'd had the chance to decide whether I was going to do it or not.

"I have no loyalty to you," I said coolly, following my instinct to answer to no one. I wasn't one to be pushed.

"You don't have any to Arabella either. And she is the one in the wrong."

True, but why would I ruin your day because your dad is a horndog and Arabella is continuously breaking Guinness records as the trashiest person alive?

"I don't owe you an explanation."

"Do you like her? Is that it?" she asked.

Sober Lenora would never ask this.

"Fucking in love with her," I said.

I was not in charge of how I was feeling, and that annoyed the shit out of me. A part of me wanted to scream that she was the dumbest smart creature I'd ever met, and another wanted to apologize for...for... Jesus fuck, why was I twisted inside out over this bullshit?

Guilt. I was feeling guilty. Goddammit.

"Wouldn't surprise me," Len scoffed. "You're made out of the same cloth."

"Don't poke the bear," I warned.

"The bear poked me first! The bear tore me to shreds. Arabella is out for my blood."

We were not talking about the same fucking bear, that's for sure.

"Yeah, well, at least she sucks cock," I deadpanned.

Len snapped her mouth shut. I heard her body shifting, standing up in the dark. She was unsteady but humming with hot energy that made me want to rip her clothes off. I heard her bump against the wall, and after a few seconds of squirming, she managed to tug her phone out of her pocket and turn the flashlight on. Her blond hair glowed like charred gold, and her face looked even younger under the white light. She moved the phone around, examining where we were.

"Christ," she breathed, pointing the phone up to the ceiling in a circular motion, her eyes bulging.

"Nice choice of words." I slipped behind her, one hand curling over her midriff and the other taking hold of her phone. I directed the light to the corner of the ceiling, where there was a line of rusty, crooked hooks. There were rope marks all over the oak beam, which was half-rotten, soggy, and damp in some places.

"It's a nine-hundred-year-old castle. You must've known there was history behind it. *Secrets.*"

The word *secrets* weighed heavy on my tongue, and we both knew why.

She said nothing. My cock pulsated, throbbing, *begging* to punish her for liking Pope, and I pushed it against her ass. I didn't even think she noticed. She was too captivated with the place we were in.

"What happened here?" she whispered, her heartbeat wild and feral against my fist.

"Story is, the castle had been standing on a pilgrim trail leading to London. The Tindall couple, who didn't have children and hated the fuck out of each other, needed a way to burn time. Didn't help that the Tindall dude lost all the madame's inheritance gambling and drinking. They needed cash, fast. They made money renting out the first floor to the pilgrims, who used it as a court of law. Criminals judged guilty of serious crimes were brought here. Any idea why?"

My lips fluttered over her collarbone. The air was chilly and moist—different from that in the cellar I worked in, which had been refurbished and air-conditioned so it could keep the mammoth statues Edgar Astalis kept there in top condition. This felt authentic. Old school. Creepy and medieval.

Her throat bobbed under my lips. Her breath still smelled like nail polish remover (damn vodka), and I *still* wanted to kill Pope, but she was mine now, which meant I no longer saw red.

"They executed them here?" she croaked.

I nodded into her skin. "Four hundred people have died here. Reputedly."

"Wow." She shuddered, her skin blossoming under my lips and fingers.

She was turned on by it. I slipped my hand into her shirt, moving my fingers up and down her stomach. She was so hot, and I was so cold, and it felt so fucking wrong, I thought I was going to come inside my jeans right there and then.

We could never be together outside these walls, for more than just these few months. Lenora would inevitably find a man who would give her the world, and I'd leave here and try to ruin said world because that's all I knew.

She was perfect, and I was nothing but a collection of flaws.

Besides, she doesn't want a goddamn boyfriend, I reminded myself. *And you don't do the monogamy crap.*

My little story kept her occupied, though, and took her mind off Arabella and Edgar.

"Can you feel the death all around us?" I curled my hand over the flashlight of her phone, so we were in the pitch-black again. I dragged my teeth and stubble over her sensitive skin. "Does it make you *wet?*"

"Do you believe in ghosts?" she asked, ignoring my question.

Her head fell sideways, giving my lips better access to travel along her collarbone.

I nodded into the crook of her shoulder.

"Really?"

"Ghosts of our past."

"Oh."

"Who drive us to be who we are. To do what we do."

She trembled as my hand slipped into her elastic sports bra. Her tits were even warmer than the rest of her body. Silky and soft. I'd sculpted hundreds of tits in my lifetime but never touched any. It shouldn't have surprised me that they were so smooth. They were, after all, anatomically, fat.

I knew that, I sculpted that, I made it look real.

But I finally *got* it. The obsession with tits. Len's were spectacular. I squeezed, breathing through my nose to keep the pressure in my balls in check. I wanted to make her forget Pope had a dick. Or anyone else for that matter.

"You didn't get me anything for my birthday," she murmured, letting me kiss her neck and up her jawline while my thumb found her hard nipple and flicked it.

Another thing she never would have said sober. I stilled, my mouth on her skin, my breath uneven.

"I wasn't expecting anything to be honest. Not even a card. But a happy birthday, yeah. I expected at least that."

I said nothing. My hand was still shoved inside her bra, but I didn't move. I wasn't sure if I was angry at her or at myself, and that was another brand-new feeling.

Just tell her happy birthday, a small, tiny, fucking crazy part of me urged. *Manners are not a weakness. And you're about to plunge into her ass bareback.*

But I couldn't bring myself to do it. It felt like a power battle, and for some reason, she always had the upper hand, even if she didn't know it.

She felt out of reach, and it made me want to throttle her.

I shook my head. She stepped away from my touch. My hand fell from under her shirt. The chill of the room wrapped against it immediately. Len turned around to face me, took her phone from my hand, and flicked her flashlight completely off.

"I know I'm drunk, and I know you said I'll regret the things I said tonight, but I honestly don't believe I will." Her voice was steady. Flatlined. "I'm done being considerate of my dad. He certainly isn't considerate of me. As for you..." She trailed off.

I waited. Since when did I wait for people to tell me what they thought about me?

Never.

Who cared?

She was just another mouth—not even a particularly good one. She sassed way too much and gave me trouble.

"Finish the fucking sentence." I loathed myself for giving her yet more power by wanting to know what she had to say.

"Our arrangement is over. Don't come to my room. Don't talk to me if you see me in the hallway. Stay out of my business. We're done. And you never asked me—I know, I know, *not* that you care"—I heard the whine of the ancient door opening, and Len took a step out—"if I believe in ghosts too. But here's your answer: I do, for the exact same reason you do. I don't believe in literal ghosts, but I believe our past unleashes dog-shaped demons upon us, and they chase us, and that's what keeps us running. Moving. Living."

I said nothing, not really in the mood to correct her and tell her I hadn't asked whether she believed in ghosts or not because I knew the answer already. It was what made her presence bearable. When we were in a room together, all our ghosts were waiting on the other side of the door. I could hear them.

"My ghost is my mum. I lost her when I was very young, and I vowed to never love someone as much as I loved her, so I wouldn't have to go through the pain of losing them too. Losing her almost broke me. But because I don't get attached to people, I wasn't scared to get in bed with the devil himself. I finally realized I can't fall in love with you, but that doesn't mean I should give you the time of the day," she paused.

I could make out the shape of her head as she shook it.

"As it happens, I really shouldn't. Now, take me to my room and lock my door after you. I don't want to see my father."

I did as I was told.

I left her with a bottle of water, two Advil, and a scowl.

"Goodbye, Spencer," she said, watching from her bed as I locked her door and slipped the key back into her room, protecting her from myself.

Yeah, good fucking riddance.

The boy snored softly when I entered his room.

He was in the upper bunk bed, in the boys' dorms on the third floor. The lower one hadn't been occupied, so I guessed his roommate was hooking up somewhere. It was embarrassingly easy to find him. Fairhurst kept his name on his phone's contact list along with a picture of him, the sloppy fucker, and I had access to every single detail on Fairhurst's phone now, thanks to the Fixer.

I was feeling a little unhinged and a lot trigger-happy from my encounter with Len earlier tonight, but I doubted it was the reason I nearly tore the boy's head from his spine when I clawed at his throat and brought his face down to mine. I wore a hoodie, a black ball cap, and a black bandana on my lower face.

His eyes popped open in the dark, frightened, like he'd just seen a ghost.

"Out," I hissed.

I wasn't hot on using too many words. He wasn't supposed to pick up on the American accent. I squeezed the back of his neck, bringing my point home. He nodded frantically, jumping to the floor with a thud and grabbing a hoodie from the back of his chair by his desk. He slipped into his slides, then waited for instructions. I poked my knife into his back from behind and opened the door for him, forever the fucking gentleman. Once we were out in the hallway, I followed closely behind him. Four in the morning or not, there was little room for error.

We took the stairway up to the fourth floor, to Fairhurst's bedroom. I knew he was staying in London tonight because he'd said as much after I got back downstairs from Lenora's room and made excuses for her. Edgar had looked wrecked, Arabella triumphant, and Poppy was bawling. Harry said he'd deposit Lenora's present at her door and take her to dinner when she was feeling better.

Inwardly, I told him I'd die a thousand deaths before I let them spend one-on-one time together.

When the boy and I reached Harry's room, I picked at the lock, broke in, and closed the door after us. I opened the double doors of Harry's walk-in closet and motioned for the kid to get in.

"G-get into the closet?" he stammered, rubbing at his arms. It wasn't even cold.

I nodded curtly.

"W-what will you do to me? I'm just... I'm not... We're not together or anything like that. I didn't know he had a boyfriend. He was just a pull."

Sure. That's why he was here. Because I wanted Fairhurst's cock all to myself.

"In," I snapped, poking the knife in the guy's throat.

He scurried into the closet, turning around and looking at me expectantly. I knew he was a senior. I knew his name was Dominic Maples, that he was originally from Edinburgh, that he'd been fucking Fairhurst for a year now, since before he was legal. Of course, dangling it in my enemy's face was futile at this point.

I didn't want to cause harm.

I wanted full *destruction*.

And locking Harry's ass in jail simply wasn't enough.

Once Dominic was inside, I used my gloved hands to place his palms on the shelves of the walk-in closet, widening his stance by kicking his feet apart.

"Get naked," I said gruffly.

"Why... How..."

Rather than answer his half-finished questions, I shoved his sweatpants down myself. He kicked them off obediently, along with the slides, getting the point and taking off his hoodie and shirt.

He turned around to look at me, and that's when I noticed he was hard. His damn cock was pressed against a drawer, purple and engorged. Yeah. He really was Harry's boyfriend. They were both sick.

Once Dominic was stark-ass naked, I took a graffiti chalk can and sprayed his back. He shivered as the cold liquid splashed over his skin, biting into one of Harry's sweaters to keep quiet, but his damn cock was still pressed into the mirrored drawer, and it was still rod-straight.

When I was done with the black paint, I tossed the can aside, took the kid's phone out, and shoved it in his face, standing behind his back.

"Unlock."

He stared into it, using face recognition. I took a picture of the guy's back, sent it to Fairhurst through Dominic's phone, and tucked said phone into my pocket.

Showtime, motherfucker, and you got a front-row seat.

CHAPTER SIXTEEN
VAUGHN

I entertained the idea of letting Len know I was going out of town before remembering there wasn't a point, because she didn't want to hear from me.

She hadn't left room for interpretation—our hookups were over.

She couldn't have been clearer if she'd tattooed her forehead with *Property of Pope* (whom I was still going to kill, because *fuck him*).

Just as well. If she was dumb enough to say I never gave her a birthday present, I really had no goddamn interest in tapping her ass anyway.

And still.

And still.

I was going to send another motherfucking basket to her room this morning, as I had every single day since Arabella sucked me off on the last day of school. At first, I'd sent chocolate because I didn't want it to be too obvious, but I figured she'd know where they came from on her birthday when I sent brownies. They were hand-made and in different shapes, for her entertainment. Clouds, unicorns, stars, animals, letters. Anything but a heart—that was my careful instruction to the chocolatier. Each was individually wrapped in fantasy-book wrappers: *Lord of the Rings*, *A Song of Ice and Fire*, *Harry Potter*, *Northern Lights*.

Cost a little extra to pull off, but half-assing shit wasn't in my nature.

It wasn't about wanting to fuck her or trying to make her feel better, God forbid. I didn't even leave a note. I just knew she liked sweet things since that day behind the fountain, and I pitied her ass because she was an orphan and friendless and fucked up.

That's all it was. Pity.

I called the chocolaterie, and the lady there recognized me by my accent and the fact that I'd used them for a few weeks now. Also, I was probably the only bastard who called before their opening hours, when they'd just started their day baking.

"Another one? You're persistent, lad." She giggled.

I rolled my eyes, watching the English countryside zip by on the first train into Hertfordshire. It was a quarter to six. Even the birds were still asleep.

"Maybe you should personalize it this time? She obviously needs a bit of thawing. You've been sending them for quite a long time now."

A note was a bad idea. She'd think I cared, and fuck, did I not give a damn about her. It was cruel to pretend otherwise. Especially now, when we were done.

"Blank note is fine," I clipped.

"Righto," she singsonged. *So fucking cheerful in the morning.* "Would that be all?"

"Yes."

"Loads of noise in the background. Are you traveling anywhere special?" She tried to lighten the mood.

Could I deduct the tip for the time she wasted trying to mingle with me? Because pretending to give a damn seemed way above her paygrade.

"Hertfordshire," I said. "St. Albans."

"You must visit London if you haven't. It's quite close."

"Great idea."

I've been to London more times than you've taken shits, lady.

I killed the call, leaned back in my seat, and tapped my knee. Harry Fairhurst did exactly what I thought he'd do once I sent him

a picture of his lover buck naked, with graffiti over his back and ass
that read **HARRY FAIRHURST IS A CHILD MOLESTER**.

He grabbed his keys and dashed back to Carlisle Prep, where
Dominic was still locked in his closet, because—c'mon, give me
brownie points for the irony—*his gay lover was locked in a closet.*

In his bid to save his ass (and maybe Dominic's, though I wasn't
holding my breath), he'd forgotten his laptop at his house. I knew
because I'd planted a little tracer on that bitch when I sneaked into
his office one day and could see its location at any given moment.

And whaddaya know? Someone just happened to block the
highway he was driving on his way to Carlisle, in case he figured out
I wasn't there and decided to dash back home.

That someone was paid nice and well by yours truly—more than
enough to replace the crappy Alfa Romeo 2001 he'd smashed right
into a Sainsbury's truck to stop traffic.

God bless hedge funds.

As for Harry's house keys? What can I say? I was saddled with
sticky fingers…and *very* slippery morals. Making copies the day I
put a tracer on Fairhurst's laptop was like taking candy from a baby.

The train stopped at St. Albans, and I got off, feeling fresh as a
daisy, other than the dull headache Good Girl gave me yesterday. But
that was probably nothing compared to the hell she was going through
this morning after outdrinking every fish in the Atlantic Ocean.

I texted the chocolaterie woman and added two bottles of water
to my order. Might as well. Len still thought the chocolate came
from someone else.

I looked down, and there were three missed calls from my dad.

He can wait, I thought, proceeding without caution.

I didn't have to hack into the laptop.

But once I sifted through the files he had on Mom—all the lies, all the pictures, all the testimonies, edited recordings of her, emails she'd never written, orders she had no idea were going to arrive with cocaine bags stashed inside the frames of the paintings—I considered it my little, final, burn-in-hell parting gift.

Once I'd deleted everything from Fairhurst's cloud and destroyed all the evidence on his camera, I smashed my boot into the laptop and tucked it into Harry's neatly made bed.

I finished off by pissing all over said bed and laptop, in case he was bad at taking hints.

That still left me a few hours to burn before my next train to Berkshire. Dad called a couple more times. Mom, too, but I didn't feel like talking to them from Fairhurst's house. I was too on edge whenever he was concerned.

I settled for giving myself a tour of Harry's house. I'd never been there before. I took it upon myself to unplug his fridge and open the freezer, letting the meat thaw. Then I opened the back door in case any wild animals found themselves itching for a treat. I finished by helping myself to some of his pricey status watches, to make it look like common burglary.

Of course I made sure to deposit the Rolex and Cartier watches at the train station, in the hands of a homeless person sitting outside, begging for pennies, charitable piece of shit that I was.

By the time I got back to Carlisle Castle, I had two emails waiting.

From: noneofyourbusiness@gmail.com
To: pleasedonttalktome@gmail.com

Vaughn,
I checked the clouds of his other account. All clear. Your father said he'll foot the bill for this job. Good luck and let me know if you need any further help concerning the matter.
T.

From: Baronspencer@fiscanheightsholdings.com
To: pleasedonttalktome@gmail.com

Son,
Either you pick up your damn phone and answer me, or I'll
make my way over there. Spoiler alert: you won't like it if I do.
Your father

Had Jaime told him about the trust-fund money? Or had
Mom found out what I did with it through her arty-fartsy friends?
I clenched both my teeth and my phone, knowing I wasn't quite
finished with my multimillion-dollar task.

Dad could wait.

He had to.

CHAPTER SEVENTEEN
LENORA

"Oh, God…oh, God. Oh, God. Oh, God."

I woke up in my bed, feeling like a fist the size of a wrecking ball had pressed against my eyelids. I was never going to drink again. Ever.

Unless drinking would make the headache go away, in which case I was fully prepared to binge-drink my way into a coma.

The room came into focus in pieces. First, I saw a pile of wrapped gifts lying in the corner. Someone had brought them in while I was asleep. I made a quick, albeit painful count. One from Poppy (probably the long one; she knew I was interested in a particular watercolor print for my room). One from Harry (possibly the fancy-looking bag, containing an equally fancy, sensible sweater I'd never wear), a tiny bag from Papa (jewelry, no doubt), and a large box enfolded haphazardly in paper. That was one-hundred-percent Pope's doing. He knew I needed new tools and had splashed out.

Nothing from Vaughn. I didn't let myself dwell on that fact.

It was truly over, as it should be. It had been a godawful idea to begin with. Don't roll in bed with a tiger and be surprised when you wake up with claw-shaped wounds. Lesson learned.

Speaking of rolling, I did just that, falling to the floor with a thud. It hardly surprised me when I couldn't even feel the hit my body suffered. After spending a full minute staring at the ceiling and giving myself an internal pep talk about not drowning in self-pity, I turned on my stomach, crawling on all fours toward my door.

Then I realized I didn't really have a plan. Who was I going to call? Officially, I was not talking to my father (was he even talking to *me?*), Poppy was probably long gone back to London, I'd put Pope in enough trouble by showing up plastered on his watch, and Vaughn—not that he had a shred of humanity in his entire ripped body—cared as much about my well-being as he did about the cobwebs under my bed now that we were over.

Whatever *we* had been.

Christ, I was good at making a mess of my personal life. *I wish I could do that for a living.*

Somehow, I scraped my door open. Another basket full of chocolate, brownies, and two cold bottles of water awaited me, along with a steaming cup of coffee that looked fresh.

I managed a smile, even through the headache. *Poppy.*

Dragging the basket inside and unscrewing a water bottle took immense effort, but after a few sips and the sugar rush of a brownie, I wobbled to my feet and hauled myself to the showers. Papa and the senior staff had plush bedrooms, with showers and built-in water closets, and at times like this, I longed for Papa's private bathroom, but of course, not at the price of accepting a truce.

I couldn't look at his face without imagining Arabella lying beneath him, purring like a cat, and it scared me to think our relationship was irreparable. I still hadn't spoken to Poppy about it, but I knew she deserved to know and that she'd be just as broken as I was, if not more.

After emerging from the showers, downing more coffee, and helping myself to another heavenly brownie, I uncovered my work in progress and stared at it, holding its dead gaze. It had taken a familiar shape, but I couldn't put my finger on it. Something about the frown of the sculpture made my heart squeeze in pain. I continued working on it all day without taking as much as a bathroom break, until someone knocked on my door.

"Who is it?"

It was probably Rafferty, checking in on me. I'd turned to the door and started walking when a voice boomed behind it, grave and serious.

"It's your father."

I froze in my spot, like a statue carved from ice. It took me a second to recompose.

"I don't want to talk to you."

"Frankly, that's exactly why we should be having a conversation right now."

Frankly, you're a fifty-nine-year-old perv, and I carry your DNA. I wish I could scrub myself clean of my association with you.

I turned around and made my way back to the statue, picking up the needle and thread for the fabric I'd stitched to its shoulders.

I didn't expect him to barge into my room.

I didn't expect him fling the door so hard it put a dent in the wall.

Edgar sucked in a shocked breath behind me. "Whoa."

At first, I thought it was because I looked like something that had crawled out of a sewer. But I turned around and noticed it wasn't me Papa was looking at.

It was my assemblage sculpture.

"You did this?" he gasped, his eyes wide and exploring.

I snorted out a chuckle. *Now* he was impressed with my work? How bloody convenient. *And* unlikely.

I returned to the stitching, ignoring his words.

"Lenny, that is—"

"Brilliant? That's quite a coincidence, considering you didn't give me the internship I've been dreaming of since I was five, and this comes less than a full day after I publicly called you a pig. Are you trying to make amends, or are you trying to cover your arse so I won't go around telling people what kind of person you are? Because rest assured, *Papa*…" I spat out the word. "I don't *want* people to find out the extent of how corrupted you are."

Strong words, but time, I found, had two opposite effects. Either it made the pain dull and evaporated the anger or it allowed you to stew in your fury, multiplying your rage. The more I thought about my encounter with Arabella yesterday morning, paired with her slipping from his room, the more I was livid with my father. She'd confessed the affair to me, and Vaughn had confirmed it. In fact, according to Arabella, Vaughn had caught them in the act. It couldn't get any clearer than that.

Papa put his hand on my shoulder, twisting me around to face him.

I swatted his hand away. "Touch me again, and I'm calling the police."

He stared at me, confused and hurt, the creases around his eyes deeper than I remembered them yesterday. He had dark circles under his eyes. He was tired. Sleepless. Pale as the ghosts of his castle. Bet it was Arabella who kept him up at night, not the showdown with me.

"Darling, what is this about? You are worrying me to death. It is unlike you to get irrationally upset. And it is definitely unlike you to lash out. What happened yesterday?" His voice was tender, crisp as an autumn leaf. My father was not an unkind person, but he was busy, impatient—a gentle giant.

I could tell he was being genuine, but just because he regretted hurting me didn't mean he was excused.

"Maybe I got bored of being good." I hitched up one shoulder, thinking about Vaughn's pet name for me. "Maybe my eighteenth birthday resolution was to be myself. And I don't like you right now. You disgraced Mum, me, and Poppy. I know it was very convenient for you when I walked around in black clothes and piercings. I got the grades, did my volunteer work, steered clear of trouble. But know what, Papa? It didn't work for me. *You* didn't work for *me*."

He stared at me, shocked. "What on earth are you on about?"

His question only riled me further. I couldn't help myself. I gave him a little shove toward the door. He was huge, yes, but he also knew social clues when they were thrown in his face. He took a step back.

"I'm talking about how you never asked me about my art. About my life. Mum died, and you did nothing to make us feel like we had someone to talk to. I was lucky Poppy took the role of a mother. But what if she hadn't? You were always too bloody busy for me. Still are." I shook my head, finding the first thing in my sight—Poppy's poster, still wrapped—and throwing it like an arrow. He dodged it, taking another step back.

"You don't understand—"

"Oh, but I do." I smiled, feeling lighter somehow, now that everything was out in the open.

Sure, I'd always felt timid and embarrassed about asking for my father's time. I didn't want to bother him. But I never quite realized the extent of the anger I'd harbored toward him until now.

I picked up another wrapped gift and aimed it at him. "I understand everything so perfectly clear. Vaughn is more important than me. Arabella is more important than me—"

"They are *not* more important than you," he cried desperately, flinging his arms in the air. "Vaughn got his internship because he deserved it."

"And Arabella?" I raised an eyebrow, cocking my head, waiting for his explanation. "The *affair*," I enunciated meaningfully.

"Arabella…" He drew a deep breath, his cheeks staining red. "I made a mistake. I cannot undo it right now."

Of course you can't, Papa.

But this was a full-blown confession. I'd said the word *affair*, and he hadn't contradicted it.

I closed my eyes, begging the tears not to fall. I didn't want him to see what he did to me, what his despicable behavior stirred inside me.

"Leave," I whispered for the second time in less than twenty-four hours.

I didn't have Vaughn. I didn't have Papa. Apparently, I was

officially at odds with the opposite sex. Well, there was Pope, but he was hardly male as far as I was concerned.

"Lenny…"

I threw the second gift at him, and this time, I hit his chest. Before he could gather his wits, I took one of my sculpting tools and boomeranged it at him too. Knowing he was a living target, he turned around, stalked to the door, and slammed it behind him.

I collapsed on the floor, the sobs ripping from my mouth.

I didn't stop until night fell.

Vaughn didn't come to see me that night or the night after.

But Pope did, just as he'd promised.

We played board games and drank cheap, boxed wine and talked about philosophy and art and celebrities we'd like to shag (he said Rooney Mara was his dream girl, while I fancied Machine Gun Kelly). He told me about the progress he was making with his piece. He also admitted, albeit reluctantly, that he'd seen Arabella sneaking into my father's office again.

Funny, my father was perfectly content leaving *me* alone, but he was still seeing Arabella.

Brilliant.

On the sixth night of not talking to Vaughn and Papa, I showed Pope my sculpture and he, too, flashed me a weird look, like I'd done something wrong. Apparently, something about the statue threw people off, but both men kept mum about it.

"Why the face?" I scowled. "If it's bad, just tell me."

He shook his head vehemently. "Oh, it's the opposite of bad. I mean, in terms of skill and technique, it is absolutely spectacular, Lenny."

"Then what's the problem?" I frowned.

"Uh…" He rubbed at his cheek, his ears pinking. "I mean…do you really not see it?"

"No!" I threw my hands in the air, exasperated.

He gave me a pitying look. "Darling, it is Vaughn Spencer. It looks exactly like him. I mean, not really," he amended, cocking his head to examine the piece more closely. "Your sculpture has more life in it than Vaughn does. It is substantially more humane, and I'd probably trust it before Vaughn with babies and weapons of mass destruction. But other than that, spot on."

I glanced at my statue, my eyes widening as I choked on my saliva.

Motherforker.

It was him. Of course it was. The sharp-as-razor cheekbones. Dead eyes. Permanent scowl. Heart pouring out of his chest like a fountain. I did this. I'd immortalized Vaughn Spencer with my own hands. The idea had come to me while I was still in Todos Santos, the day Arabella sucked him off, the day Poppy started sending me chocolate. He'd humiliated me, and I, in return, had somewhat worshipped him.

My clammy palms choked the hem of my shirt. My fingers twitched. A part of my brain—the sane part, presumably—told me not to do it, that it didn't matter, that the piece was beautiful and enthralling and could open many doors for me. But the rest of me didn't listen.

I pounced on the statue, ripping it with my fingernails on a roar. The stitched shoulders, the paper heart, the crown of thorns. The only thing I couldn't smash and ruin was the face, for it was made out of bent metal. Resilient and patronizing, it stared at me coldly as I ripped everything else about it.

He wasn't even here, and he still watched my every step, ridiculed me, made fun of me.

As I shredded his shoulders and ripped his heart from his chest, I felt arms wrapping around my waist, and before I knew what was happening, I was kicking the air, growling and screaming at the top of my lungs.

I tried to escape the grasp, but Pope hurled me onto my bed like I was a sandbag, taking something out of his trousers pocket and jamming my wrists to my metal headboard. I growled like an animal, bucking in the air and trying to kick him.

He *handcuffed* me to my own bed. *Wanker!*

"Take it off. Immediately!" I demanded.

To be honest, I was mad at myself, not Pope, who was just trying to make sure I didn't ruin all my hard work in a moment of insanity. But still.

I am insane, aren't I? I thought rather grimly. *All arrows point to the same conclusion. How shameful that white is my least favorite color to wear.*

"I don't think I will," he said evenly, straightening up and examining me with hands on his waist, like I was a wild coyote he watched through a secured cage. "Don't take this the wrong way, but you are a bit unhinged."

He said "a bit" for the sake of civility. Truth was, you couldn't be a bit unhinged, just like you couldn't be "a bit" dead. Being crazy demanded commitment, which I certainly showed.

"I guess you like him," he said mildly.

I did not answer. I didn't want to confirm Pope's theory, but it would be stupid to deny it. Vaughn occupied my thoughts more than he ought to. Even subconsciously. I'd made him into a statue without meaning to.

"You had a plan in motion. Why didn't we execute it?" Rafferty asked.

"Because he never showed up in my room." I sulked. God, I was such a teenybopper, and it was all Spencer's fault. He turned my mind to goo. I'd become someone Arabella would get along with nicely.

"Remind him that you exist, then," Pope said, not backing down. "You're making it easy for him to forget you. You stay in your room all day working. Both of you are such hermits, you lock yourselves in your corners of the castle. He couldn't forget you when you were in high school, and I very much doubt he can here. Difference is, you're not dangled in his face, a forbidden fruit, a taunting reminder of everything he wants. Be that fruit," Rafferty said, clapping his teeth together in a teasing bite. "Remind him he wants to eat you."

I swallowed. He was right. Vaughn kept away because he could. But he was also wrong.

Because Vaughn was definitely coming back. This week, the next, or in a few years.

Whether it was in a bloody bath or hovering over me one night, for some reason, his need to be next to me was stronger than he was.

And I was going to wait. Bide my time.

If he truly wanted me, he'd come here again.

And I'd be waiting.

Fully loaded and ready to fire back.

CHAPTER EIGHTEEN
VAUGHN

He went to her room every night.

Not that I was keeping tabs or anything.

I was just in the neighborhood when it happened.

And by in "the neighborhood," I mean in her hallway, lurking.

And by "in her hallway, lurking," I mean clearly I needed professional help, an intervention, and a fucking *life*. I found myself standing behind a Louise Bourgeois statue for hours daily, waiting like some kind of a rabid Belieber.

Sure, I had my reasons. She was the first thing that had resembled a crush for me, no matter how cringeworthy I found the word (or the girl). It made sense that I would feel somewhat possessive of her, now that she'd opened her legs to Rafferty Pope, who, according to whispers at Carlisle Prep, was working on one hell of a painting.

The pathetic part was that I *wanted* to visit her.

Lenora didn't want to see me. But I was notoriously uninterested in what people wanted. I'd have come to her earlier, but I'd I held back because I wasn't supposed to be at Carlisle Castle.

Shortly after I paid a visit to my little friend Harry Fairhurst, I left a letter on Edgar Astalis's desk informing him that I'd be gone for the rest of the week to find inspiration. This, of course, was bullshit with a capital B. I didn't need inspiration. My piece was almost done, months ahead of schedule, and by far the closest thing to perfection I'd ever created.

What I needed was to buy time until the money Jaime released from my trust fund had wrapped around the possessions I wanted to purchase like an octopus. I had a very clear idea of how I wanted to play this out, and it was important that Fairhurst thought I was untraceable during that time period.

Plus, I needed to lay low in case the boys in blue paid a visit to Carlisle Castle after what I did to Fairhurst's lover. No one had filed a complaint in the days that followed, but life had a way of surprising me, especially with a curveball from Fairhurst.

Harry hadn't reported any missing items from his house. He must have been waiting for our long-overdue conversation or pulling his own tricks out of his sleeve.

Now that I'd done what I had to do, I'd thought I'd torture him a little by letting him stew until Monday. But as it happened, I didn't feel like keeping away from Lenora for that long, so Friday—today—would have to do.

I pushed open the door to Fairhurst's office without knocking first thing in the morning, striding straight to the chair in front of his desk and taking a seat. I had a cup of steaming coffee in my hand—the other one I left by Len's room every morning, not that she deserved anything from my ass.

Making myself comfortable, I took out a joint and tucked it into the side of my mouth. Technically, it was illegal in the UK, but I still didn't give much of a crap. I could take a shit on Harry's desk and he wouldn't bat an eyelash. Fairhurst knew I had him by the balls.

He was on the phone. When he noticed me, he apologized to the person on the other end, hung up, and tossed his phone across his desk. Making a point, I crossed my legs and rested my feet on said desk, leaning back and enjoying the view of a pale-ass Fairhurst waiting for the verdict.

I glared at him with a shit-eating smirk.

Finally, he knotted his fingers together, sloping forward and trying to look like the responsible, rational adult he *wasn't*.

"*How?*" His face twisted in disgust.

If nothing else, I appreciated his desire for knowledge. I'd just taken away his leverage, destroyed his false evidence, pissed all over his house—not just metaphorically—and stolen his valuables. And he asked me *how*. Curiosity was vanity, though. We wanted to know things so we could control them. *Destroy* them.

"Next question."

"What makes you think Mr. Maples won't press charges? I'd be happy to confirm it was you behind that prank in my walk-in closet."

"And I'd be happy to confirm why I did it. Which, coincidently, is how I know you'll keep your lover's mouth shut."

He snapped his own mouth shut, his jaw clenching. I tipped the ash from the joint onto his floor, looking around. It was a fine-looking office, with one of his paintings hanging in front of his desk.

"No files. No laptop. No camera. No *leverage*." I counted with my fingers. "Sucks to be you these days, Harry. A part of you probably wishes you'd executed your plot and fucked my mother over before I could ruin you. You know I never told her about your shitty scheme? Her heart doesn't deserve to be broken. She actually likes you."

Goddammit, Mom.

He looked away, probably recalculating his next step. My feet were in his fucking face, and behind them, I knew he could see the golden victory in my expression.

"I guess you came here to lay out your demands. You know I'll cooperate. I *did* get you into this program, didn't I?"

He'd accepted me because I blackmailed him.

I shrugged. "Anything you have to give, I have no interest in."

"Is that so?" He quirked one eyebrow, standing up. "You'd be surprised. Money, sex, and power speak. I offer plenty of all three."

"There are no bargains between gods and mortals. You will kneel, and as we're both well aware, you're also going to fucking enjoy it."

It was my turn to stand up. He assessed my face, refraining from making a move. I remained calm, stony, and tranquil. He rounded his desk and stood in front of me, then began lowering himself to the ground, an act of goodwill.

Before his knees touched the floor, I spun on my heel and gave him my back, walking over to the painting hanging on his wall—the one I couldn't get—and put my joint out right in the eyes of the pretty Italian girl with the perfect tan in 1950s summer in Ischia.

He stared at me from his place on floor, silent.

"How's business, Harry?" I asked conversationally, staring at the girl.

She had deep brown hair, a sad face, and now two cigarette burns for eyes. Harry Fairhurst's technique of painting eyes was what had made him famous. They looked so real, you sometimes looked down to avoid eye contact. I knew that better than anyone because I was well-versed in escaping the eyes he'd painted that stared at me in my own house.

He also loved to paint sad faces. I always thought there was something sadistic about his art. I was surprised Mom couldn't see it.

"Fine," he clipped impatiently, standing and hurrying toward me before I tarnished the rest of his precious baby. His art. His painting. I made a V sign with my fingers, digging them into the girl's eyes. The canvas was rich and thick, the paint over it dry and resistant, but I managed to pierce the holes deeper, slashing her face with two strokes of my fingers. The painting was officially ruined now.

"Clumsy me." I turned around, flashing him a smile. "You were saying? Just fine? Sounds a bit lackluster."

"Actually…" He cleared his throat, lacing his fingers behind his back, trying to salvage some kind of pride as he stood in front of me. "It's been a very good year. My paintings have just been purchased by a private curator—nearly all of them, across the world. My guess is they're going to open an exhibition, perhaps even a museum."

"I wouldn't count on that," I said smoothly.

He frowned but said nothing.

"See, I'm the investor, and I already found a fitting purpose for your paintings," I said, taking my phone out of my back pocket and sliding my thumb across the screen. "It took a bit of effort. I even had to break into my trust fund, but I got my hands on them. All one hundred ninety-three paintings. Wanna guess what I'm going to do with them?" I looked up, my voice cheerful, my stance confident.

His Adam's apple dipped with a swallow, and his face drained of color.

"Don't be shy now, Fairhurst. That's not who you are." I shoved my phone in his face, showing him exactly what I'd been up to in the days following my breaking and entering his house. All the paintings had been shipped express to Knight's address, which had cost me dozens of thousands of dollars. After that, my best friend was all too happy to make a bonfire on a local beach and feed the flames with rich canvas and elaborate paint. They'd all melted spectacularly into the sand, the ocean washing away whatever was left in them.

Fairhurst grabbed my phone and scoffed, watching the video of teenagers running through the fire, laughing and pouring gasoline onto the flames. After a few seconds, he tossed it back to me.

"You're dead! You are fucking dead. I'm going to kill you!"

I tucked my phone back into my pocket, yawning as he paced the room, back and forth. His entire career, up in flames.

He stopped abruptly in the middle of the room. "You ruined all of them, but not the one you want gone more than anything else— the one hung in front of your childhood room." His voice was laced with venom.

I laughed, ignoring the dull pain in my chest. "Working on it."

"You wouldn't."

"I wouldn't?" I rubbed at my chin. "Or shouldn't? Those are two very different things. I could kill you right now and you wouldn't even stop me. Because if I spill the shit I know about you out in the open, you'll be as good as dead anyway. Jailed, stripped of your money and prestige, living in solitary confinement so your fellow prison mates don't kill you."

"I'll deny everything you say. Every single word. I will start from scratch. I can—I can paint new paintings!" he screamed in my face. "I'll work twice as hard."

I frowned. "That'll be a bit difficult."

"Why's that?" He took the bait again.

I grabbed his left hand, his darling, moneymaking hand—funny how we were all left-handed in this business—insured for two million bucks, and found his pressure point, squeezing hard. He shrieked in pain, tears running down his cheeks. I raised his hand to my chest, shoving my hand forward until I heard the crack of his thumb breaking. Satisfaction shot through me. *Revenge.*

Our eyes met, and his were so shocked and horrified, I wondered what he'd feel like when I had my knife at his throat. Expressionless, I made a ninety degree angle with his wrist, moving it to the other side of my chest. With my forearm on his elbow, I applied pressure until I heard his arm snap. He screamed to the fucking roof before I shoved him against the wall and let him drop to the ground. Whimpering, he stared at his twisted thumb and the bone poking out at his elbow. I darted to his desk, grabbed my untouched cup of coffee, and poured it on the floor beside his sagging body.

"Oops," I said dryly. "Better be more careful. You could slip and break your other arm too. Worse still, you could have a fatal accident. Now that'd be a shame."

His eyes were blurry with tears, his body shaking and arching with pain. When your entire existence is hanging by a thread, by the revenge you seek, you sometimes ask yourself if it's worth it, if you'll ever get the satisfaction you're after.

The answer is yes.

I was hard as marble and ready to remind Lenora she was not in the business of depriving me. I turned around, leaving Harry high, dry, and ruined for the next year or so, artistically speaking.

"Tell anyone what happened, and rot in jail for the rest of your life," I reminded him as I slammed the door behind me. The wail he let out soaked the walls of the castle, and all I could think was, *Once upon a time, I cried just as hard, and I didn't even shed a fucking tear.*

———

I spent the rest of the day working, ignoring the sound of the ambulance upstairs as Harry was rushed to the hospital. When the clock hit seven p.m., I went back to my room, took a shower, and headed straight to Good Girl, skipping dinner. I felt on edge. Each day we hadn't spoken had left a gap. If all it took to pacify her ass was telling her happy birthday, I guessed I was willing to bite the bullet.

I mean, I knew her birthday had been shitty, so this was plain courtesy at this point.

The thought that Lenora might have plans with Pope occurred to me but did not deter me. Pope was an ongoing issue, but I could handle him.

I was at Len's door when my phone started ringing for the thousandth time today.

Dad.

What was his problem? I'd spoken to my mom three times since breaking into Harry's house, expecting her to mention that Dad wanted to talk to me, but she never did. One time she'd tried to give him the phone, and he'd said he'd call me later.

The fact that he'd kept something from his wife (Dad never kept anything from Mom) made me uneasy, and *that* meant the conversation we were going to have wasn't one I was eager to participate in.

I hadn't been planning to ghost him tonight, but *fuck*, I wasn't going to turn around and take the call. I needed to devour Good Girl to make my Bad Life a little less miserable.

I knocked, knowing full damn well I wasn't in any position to barge in anymore. She wasn't the same girl from six years ago. Although, privately, I had to admit, both versions of her turned me on.

Sweet and innocent.

Feisty and psychotic.

A combination that made me want to dick her *more* than I wanted to keep said dick away from anything remotely intimate.

"Come in," her sweet voice called.

I'd started pushing the door open when it occurred to me that the invitation was likely for Pope, who had been visiting her on the reg, and not for me.

What if she's naked?

She fucking better not be. I'd slap her ass silly after I fucked her.

But I was experiencing something strange and uncultured called *restraint*. I didn't want her to throw my ass out of her room like leftover Chinese takeout again.

"It's Vaughn," I said as wryly as possible, waiting for her to shoo me away.

A few seconds passed before she answered. "Well? What are you waiting for?" she responded blandly.

What *was* I fucking waiting for? Goddamn.

I pushed the door open, hoping to find her working or reading or converting to a religion where she could only have sex with people named Vaughn Spencer. Instead, she was perched against her drafting table, wearing something I'd never seen on her before: a silky black nightgown tied together with a powder-pink ribbon at the tits, a slit revealing her milky side ass.

Standing like that, she looked like Aphrodite, rising from the sea, fully formed and made to godly perfection. Confident. Gorgeous. Pleasurable and lustful.

And knowing that wasn't the case—that she had an insecure, irrational side to her—made her even more desirable and raw.

"Shit." The word was breathed in awe.

I frowned, waiting for her to complete the sentence, then realized I was the pathetic motherfucker who'd uttered it.

She crossed her legs at the ankle, looking at me funny.

"You may pick up your jaw at any time, Spencer."

I blinked, resisting the urge to say something offensive and disgusting. It was an instinct, but that wasn't the way to her pussy, which was my final destination tonight. So what if she called me out for wanting to screw her?

A thought occurred to me—an alarming one, at that. Namely, having full-blown sex with her. And maybe even enjoying it. She was the kind of girl who would never throw it in my face if something went horribly wrong—like if I put my junk in an unauthorized trunk accidentally. Not to mention, she was a virgin too.

Maybe.

Hopefully.

Fuck.

"Vaughn?" She tilted her head, waiting for signs of life from planet My Goddamn Brain.

I clapped my chin up with one hand, pretending to put my jaw back in place. "Happy?"

"Very." She pushed off the table, walking toward me.

I stood there, waiting for the catch. She'd told me not to come here again, and I knew better than to think she'd changed her mind. Lenora was a lot of things. Flaky wasn't one of them.

"Close the door after you," she whispered into my face when we were toe-to-toe. "Then get in my bed."

And the stupid, horny, teenage asshole that I was, I did.

CHAPTER NINETEEN
LENORA

"I said if you pushed me, I'd push harder." I clucked my tongue, striding to Vaughn in my sexy lingerie. "Actually, I said it many months ago, when we were still seniors. Remember?"

Because I do.

Vaughn sat on my bed. The metal headboard behind him was round, thin, and perfect for my plan. I produced the handcuffs Pope had given me from my nightstand drawer—I hadn't dared ask where he'd gotten them—and straddled Vaughn's narrow waist, feeling his abs contracting under his shirt as he sucked in a breath.

His throat bobbed, but his lips stayed pursed and sullen. He had this upper-class quality about him no new-moneyed man could buy—a rich boy's pout that stirred something between your legs.

Mine, anyway.

He watched me through hooded, predatory eyes, probably thinking my plan was to kneel like the rest of them and service him chained to my headboard, unable to push my hair out of my face. He was predictable and entirely too used to getting what he wanted.

But the things we want aren't always the things we need. Vaughn needed a reminder that he didn't rule the world—a nice, generous dose of reality check. Most of all, he needed to learn a thing or two about intimacy.

"Finally wrapping those lips around my cock?" he taunted, his voice thick with lust, strained.

We still hadn't broached the subject of our last conversation, in which I'd told him to take a hike. He seemed to have forgotten all about it. That was unlike observant, sharp-witted Vaughn. Not even asking what I was doing in a sexy nightgown? Why I wanted to chain him to my bed? Why the change of heart?

Your heart has nothing to do with this, I scolded myself. *You're just teaching him a lesson.*

My sculpture—partly salvaged but mostly ruined, with just the face remaining perfectly intact—was covered by a simple beige cloth in the corner of my room. Funny, I felt just as torn as it was.

I shrugged at Vaughn's question. "Only one way to find out, right?"

I took his hand in mine. His arm was heavy with muscle but lax, ready to cooperate, and a thrill shot through my lower belly, exploding in my heart.

Locking his first wrist against the headboard, I leaned down to him, my breasts pressed against his mouth through my nightgown. I worked his other wrist, my body humming with sweet ache. Vaughn didn't try to touch me. He seemed enchanted, following my every move through heavy-lidded eyes.

You poor sod.

"Don't worry, Good Girl, I'll give you pointers. It's not that hard to give head."

"Suppose it's going to be a lesson for both of us," I said cheerfully, standing up and turning my back to him.

I waltzed toward my door, my heart beating so fast I could feel it in my throat. The atmosphere in the room changed and thickened with danger and anticipation.

I doubt you'll call me Good Girl after tonight, Spencer.

"Where are you going? Get your ass back here."

His tone held a threatening edge. But there was nothing he could do to me from his position, chained to my metal headboard. That was the beauty of the entire situation—his complete lack of power.

I flung the door open, stepping aside. Pope walked in—perfect timing—still wearing his gray, stained slacks and a dirty white shirt. He smelled of paint fumes, varnish, and labor.

"Spencer, mate. Fancy seeing you in a compromising position." He wiped his face clean of sweat.

I looked back, watching Vaughn twist on my mattress, his arms locked above his head. He tugged, moving the bed an inch. Even though he didn't wince, I knew the handcuffs must have cut into his wrists.

"Go eat cow shit, Pope."

"Oh, I think I'll settle for Lenny. She seems much more edible. Not to mention sanitary." He snapped his fingers, pointing his index at Vaughn with an easy wink.

Vaughn's eyes expanded, zinging with rage. It was the first time he'd looked genuinely disturbed. Stifling a giggle, I walked over to my drafting table, perching my bum at its edge and curling my fingers around its sides. Pope advanced toward me, peeling his dirty shirt off and throwing it on the floor midstride.

"What the fuck is this?" Vaughn seethed from his spot on my bed, tugging at the handcuffs again.

It was the same bed he'd approached when I was weak and young and scared. The tables had turned, just like I'd promised they would.

And whaddya know? Spencer didn't like the view from that angle.

Pope stopped about a foot from me, waiting for further instructions, his muscled back to Vaughn. We'd talked about this before my birthday. This was what I wanted. My present. *Payback.* I wanted Vaughn's heart to bleed the way mine had that final day of school.

I wanted him to feel like someone had clawed his soul out and dumped it on the floor, left for the throng to step on with each laugh, taunt, and hoot.

I turned my face to my enemy, businesslike.

"Told you there would be consequences. You let Arabella give you head in front of everyone the last day of school. You flew to Indiana for your neighbor's proposal, taking her with you, knowing word would spread and get to me, that I would know you took my bully, my tormentor, with you. *Then* you brought her here. And now she is having an affair with my father—my only family, aside from Poppy and Harry. That really did it, Vaughn. You play with fire, you get burned."

God or not.

I wanted to awaken something in him, something human and feral and shameful. *Need.* Carnal lust.

He was a virgin, even if he wouldn't explicitly admit it. And I didn't know why, but sex disgusted him. Intimacy frightened him. Yet for some insane, screwed-up reason, I wanted him to be my first. I knew Vaughn was incapable of falling in love, but I wanted to steal pieces of him. His time. His talent. His words. His smiles. And yes, his virginity too. I was a thief of everything Vaughn Spencer.

He was stunningly untouchable. A demi-god. Unreal.

"You were weak," Vaughn sneered, his voice dry and calm, his biceps bulging beside his head, highlighting his proud posture, even in this position. "I made you strong. I made you resilient. I made you one of us. Now you take no one's bullshit—not even mine. All in the span of one year. By the time I was done, you no longer needed the black hair and Goth bullshit. Everyone feared and respected you. I took away from my power and gave it to you because every time you disrespected me, challenged me, it weakened *me*. I worked hard so you'd stand up for yourself. I saved you, Astalis, and not for the first time."

There was a beat of silence.

What did he mean? When else had he saved me?

I knew he actually believed his backward logic, that every time he was cruel or offhand with me, he excused it by thinking he was toughing me up.

I smiled. "Well, Master, I think you did too good a job. Turns out I, too, am partial to public sex displays."

"We weren't together then," he snapped before I'd managed to pronounce the last vowel.

He was right. We weren't. But I'd still felt like he belonged to me no less than he'd claimed I belonged to him.

"We aren't together now," I retorted.

He laughed, like this was all a big joke. "Get real."

"Now's not the time to get real. Now's the time to get *even*."

With that, I grabbed Pope's face and brought it to mine. Our breaths mingled, sweet and warm. His arm circled my waist, his fingers fanning in mock possessiveness over my lower back. His other arm snaked between us, cupping my face.

"*No*," Vaughn growled from the bed, his pitch feral.

Pope put his lips to mine, kissing me softly, slipping his tongue into my mouth at an angle Vaughn could see.

Truly, the hottest thing about our kiss was knowing he was watching—not that Pope wasn't a good kisser, but I barely felt his presence in the room. Revenge was sweet and pungent, and it made me throb between my legs.

I'd nearly died watching Arabella service Vaughn. But I couldn't deny, a part of it had turned me on too.

"Don't you dare fucking take this where I think you're about to, Good Girl. I will kill your little prodigy friend and won't even bother to leave ashes for his family to scatter around his hometown of Cuntville."

It broke my heart that until this day, Vaughn hadn't experienced true, raw jealousy. He thought he hated me, but he couldn't let me go. He always sought me out. It drove him crazy when I was away and annoyed the hell out of him when I was too close. His feelings toward me had a word, and I was going to teach him. Even if it was the last thing I did.

Even if I could never love him back.

My kiss with Raff deepened, and as it did, I rolled my black nightgown up so my matching lacy knickers were exposed. I normally went for the elastic, cotton ones—the comfy option—but I wanted to taunt Vaughn. I heard the handcuffs clinking against the metal bars, the scrape of the bed moving an inch toward us, then another inch. I smiled into my kiss with Raff.

"I'm going to smoke this bitch to the goddamn ground. You know I will," Vaughn hissed, his eyes two slits of ice. "Take a step back right now, and I'll end this with two shiners and a warning. Let me save you from yourself, Pope, because right now? You're fucking yourself more than you're about to do her."

Raff pulled away from me momentarily, fingering my face with a tender smile. He was a good friend for helping me with this. He had no skin in this game, other than helping me reclaim my pride and power in this twisted power struggle Vaughn had started.

"But, Spencer, mate, she is *so* bloody sweet."

Pope began to lower himself down my body, kissing a path between my breasts and along my stomach through my nightgown.

"That's *enough*," Vaughn snarled. "Lenora, you made your point. I haven't received a public blowjob in months. Unchain me."

I ignored him. I knew that in all probability, Vaughn had been completely celibate since arriving at Carlisle Castle, save for our encounters. But in my mind, he was the one who'd brought disaster to my doorstep. Arabella was here because of him.

Plus, there was a slightly deranged theory I'd been nursing privately since I was a kid—one that believed we'd had a special bond, a carnal connection, since that moment behind the fountain, sharing a stupid, half-melted chocolate bar under the pounding sun.

And Vaughn had let dozens of girls suck him off him since then.

He'd betrayed me every time he'd let someone else touch him after the day he'd threatened to kiss me, after showing me the first traces of his humanity, after we looked at each other and knew—*knew*—anyone else was a terrible mistake. We weren't coincidence.

We were fate. And our bodies—though not our souls—belonged to each other. But he'd broken the pact. Numerous times.

Vaughn wasn't the only one allowed to make mistakes.

If we were going to need each other's forgiveness, I had to sin too.

He'd wronged me many times. I'd wronged him never. Perhaps until now.

He needed to forgive too.

This was *me* helping *us* go back to being screwmates.

I felt the breeze of cold air on my swollen clit as Pope pulled my knickers down. I kicked them aside, and they hit the wall. Raff lowered his face between my legs and took a long, greedy breath.

"Hmm," he shuddered into me.

Vaughn regarded the scene wordlessly. I looked up from Raff's mane of wild, blond curls and watched him watching us. He'd stopped resisting the handcuffs. He simply watched, his jaw ticking.

"What can I say to make you stop?" he growled.

Bargaining. The god who descended to earth and tried to strike a deal with a mortal.

"What is it that you want, Lenora? Exclusivity? Dinner dates? Your precious internship back?"

"An apology," I said, unsmiling.

Pope held back. His mouth was so close to my groin I could practically feel it on me.

"For starters," I added.

"I apologize." Vaughn spat the word like it was poisonous, taking a few seconds to get used to its taste.

"What for?" I asked conversationally.

"For letting randoms give me head both when you were an ocean away and a few feet from me. I apologize for bringing Arabella here. I thought she'd be just another pawn in our game. I had no idea she'd fuck your dad. What else?"

I stroked my chin, pretending his words didn't slice something deep inside me. "No more treating me like I'm your property. We both know I'm your equal."

"Fine," he replied, seeming eager to move on with the plan. "Now kick his fucking face in before I do it from across the room."

I shook my head slowly, going in for the kill. He couldn't give me his internship, I knew that, but everything else I'd asked for was already given. That's why he kept coming back. He couldn't deny me.

I needed something else. Something big.

"I want to see your secret sculpture," I added. "Your mysterious art."

Vaughn closed his eyes, letting out a ragged breath. It looked like he'd been punched in the face. *Too far*, I thought.

"Anything else, Len," he grumbled quietly. *"Anything."*

"No."

He squeezed his eyes shut, looking pained, his chest rising and falling. When he opened them again, his expression was dead and hollow. He truly was a black swan.

"Make it quick," he said, resigned.

"Keep your eyes open, *Clockwork Orange* style."

"Fuck you."

"Is that a promise?" I taunted.

"After tonight? You'll be lucky if I spit in your direction, Astalis."

And just like that, Raff's mouth disappeared between my legs. I threw my head back, shocked by the hot, wet sensation of his tongue as it pried my pussy open, slipping in with confident expertise. He made a moaning sound as he grabbed both my bum cheeks. I propped myself against the table, looking down as he feasted on me.

A whimper escaped my mouth when Pope ran his tongue in circles all the way from the base of my sex to my clit, flicking it over and over again. I trembled, my nipples puckering, my breasts swollen, sensitive, and sore with need. I grabbed one of my tits and squeezed, imagining it was Vaughn, wondering if he would ever do something like this—give without taking.

"Oh God," I muttered.

"An angry one," Vaughn's metallic voice hissed from afar. "Just remember, it's me who's doing this to you, not him. We both know that. That's who you're imagining underneath you, Len. Me. Past. Present. Future. It will always be me."

I wrapped one thigh around Pope's shoulder, running my fingers through his silky hair. The pleasure built inside me like a hurricane. Every inch of me burned with lust.

"Just like you've sucked me off thousands of times." He continued talking, hijacking this moment with Pope. "From the first blowjob till the last, it was you I saw."

Pope sucked on my lips, hoovering them into his mouth, darting his tongue out and massaging my clit.

"Since that day behind the fountain, we've wanted to get our rocks off. We just didn't know how to name it. Now we do."

I exploded with a near-violent orgasm, seeing stars, rocking my body back and forth, my groin chasing Pope's lips, but it was Vaughn's name in my throat. Wave after wave of pleasure coursed through me. I looked down to see my best friend smiling devilishly at me, his lips swollen and glistening with my cum.

"Delicious." He swiped his thumb inside me one last time, gathering more of my juices with his eyes still on mine.

Pope was beautiful like a poem. You could read his face every day and still find something new to admire. One day, someone was going snatch this talented, gorgeous man, and she was going to be so lucky. Luckier than I would ever be, because I was undeniably fixated on Vaughn, the most complicated guy in history.

I looked up at Spencer. He was quiet, his gaze holding mine. I didn't expect an extravagant show of emotion, but his lack of response was high on the Creep-O-Meter.

"Pope, get the fuck out," he clipped.

Pope sent me a questioning look as he stood, and I nodded, rising on my toes and kissing his lips softly. He flicked my ear, turned around, and walked to the door. There he halted, tapping the doorframe, his back still to us.

"I'm not scared of you, Spencer, and your little I'll-fuck-you-up speeches do nothing to interrupt my sleep at night. But just for the sake of full disclosure, I have no romantic interest in your girl. She's my friend. Which means I will always have her back. Which *also* means that if you make her happy, I'll have no problem with you. But if you hurt her…" He trailed off, shaking his head on a chuckle. "Your big mouth and rich daddy won't be able to save you from what I'll do. Night, kiddos." He shut the door behind him.

Vaughn stared at me, so furious his smooth skin was lined with wrinkles around his pinched eyebrows and twisted mouth.

"Take the handcuffs off," he ordered.

I grabbed the keys from my nightstand and released him, forced to lean against him as I did. I could still feel the dull, pulsing heat of Rafferty's mouth on my pussy, and it made me shudder above Vaughn, who clenched his tense jaw to the point of snapping, not even daring to breathe in my direction. As soon as I released him, he stood up, tightening his boot laces.

He was leaving.

I pretended not to care, throwing myself on the mattress and picking up the fantasy book on my nightstand, taking out the bookmark where I'd left off. If he wanted to be a hypocritical bastard, he very well could, but not with me.

I thought he was going to walk out the door and come back once he'd cooled down, which would be in approximately a decade, judging by his mood. Instead, he launched toward the corner of my room, grabbed the drafting table, and smashed it against the wall, breaking it in half. Next came Pope's shirt, which was still lying on the floor. He opened a window and threw it out, proceeding to turn to the wall and slam his fist against it. I heard the crack of bones and darted up, swallowing a yelp.

His hand.

"What are you doing?" I cried. "You're going to hurt yourself. You're not going to be able to work."

Ignoring me, he walked toward the beige cloth, his hand dripping blood across my floor. He picked up the cloth and threw it aside, exposing my biggest weakness.

The sculpture.

Ruined. Destroyed. Yet somehow still perfect in its own way.

He stood in front of it, tipping his chin up, whistling low, finally regaining some of his self-control.

"Someone caught feelings and decided to throw a fucking fit," he bit out, not an ounce of pleasure in his tenor.

I ran to him, grabbing the cloth from the floor and shoving it back over the assemblage.

"You had no right." I pushed his chest.

"Right?" He laughed bitterly in my face, pushing me back.

It was the first time Vaughn had been physical with me in a way that wasn't consensual or warranted, the first time I'd ever heard him raise his voice. "There's some dudebro walking around these halls with pussy breath and a shiny-ass mouth because you used his face as a seat, and you talk to me about *rights*? You're fucking insane." He shook his head, like he couldn't believe he'd gotten involved with someone quite so deranged.

I hitched up a shoulder. "Speaking of double standards, how's Arabella doing? Seen her recently? You know, not from above?"

Was she exclusive with my father? Christ, I didn't even want to think about the details.

Vaughn moved his hand from his cheekbone to his chin, rubbing his skin with frustration. He smeared blood from his injured knuckles all over his face. "How the fuck should I know? I've exchanged six words with her my entire life, including the trip to Indiana. You're seeing this guy every single day. Did you have a good practice all those nights?"

I cocked my head, blinking. "How did you know he was here every night?"

His cheeks turned scarlet, lush and youthful. He looked sideways, scowling. "This was a mistake."

"Remedy that, then. *Leave.*"

He turned toward the door, putting knots in my chest.

Don't listen to me. Don't leave.

He walked, stopped, then spun back on his heel.

"I can't," he growled, standing perfectly still, like the statues he made. "God fucking dammit, I can't leave!"

"You sound like an abused wife." I fought a smile.

"I feel like one." He let out a long-suffering sigh. "This thing between us…" He motioned with his hand. "It's like a failed organ transplant. My body is rejecting whatever it is I'm feeling. It's foreign and strange in every one of my cells. But it's there. It's like cancer, and it's spreading. I want to purge it out. I want to purge *you* out, Lenora. You're a distraction I don't need."

"Am I no longer a good girl?" I felt hysteria bubbling up my throat but stayed calm. I didn't know whether I wanted to keep the title or not. It meant something to him, which filled me with unexplained pride, but it was also a degrading pet name of sorts.

"You will always be Good Girl."

"Even after this peep show?" I wiggled my brows, trying to lighten the mood.

He groaned, a human sound from a man much more than a human. "You were never Good Girl because you are good. You're Good Girl because you're too good for *me*, and we'd both be wise to remember that."

"What makes you think so?" I asked, surprised. He didn't seem to lack confidence. I stepped forward, placing a hand on his shoulder. "I don't think many people would agree with that assessment. You have more talent and money, more prospects and looks."

"And issues and anger-management problems and enemies. The things I'm capable of…" He took a step away from me, letting my hand drop between us. "You shouldn't be with someone who can do what I'm about to."

I had no idea what he was talking about, and still, somehow, I knew he was not exaggerating. I'd always had this feeling Vaughn was going to kill someone someday. It had gone through my head the night he came to seek me out after I saw what I saw. I'd wondered if he'd slit my throat.

"I can take care of myself."

"We have a past and a present, Len. No future."

"I never asked for a future," I said, sounding a lot more confident that I felt.

"Goddamn shame." He *tsked*.

I didn't understand what he wanted from me. Sometimes it felt like he was after everything, and sometimes it felt like he wanted nothing at all.

There was a beat of silence.

"Then don't do it," I whispered. "Be good enough for me."

What am I asking? my mind screamed. *I don't even want a relationship.*

But this had nothing to do with me. I had a feeling Vaughn was not going to recover from whatever he was about to do.

He shook his head. "I have to."

"Why?"

"Because I swore it to myself."

"Break your promise," I snapped.

He took a step toward me. The never-ending tango of Vaughn Spencer and Lenora Astalis. He cupped my cheek, and I didn't know why, but it felt a lot like a breakup.

"If we keep this going and something happens, goodbye would be too much to take. I already want to rip the world apart when someone else touches you."

"Every painful goodbye starts with a wonderful hello." I smiled sadly, leaning into his palm, feeling my eyes bright and vivid with unshed tears.

His chest caved, and he took a ragged breath, jerking me to

his body. "I don't know what to do with wonderful things. I always stayed away from them. You kill me, Astalis."

You killed me when I was twelve. The part that was supposed to like other boys? You took it with you.

I looked up to him, so unbelievably mad that he was making me feel things I had no business feeling, and whispered, "Then *die*."

He grabbed the back of my head, twisted his fingers into my hair, and pulled me into an open-mouthed, punishing kiss—scalded by bitter, hot jealousy. His menacing hiss when our tongues touched for the first time told me he wasn't ready to forgive my little stunt with Pope.

"Mine." He grabbed my jaw, kissing me so deeply I thought I was going to choke.

He was staking his claim and marking me, not making either of us feel particularly good. He backed me against the wall, and when I was pressed to the cold concrete, he tugged at the cloth on the statue again, angling my face and forcing me to look at it.

"See this?"

I swallowed wordlessly.

"This hurts," he said angrily.

Pain. I'd doubted he was able to experience the feeling until now, much less confess it.

"Why?"

"Because you're better than me. And it's fucking killing me."

My heart soared, butterflies taking flight around it in circular motions. He'd never acknowledged my talent before.

"What'd you use?" He released my jaw.

"Tin cans," I breathed as he sneaked his hand between my thighs, stroking the area around my pussy, though not giving me the satisfaction of plunging in.

But I knew he would. I knew he'd erase Pope from my DNA before he left here, no matter what.

"What happened to the rest of me?" he asked.

"Destroyed."

"How fucking fitting." His fingers found my walls, and suddenly, I was wet and aching again.

He slapped my pussy once when I whimpered, then got back to fingering me with expertise that surprised me, considering his lack of practice. I clenched around his fingers, biting down on my lower lip, knowing he didn't want me to come—he wanted to mark me.

He fingered me slow and deep, curling his fingers when he reached a sensitive spot and rubbing it teasingly. My nipples hardened as I watched his dead, cold expression in awe. My legs were weak, my knees shaking, but I knew he wouldn't let me get comfortable.

"Why won't you show anyone your statue?" I asked, the lust thick in my voice. "Is it not going well?"

He smirked at me like I was a silly, silly girl. But he couldn't fool me anymore. I'd gotten under his skin and found something wonderful. His blood was red, just like mine.

And hot.

And so very, terribly human.

"Why, then?" I pressed.

"Because," he said, leaving me hanging.

His eyes roamed my face. They promised trouble. I didn't know if I could take more than we were currently dealing with.

"I'm going to fuck you." He fingered me faster. I moaned, lolling my head against the wall. "Fuck you before he does. Fuck you so you'll always remember I was the first. Fuck you just like you've fucked *me*, over and over again, since I was thirteen."

I came hard around his fingers, whimpering with ecstasy. It felt different than it had with Pope. The stakes were higher. I cared. I cared what he thought when he looked at my face as I came. I hoped he liked the scent of my pussy. I wanted to please him, and that bothered me.

Instead of licking his fingers, like Rafferty had, Vaughn wiped them on my cheek, still looking at me with disdain.

"For the record," he said, just when I was about to tell him to bugger off, I wasn't going to sleep with someone who treated me the way he had, no matter how much I wanted to. "I didn't tell you about Arabella and your father because I didn't get the chance. Although I can't promise I would have for sure. Thrusting oneself into drama is more your sister's thing. But it wasn't some elaborate scheme against your ass. As for your birthday gift, my *sweet*…" He leaned into my face, brushing the fingers he'd used to pleasure me across my lips with a smirk. "Figure it out. You're a big girl. Tomorrow. Seven p.m. at the cul-de-sac."

He left without another word.

CHAPTER TWENTY
VAUGHN

The next morning, I rewrapped my hand with gauze, sneering when I saw the state of my busted knuckles.

I wasn't pissed at myself for punching concrete. I was actually pretty pleased that was the only thing I'd punched in that room. Killing Pope had been high on my agenda. The fact he was still breathing should have earned me a Nobel Prize.

Moving out to the corridor, I checked that the coast was clear before I paid a little visit to his room. He was still asleep. I pushed his door and walked right in like I owned the fucking place.

"Mornin', motherfucker," I greeted, smiling politely down at him.

He opened his eyes and mouth to answer, but of course, it was a little difficult, considering I had my elbow shoved against his throat.

Pope's eyes widened when he realized I was blocking his air pipe, leaning close to him, almost like I was going to kiss him. His brows pinched together, and he turned red.

"You said you weren't scared of me yesterday, but I fail to see how that's relevant. I would need your fear if I were planning on throwing around idle threats. As it happens, I fully intend to follow through on every single thing I'm about to say, so listen closely. Yesterday, you tasted what was mine. Whether you fed yourself some bullshit excuse about helping a friend or not, it happened. And I wasn't happy. But I also realize Len is fond of you and wanted to get this shit out of her system. I get that. I do. I'm not an unreasonable person."

Although, considering that his red face was slowly taking on a nice shade of purple, I wasn't sure he'd agree with my last statement. I pressed harder, knowing I had just a few more seconds to relish his fright and fury. I wasn't going to push until he choked to death. I didn't know much about women, but killing their best friend didn't seem like a good courting move.

Not that I was courting Lenora.

I was just going to fuck her, take what I needed, and leave.

"You're never going to touch Lenora again—during my time here or after. No kissing. No fondling. Not even flicking her ear, like you did yesterday. And you definitely aren't going to get anywhere close to her pussy or tits if you want your tongue to stay in your mouth and not be shoved up your ass. You can be her friend, her *platonic* friend— the one with zero benefits. Also, we never had this conversation. Am I understood? Blink twice if I am, once if you really want a nice visit to the ER and an oxygen mask for the next week or two."

He blinked twice, and I released him. I was sure he had plenty to say to me, but as it happened, I didn't have the time or will to listen.

I stalked out and locked myself in my cellar for the remainder of the day, working.

I felt this weird, hungry, impatient lust for life that hit me like a tornado. It was strange, new, and raw. I finally understood that Iggy Pop song. But to feel lust for life, one must be alive first, and I wasn't sure I'd been living before Lenora moved into Todos Santos.

Which was a pile of steaming bullshit. What was wrong with me? I wasn't feeling alive.

I was feeling horny. That's it. I just wanted to get my dick wet.

I called it a day a little early—three thirty. I locked the cellar behind me and took a trip downtown, shouldering past students and professors who begged to see my work.

I bought brownies, wine, and flowers, then threw them in a

garbage can before I made it back to the castle. I was torn between wanting to impress her and wanting to kill her.

As I continued on, furious at myself for yet again letting a *girl* fuck me up, my phone rang. I thought it was Dad, but no, it was Knight. I took the call.

"What?"

"Don't *what* me like I'm interrupting your goddamn schedule of scowling at places, people, and your own reflection. You texted you wanted Hunter and me to come to London. Everything cool?"

He sounded sober, which meant he'd been keeping up the good work. I Skyped with him often, but it still surprised me to talk to Knight without some sort of slurring involved.

"Berkshire, and yeah, everything's going according to plan. Just need a solid."

"In person?"

"The fucking flesh."

"Aight. Hunter's travel agent is booking us tickets now. How are things with Drusilla?"

I heard the smile in his voice and clenched my jaw. Who the fuck knew? Admitting to having something with her would only invite unwelcome questions when I eventually put a stop to it. No way was I going to drag her down the dark rabbit hole I was about to dive into.

"There aren't any *things* between us," I told him.

"Hot damn, Spencer. I thought I was the romantic. Turns out, you were the one to drag your ass across the world for a pussy."

"It had nothing to do with her. I came here for the internship."

He laughed. I was too distracted to give a damn, though.

"Suuuuure. And I'm doing Meatless Tuesdays because I like quinoa, not because of my vegetarian bae. You're drowning in a river of denial, too proud to ask someone to pull you out."

"Clearly Luna likes you for your dick, not your ability to form a fucking sentence. Stay away from writing poetry."

"Clearly." More laughter. When he finally calmed down, he said, "Oh, and it's good you're not too hot on Astalis, because rumor has it your mom wants to hire her for her gallery in LA when she finishes this little stint. And you told anyone who's willing to listen you were never coming back to California, *amiright?*"

"What?" I nearly shrieked, standing in front of the castle now. It infuriated the living fuck out of me that Mom would make this decision without consulting me first. Especially seeing as she didn't even *know* Lenora.

Then again, that was exactly why she didn't tell me. I'd never told Mom how I felt about Astalis.

You don't feel nothing for Astalis, dumbass.

It was quarter to seven, and I was feeling on edge. Pacing back and forth on the front lawn, I shook my head.

"Mom can hire her. None of my business."

Knight was cracking up at the other end of the line. "Dude, it took you ten minutes to say it. Just admit you believe in a thing called *looooove*," he sang. "By the way, this was a test. Your mom said no such thing. But it's good to know how you really feel. See you in England, fucker. Stay safe."

He hung up.

I looked at the time on my phone. I had fifteen minutes to shower. My room was all the way on the third floor, the communal showers another good ten minutes from there, down in the dorms. There was no way I was going to make it. I had two options: wait for her and invite her to stay in my room while I cleaned up or leave her waiting for me.

It wasn't a particularly chilly night. And she *did* make me watch her coming in another man's mouth...

Thing was, I no longer wanted to punish her.

I didn't want her pain, her insecurity, to scratch at the things that made her tick.

I stood there for twenty minutes, and at five past seven, when she showed up, her back to me, I approached and kissed her shoulder, watching the surprise and delight in her face when she turned and faced me.

"Whoa." She grinned.

"I need to shower. Wait in my room?" I asked, like a normal person or something.

She smiled, saying something equally as ordinary. "Sure."

I found her lying in my bed, flipping through my anatomy and sculpting books. The room was bare of any vibe or personality—I preferred it this way—but I still had my sculpting bullshit lying around. I stopped at the door and watched her, wearing nothing but a towel wrapped around my waist.

Mainly I couldn't understand the way this made me feel—observing her on my bed, which smelled like me, going through my shit. The pleasure was unexpected. Foreign. My chest constricted, and I tried to take a deep breath, thinking maybe I'd pulled a diaphragm muscle.

Still, I couldn't draw enough air to satisfy me.

"Oh, hey." Her voice was raspy. Hoarse.

I strolled in, pretending I didn't hear her. I grabbed a rolled-up pair of black jeans from my closet, planning on getting dressed behind a small recliner in the corner of my room.

"Thanks for the new drafting table." She put the anatomy books aside.

"I broke yours, and you have to work on something," I reminded her.

Hardly a charitable act.

"Drop the towel," she said all of a sudden.

I looked up, half my leg already in my jeans. She sat up in my bed, propped on her forearms, a summer-dream smile touching her face. I couldn't explain it, but I could breathe her from across the room: lavender, cotton, and my own fucking demise.

"Drop it," she repeated, all mischievous and…cute. Yeah. Okay. She was cute and pretty. Big fucking deal.

"What for?"

"So I can see you." She wiggled her brows. "After all, you've seen me plenty."

"I'm about to be balls deep in you in less than fifteen minutes if I have my way," I said. "Naked."

"Hardly the same." She licked her lips, her freaky, multicolored eyes glittering like marbles. "There's something vulnerable about standing naked in front of somebody."

"*Precisely*," I scoffed. "Why would I put myself in a vulnerable position?"

She held my gaze, her voice turning serious. "Because I asked you to."

Momentarily speechless, I regarded her. She was serious. I stepped from the recliner, dropped my towel, and straightened to my full height, hands on hipbones.

Stark fucking naked.

The first time I'd been naked in front of a stranger since… Never mind.

Completely naked. And I couldn't even figure out why I was humoring her ass.

The silence wrapped around us, and I let it, because it was her fault shit had gotten weird.

"You're ashamed." She cocked her head, a curious expression on her face.

I scoffed. *Right.* She'd be lucky to see a fitter body on a health magazine cover.

"What are you ashamed of, Vaughn?"

I sneered. It didn't matter.

She stood up and walked toward me, cupped my face with her

tiny hands. It almost felt maternal. "You're beautiful." She kissed the tip of my nose, closing her eyes. "So beautiful," she whispered.

A tear rolled down one of her cheeks. I didn't understand what was happening, and yet somehow, I wasn't surprised when she cried. I just didn't want to fucking *see* it.

I wrapped my arms around her, trying to comfort her because she… What? Pitied me? Em-fucking-barrassing, but apparently I was willing to go this far to be inside her. My knee-jerk reaction was to kick her out. My plan was so close to execution, and this was going nowhere fast.

But I couldn't.

And not for lack of trying.

We hugged—me naked, her wetting my shoulder with her tears—for what seemed like ten minutes before she pulled back and kissed my lips.

"Thank you," she said.

"For what?"

"For allowing yourself this one moment of being a boy. And for letting me witness it."

———

Down in my cellar, I lit a joint and passed her one of two cans of beer I'd taken from Harry's fridge. He was still in the hospital, and he'd been transferred to one in central London, so getting drunk around here wasn't really in his near future.

Len cracked the can open and put it to her lips, not taking a sip. Her eyes roamed the dark, cold place.

"It's perfect for you," she said.

"Said the vampire." I spoke with the joint between my lips, throwing my Zippo against the bench she was sitting on. It was made of cobbled stone. Medieval as fuck. My sculpture, now almost completely done, was clothed in the center of the room by two separate sheets, so she couldn't see it.

"You invited me in."

"As per usual," I said seriously. "You'd be smart to decline next time."

She smirked, putting her beer down. I sat next to her, feeling on edge. I resisted the urge to rub my thighs, like Mom did when she was nervous. I nailed my palms to the bench on either side of my body.

"Why are you not drinking?" Small talk. I was starting small talk. *Willingly.*

"Because I almost died on my birthday from alcohol poisoning."

"I got you." I gave her beer can a push in her direction.

She studied my face.

"I mean it. Do you want a trust-fall exercise before we do it?"

"No, thanks. I'll crack my head." But she downed the beer so fast, I thought it was an optical illusion. Then she sat back, staring at the covered statue.

"I know you're not going to show it to me, but I'm sort of okay with that. Because I know I'll see it at Tate Modern. As long as I know something's not gone forever, I don't miss it."

She wasn't talking about my sculpture anymore, and we both knew that.

"You miss her," I said. *Fucking duh.*

She nodded. "Every day. Losing her was worse than losing my limbs. I promised myself to never get attached like that again. It's dangerous, you know? Better to keep people at arm's length."

"You already are." I sucked my teeth. "Attached, I mean."

"No, I'm not," she protested, but her face was bright red.

"So you just happened to suck my blood? Ride someone else's face with me handcuffed to your bed? To *sculpt* me?" I grinned. "You're either attached or a certified psycho. Your pick, Good Girl."

"Neither. I'm just a normal girl with normal needs." She tipped her chin up. "You bullied me in high school, and so yes, in a moment of insanity, I sucked your blood. In another, I let Pope go down on me. That doesn't mean anything, Vaughn. I'm ordinary."

I snorted. "The fuck you are. You wouldn't be here if you were anywhere on the ordinary spectrum."

"Because I'd be too boring to fit in your man cave?" She cocked her head, grabbing my half-full beer and tipping it into her mouth.

"Because you wouldn't willingly come to my man cave," I snapped. Not after everything she knew about me anyway.

I picked up a chisel from the floor, poking at the strap of her top and pulling it slowly, knowing I could snap and tear it at any moment if I pressed the pointy tip to it.

"I'm normal." She licked her lips, looking down at her hands. Her nipples puckered through her top, and she twisted her legs together, refusing to look me in the eye.

Nuh-uh. "Sure you are. You don't like blood," I goaded her.

She was a beautiful liar. Luckily, I didn't mind a little deceit. People were obsessed with the truth, like they could fucking take it. Me, I liked messy and manipulative.

She shook her head, still inspecting the blade in my hand.

I slid the chisel from her top, put it to my upper wrist and cut a shallow wound horizontally, not even flinching. She let out a little gasp, her breath hitching. I smirked, standing up so I stood between her legs, bringing my wounded wrist to her face.

"This doesn't turn you on."

"No." But there was no power in that statement. Her voice was throaty and full of need.

"How about when I do this?" I pressed the pointy part of the chisel to one of her puckered nipples through her shirt. It was so sensitive she couldn't help herself. She closed her eyes and let a moan escape those pretty pink lips. I swirled the blade around her nipple, watching her tremble in her seat.

"No." She squeezed her eyes shut, panting. "No."

"You can always leave," I challenged, knowing she wouldn't. Couldn't. Every encounter we'd had since we were kids had led to this moment. We were finally showing each other our dark sides—the shadowy, twisted carnival in our souls no one had ever been invited to.

This was a golden ticket, personally handed over by our very own Willy Wonka. Us. Alone. Where no one could find us.

She was seeing this one through.

"Fuck you, Vaughn." Her voice shook.

The third time she'd told me this.

Each time, I had a different answer.

"*Gladly*, Good Girl."

With a well-mannered smirk on my face, I tore her top off in one, swift movement—like a gash. A little inaccuracy could've caused her serious injury. She yelped, squeezing her eyes shut and leaning back. She clutched her midriff, her shaky fingers looking for a wound. After a few seconds, she opened her eyes and looked down, examining the damage.

Her skin was milk and honey, smooth as freshly fallen snow. She blinked, looked up at me.

"Still not turned on?" I asked.

"*No.*" She enunciated the word venomously, waiting to see what I'd do next.

I laughed. She did too. The crazy, humorless laugh of two people who understand each other perfectly, yet are stuck in a world that makes no sense to them. I never thought I'd have this with a girl. Or a guy. Or any fucking human for that matter. Not even my parents fully understood me.

I pushed her shoulders, and she slid over the bench, lying down.

I put the chisel to her jeans and used it to pop the three buttons free, tugging the denim down her thighs with my free hand. Still looking her dead in the eye, I clipped her panties from each side, letting them fall beneath her, and put the pointy end of the chisel to her pussy, waiting for her to stop me.

"Not horny for this blade, baby?"

"Not even a bit." Her eyes leveled with mine, daring me.

Show me more of your crazy. My veins hummed with exhilaration. *It's turning me the fuck on.*

I was so hard I didn't even have time to be worried about what I was about to do to her. *With* her.

I looked down and again noticed her tattoo.

Ars longa, vita brevis. I could finally read it, and I knew exactly what it meant, why she'd put it there. Something inspired me to kiss it. I did. She shuddered.

"There will be other pleasures worth chasing, and they'll have nothing to do with art," I whispered into her skin, unable to pull away from it.

"Show me," she rasped.

I slid the chisel into her pussy, stopping a quarter of the way in. I wasn't going to hurt her, not really, no matter how much she craved it. I found her hot and wet and ready. *Drenched.* Her cunt produced wet sounds that drove me mad and made my dick so hard I got dizzy from lack of blood to my other organs. The slightest stroke of her hand and I was going to jizz like a broken sprinkler system in a country club. This wasn't going to be a twenty-minute session of virtuous lovemaking. I'd be lucky not to come in my goddamn jeans.

Len braced herself on her forearms and watched my hand sliding in and out of her with the chisel, keeping the penetration shallow. She closed her eyes, her head falling back, and shivered, her entire body blossoming in goose bumps.

I wrapped my injured arm around her neck, bringing her closer, kissing her slow and hot and deep, getting her all sex crazed. Her mouth slid across my wrist, like I knew it would, and her eyes rolled back in their sockets the minute her mouth touched my blood.

"God…" Her voice cracked like an egg, spilling with lust.

"God, what?"

"God…have sex with me."

"I'm afraid that won't do," I lamented. "Say the magic word."

"Please?"

"Fuck. *Fuck* me."

I was buying time so I wouldn't come prematurely before my briefs were shoved down to my ankles. She closed her eyes, drawing a shaky breath. I slid the chisel half an inch deeper into her pussy. She was so wet I doubted it was enough for her. She couldn't squeeze around it, choke it with her walls. No. My cock was the only thing that could do the trick, and we both knew it.

"Please fuck me." The words fell from her mouth, which tasted salty and warm, like my blood. I kissed her again.

"Why?" I asked, my lips moving down her neck, sucking. "You're not turned on. Seems pretty pointless."

"Vaughn," she moaned.

She was so close to coming, and suddenly, I realized I wanted her to. I wanted her to walk out of here satisfied.

Not because of my sculpting tools. But because of my *cock*.

I pulled away, dragging the chisel out of her pussy. My mouth disconnected from her neck. I got up and left her to fall against the bench with a thud, staring at me, sober eyed, mouth agape.

"You say you don't like blood, but I tasted your lips, and you're a little demon. It's on your breath. I think you're far from normal. I think you're every shade of screwed up in the coloring book, just like me, and I knew—*saw* it—when I gave you that brownie all those years ago. But the biggest lie you tell yourself is that you're not mine. Get a clue, Astalis." I threw the chisel at her feet, turned around, and walked out of the cellar, leaving her there alone.

I wasn't worried for one second that she was going to peek at my work, see my statue.

She was a liar, yes, but she was *my* liar.

I didn't need a trust fall. I'd dive headfirst and know she would catch me.

Len galloped toward me, out into the hallway. She spun me by the shoulder and frowned. "You have sex with me now, Vaughn

Spencer, or I swear to God, I will leave this place tomorrow morning and never see you again."

"There she is," I murmured, "the girl from the fountain, all grown up."

I crashed my mouth down on hers, lifting her by the backs of her knees and shoving her against the wall, my lips on hers throughout the process. Her shirt was in tatters, and she was spread wide and naked from the waist down, tugging at my jeans with intent.

"Condom," I mumbled into her mouth, reaching for my back pocket to grab my wallet.

I'd believed Dad when he said he was going to rip me a new one if I made them grandparents before retirement, so I'd visited a local Boots a week ago to stock up on rubbers.

Also, I was stalling.

Okay, mainly stalling.

"No condom," she pleaded into our kiss, grabbing me through my briefs once my jeans fell off, in a vise grip that surprised me. Girls were usually more timid than that. "I'm on the pill."

I unglued my mouth from hers, frowning. "It's your first time, right?"

"Yeah," she panted, her lips unbelievably swollen and pink from our bruising kisses. "You?"

"Why are you on the pill, then?"

I was kind of hoping my choke count would stay at one with Rafferty Pope but knew damn well I was about to finish every motherfucker who'd touched her if I didn't like the answer coming from her mouth.

"To regulate my periods, arsehole." She rolled her eyes, annoyed.

I laughed when I kissed her again, plunging into her without analyzing what I was doing.

I didn't expect to moan so loudly into her mouth. Almost like a plea.

But she was so tight—much tighter than a mouth or my

fist—and warm and wet and delicious. A tremor ripped through me, and I felt my balls tightening so hard, even my ass muscles were clenched.

God. Fucking. Damn.

I counted to five Mississippi while inside her, taking a few labored breaths to regulate my pulse and the premature-spunk situation, and then I began to thrust, my desire so achingly prominent I couldn't help but squeeze my eyes shut.

In. Out. In. Out. How could something so simple bring so much pleasure? It didn't make sense. She moaned into our kiss, and I tugged her ribbons of gold hair to extend her neck, before deciding that watching her beautiful, infuriating face was distracting altogether and flipping her over, so her back was to me.

I angled my wet, hard dick into her, plunging again. *Much better.*

"Ugh!" she cried out, even though I went slow, and I dropped my lips to her shoulder, refraining from kissing it, but just barely.

"Should I go slower?"

"I'll die if you do. I think I'm going to come. It just hurts a little."

"I'm sorry." For some reason, I still hated saying those words.

"I expected it." She was talking to the wall, bracing her hands against it, and I felt like such an asshole for flipping her.

I kept thrusting, tool that I was, knowing I was going to blow my load. It became excruciatingly painful not to come, like trying to hold back a sneeze halfway through.

"Oh, fuck, Len…"

"Hmm…" She was into it, slamming her ass against my groin, begging for more. Her ass cheeks were completely wet from her juices. So were my dick and balls.

"Keep going, I'm close."

"I can't, baby, I'm sorry." I cringed. It'd been…what? Three minutes? And I was being generous with myself here. Oprah-gifting-people-cars generous.

"Damn." My head fell back as I came inside her, emptying my

entire three gallons of cum into her sweet pussy. I hadn't realized just how much I needed my body against hers until I came.

We stood like that, both of us facing the wall, for just a second before I spun her around. She stared at me with those blue-green-hazel eyes of hers, which always fucked me up like no other rival ever could.

"I'm sorry," I told her.

"Yeah, you said." She flashed me a mischievous grin.

She didn't look mad. I mean, not that she should be. But she didn't come. I wanted her to come.

"I'll make it up to you." Fuck, I hated myself more with each apology.

"You can start by getting me some tissue. I'm leaking."

She opened her legs slightly, and we both watched in the dim, faint light as thick, white cum slithered down her inner thigh, along the tattoo. There were traces of blood there too. Not a lot, but enough to tint the liquid pink in some places.

I swallowed. "Did it hurt a lot?" I looked at her. Not that she gave a shit. She liked pain.

She shook her head. "Nah. I enjoyed it for the most part."

For the most part.

Silently, I backed her up until her knees hit the bench, cradling her waist and head to lay her down gently, her ass perched on the edge of the bench, half in the air.

I kicked her legs apart and kneeled in front of her, using my thumbs to open her pussy lips. More white liquid spilled from her. I brushed it aside with my thumb.

"What are you doing?" she gasped, staring down at me with a mixture of horror and amusement on her face.

Saving my goddamn pride.

I put my tongue to her pussy. It was salty and warm—my cum, her blood, and her juices swirled together. It wasn't exactly Jamba Juice, but it was me who'd spunked her nice and good, so I couldn't complain. Besides, the actual pussy-eating was kind of rad. Everything was pink and soft and warm. Not a bad pastime. I started nibbling on her lips, licking her crack to clit.

If I'd been a little less of an idiot, I'd have asked Knight or Hunter how to go down on a girl. Or even watched a video or two. But no. I never had the slightest interest in pleasuring a chick.

Yet here we were.

Still, Lenny moaned, writhing in front of me, her eyes closed. I wanted to be better than Pope. Stupid, I know, but he'd had his mouth here yesterday, and when she'd come, she'd been loud enough to wake the dead.

I rubbed her clit with my finger, diving into her pussy with my tongue, battling her tight walls. Her moans intensified, and she laced her fingers through my hair.

Better.

"Tell me how to make this good for you, Good Girl," I mumbled into her pussy, licking her clean of everything we just did.

I recognized that it was gross as fuck to 99.98 percent of the population, but I'd always been the rebellious 0.02 percent. I knew she liked it, that we were on the same wavelength.

She purred. "Squeeze my clit."

I did.

"Harder." She gasped, her breath coming harsh and fast.

I massaged her swollen clit in circular movements, fucking her with my tongue until it slipped down to her ass crack. That's when she *really* moaned. Right. She was into ass play. I recalculated my internal GPS and started tracing the tip of my tongue around her crack.

"Feels nice." Her voice was thick and sweet, full of indulgence. I wanted to kiss her lips and tell her I'd always lick her ass. But I knew realistically that now wasn't the best time to french kiss her.

"Come for me, Len."

She came on demand, her thighs squeezing my face, her entire body jerking, her pussy chasing my mouth. It was the most beautiful thing I'd ever seen, and I'd seen some sick shit in my limited time on earth. Lenora coming with her ass and pussy in my mouth, her clit under my thumb, however, not only took the fucking cake but the entire bakery.

Three minutes passed before she came down from the high. After she did, we stared at each other, me still on my knees, her legs open in front of me.

We started laughing.

She slid down, holding her stomach, laughing her ass off. We rolled on the floor, getting covered in stone dust, with Len wiping tears of mirth from the corners of her eyes. I didn't even know what we were laughing about. I wasn't the laughing type. Nothing was particularly funny to me, even then. I think we were just...*happy*.

"You need to wash your mouth before you kiss me again." She coughed when she finally calmed down.

I side-eyed her. "Why?"

"Because you have arse breath."

"I would kiss the shit out of you if you ever ate my ass."

"Nice choice of words." She tapped her chin. "Would you like me to eat your ass?" Her eyes widened, with surprise more than terror.

I knew she'd do it. I knew her crazy ass would do just about anything. And I needed to calm myself down because I was beginning to get ideas. Unlikely ideas, like taking Len with me on my quest to live on every island in Italy and France and Greece, like touring European museums together, and bungee jumping, and scuba diving—all the things I'd wanted to do alone after my business here was done.

Because doing them with Len could be so much more fun.

"Not particularly." I shook my head, kissing her cheek and wrapping my arm around her on the cold floor. I didn't want to be too adamant in case she had a weird, unexplained taste for ass, but it didn't sound like my jam.

I stared at her for a while.

"Thank you," we said at the same time.

We didn't have to explain why. It was obvious.

I was her first.

She was mine.

———————

The night was too good to be true, that was for sure.

Still, I shoved the bad inkling to the back of my mind, thinking maybe karma was so busy fucking Fairhurst with a twelve-inch dildo, she'd forgotten about me.

Len and I went up to my room, where I got my toothbrush and a towel. We went to the communal showers, I brushed my teeth, and then we took a shower together. I didn't fuck her again, because I knew she was sore, but we kissed a lot and I bit her nipples, testing how far I could go before it became unpleasant (very fucking far, as it turned out).

Once we were both clean, she said she was going back to her room.

"Fine. Let's go," I heard myself saying.

Even though I'd already pissed on every single rule I'd made concerning the opposite sex tonight, and I knew spending the night together was the final nail in my pussy-whipped coffin.

She put her boots on, not looking at me as she asked, "You mean, walk me to my dorm?"

"I mean…" I clenched my jaw, resenting her for making me say it. "To sleep in your room. Same bed and all that fucking jazz."

She looked up with a smile, tossing me a pack of gum she'd found under my bed. "Cute."

"Ain't gonna spoon you, Good Girl."

"But you are going to fork me." She laughed. "And yes, you were thinking of spooning."

"Don't embarrass yourself."

Yes, I was. I was glad Knight didn't have mind-reading abilities. He'd ride my ass until retirement if he knew I'd wondered how it felt to sleep with Len in my arms.

We walked down the hall toward her room. Save for the owls hooting outside and the crackling of fire in the rooms, the place was silent. We rounded the corner leading to the staff area, where Edgar, Harry, Alma, and the rest of the fuckers resided. Len slipped her hand in mind, lacing our fingers together. Then she froze in her spot all of a sudden, her boots squeaking on the floor.

I turned around to face her. She cocked her head toward her dad's room. We listened carefully. Voices seeped under the closed door.

Arabella? she asked voicelessly, her lips shaping the name.

I advanced toward the door, pressing my ear to it. She did the same next to me. It was risky, but what did I really have to lose? Nothing.

I wasn't even that hot on the internship.

I was close to executing my plan with Harry, and between pissing Edgar off and letting Lenora down, I knew which side I was on: the one that didn't fuck someone thirty years their junior.

We heard sniffling, whining, and shuffling, then the uncanny sound of Arabella moaning loudly.

"Darling," Edgar said, his voice tender and raw.

Arabella moaned again.

"Get off of me, please."

I unglued myself from the door, taking Len by the arm and dragging her away. She fought me on this, her legs heavy against the floor, trying to shake my touch off. She slapped my hand away when I tightened my grip on her.

"Let me be!" she whisper-shouted.

I turned around, baring my teeth. "So you can hurt yourself some more? The fuck I will."

"Vaughn."

"*Len.*"

We stood like this for a moment before I scooped her up by tackling her midriff, flinging her over my shoulder, and marching down the corridor like a caveman. She pounded her little fists, clawing with her nails into my flesh through my shirt.

"Let me down!"

"Enough people have done that recently. I think I'm gonna stick to being the voice of fucking reason. My first executive decision is to leave."

"What about my father?"

My father. Goddamn posh people. She very rarely called him Dad. Every time she called him Papa, I had flashbacks to an *Oliver Twist* musical my parents once dragged me to.

"I'll deal with him."

"He's my problem," she scoffed, still draped over my shoulder as I rounded the corridor toward her room.

"Well, now he's *ours*."

"Put me down, Vaughn. I mean it."

She was already walking the tightrope between deranged with anger and emotional, and I didn't want her to feel more powerless than she already felt, so I lowered her to the floor. She looked away, refusing to let me see her tears. I pawed both her cheeks, relishing how small she was in my hands.

"Look at me."

She dragged her eyes to mine reluctantly, blinking away tears. I pressed my lips to hers as gently as I possibly could.

She'd opened her mouth to say something when a voice behind her cut through the air, interrupting.

"Well, well, the heartless prince not only lives past nineteen; he also *loves*. That's a twist in the story I didn't see coming." Harry Fairhurst strode forward, climbing the stairway and stopping in front of us. His arm was in a cast and sling. He had dark circles under his eyes and looked even thinner than his usual malnourished self. There was no humor in his voice, just malicious intent.

But the real kicker were the words he'd carefully used.

Prince.

Heartless.

Lives.

Loves.

He remembered every single one of our encounters. Each verbal exchange. Shouldn't have surprised me.

I glowered. Him seeing this was not in my plan.

Lenora turned around, flashing him a smile.

"Uncle Harry! You're back from hospital. How're you feeling? No more coffee for you, you clumsy thing," she joked, running to him and flinging her arms over his shoulders.

Two things happened simultaneously. One, I realized that Len truly liked her uncle, and there was nothing I could do to change that. Two, she was never going to forgive me for what I was about to do.

I leaned against the wall and shoved my hands into my pockets, watching as he kissed both her cheeks and flung her blond ponytail with a familiarity that told me he'd done it a thousand times before. And why wouldn't he? He was her uncle.

"Thank you for the new jumper, by the way." She took a step back, seeming to forget all about Edgar.

I knew she'd been raised here, in this castle, so it made sense that she was close to him. I just hadn't thought of that.

Fuck, fuck, fuck.

"You're never going to wear it." He flicked her ponytail again.

Stop touching her.

She shrugged. "It's the thought that counts."

They both laughed.

Harry ran his cool eyes from me to her, a vicious smile tugging at his lips. "So, Lenny, are congratulations in order? Is the talented Vaughn Spencer your new beau?"

She frowned, about to deny it, and at this point, denial was exactly what I needed. He shouldn't think he had leverage on me. Especially in the form of a pussy. Unfortunately, I wouldn't put it past him to hurt her to get to me, and he needed to know she was off-limits.

I took a step forward. "Yeah, I'm the boyfriend. Nice to see you again, Mr. Fairhurst. Oh, wait…" My eyes flicked to his cast. "You can't shake my hand. Never mind."

Lenora's head shot up, her gaze chasing mine. Fine, I'd declared us as a couple without consulting her. But really, we were exclusively fucking each other and throwing fits whenever the other breathed in another person's direction. It wasn't farfetched.

"Is that so?" Harry lifted a brow.

I could already see the wheels in his brain turning, trying to figure out a way to use it in his advantage.

"No other way for it to be," I said wittily. "And you'd be wise to remember that."

Yet again, I threw myself in the fire to save her skinny ass, dumb motherfucker that I was.

"Nice," he said, taking the hint.

"Haven't been called that before, but I'll take it." I threw an arm over Good Girl's shoulder, taking off toward her room again.

Len turned around to look at her uncle, then looked up at me, confused. "What was that all about?"

I ignored her question.

That was one secret I was taking to my grave.

CHAPTER TWENTY-ONE
LENORA

I woke up alone.

Vaughn's warmth had evaporated right along with his hard frame. I scrubbed the sleep out of my eyes and sat upright, trying to ignore the painful echo of Papa's whispers to Arabella last night. There was no mistaking what had been happening there. He'd told her to get off of him. That meant she *was* on top of him—and not to play chicken fight, presumably.

I stretched, trying not to worry about what last night with Vaughn had meant. He'd said I was his girlfriend, but Vaughn was a master manipulator and had many reasons to say things—many reasons that had nothing to do with his actual feelings.

I stood up and opened my door, knowing I'd find a steaming cup of coffee and a basket of something sweet. This time, it was a tray of muffins. The scent of banana bread and blueberries wafted in the air, and my mouth watered as I grabbed the tray and coffee, ushering them to my new drafting table. I was grateful my sister had kept up her daily tradition. I set everything aside and called her.

"Heya," I said when she answered.

"Hey! What are you up to? I was meaning to call you yesterday to check on you." She sounded like she was out and about in the big city. A bit breathless.

I ran my hand over the table, mentally going through the pros and cons of salvaging my assemblage statue.

Pro: It was a magnificent piece. It was going to help me put a mark in this industry. There was something iconic and different about it.

Con: Putting this piece out in the open meant admitting to feeling things I swore I wouldn't feel, to a man I swore I'd never even acknowledge.

"How's London?" I asked.

Listening to Poppy's voice soothed me. I didn't know how I could break her heart by telling her about Papa and Arabella, but I knew I had to.

"Lovely, albeit gray. And Carlisle?"

"Same." I chuckled, picking invisible lint from my pj's. "Listen, I know you're busy; I just wanted to say thank you for all the chocolate and pastries. Aside from the type two diabetes I'm bound to have by the end of these six months, it's a sweet gesture, and it reminds me someone cares, that somebody is thinking about me every day."

Silence stretched on the other side of the line.

Should I have said something sooner? Probably. It'd been months since she started doing it. I hadn't wanted to embarrass her by talking about it. This was obviously a mistake. A gesture better left unspoken.

"Look, I—" I started at the same time she began speaking.

"It isn't me." Her words came out in a rush.

"What?" I paused.

"It isn't me who's been sending you the sweets."

"But I thanked you on my birthday. You didn't seem confused."

"Yes, I wasn't. I sent you a teddy bear, and I was planning to give you your real gift later that evening. But I never sent you any sweets, Lenny. It's just now that the penny dropped. You've been getting many gifts you thought were from me, but I can't take credit for them. Can you guess who it might be?"

Could I?

It wasn't Pope or Papa. They were both too busy with their lives, and anyway, it wasn't their style. Uncle Harry and I were close, but not *that* close. This took commitment. Obsession. This took discipline and care. I didn't know many people who were capable of those things, who would keep this a secret and not mention it.

I knew one person like that actually.

But it made no sense at all. This dated back to our time in Todos Santos. Impossible. But then…

As for your birthday gift, my sweet… The memory of his voice coated every part of my body. It had been a hint.

"Lenny?" Poppy probed. "Who could it be?"

Something pricked my thumb just then, dangling from the edge of the drafting table. I frowned, sucking on the blood and leaning forward to get a better look.

A crown of thorns. Elaborate, thick, and completely perfect in every way. For my ruined sculpture. Jesus, he must've worked all night to make it happen. Did he even sleep?

"I have to go." My voice quaked with emotion. "I'm sorry, Poppy. I really must. I'll talk to you later."

"Okay…you're not angry, are you?" she asked.

I laughed. I couldn't help it. I was going to give her some bad news, but I didn't even have it in me to do that anymore.

"No, Poppy. I'm the happiest I've ever been actually."

I ran the length of the corridor, down to the cellar. I had to tell Vaughn I knew, ask him why he'd done that. It was ten in the morning, and everyone was in class. The clinks of my boots thudded in the empty hallway. I got to the first door of the two leading to Vaughn's cellar and raised my fist to knock, but I heard a familiar voice coming from inside.

"…will never forgive you. I know my niece, and she is good. Pure. Her artistic nature is not to be mistaken for insanity, as in your case."

If I had to guess, I'd say my uncle and Vaughn were standing on the stairway leading to the second door of the cellar. It made sense. Vaughn wouldn't let anyone see his statue.

"She'll have no way of knowing," Vaughn replied.

"I'll make sure she does. Not a difficult task, I assure you, with or without my laptop. I can go to her right now."

"I don't care," Vaughn said after a beat of silence.

What were they talking about? I could feel that things were tense between them yesterday, but I'd been too occupied to poke.

"Yes, you do," Uncle Harry said through a smile I could hear. His voice was low. Mocking. "Oh, how the mighty have fallen. Vaughn Spencer. In love. And with a timid English rose, no less."

My heart rioted in my chest. They were talking about *me*. Uncle Harry regarded me dismissively, like I wasn't worthy of Vaughn's affection—very unlike the Uncle Harry I knew, who'd taken me to galleries and carried me on his shoulders when I was younger.

Vaughn let out a bitter laugh. "I'm not in love with your niece."

"You just happened to kiss her publicly?"

I could practically hear the shrug in Vaughn's voice. "I see a lot of girls, publicly or not."

"You let them suck your cock casually. Yesterday you were afraid I'd hurt her." Yet another taunt left Harry's lips. "Don't pretend like we haven't been keeping tabs on each other over the years. I know exactly what you do and who you do it with. No. Lenny's different. Plus, you aren't the only one fond of snooping around—got a bit of quality time with your nightstand drawer while you were playing French lover. Over twelve thousand quid in chocolate and brownies in the last few months? Are you trying to kill the girl?" He let out a humorless laugh.

My stomach twisted. Everything inside me screamed to pound on the door and demand answers.

At the same time, I knew both of them, and I had no doubt I couldn't pry secrets out of them with theatrics.

"Stay away from your niece. I mean it."

"I don't take orders for you. I mean that too."

"Screw you, Harry."

"Almost did, lad. Almost did. It's not too late by the way. I like your fire."

"When I fuck you," Vaughn growled, low and untamed, his voice seeping bone deep, "it's not your ass I'm going to break. It's your spine."

A loud thud filled the stairway. Harry whimpered in pain, and it sounded like his body had collapsed against the stone stairs.

I closed my eyes, drawing a shaky breath as the pieces of the puzzle finally fell into place, each of them clicking and locking against one another with chilly finality.

The stolen internship. The threats. The hatred. The taunts. The secret Vaughn thought we shared.

Turns out we had very different ideas of what had happened in that darkroom.

I turned and ran, my legs failing me twice before I finally made it to my room.

No, Uncle Harry, I thought bitterly. *I wouldn't blame him if he kills you.*

Three nights passed before Vaughn came to me.

On the fourth one, he crawled into my bed while I pretended to be asleep and kissed my lips. It felt like goodbye. Maybe for him it was. But not for me. I opened my eyes midway through the kiss, staring back at him. He pulled away, his slanted eyes widening in surprise.

"Whoa. Should've kept that balloon floating tall on the last day of school. You *are* a creep."

I grinned, stretching to try to ease the tension in my shoulders. Vaughn's history with Harry explained so much about his behavior. My heart was in tatters just thinking about it, so I'd given him the time he needed, letting him come to me. I'd spent the last few days heaving into the toilet, trying to stop my tears from running.

"Kiss me, arsehole," I demanded, tapping my lips.

Vaughn leaned down and gave me an obedient peck.

"You're grinning. Why are you grinning?" He frowned.

Why, indeed? My father was a total perv, my uncle a child molester, and I was stupidly in love with the boy I hated.

The boy I'd never *really* hated.

The boy I'd convinced myself I hated so I would never have to face the feelings I felt right now: sheer fright that he was going to snatch my heart from my chest and stomp on it with his army boots.

"Because I realized something in the days you were away."

"I—" he started, but I put my finger to his lips.

I didn't want his apologies.

He perched his forearm on my pillow, staring down at me, his lips naturally pouty to perfection. "I'm listening."

"You are the one who keeps sending me all the chocolate, brownies, and coffee every morning."

He kept staring at me, like he was waiting for the punch line. I swallowed. What if I got it all wrong? But of course it was him. Even Harry had said he saw the receipts.

I cupped his cheek, bringing him to my lips again, whispering against his mouth. "To what do I owe these morning gifts, Vaughn Spencer?"

His breath was ragged and shaky as he grabbed my jaw, angling my face to his.

"I am hell bound, and you are heaven sent. You're the first girl I ever looked at and thought...*I want to kiss her.* I want to *own* her. I wanted you to look at me the way you look at your fantasy book—with a mixture of awe, anticipation, and warmth. I gave you a brownie, hoping you'd remember me sweetly, praying the sugar rush would spin a positive feel around that vacation. I remember how you looked at me when you saw me killing jellyfish. I never wanted you to look at me like that ever again."

"I won't." I shook my head, tears falling down my cheeks. "I would never look at you like that again."

He licked his lips. "You did. For an entire year. But somehow, it made shit bearable. It felt like proving a point to myself—that you weren't worth the work, that we were doomed."

"We're not," I insisted, swallowing back the L-word, which kept rising in my throat, demanding to be said.

I didn't want to freak him out, but I felt it. I felt it humming in my body, threatening to burst forth.

"We are." He dropped his forehead to mine, shaking his head. Our noses brushed together. "Fuck, we are, and soon I won't be good enough for you. But tonight? Tonight I can convince myself I still am."

"Tell me everything. I want to know." Tears ran over my cheeks now.

I kissed the tip of his nose. The corner of his lips. His cheek. Forehead. Eyes. Everything about him screamed *boy* all of a sudden, and things I'd thought I could never forgive—the way he'd acted toward me, Arabella sucking him off, him snatching the internship—seemed so trivial now.

He shook his head, pressing his hot lips to mine. His eyes shone. Even in the dark, I could see how close he was to letting it all out.

"I would never put you in that position."

"I'm asking to be in this position."

"Let's pretend tomorrow never comes. Because for me, it doesn't."

I was about to answer when his mouth descended on mine. I wrapped my arms around his neck, raking my fingernails along his working muscles. They bulged as he removed my top and jammies.

Rain began to drum on the windows of my room. It had been an exceptionally dry fall, and as winter wrapped around the castle, I was expecting more storms. But it seemed eerily quiet. Like nature held its breath in anticipation, just like us. The cards were about to be revealed, people were going to get hurt, and the thunderclouds let the rain loose.

Vaughn kissed his way from my lips to my jaw and down to my neck, sucking one of my nipples into his mouth. My legs wrapped around his waist in a vise.

"Fuck, you're beautiful," he moaned into my nipple, flicking it with his tongue. "Funny," he murmured against my flesh as his lips moved back up, while he kicked his trousers down. "Talented as fuck." His mouth dipped into the hollow place between my neck and shoulder, tasting me. "And mine," he finished, thrusting into me in one go, so deep and carnal, I arched my back and let out a yelp. "A million times over, forever mine."

He moved inside me in smooth, continuous thrusts that left me clawing at his back with impending insanity. Everything about what we did felt delicious and final and completely different from our previous encounters. This was not Vaughn taking his anger out on me or the time we lost our V-cards together. This was Vaughn apologizing for the past decade—and for what was still to come.

And it was me accepting that I couldn't keep him.

I couldn't ask him not to do what he was about to do. I just needed closure before he left. Because he *was* leaving. All this time, I thought he'd stolen the internship to spite me. Turns out, he had a much bigger plan. I was just a bystander.

A casualty. Collateral damage.

After he came inside me and rolled on his back, staring at the ceiling, I found his hand under the duvet and squeezed.

"Why do you always do that?" he croaked. "Stare at the ceiling. What's so interesting about it? I always wanted to ask."

It warmed my heart that he cared. That he wondered. I smiled sadly. "That's where I keep all my memories of her. They're written in all the ceilings, of all the places all over the world." I pointed at my blank ceiling. "At night, I pluck a memory out, relish it, play it like a video, then put it back. I never run out."

"You," he whispered, kissing my cheek, "are so effortlessly yourself."

That was the greatest compliment someone could give me. I turned to face him in bed. "I know what you're about to do. I just need to hear your story."

He swallowed.

"The minute it's done, I'm leaving. I can't let you waste your life with someone like me. You deserve more, and if trouble ever finds me, it sure as fuck isn't going to touch you."

Some things you just need to power through. Losing each other before we'd even had the chance to have one another seemed to be one of them. I didn't fight him.

"Tell me," I whispered. "I want to know why you're leaving."

He did.

CHAPTER TWENTY-TWO
VAUGHN

The first time it happened, I was eight.

I'd always had the tendency to disappear. I never stood still, forever on the go.

Mom called me Houdini because I used to vanish from her sight everywhere we went—parks, malls, country clubs, restaurants, SeaWorld, Disneyland. She'd clutch my palm, nearly crushing my bones to dust, muttering about how the things we loved the most were often so slippery and hard to keep safe.

She called me her little explorer, said I'd turn her hair gray, but I was worth it. The world felt like a swollen piñata full of shit I wanted to touch and smear and eat.

That day, though, I should've stuck to my parents' side.

We were at an exhibition in Paris. The gallery had a fancy, five-word name I couldn't remember, let alone pronounce. There were a handful of children in the gallery, all of them glued to severe-looking au pairs with dark circles around their eyes. There had been a public auction for some rad-ass art pieces collectors and curators had been frothing at the mouth for. Problem was, it was stuck smack in the middle of summer vacation. My mother had been very keen on coming back home with something new for her gallery, so she'd dragged me and Dad along.

We'd go with her to hell, if need be, sans sunscreen.

Back then, I had a nanny whose job was to keep me alive and within reach. I hardly spent any time with Maggie, and when I did, it was for the odd hour here and there, when Mom needed to do something—like participate in this auction. Maggie, a fifty-five-year-old grandma who resembled Lady Tremaine of *Cinderella*, took me to the downstairs restaurant at the gallery and bought me a healthy pastry that tasted like wood and a carton of organic, sugar-and-taste-free chocolate milk.

The gallery was big and full of rooms I was itching to explore. I deliberately squeezed the chocolate milk against my white shirt, creating a stain the size of Texas.

"Shoot," I said wryly, squeezing the rest of the liquid onto my hands. Sticky fingertips were my favorite.

"Oh, honey, don't worry about it. Stay here." She got up, patting my knee. "I'm just going to grab some napkins, okay?"

"Sure."

The minute she turned around and made her way the counter, I jumped off the chair and raced into the nearest open room across the corridor. It was big, white, and cold—full of mammoth sculptures lurking like monsters. Their stones were dry and comforting. I touched one of them, relishing its texture. The still, humanlike statues reminded me so much of death, and death fascinated me because it was stronger than me. Even my dad.

I didn't think anything could be stronger than my parents.

I strode easily, fingering, touching, brushing my nails against the expensive pieces, eager to make a dent. I could hear the echo of Maggie's voice carrying into the open room as she searched for me, her footsteps fast and hysterical. A twinge of sorrow pinched my heart, but this wasn't my first rodeo. I figured I'd get out of here before my parents were done and return to her, like I had so many times before.

No one had to know.

There was one sculpture in particular that held my attention in a vise. I ran a hand over its face and for the first time, shivered with excitement. It was brutally beautiful. Bold, menacing, yet tranquil. The sign underneath it said *Tutankhamun's Death Mask by Edgar Astalis*. It looked back at me with a hint of a smile.

I smiled back.

"You know," a voice boomed behind me. English accent. Male. Old, at least in the ears of an eight-year-old.

I didn't turn around. I hated giving people the satisfaction of getting the reaction they wanted from me. In this case, surprise.

"This is one of the pharaohs of ancient Egypt. He died at the tender age of nineteen."

No one had ever spoken to me about death before, and I wanted to gut the subject open, let every secret and fact gush out. Where did we go afterward? Did it hurt? When did it happen? Could moms die too? I knew Knight's mom, Auntie Rosie, was always sick. I couldn't imagine my life without my parents, but I knew death grabbed everyone by the throat eventually. Some part of me wanted to look it in the eye and spit in its face.

Later, it'd earn me the title of daredevil—a rash, bold, careless bully.

I remained silent, my back to the stranger, but I heard his voice getting closer, his shoes clicking on the granite floor with ease and confidence.

"They made him a golden veneer called the Death Mask and installed it on his head before burial. The original mask consists of hundreds of sheets of gold and was made in less than ninety days. Its creation is so miraculous and outstanding in the art world, some believe the Death Mask wasn't meant for Tutankhamun at all."

I didn't know why he was telling me this. He sounded smart. Not as cold and intimidating as my dad. Not that my dad was like that to *me*, but I knew he scared some people, and I could see why.

Fear equaled limitation. Restraining people, controlling them, appealed to me. There was wild, raw power in it. Infinite possibility.

"What's your name?" The man was now standing next to me, his hands laced behind his back, both of us watching the statue.

"Vaughn," I said.

Vaughn meant *junior* or *younger* in Welsh. Mom said when she first held me after I was born, I was the spitting image of my father. So shockingly similar, her heart almost cracked and burst with love.

She'd also warned me not to talk to strangers, let alone give them my personal details, but I wasn't scared. The man looked harmless: tall, thin as a shoelace, and soft-spoken. He wore an eccentric suit—green on yellow, I remember.

"I'm Harry. Do you know what mummies are, Vaughn?"

"Course," I scoffed, running my finger along the statue's nose. "Tutankhamun was mummified, right? Because he was Egyptian."

"Smart kid."

Couldn't dispute the obvious, so I shrugged.

"But there was something very different about the way they mummified Tutankhamun. He was the only mummy ever found who didn't have a heart. The Egyptians never removed the heart when they buried their royals. But they did with him."

Looking back, I could see how inappropriate the conversation was—talking about death, the removal of inner organs, and the mummification of bodies. However, I'd been fascinated. He'd told me more about the real Tutankhamun, and I'd gulped the information thirstily, struggling to keep my face bored and expressionless.

It was only when he took his first breath that I realized he was standing far too close to me, that with every fact he'd volunteered about the young prince, he'd taken a step toward me. His thigh was now pressed against my arm. I took a step back, squinting at him.

"Personal space here," I quipped.

His face opened with surprise. People weren't used to sarcasm from kids my age.

"Sorry," he mumbled, moving away.

"I want to be mummified without a heart." I pointed at the sculpture, changing the subject.

"At nineteen?" He looked down at me, smirking.

He seemed entertained by me, which was unusual. People typically said I was mouthy and had an unruly streak.

I shrugged. *Sure.* Nineteen seemed centuries away.

"What about your parents? They'd be sad if you died so young."

"They wouldn't care," I lied. I didn't know why I said it. I just wanted to sound grown-up and sophisticated.

"You sure?"

"Yup. Who are you anyway?" I narrowed my eyes at him.

"I own this gallery. And you, my little friend, are in big trouble." His tone turned frosty as he grabbed the statue of Tutankhamun and threw it on the floor. The statue broke into three pieces.

I stared at it, wide-eyed, my mouth slacking.

What. The. Fuck?

"This statue is being auctioned off for six million dollars upstairs," the man said in the same monotone tenor one would use to discuss the weather. "My cousin's most sought-after piece. And *you* just broke it."

"I didn't!" I gasped.

For the first time in my life, I felt something foreign, powerful, and pungent. *Hatred.* It was so thick I could feel it bursting on my tongue. He was going to pin it on me, and people were going to believe him because he was older and wore a suit, even if it was a funny one. I was just a kid who couldn't help himself and had bailed on his nanny—and not for the first time. I had trouble written all over me.

"Yes, you did. I saw you."

"That's a lie!" I kicked the air in frustration, my throat burning. I was so angry I wanted to hit him, but I knew I couldn't.

I heard Maggie's voice calling my name desperately. The man heard her too. He smiled.

"They left you with the au pair. How bloody cliché." He shook his head, chuckling to himself.

At the time, I didn't know what he meant. I knew now. He'd thought my parents had little to no interest in my life. That I was easy prey—a decoration they plucked out of the wet nurse's arms once in a full moon, to show their friends and colleagues they had an heir.

"Is your father going to hit you when he finds out?" he asked me.

"What?" I spat, surprised by the idea. "No. No, he won't."

"But he'll be livid that you broke it. Does he even have the money to pay for it?" He eyed me.

Maggie's voice grew closer. She was coming. *Fuck.* She was going to tell on me, and my parents were going to give me so much shit. If Dad would need to pay for this, I was guessing he'd fire her too. Maggie was someone's grandma. That someone was sick. I didn't know what the kid had, but I knew his name was Johnny and that Maggie needed this job. My mom sent flowers to his hospital when he was going through treatments and visited them often, but she never took me because she said she didn't want me to see certain things.

Everything became so complicated in one catastrophic moment. I had no idea life could take such a sharp turn in a fraction of a second.

"You're a liar!" I roared in his face, shoving him with all of my nonexistent strength. My noodle arms bounced back comically, hitting my sides. Not only was I eight, I was also on the skinny side.

He grabbed my wrists and brought them to his stomach, laughing in a low, gravelly voice.

"How about we strike a deal, little man?"

"No!" I tried to resist, kicking his nuts, but he was faster, dodging my advance. I was delirious with anger, kicking without aim.

"I can make this all go away. Take the fall. Forget it ever happened and talk to my cousin. On one condition."

I stopped struggling, frozen. Every bone in my body told me not to take whatever he had to offer, but Maggie's voice grew even closer and more unsteady. She was in tears now, sniffling my name in panic. *Fuck, fuck, fuck.*

"All I need you to do to make it go away is…" He trailed off, taking one of my wrists and putting my palm against his groin. "Slide your little hand into my trousers and squeeze my penis. That's all. Just a bit."

I'd touched myself thousands of times. Obviously not to jerk off, but me and my wiener were on good terms. Then again, my parents had told me my privates were mine, for no one else to touch.

They never said anything about me touching someone else's, though.

"No. That's gross," I said on impact, pulling away. "You're old. Besides, I only like my own penis."

"You'll like mine more for six million dollars, little one." He laughed, unzipping his cigar pants but leaving them on.

Maggie was directly outside the room now, and I was wild with adrenaline. Everything could go so wrong. My mother would be crushed that I'd snuck away again, my dad furious when he had to foot the bill for this. I didn't want them to feel that way.

And Maggie—what if they fired her? Mom wouldn't. But Dad could and would. Even Mom wouldn't be able to convince him otherwise. It wasn't the first, third, or even fifth time that I'd run away when Maggie was in charge.

"Okay, okay," I breathed out, shoving my hand into his pants. His penis was thick and big. It felt weird and unnatural. The wooden pastry made its way up my throat. I needed to puke.

"Now *squeeze*," he instructed with his breezy English accent.

I did. I squeezed again and again and again, pumping it like a stress ball, wanting to hurt him badly. But the more I tried to make it painful for him, the more he seemed to like it. It all happened really fast. Ten seconds flat. His eyes rolled in their sockets, dropping shut, and he shuddered.

He pushed me away all of a sudden, a jerky reaction. I fell on the floor and watched as he took a multicolored handkerchief from his breast pocket and shoved his hand into his opened zipper. When the handkerchief reappeared, it was wet and sticky.

"Bloody hell," he breathed heavily, wiping his brow. The look on his face when he saw me on the floor, staring at him, was confused, then angry.

"On your feet now." He clapped twice.

I shot up the minute Maggie walked into the room. She wasn't alone. Mom and Dad were with her too. One look at the three of them, and any regret I might've had for doing what I did with this man vanished. Mom and Maggie had tears in their eyes. Maggie's brow was dripping with sweat. Dad looked like he was about to kill someone. If they thought I'd snuck away to break a six-million-dollar piece of art, I'd be grounded well into my midforties.

"Vaughn!" Mom cried with relief. She ran to me, scooped me up, and held me tight, like I was a baby. My limbs flailed helplessly as she squeezed me to her chest and pressed me close. I felt her heart pounding violently against my own—and the trace of something gluey in my left palm.

"God, I was so worried. What am I going to do with you, Little Houdini?"

"Chain him by the ankles and throw him in the basement until he hits eighteen by the looks of it," Dad commented, striding toward us and plucking me from her arms. He put me down and crouched to my eye level, his face full of thunder.

"Who is this guy?" He tilted his head sideways, motioning toward the guy who'd asked me to touch his penis, but still staring at me.

I'd just opened my mouth when the man cooed, "Emilia LeBlanc-Spencer! We finally meet. Huge fan over here."

"Harry Fairhurst. Same could be said about you. I just bought one of your paintings." Mom had recovered from her earlier hysteria but still gave him a suspicious look.

She glanced at me, waiting for cues. Dad stood up, frowning. He didn't like something about this scene, either, but couldn't place what it was.

But me, I was ashamed.

Ashamed I'd screwed up.

Run away.

Fell into this person's scheme.

I felt stupid and juvenile and more destructive than I ever had been, with Maggie on the line.

She could've lost her job, and Dad could have paid six mill for my stupidity. And anyway, I wasn't going to see this asshole ever again.

"What was my son doing in this room with you, Fairhurst?" my dad asked.

Maggie snatched me into her arms. Mom turned to the Fairhurst guy, her body tense. "Harry?"

He looked between them, at everyone but at me. His eyes glittered with something desperate, but I didn't know what it was. He pointed to the broken statue at his feet, and my heart skipped a beat.

The motherfucker.

"I accidentally dropped this," he explained nonchalantly, the smile returning to his voice. "Vaughn here heard the crash and rushed in. He said he'd help me clean up. I told him that was not necessary, that he needed to go back to whoever was calling for him."

Lies. But I thought they worked in my favor, so I kept my trap shut.

Dad turned to me. "Is this true?"

Harry Fairhurst did not dare to breathe for the duration between Dad's question and my answer. Mom took a step away from Fairhurst, her eyes wild with something I couldn't read—not just worry. She was aghast. I couldn't do it to them, not when I knew Harry still had a napkin with that wet shit on it in his breast pocket.

"Yeah," I answered finally. "I wanted to see what happened."

"You can tell us the truth," Mom said quietly. She had that look, like she was going to cry.

"I am," I scoffed. "I am telling the truth."

That day, I unraveled two amazing discoveries:

1. I had the ability to destroy my parents. All I needed was to tell them the truth. The guilt and prospect of my being all fucked up about it would do the rest.
2. I would die before destroying them.

Harry Fairhurst was right about one prophecy, though. I was a bit of a Tutankhamun. At nineteen, I no longer had a beating heart. I wore a death mask everywhere I went, and I was thirsty for revenge. For his blood.

There was just one tiny problem that did not occur to me beforehand.

Namely, his niece, Lenora, who'd shoved a heart back into my chest. Now that it was beating again, I didn't know what to do.

———————

Fairhurst abused me two more times.

The next was a few years after the gallery incident—on that vacation in the South of France when I gave Lenora the brownie. In the private beach's restroom.

I came out of a stall just when he walked in, both of us in swimming trunks. He grabbed my arm, squeezed it, and smiled. I thought he was probably grateful I hadn't told anyone about what happened.

After all, years before, in the gallery, he'd looked like he was ready to piss himself when my parents walked in and he'd realized who I was.

But now, when he knew I wasn't going to tell on him, I soon realized he wondered if he could get away with it a second time.

"How's life treating you, Tutankhamun?" His thumb rolled down my cheek.

Heartless prince, he implied. *Empty-chested mummy.*

I jerked my arm free, turning my face the other way. I no longer cared that he talked to me and treated me like a grown-up. He was the same asshole who'd threatened to tell my parents I'd done something I didn't. I advanced for the door, every fiber in my body shaking with rage.

"Oh, Vaughny boy, I would not do that if I were you, my dear lad."

I stopped but didn't turn around. I'd changed in the years since he'd demanded I do what I did to him. It was gradual but persistent. I'd come to feel less everything—jealousy, love, compassion, happiness—and therefore needed to hurt more.

I'd started picking fights at school. Got suspended three times. Cut myself a little where no one could see—upper thighs, stomach, chest. It felt like feeling *something*, and feeling something was better than feeling nothing.

As it happened, I liked to bleed, and Len liked the taste of blood. We were, without even knowing it, very fucking suitable for each other in the worst and best possible ways.

All this time Knight had bantered about putting hats on hamsters, but I knew no social circle or blowjob could hide the very apparent fact that I. Couldn't. Fucking. Feel.

"Take a hike," I said without turning back to look at Fairhurst. I took another step toward the bathroom exit, but what he said made me pause.

"Your mother is going to be vastly disappointed when she discovers I've blacklisted her from all of my galleries and refuse to work with her—especially now, when she's on the brink of a once-in-a-lifetime deal."

I turned around and stared at him, dumbfounded. By this time, I knew my mother adored the ground he walked upon. He was the epitome of talent in her opinion—in many people's. That gave him an untouchable shine I couldn't pierce through.

"I'm going to tell them what you made me do," I said, my voice low and steady. I only half meant it.

He smiled, rearranging the waistband of his swimming trunks suggestively. He'd done some growing up the past few years himself. His eccentric style had been replaced with the generic look of a self-made millionaire.

"I'd like to see you try, two years after the fact. Especially when your mother is trying to enroll you at Carlisle Prep for summer session. Seems a lot like the boy who cried wolf because he didn't get in." He pouted theatrically.

"I don't care about the prep school."

"Do you care about your *family*, though? Their reputation?"

This time, the only thing he asked was for me to get naked in front of him in one of the stalls. He didn't touch me but seemed well-versed in the ritual when he bent me against the wall, jerking off behind me. I wondered how many boys he'd done that to at Carlisle.

The last time, at thirteen, it had happened in the darkroom.

That was the time Len caught us red-handed, and I'd wanted to die, because out of all the students, of all the schools I ever went to, she was the one person I didn't want pity from.

She'd walked in when his lips were wrapped around my cock, no less. I was half-mast, desperately trying to get hard so we could get it over with. Harry and I were tucked in the shadows of the room, my arm braced against the wall.

I wasn't hard when she walked in.

But I sure as fuck was when she ran out.

I imagined it was her, grabbed his hair, and fucked his mouth mercilessly, irrationally mad to a point that all I could see was red. He took it with little, helpless, joyful moans, and I slapped him, shutting him up so I could pretend he was Lenora. He came when I did.

That time, he promised me the internship at Carlisle Prep when I graduated high school. And by then, I knew what I wanted to do to him, what needed to be done. I was too young to do it then, but I swore I'd come back and avenge what he'd done to me.

What he'd done to all of them.

That darkroom had been occupied every single night, I noticed. The boys of Carlisle Prep always looked red-eyed, tired, broken. Haunted. Ghostlike. Not unlike me.

I was going to kill the fucker and make sure he couldn't touch anyone ever again. But when his lips were around me, I'd thought about Lenora Astalis.

The girl who peeked at me every day during summer session and hadn't realized I'd glanced at her too, because I was better at hiding it.

That's what I never told Len. That she was the only reason I received blowjobs.

Because they reminded me of that day, and it was a screwed-up way to avenge what she saw.

What she must've thought of me.

The sweet, beautiful girl who'd occupied my mind since the South of France grew pointy devil horns, and I was fine with it. If I hated her, I didn't care what she thought about me.

Simple.

I'd spent the rest of my adolescent years trying to prove to everyone and myself that I wasn't appalled by human touch. That I was straight. That I was in charge of my sexuality. I received public blowjobs and talked about sex all the time.

No one could imagine the unimaginable.

That I was a virgin.

That I never wanted to have sex.

That every single time I became hard on demand, I'd had one thing and one thing only on my mind—ever since that night in the darkroom:

Killing Harry Fairhurst.

CHAPTER TWENTY-THREE
LENORA

Vaughn left my side sometime after I fell asleep, exhausted by absorbing what had happened to him without falling apart. The place where he'd kissed my forehead was still warm, the only souvenir of the last time we'd spend together.

I didn't bother leaving my bed the following morning. I felt like crying for eternity, curled inside myself, my body rocking back and forth as the sobs rattled through me. Turned out that Vaughn looming over me and threatening my life wasn't half as devastating as hearing what had made him want to kill me—and the rest of the world—in the first place.

I allowed myself the better half of the day to fall apart privately, letting out all the emotions I couldn't show him. Then I stood, picked myself up, and finished my statue.

What I did next would shock everyone.

Including myself.

VAUGHN

Instead of going back to my room the following morning, I headed straight to Edgar. I was running out of time to do everything I wanted to do to take care of Lenora before shit hit the fan. Confiding in her had felt eerily similar to handing her my balls in a nice, cellophane-wrapped package, but strangely necessary.

All that we were would die right along with Harry Fairhurst tomorrow, and Hunter and Knight were due to land at Heathrow later tonight.

I barged into Edgar's office without knocking, ignoring the fact that Arabella was sitting in front of his desk. They were engrossed in deep conversation, hunched forward and exchanging hushed words over raised tones. Planting my hands on my hips, I jerked my head to the door.

"Outta here," I barked. Didn't take a nuclear scientist to know who I was talking to.

Arabella twisted her head to look at me, wiping her cheek—from tears or cum, anyone's guess would be as good as mine.

"You're not the boss of m—"

"Ass. Outta. That. Chair." Each word was pronounced with dripping mockery. "Before I drag you by the hair, and believe me, Arabella, I won't even think twice before tearing those expensive extensions—*and* your real hair—from that empty skull of yours."

That was a lie but a believable one nonetheless. She turned her face to Edgar, expecting him to fight her war, but he was too stunned to react, his eyes on me. Reluctantly, she stood, her chair scraping back, and walked slowly out the door. She stopped when her shoulder brushed my arm.

"I know something fucked you up, Vaughn. Everyone knows that. And you're not the only person who's bad for a reason. I'm not the devil," she whispered.

"No, you're not," I rasped under my breath. "The devil's smart and calculating. You're neither." I slammed the door in her face.

"What do you think you're doing?" I scowled at Edgar the minute we were alone, leaning forward and bracing my hands on either side of his desk.

It was covered with bullshit—sketches, documents, coins, a picture of Lenora, Poppy, and their mother smiling back at him. Fake fucker hadn't checked on his daughter in weeks.

"I beg your pardon?" He sat back, blinking. "Who do you think you're talking to, Mr. Spencer? I strongly advise you check yourself before you're checked out of this institute. I am not impressed with either your manners or your profess—"

I cut him off. "Fuck my professionalism. You're fucking your daughter's enemy." I wiped his desk clean of everything there in one harsh movement, just barely holding back from smashing the entire thing in his face.

He pulled back and coughed, seeming surprised by my outburst.

"Your *teenage* daughter's enemy," I added. "So don't lecture me about manners. Len is not even talking to you, and instead of making things right with her, you go around spending time with that bitch? What is wrong with you?" I straightened up, pulling at my hair with both hands as I paced across the room.

He stood, his voice booming so loud it rattled the glass windows. "What are you on about, you silly boy?"

I whirled to face him. "Don't play dumb. Arabella told both me and your daughter that you guys are having an affair. How long has this been going on? Since you were in Todos Santos? Was she even legal when you first had a taste?"

"I...I... *Wait.*" He frowned. "Lenny thinks that's what I'm doing when I'm meeting with Arabella?" It was his turn to run a hand through his mass of gray curls. "She thinks I'm having *sex* with her?"

By the way he said the word *sex*, I gathered that he viewed the concept as about as appealing as I did. In other words, he'd rather be chopped up and thrown in the ocean than tap Arabella's ass.

Then what was he doing with her alone all the time? She wasn't my first choice for intellectual conversation.

"Are you saying you're not?"

"No!" He slapped the desk, roaring.

"Enlighten me, then. What possesses you to spend more time with Arabella than you do with both your daughters combined?"

"I cocked up!" Edgar pushed his desk away completely, causing it to skid over the floor until it almost hit me. He shook with what looked like years of built-up rage. "I cocked everything up in Todos Santos, but not the way you think. I didn't have an affair with Arabella. I had an affair with her mother, Georgia—the first woman I've been with since Lenny's mother died. I got carried away, not thinking. Not thinking she was married, that she had kids, that I was destroying another family while trying to keep mine together. Arabella caught us in the act one day and told her father. This spun the next year in my life out of control. Apparently, Georgia had been battling an addiction to painkillers and alcohol, and I was one of her continuous bad decisions. She cried rape to save her relationship. And I got thrown into a behind-the-scenes legal battle with Arabella and her father, who wanted to avenge Georgia's indiscretions. He whisked Georgia off on a so-called vacation, but really, it was a lengthy trip to rehab, while Arabella stayed in California with her sister. That's when her mother admitted she had an affair with me and wanted a divorce. When her husband threatened to drag her through a nasty process and waved the prenup in her face, she tried to cut her wrists, unsuccessfully. Arabella and her sister were crushed, and guilt consumed me, so I found myself helping the family through this period. When I learned Arabella had found a way to get here, I knew she was after revenge. That's why I've been distant with Lenny. The less I drag her into this, the less chance Arabella has to get to her. She's been making every day a living hell. I think she has this idea that if she ruins my life, she'll feel better about the fact that I ruined hers."

"Is that what's happening right now?"

"Yes. She barges into my office and room unannounced, throwing accusations in my face. She's walked in on two dates I've had since coming here. Shattered two of my sculptures. Then there's what she did to Lenny and Poppy, of course. I knew that. I knew. That's why I kept distance from them. I told myself it would all be over in a few short months and things would go back to normal."

"Bullshit. Lenny and I both heard you in your room," I challenged. "You told her to get off of you. You had sex."

"She was trying to seduce me!" he shouted. "She gets into fits where she tries to have sex with me, but I always push her off. I've called her father a few times. Her sister too. They said I deserve it for what I did to their family. She's a martyr, dragging me through every single sin I supposedly committed."

"Why are you allowing her to spend so much time with you, then?" He didn't seem the type to bone a teenager, but I was still skeptical.

He swallowed hard. "More time with her means less time for her to target Lenny. Children shouldn't suffer for their parents' misdeeds. I'm humoring Arabella's destructive side until her time here is up. But I am not touching her, and I am horrified that my daughter would think that. Does she not know me at all?"

"Have you taken the time to get to know her recently?" I retorted.

His head hung low, like a half-mast flag.

"Has she shared this with Poppy?" He sighed.

I shook my head. Len hadn't gathered the strength to upset her older sister. When you care about someone—and at this point there was no point denying I cared for Lenora—you really don't want to be the bearer of shitty news to them.

"Thank God."

"Don't thank God, thank your daughter. You have to make amends with her." I pointed a warning finger at him from across the room.

"I don't know, Vaughn. Parenting is bloody hard, okay?"

He wiped sweat from his brow, dragging his massive back against the wall and squatting down. I did the same, crouching across from him on the other side of the room.

"The truth is, kids don't come with a manual. I'm not always sure when she's acting up because she needs to, because it's normal, and when it's serious. Lenora has always been so inherently good. Both my daughters are, really. But Lenny has loads of common sense and a spine for miles. I'd never been particularly worried about her. I thought I was merely allowing her a rebellious period, thinking she was mad about the internship again."

The internship. I almost winced. That one was all on me.

"You need to talk to her today. Set the record straight. Tell her exactly what's up."

He nodded.

"As for the internship..." I continued, the words leaving my mouth of their own accord. "The plan has changed. I need your help with something."

Edgar frowned. "You're still going to show the sculpture, right?"

Of course. Edgar loved Len so much. That's what she didn't know. She thought him giving me the internship was him disregarding her. She didn't know he'd made the greatest sacrifice *for* her. It was me who'd deceived them. At first anyway.

I'd told Edgar I would make his daughter fall in love with me and get her out of her emotional funk. That I would court her, love her, cherish her, and be a friend to her. He, in return, sold her dreams to buy her happiness. With me.

We'd both lied to get what we wanted, and it had blown up in our faces in a spectacular fashion.

"I'm not showing the statue." I flicked my Zippo, letting the flame lick up and pressing it to the tip of my tongue, fully aware he was going to put me on fucking blast. The secret to extinguishing fire with your tongue is a lot of saliva. And very little fucking common sense. "But we are going to show them something, all right."

My meeting with Edgar somehow bled into late afternoon. I gave him careful instructions on how to handle everything with Len.

It felt like placing your toddler in the irresponsible hands of an untrained monkey, but I knew I had to get the hell out of there, and fast, after I executed my plan.

When I finally returned to my room, all I wanted was to kick my boots off, close my eyes, and pretend tonight was going to be just another night of me sneaking into Good Girl's room.

But of course it wasn't.

As it also happened, I had a surprise waiting for me in my bedroom, which had nothing to do with my two asshole friends.

"Evening, Son." My father turned around in the recliner by the window, his movements smooth and nonchalant. There was an unlit cigar tucked between his teeth and a glass of something strong in his hand.

"What are you doing here?" I felt my jaw ticking with irritation.

Talk about shitty timing. The last thing I needed was another distraction. With my luck, my mother was here too, along with the entire goddamn family.

"Sit your ass down." He jerked his chin toward my unmade bed.

"Or?" I draped a muscular arm against the wall, challenging.

"That's an easy one," he sneered. "*Or* I will stand up and make you very goddamn uncomfortable by hugging your ass. Because that's what you need right now, isn't it, Vaughn?" He slanted his head sideways. "A hug?"

I sat down, resting one boot over his recliner in my small room. I'd been hugged by my dad more than a fucking tree in Woodstock, but there was something about his expression that threw me off. He knew something.

"Here. Sitting down. I'll ask again: What are you doing here?"

"You've been ignoring my calls."

"I spoke to Mom every day. You never took the phone. Gotta hand it to you. You know how to master the hard-to-get act."

That was the strangest thing about the entire Dad ordeal but also precisely what made me not answer his calls. He was onto something, and whatever it was, he didn't want Mom to hear it.

Dad sat back, but he didn't look smug. A pang of worry pinched my chest. He had the constant air of someone who'd just fucked your wife, emptied your safe, and taken a shit in your bed. Now he looked surprisingly somber. Somber meant trouble.

"We had to talk privately," he said.

"Clearly." I scanned his face, looking for clues.

"I figured it all out, Son. I'm sorry. I'm so. Fucking. Sorry." His voice broke midway, and he turned his face away, his jaw clenching like mine did. His throat bobbed.

No.

No.

I dropped my head into my hands, elbows on my knees, and shook it.

"Troy Brennan?" I asked. It had to be that fixer he'd hooked me up with. How the *fuck* else did he figure that out?

"No. I made a promise and kept it."

"Jaime, then?" I snorted in false amusement. He must've told Dad I was in some kind of trouble. I didn't even have it in me to be mad at him. It was the logical thing to do. Still, shitty as hell. He'd signed a contract.

"No," Dad said, standing up and taking the necessary half step toward me.

I didn't want any of what he was about to offer—not the pity, the pain, the shame, the feeling that accompanied those things. Still, he sat next to me on the bed.

"I think Jaime was planning on telling me after the fact. But one night I got into my bedroom and your mom had fallen asleep with the lights on, an art magazine half-open under her arm. I tucked her in and was about to turn off the light when I picked the magazine up and saw an item about how all of Harry Fairhurst's paintings had been bought by a mysterious collector. I wondered why we hadn't been approached about the paintings in our house—everyone else had been, after all—but the answer was simple. You had access to our house, and to the paintings in it. I threw the magazine away so she wouldn't know, wouldn't do the math herself. I racked my brain trying to figure out why you'd want to own all this motherfucker's paintings. Better yet, how you could afford them. So I checked your trust fund, and sure enough, it was empty."

I swallowed wordlessly. I'd been sloppy in that regard. All I could see was the end goal, and that had backfired in my face.

Dad put his hand on my back, both of us hunched over, seated on my bed. My face was still buried in my hands. I felt like a stupid kid and hated every minute of it.

"What could drive a man to buy an entire, eight-figure collection of paintings he's not even fond of?" My father's voice drifted in the air like smoke, lethal and suffocating. "There was only one answer: vengeance."

I stood up and walked to the window, refusing to face him.

He knew.

Lenora knew.

My secret was no longer mine. It had broken free. Run loose. I had no control over it. It was probably pounding through the alleyways of every ear in my inner circle.

"You want him forgotten," Dad said gently behind me.

I appreciated that he didn't say outright the things Harry had done to me. It made the situation a little less unbearable somehow. I sniffed, ignoring the statement.

I wanted to forget Harry Fairhurst had ever existed, yes, but I knew I couldn't. So I'd settled for erasing him from the memory of the rest of the world.

Ars longa, vita brevis.

But not if all your paintings are torn, burned, and floating in the Atlantic Ocean. Then you're just another mortal.

Dad stood up and came toward me. He planted his hands on my shoulders from behind. I dropped my head to my chest. He hadn't ridden my ass like I thought he would for ghosting him for eternity.

Or spending a sickening amount of money on art I had burned.

"Let me do it," he whispered.

"Huh?" I spun, my eyebrows diving down.

"I know what you're about to do, and I'm asking you to let me do it. Not for you, for me. When we talked about your problem before, I told you I wouldn't pry, but if I found out who was involved, I'd deal with them myself. And you agreed. We shook on it. There's a lot on the line for you, Son. Let me shoulder your burden. Let it be on my conscience, not yours. After all, I was the one who fucked up. I was the one who let it happen. I was the one who didn't figure it out in that Parisian gallery, the idiot who sent you to Carlisle Prep when you were a young boy. My fuckup. My mistake. My payback."

I appreciated how, even now, he did not bunch Mom into the colossal fuckup that was Harry Fairhurst. He took full responsibility as the head of the family. Some people thought flowers and hearts were romantic. Me, I thought being a badass who took the fall for his entire family and shouldered all their sins was far better. Not that it was really my parents' fault. They'd prodded, asked, begged, and questioned. They'd provided me with a magnificent childhood, and not just materialistically.

"Thank you," I said curtly. "But no."

"You don't know what killing a person does to your soul."

"And you do?"

He squeezed my shoulder again, refraining from answering me. *Interesting.*

"You have a girlfriend." Dad changed the subject. "Isn't she his niece? That would complicate things."

"We're not staying together." I swallowed the lump in my throat. That would be beyond awkward, now that she knew my plans for her uncle.

I'd given her all my secrets.

I'd trusted her then, and I trusted her now.

She'd never opened her mouth. And as it turned out, she hadn't even known what she saw back then. When I told her about Harry's abuse, she'd confessed to me that what she saw in that room was completely different.

"I didn't see Harry's head underneath you. I just thought it was a girl. I didn't know anything about oral sex. I thought you were young and angry, and doing things you shouldn't be doing and going to regret. I felt sorry for you. At thirteen, you shouldn't need sex and booze and blowjobs to feel. At thirteen, you're learning the hang of feelings. It's life on training wheels, you know?"

I didn't know. Harry never gave me the chance to know what it felt like to feel.

"Besides"—I moved around Dad, changing the subject—"how do you know about her?"

"Knight sent a family newsletter," he said matter-of-factly.

Fucker, I mouthed.

"Watch your mouth."

"I was making a general statement. What do you think he does with Luna? Play poker?" I flung myself over the bed, staring at the ceiling. I felt like a real teenager for the first time in forever. My dad was on my case, offering to get me out of the shit I'd gotten myself into. I had girl trouble. I made sex jokes on my best friend's account.

Dad stood in the middle of the room, looking a little lost all of a sudden—for the first time ever actually.

"It doesn't have to be that way, Vaughn. You don't have to lose her. You don't have to lose anything."

"It's a done deal, Dad. Drop it."

"Son…"

I turned to look at him. "Whatever you do, don't tell Mom. It would break her."

He held my gaze, nodding gravely. He got it. He got why I needed to do it myself.

"I won't," he said. "I didn't when I saw the article. This stays between you and me. What happened doesn't define you, you hear me? Once upon a time, I held on to a dark secret too." He leaned down, brushing my ink-black hair from my forehead and frowning. A mirror image, father and son, with nearly three decades between them.

"How did it end?" I blinked.

He kissed my forehead like I was a toddler, smiling.

"I killed it."

CHAPTER TWENTY-FOUR
EMILIA

I was raised to find beauty in everything.

Growing up in Virginia, we didn't have any money. We used buckets as small pools in hot, humid summers and trash bags to collect oranges and peaches in spring. An old tablecloth was destined to become a fine-looking dress once it ceased to serve its purpose. Two empty tin cans turned into a very short-distance walkie-talkie. An evening without electricity quickly rolled into an all-nighter full of scary stories and truth or dare.

Years later, after I married my billionaire husband, I'd stumbled across an article in the *New Yorker* asking if the poor lead more meaningful lives.

I didn't agree with the sentiment altogether because I was happier now—happier with the love of my life, with my beautiful son, and surrounded by friends I could host and spend time with. But then again, I wasn't really rich, was I?

Even with many millions in the bank, I would always be Emilia LeBlanc, who wore knockoffs and shook with exhilaration when opening new tubes of paint. There was something about the unavailability, the unattainability of buying new painting gear I'd grown up with that made unwrapping new equipment almost orgasmic. I never lost the joy I found in small things.

That's why I fell in love with Harry Fairhurst's paintings the moment I spotted the first one. It was a lone figure, walking in an alleyway, the buildings around it melting downward in an arch, ready to swallow the person who dared take that path whole. Regardless of his precise technique and striking execution, it just seemed like a sad painting of a sad person.

When I met him and found out he was gay and that he'd been bullied for it in school, I immediately took a liking to him. But something always lurked in the background, something dark and feverish I couldn't pinpoint.

He'd asked me a couple of times, while we were on vacation in the same city or island, if I needed some time off from Vaughn, if I needed him to babysit my kid. My answer was always no. But when I asked Vaughn about it, he was adamant everything was okay, that he liked Harry, and that nothing had happened in that room.

I believed him. After all, my kid had always been very much outspoken when things *weren't* okay.

Now, as I walked aimlessly in my grand, empty house, my husband miles away in England on a business trip, I decided to occupy myself by cleaning a little. I discharged our staff early, surprising them with tickets to *Hamilton* in San Diego, and began to scrub the kitchen floors. It was weirdly therapeutic—maybe because I'd been used to helping my mother clean the Spencers' grand kitchens when I was a kid and she worked for them.

After that, I took the trash cans out. I flipped them open to make sure nobody had put anything in the wrong place. California was big on recycling, but it seemed like our neighborhood was practically obsessed with it. I was too. I'd always been frightened about the world we're going to leave for our grandchildren.

As I peeked inside, everything looked kosher. In the brown trash can, appointed to recycling, lay the art magazine I'd never finished reading. I frowned. I didn't remember throwing it away.

Something willed me to reach into the bin and take the magazine out. Confused, I began to thumb through it, my forehead so tight with a frown, my entire face hurt. It was unlike Ronda and Lumi, our housekeepers, to throw such a thing away without asking me first. I wasn't mad. I was curious.

I stopped when I reached the last page, in the section about new art deals taking place around the world. The page was more wrinkled than the rest. I skimmed through the text, my heart stopping in my chest.

The magazine dropped from my hands, and I felt my mouth going dry.

For all the things I'd missed throughout my life, which weren't many—the occasional friend's birthday, a wedding, and a couple charity events I couldn't attend—I'd never missed something so big.

Fairhurst's paintings had all been sold to a secret bidder.

Almost every one of them—other than mine.

I ran back into the house, up the stairs, and to the main hallway of the second floor. I stopped at my favorite of Harry's paintings, the one in front of Vaughn's room.

Heartless Prince

Fairhurst had told me he'd titled the painting that because it was a replica of the Death Mask of Tutankhamun. But the eyes were the real kicker. They looked so completely human and deliciously frightened—shocked and panicked, ice cold and blue as the brightest summer day's sky.

Something dangerous began to hum in my blood. I stared at the painting, and before I knew it, my entire body was shaking with wrath, nausea coating my throat. I could feel myself breaking out in hives. I looked down, and my skin was patchy, red, the hairs on my arms standing on end.

My husband was in England.

The magazine was in the trash.

My son was different from other boys—always had been, but particularly since our trip to the Parisian gallery.

This is not a coincidence.

Vaughn, Vaughn, Vaughn.

My precious son who'd had to see this painting for months, day in, day out. Face it, brave it, overcome it. My boy, made out of frosty exterior, with fire in his heart. Just like his dad. I'd waited so long for him to fall in love, to blossom into the man I saw behind his anger and pain.

I'd never thought my predator son could be someone's prey.

I pounced on the painting, ripping the thick canvas with my bare hands, feeling my nails breaking, my flesh bleeding. My fingernails ripped from some of my fingers, dropping to the floor, but I didn't stop. Like a declawed cat, I persisted, tearing at the fabric. I only realized I was screaming when my throat began to burn. Once the painting was on the floor, in tatters, I began to kick it.

Only when there was no way to distinguish what had been in the painting, when the eyes were completely gone, did I ball on the floor and began heaving and crying. When I could, with shaky fingers, I withdrew my phone from my dress's pocket and booked a ticket to Heathrow, a red-eye flight taking off in less than an hour.

My son was not a heartless prince, placid and beautiful and lifeless.

He was misunderstood, wild, and alive.

And he had a mother—a very angry one at that.

One Harry Fairhurst should not have crossed.

CHAPTER TWENTY-FIVE
VAUGHN

"Holy shit, this place is colder than Vaughn's heart," Knight complained, pretending to rub his arms, even though he was clad in a peacoat that probably cost more than a Fairhurst painting.

Hunter, a Boston native, wore a light bomber jacket and a patronizing smirk, wheeling the one suitcase they'd brought with them.

"Did you bring what I asked you for?" I hissed, flipping the keys of the rental car I'd picked them up with from Heathrow.

Dad had asked if I wanted him to do it—he was staying at the same cottage Mom and he had rented when I'd moved in here—but I'd told him I didn't want him to get involved. Unlike Knight and Hunter, he asked questions. My friends were another story altogether. Knight had trashed art worth millions of dollars, burning it to the ground, and didn't even wonder why. That's why they were perfect for this job.

The automatic doors of the airport opened, and we all walked across to the Vauxhall Astra I had waiting. My friends looked at the silver car with a mixture of disgust and horror.

"Shit, man, you really don't want to get laid here." Hunter shook his head. "Do you have something against British girls or...?"

"It's a rental," I barked, grabbing his suitcase and hurling it into the open trunk of the car. "And chasing tail is not an Olympic sport for me as it is for you. Now I'll ask again—did you bring it?"

He knew exactly what I meant. It was too specific for me to buy here, in the UK. It could be traced back to me, and that was a risk I couldn't run. Hunter, on the other hand, had no problem buying it from a Canadian dude who drove all the way to Boston to hand it to him in person. Untraceable.

"Of course we brought it, fucker." Knight laughed, tapping the roof of the car and sliding into the passenger seat. "Why else would we bring a half-empty suitcase? So we can shop at goddamn Primark?"

I slid into the driver's seat, buckling up. Hunter got in the back.

"Tell me you don't shop at Primark," Knight said, dead serious, after a beat.

I shrugged. "They have good socks and jeans."

"Jesus." Knight dug his palms into his eye sockets at the same time Hunter laughed and said, "Goddamn, you are something else."

We spent the rest of the drive catching up. Knight seemed genuinely happy, which didn't surprise me, because he'd finally gotten what he always wanted: Luna Rexroth. Hunter lived in Boston and seemed mysterious about his time in college. I knew he had a job lined up, working for his family business once he graduated, and that his future had been written in blood the day he was born, but he never seemed to want to talk about it. And naturally, I wasn't one to poke.

When we got to their Airbnb condo in Reading, everything had already been readied. The security cameras upfront were working, blinking their red dots at us and recording everything. I slid into the garage, took the thing I needed from their suitcase, and drove back to Carlisle.

I couldn't help but make a stop at Lenora's room. I got as far as her door, pressing my forehead to it and taking a deep breath.

There wasn't any point in seeing her again.

It would just make shit harder.

I knew she was on the other side.

Alone. Soft. Beautiful. Mine for now.

I turned and walked away, feeling for the first time what it meant to have a hungry heart.

Harry Fairhurst wasn't born yesterday.

Shortly after I broke his arm, he'd booked a ticket to Brunei, in Southeast Asia, known for its beautiful beaches, exotic rainforest, and ability to hide there without a trace—the perfect haven for a child molester. Luckily, I'd calculated his moves, no matter how fast, swift, and smart. Right now he was still in his St. Albans house, packing up and getting ready to leave for the airport.

The first thing I'd done today was slide a letter under Len's door. I wasn't dumb enough to discuss what I was about to do in said letter—I trusted her, but how was I to know it wasn't going to find its way to unfriendly hands? The second was to head to my cellar and pretend to work as if nothing had happened.

When the clock hit three, I went to Hunter and Knight's apartment, passing the security cameras and making sure my face was visible. *The perfect alibi.* Once inside, I jumped out the back window, ran across the street to another rental car—this time a Kia—and drove to Harry's.

I parked at the fringe of the neighborhood, where the houses kissed the woods, took out what Hunter had gotten for me, and walked the rest of the way to Harry's house. Rather than open the door with the key I'd gotten my hands on, I jabbed my elbow through one of the windows, making it look like burglary. I stepped through the shards of glass, a replica of Tutankhamun's Death Mask on my face and shoulders—the mask my friends had brought from the US—gloves on my hands, and my weapon dangling from my fingertips.

Harry was standing in the hallway, surrounded by three suitcases.

"Christ!" he yelped, immediately backing himself against the wall.

He was such easy prey. If I hadn't been so young, so impressionable, and such a fuckup, maybe all of this could have been prevented when I was a kid.

Maybe I could be with Lenora now the way I wanted to.

Maybe I'd have a future that wasn't all bleak.

"Vaughn?" he asked. "Is that you? How did you get your hands on that mask? This is... Oh God. Oh God."

"God's not going to save you," I *tsked*, well aware of how creepy I looked with the mask.

This was one for the fucking books. If nothing else, the great Harry Fairhurst, creator of the most humanlike eyes in the history of art, was going to go out in style.

"What is in your hand?" he gasped, wincing visibly. "God, I don't want to die. Vaughn, I was young. I did some horrible things, but I...I...stopped. You know I did. You saw me with Dominic Maple. I haven't done those other things in nearly five years."

I lifted the khopesh—an Egyptian sickle sword—examining it from all angles. I'd forged it myself in my cellar after hours. It took me weeks to get it just right. It was small and sharp. I looked down, examining it through the slits my mask provided, feeling hot and sweaty under it.

"Let's talk about the heartless prince," I said with a calm I couldn't really feel. Not killing him wasn't an option. This was what I'd been waiting for since I was eight. But it wasn't as climactic as I'd thought it would be.

He was sweating and shaking, his back against the wall, but seeing his fear didn't bring me as much pleasure as seeing Len's face when she opened the door for me.

Harry pissed his pants just then. He couldn't even cover it, because one of his hands was stretched up, begging me not to hurt him, while the other was still in a cast and a sling. Also my doing.

"I just said some things. I didn't mean them..." he started.

"Remember our conversation that day?" I strode to him purposefully, ignoring his words. "Because I do, very damn well. According to one researcher, the death mask was originally intended for someone else, not the young prince. The artistic accuracy and skill is so precise, people find it hard to believe it was made in such a rush." I took another step, watching him collapse on the floor, against the wall. "They think it was intended for his stepmother, Queen Neferneferuaten. So really, it was someone else who should have died and put on a mask."

I carefully removed the mask from my face, waiting for the sick pleasure to kick in.

But it wasn't there.

I went through the motions, cradling the mask against my waist. My hair stuck to my forehead, and when I looked down and saw Harry weeping, all I wanted to do was kick his face, turn around, and go straight back to Lenora.

It was frustrating as shit because there was nothing I craved more than to be present in this moment, which I had planned for over a decade.

I put the mask on his face, and he was so scared, he didn't even try to struggle. With his face covered, he squeezed his eyes shut, sobbing, in hysterics.

"Please. I know you're not a murderer. Please, Vaughn, please."

I stared at him, clutching my weapon, turned off by the idea of slitting his throat and letting him bleed dry. I was going to make it look like burglary. I *did* have the perfect alibi.

"Lenora will *loathe* you," he spat, trying another tactic.

"Lenora knows," I corrected. "She understands me."

He laughed humorlessly, shaking to the core. "That doesn't mean she'd ever look at you the same way. You think she'd want to be touched by a murderer? Kissed by a cold-blooded killer? You think she's going to *marry* one? Have his children? Do you think my sweet, beautiful niece is able to fall in *love* with the man who killed her uncle?"

When I remained silent, debating whether this question was even relevant, he took it as a sign of my weakness, regaining some of his confidence.

"We can make this all go away. I sucked your cock and came into your hand. Big fucking deal. I didn't sodomize you. You didn't fuck me. Other boys had it a lot worse, Vaughn, so stop being such a bitch about it. Let me go, and I promise to stay in Brunei for the remainder of my life. I have the means to sustain myself there."

"You'll just harass other boys."

That was part of why I wanted to kill him. Not only because of all the things he did to me, but because of the prospect he might do them to others. He'd said he hadn't touched an unwilling victim in five years. I had no reason to take his word for it.

"Can't." He shook his head in the mask violently, probably making himself dizzy. "Not in Brunei. I won't even be able to have a relationship. It's strict over there. They would kill me if they find out I'm gay."

"You're not gay; you're a pedophile."

"That's illegal there all the same." He didn't try to deny it.

I knew it was stupid to stand here and listen to him. If he didn't follow through with his promises, I was going to be in deep shit for attempted murder, no matter how solid my alibi was.

Besides, I wanted him dead.

I did.

I just didn't want Lenora to be secretly appalled by me, and I didn't understand why I cared so much. I knew she would *understand*, but I could already feel her disappointment everywhere. It scorched my skin.

It seemed like I couldn't will my heart to stop wanting her any more than I could will it to stop beating. They had a word for what I was feeling, but I didn't want to say it. Think it. Consider it.

Love. I was in love with Lenora Astalis. Had been from the goddamn get-go.

I'd offered her a brownie because I wanted to talk to her.

I'd followed her back to her room at Carlisle after she'd entered the darkroom because I wanted to thrust myself into her life with a dirty pact. A bargain. A silent contract.

I bullied her because I loved her.

I loved her because she was the only girl who looked at me and didn't see money or status or violence or a heartless prince.

She saw *me*.

I took a step back. Harry saw it. I hated myself for choosing love over hate. I hated myself for fucking myself over, for not going through with it because of a pussy.

But she wasn't just a pussy, was she?

"That's it, lad. That's it. Do the right thing."

As he said it, the front door opened and closed behind me. I turned around, my eyes widening in horror when I saw who stood on the other side.

My father walked in, his face a blank mask of death.

"Vaughn, go back to Berkshire and call my PA on your way home. Tell her to get someone to come fix that window. *Today*," he enunciated, his voice steadfast.

I jerked my chin up. "I don't want you to interfe—" I started.

He plucked the weapon from my hand and pressed it to the base of my neck, exactly on my vein. "I don't care what you want. Go."

I did the thing I should have done when I was eight.

When I was ten.

When I was thirteen.

For the first time in my life, I let my father take care of me. Deal with my bullshit. Help me.

I closed the door behind me, shaking my head.

Family is destiny.

CHAPTER TWENTY-SIX
VICIOUS

"You told my son he wouldn't get the girl if he got revenge. Well, lucky me, I already got the girl. I get to have *both*."

I ate the distance between me and Harry Fairhurst in two steps, deliberately stepping on his fingertips. He arched his back, yelping. An injured animal. I removed the mask from his face so he could have a front-row seat to what I was about to do to him.

"Baron," he whimpered, his face red, swollen, and blotchy with hysteria. "Thank God you're here. Vaughn clearly needed a voice of reason."

Nice try, motherfucker.

I crouched down, digging my heel into the fingers of his healthy hand and meeting his gaze. I heard them crack under my shiny loafers. As soon as he saw what was behind my eyes, his face turned from panicked to ashen. I wasn't here to strike a deal or to relieve him of his destiny.

I was here to collect a debt.

Vengeance.

My son's pride, my son's life.

And it's been long overdue.

"You can't... You don't know... P-people will..."

"Find out?" I finished the sentence for him sardonically, flicking his chin up and forcing him to hold my gaze. "Fat chance, considering you're currently in the midst of committing suicide."

"But I'm not…"

I grabbed him by his blond hair, cut expensively and touched up to disguise any grays, dragging him to his dining table and sitting him down. His skull and forehead were bright red. I plucked a grocery list notepad and a pen from next to the fridge and placed them on the table, grabbing the seat opposite him. My son's dagger burned a hole in my hand.

"Start writing."

Ten minutes later, his suicide letter was done. The handwriting was legit, and he got a nice incentive to play along, seeing as I gave him a deal he couldn't refuse.

"Write the letter and go peacefully, swallowing a bunch of pills. Don't write the letter and I slit your wrists in your bathtub and watch you bleed. Either way, you'll be dead before dinnertime, and it will look like suicide. The awful, messy way or the peaceful way? Up to you."

He chose the pills.

When he was done writing, he looked up from the notepad expectantly. His eyes were red, hollow, soulless. I tried not to think about what they'd seen when he was alone with my son. I tried not to think about a lot of things in that moment. My wife—my beautiful wife that I loved more than life itself, who gave meaning to my existence—liked Harry's work, and I'd let him into my life. Into my house.

If she ever found out, she was going to kill him herself. Then fling herself off of a rooftop. I knew Emilia LeBlanc-Spencer better than she knew herself.

There was only one person she loved more than me.

Our son.

"Medicine cabinet?" I angled an eyebrow. I wasn't prone to big speeches. I wanted to get it over with. I heard a truck parking outside the house, the sound of the vehicle automatically locking, and knew it was the glazier who'd come to fix the window. We had to slip away from the first floor quickly. Luckily, Fairhurst was too far gone inside his own head to notice potential help could be on the way.

"U-upstairs," he stuttered. He smelled of piss and desperation. *Thank fuck.* "Let's rock 'n' roll."

The glazier walked in through the half-open door exactly a second after we went up the stairs. We slid into Harry's en suite, and I locked the door behind us. Emptying the cabinet's shelves, I grabbed everything at hand—paracetamols, aspirin, nefopam, ketamine (wasn't sure what business that had being there, but I couldn't complain; this shit could kill a horse with a bit of enthusiasm and the wrong quantities), and the usual variety of Xanax, Ativan, and other benzo drugs.

I emptied the pills across his gray marble counter and nodded toward them. "Any last words?"

"I—" he started.

"Kidding. I don't give a fuck."

"No, you don't understand. I don't have any water." He side-eyed me with a pouty frown, the piss stain on his pants drying and stinking up the entire bathroom. I heard the guy downstairs whistling to himself, working quickly, and knew he had no idea we were upstairs. His invoice had no doubt already been paid by my PA. As far as he was concerned, he was all alone.

"You have a fucking sink in front of you," I retorted.

"I do not drink tap water."

"You're about to die, you idiot." I grabbed the back of his head and smashed it against the mirror above the sink, turning the tap on in the process. Blood trickled down his forehead when his head bobbed back up. The mirror in front of him was shattered.

"That's seven years of bad luck. Your death couldn't come at a timelier moment," I chirped.

I began shoving pills into his mouth. I didn't have time for this. I wanted to call my son and see that he was okay, talk to my wife and assure her everything was fine.

After his mouth was full of pills, I pushed his head under the water, forcing him to gulp down or choke up. I repeated the action three times, until I was sure he'd swallowed enough drugs to kill a *Game of Thrones* dragon. His bloodstream would soon be more contaminated than Chernobyl circa 1986.

When it was done and dealt with, Harry sat on the edge of his massive bathtub, clutching the edges to the point of white knuckles. I leaned against the sink, watching him die impatiently.

"So this is how it ends?" He looked around him, quietly stunned.

I crossed my arms. Expecting small talk from me after what he'd done was a fucking stretch.

"Ever wondered what it feels like?" He scrubbed his cheek absent-mindedly. I don't think he noticed his hand trembling. "Death, I mean?"

"No," I answered. "I lived through it during my teenage years and most of my twenties. I know exactly what it feels like."

"Do you believe in the afterlife?"

"No more than I believe in unicorns." I stopped to think about it. "Actually, unicorns could potentially exist. Some dumb, millennial scientist is bound to fuck with a horse's DNA and manage to get it to grow a horn and a pink, fluffy tail. Of course, you won't be here to witness it. I'd send a picture, but sadly, USPS doesn't deliver to hell."

"I always thought—"

"Shh." I pressed my index to my lips. "Your thoughts don't interest me. You're a pedophile. At least have the dignity to die silently."

He was quiet for exactly two minutes, then spent the next ten minutes compulsively blabbing about his dark childhood—with his drunken father and MIA mother. I spent the next ten minutes flicking dirt from under my fingernails and checking the time on my Bvlgari. When the minute hand on my watch signaled it had been twenty minutes since the asshole gulped down a pharmacy, and I heard the truck downstairs disappearing in the distance, the glazier with it, I picked up Vaughn's dagger.

"What are you doing?" Harry looked up from the floor, blinking. He looked so broken, a part of him was already dead. He'd accepted it. It surprised and frustrated me that it hadn't happened yet.

"Turns out the pills aren't quite fast enough for my taste," I said roughly, picking him up by his neck.

"You promised me you wouldn't let me bleed out. We had a deal."

I propped him back on the edge of the bathtub, grabbed his wrist, and cut a deep gash. He shifted his gaze from his wrist to his other arm—the one with the cast—mouth agape, eyes flaring with alarm.

I'd cut a gash that would drain his body of blood. And he couldn't even *try* to stop it because my son had broken his other arm.

Poetic. Precise. Perfect.

"I did? Well, I don't negotiate with child molesters, much less those who hurt *my* child. Have a nice death." I gave his chest a shove, watching him collapse into his bathtub, jerking and convulsing like a fish out of water.

I grabbed his shaving razor through a towel to avoid leaving fingerprints, took out the blade and threw it into the bath, not bothering to close the door after me.

I felt heavier than when I'd walked in.

That's how I knew I'd done right by my son.

———————

Some hours later, I parked in front of the cottage I'd rented downtown near Carlisle Castle. Vaughn wasn't answering his phone, and I was ready to burn the world down. I'd shoulder a million deaths to protect him and Emilia. All I asked—*all* I fucking asked—was to know they were both okay at any given time.

I walked into the cottage, dropping the keys on the rustic kitchen island that bled into the open-space interior, and spotted my wife sitting on the couch, cross-armed, fire in her peacock-blue eyes.

She stood up and stormed toward me. I opened my mouth, my expression automatically easing at her sight.

"Sweetheart. I was going to—"

The slap came out of nowhere. It wasn't the first time Emilia had slapped me. But this time, I didn't know what I'd done to deserve it. Upon closer inspection, I could see she had tears in her eyes, dark circles beneath them, but the rest of her was as pale as a ghost.

"Baby…" My mouth fell open when she dropped to her knees, burying her face in her hands. I lowered myself to the floor as my mind caught up with her actions. The word *no* carved itself into every cell in my brain.

She couldn't know.

I'd tossed the magazine, and she hadn't been in touch with Harry lately.

"How could I be so stupid?" she wailed.

She knew.

"And how could you hide the magazine from me? What did you think was going to happen? God, I did this. I did this to my own son. How could he even look at me?" She sniffled. "I put a painting of his sad eyes in front of his room. I'm a monster."

"You're not a monster." I scooped her into my arms on the floor, kissing her forehead, threading my fingers through her hair. "You're the farthest thing from a monster. You *heal* monsters. You set their hearts on fire and make the bad shit perish. Vaughn loves you very much. I do too. This is why we couldn't tell you. And I only recently learned myself."

"Is he okay?" Her question came out muffled.

I felt my dress shirt soaked with her tears. I hated to see her like this. I'd kill a few more Harry Fairhursts with my bare hands if it meant making her happier.

"He is fine," I said with conviction I didn't feel, because *where the fuck* was *he, anyway?* "Absolutely fine. He is thriving. He is healthy. He is in love."

The wreckage storming through her body subdued a little. I was on the right track.

"And Harry?" She unglued her head from my shoulder, looking up and blinking at me.

It never ceased to amaze me, the effect her eyes had on my heart rate. She was a wingless angel—divine and saintly, but not in a prude way that made you want to fuck her dirty just to prove she was less than perfect.

I dragged my thumb across her lips. "Dealt with," I said.

She closed her eyes and took a ragged breath. "Did Vaughn—"

"No. I did." I refused to let her finish the sentence, knowing how much it pained her to even *think* it. "Vaughn went back to his girlfriend, Lenny. He is fine." *A lie.* Who the fuck knew where my son was right now? "We didn't tell you because we knew you'd take the blame."

"I *am* to blame." She shook her head.

I shut her up with a bruising kiss. "No. Harry Fairhurst is responsible. The responsibility for child abuse is on the abuser. Vaughn was surrounded by top-of-the-line nannies on the rare occasions he was out of our sight. We sent him to the best establishments. You gave him everything you could. Despite what happened to him, he grew up to be a boy who adores his mother so much, he couldn't even tell you to remove that stupid painting from the wall opposite to his door. *This* is the mark you left on him, Em. Not the ten minutes he was out of your sight. Not the time he moved to Carlisle Castle for the summer after *begging* us to go there. You couldn't have known."

As I spoke the words, I realized I couldn't have prevented this from happening either.

I couldn't shoulder the responsibility because I'd tried to protect my son with the ferocity of a thousand blazing suns. I knew that because I, myself, had been abused.

In a very different way, but nonetheless.

"The best thing we can do for him is pretend it never happened, that you still don't know. Allow him his dignity, Em. It's the most important thing a young man can have. Now, let's go home and leave the two lovebirds to clean their own mess. We're due back to see his exhibition anyway."

I picked her up and took her home.

My trophy.

My girl.

My heart.

My everything.

CHAPTER TWENTY-SEVEN
LENORA

The entire courtyard was full of them.

Posters of my uncle, Harry Fairhurst, smiling, with the caption: "Rip me if I hurt you."

The idea was to let people speak up without expecting them to come forward and admit to something still considered shameful and weak in our society. To me, admitting you'd been sexually abused was brave, but I understood it wasn't my place to judge how people handled their personal tragedies.

I'd printed out one hundred and fifty copies of the posters and hung them all over Carlisle Prep. By the next morning, many of the posters had been ripped apart. Some stomped on. Some now included a Hitler moustache, horns, or acne on his face.

I'd spent all night putting these posters up. At sunrise, I'd marched downtown on foot, picked up a coffee and a pastry, and gone back to the castle. That's when I saw what they'd done to the posters.

I poked my head into classes, went down to the cellar, and threw office doors open on the main staff floor.

Harry Fairhurst was nowhere to be found.

Neither was Vaughn Spencer.

My heart galloped against my rib cage. I rounded the corner to Harry's office, even though he'd missed the class he was supposed to teach and was about to open his door when fingers curled around my shoulder. I looked back exactly at the same time I was shoved into his empty office. The door slammed behind me. It was Arabella, and she was still wearing her pajamas, her hair a mess.

"Hi, trash," she greeted with her fake, cheery voice.

She'd chosen the wrong place and wrong time to mess with me. I was on edge, at war with my father, worried sick for Vaughn and what he'd done, and burning with rage about my uncle. She'd just added fuel to the fire already blazing high and dangerously out of control inside me.

"Thought it was a good opportunity to tell you I decided to leave before that stupid exhibition started. Raphael bores me to death, your dad sucks in bed, and Vaughn is MIA—" She was about to finish the sentence, but I didn't let her.

I pounced on her like an untamed feline, claws first, pushing her to the floor. She fell with a thud, a scream ripping from her plump lips. I straddled her, like Vaughn had done to me so many times when he wanted to disarm me. She reached for my face, and I jammed both her wrists to her sides. I couldn't believe what I was doing *as* I was doing it. I'd never gotten into a fight (if you don't count the showdown with Arabella *herself*). I could only imagine what my parents would think about such thing.

But your parents aren't here to judge you. They've been out of the picture for a while.

Mum was dead, and Papa turned out to be someone I had no desire to impress. Plus, it'd been a long time coming. Arabella had taunted and bullied me every step of the way for the past year and a half.

I leaned down and breathed into her face, trying—and succeeding—to sound crazy. Perhaps I'd always been dancing on the invisible line between insanity and despair. "Scream, and I'll make you sorry you were born with a mouth."

She spat in my face. I could feel her warm, thick saliva running from my chin down to my neck. I let go of her wrists, curling my fingers around her neck and straightening my spine, leaning back so her hands couldn't reach my face or neck.

I squeezed her throat, adrenaline swimming in my bloodstream like a drug.

"Everyone snaps, Arabella. Even—and especially—aggravated vampires. Now tell me, why do you hate me so much?"

She opened her mouth, but all I could hear were muffled gurgles. Her face was red, her eyes watery. I wanted to stop choking her, but I couldn't. Suddenly, I understood just how hotly Vaughn had hated Uncle Harry. I couldn't blame him for what he wanted to do to the man who'd ripped the innocence from him when he was only a wee boy.

"Answer me!" I slammed Arabella's head against the floor.

She'd hit me before. I never retaliated. Never fought back. Not really. I just sassed and made her feel intellectually inferior. As if she cared. That didn't do me any good.

Arabella desperately tried to pry my fingers off of her neck now. Finally, I let go, pinning her hands to the floor again. Her neck was marred with purple and black Dalmatian dots. *My fingertips.* I swallowed, refusing to dwell on what I'd done to her.

"Why!" she screamed in my face, twisting like a snake behind me, trying to break free. "Because your asshole father had an affair with my mom, and now my family's falling apart, and we're about to lose everything! That's why! Because one day he came into our house to drop Poppy off, and he never got out of there. My mom is suicidal. My dad is MIA. My sister has no one. All because of you and your stupid family. You should've stayed in England!" she roared, throwing her head back and bursting into a sob.

Too shocked to decipher exactly what she was saying, I let her slip from my grasp. My body slacked, and she took advantage of my surprise, pushing me back.

She shook her head. "You are so fucking gross. Like I would ever touch your dad. But I want you and Poppy to burn in hell. You came in with your stupid accent and clothes and bullshit and torched everything I knew and loved. You tore my family apart. Poppy stole Knight. You *have* Vaughn. What was I left with?" She pushed my chest again, harder. "Nothing!"

"So you and my dad…?" I tried to make sense of what she was saying, let it all sink in.

"Nothing," she ground out, throwing her arms in the air. "Your dad and I are nothing. But my work here is done. He is miserable. You are going crazy. Poppy lost Knight, the only thing she cared about in America. As for Vaughn? You're crazy to think he won't dump you if he hasn't already. He's wired differently."

I watched her scramble to her feet from my spot on the floor. She wiped her face clean, patting her neck and wincing as she felt the bruises.

"I'm sorry your family is falling apart, Arabella." Genuinely, I was. Compassion didn't cost a penny. I knew what it felt like when my family collapsed and I couldn't do anything to stop it. I didn't wish it upon anyone else—not even my enemies.

So many things collided together in a burst of realization and understanding.

Papa hadn't touched Arabella.

He *had* moved on from Mum, eventually, and had an affair.

And the truth behind Arabella's declaration that Vaughn was different from other boys, that he would leave me. Frankly, he already had.

"Whatever, Lenny. I don't need your pity." She flipped her hair, as she did when she was pretending not to be upset, huffing.

Lenny. Not Drusilla or Vampire Girl. That was new.

"You have no idea what it feels like to be me," she added.

"Do I not?" I stood up, bracing myself on the edge of Uncle Harry's desk. I was dizzy from all the things that had happened in such a short period of time. "I lost my mum a week before I got my first period. I had no one to talk to about it. Poppy was so upset, she wouldn't leave her room for four months afterward. I arranged toilet paper in my knickers to absorb the blood every month until I found Poppy's sanitary pads one day. I woke up every morning for a year expecting to see my mum, before remembering she was dead. I secretly hated my father for a while for not being the one to die. He was the one I needed less."

She swallowed and looked away, blinking at the bare wall where Harry's painting had once been.

"I stayed here and let my father and sister move away because the day my mother died was the day we stopped being a family and became a man and his two daughters. Nothing seemed to matter anymore. I didn't feel connected to anything, anyone."

Arabella sucked her cheeks in. "Sorry," she muttered.

"Not your fault. I came to All Saints High already saddled with an open beef with Vaughn Spencer." I refrained from getting into the details. "The black eyeliner, hair, piercings, and wild stories about trips to Brazil were camouflage. Obviously, they didn't do the trick."

"Obviously." She rolled her eyes, and I chuckled.

I needed to get out of here. To find Vaughn and Uncle Harry. To speak to my father. Make sure I hadn't gotten myself into terrible trouble by spreading those posters everywhere.

I walked toward her, brushing my fingers over her arm. She looked up in surprise, a little gasp escaping her wounded throat.

"I hope it all works out when you get back," I said grimly, despite everything. "I think we both haven't had it easy, and I hope we can prevail. I think we can, Arabella. I think the best is yet to come."

"I hope..." She trailed off, pressing her eyes shut. "I hope you'll be fine too, or whatever."

I laughed, shaking my head. "I'll take it."

We both hobbled toward the door at the same time, pouring out of it in different directions.

I spent the next hour looking for Vaughn everywhere. I tried calling his cell. It went straight to voicemail. Exhausted, I crawled up to my room, flinging myself over my bed and closing my eyes.

"Not so fast," a voice boomed. "We have to talk."

"Papa?" I whispered.

He stepped out of the shadows, a deep frown etched on his face. He looked so much older than he had before my birthday. Before our falling out. Before we'd both slinked entirely to our separate corners of the world, ignoring each other's existence.

I could see now that he didn't know what had riled me up, and I hadn't known why he didn't crawl back to me, begging for forgiveness.

It was a huge misunderstanding, and we could have talked if it wasn't for the fact that we *didn't* talk. Ever. Not really. Communicating our feelings had never been our strong suit, especially since Mum died, and now we were paying for it.

I felt my bed dipping and held my breath, the weight felt familiar all of a sudden. Flashbacks of hundreds of nights when he'd sat by my side to read me a story or tell me a Greek legend flooded my mind. My throat went thick with emotion.

"Lenny."

I pulled my lips into my mouth, trying not to cry.

"I should've come sooner, darling."

I felt the mattress move beneath me as he shook his head. Everything about him was massive, imposing, out of this world—even his sculptures. Maybe that was the problem. My father was always so much bigger than life in my eyes, I'd had to reduce him to nothing before I could look at him as a complex, flawed person. As an equal. *Human.*

Wordlessly, I began to twist my fingers together, just to do something with my hands.

"I wanted you to know, this thing you said…you talked about… with Miss Garofalo…"

"I got the wrong Garofalo." I sighed into the dark, feeling my shoulders slump. "I know. She caught me up to speed. A married woman, huh?" But there was no power to my judgment. I felt soggy with despair. Tired.

"Would it matter if I said I was lonely?" he asked.

I could hear the defeat his voice was soaked in. I shook my head again, knowing he could feel it in the movement of the mattress underneath us.

"I am devastated over the decision I made."

Decision, I noticed. Not *mistake*. The devil was in the details, and my father still believed he needed what happened there to happen— maybe to feel like a man again and not just an artist.

What he did was awful, but it wasn't unforgivable. To me, anyway. His daughter. I didn't have a choice. I wasn't his wife. He *had* no wife. It wasn't me he'd betrayed.

"It's not the only devastating decision I've made since moving to Todos Santos."

"Oh?" I asked.

He scooted over, pressing his back against my wall. My face heated in the dark when I thought about all the things this bed had seen recently. Vaughn handcuffed. Me and Vaughn having sex. The room was soaked with him, every crack in the wood floor filled with Vaughnness. The undertone of his cool, fresh scent still stuck to the walls. His rare smiles inked to my ceiling. I wondered if Papa could feel that he was here with us.

"I gave Vaughn the internship, but not because he deserved it, you see. I gave it to him because I knew you didn't want to fall in love—never wanted to fall in love—thinking it was safer and that you'd be happier. I couldn't take that chance, seeing you lead a lonely life. I'm lonely, and it's killing me, Lenny. So I summoned him here."

I choked on my own breath, coughing. "You…"

"No. Don't. Please don't scold me or ask me why him. There was something about the two of you in a room—any room, at any point of your childhood—that made the air sizzle, seconds before you put your hand to the material and made a masterpiece. There was magic there, and it was tightly woven. I wanted to pull it thread by thread by thread until I unraveled it completely. Your mother noticed it too, the day Vaughn sneaked you a brownie."

My mouth fell open. I saw the corners of his mouth lift, even though it was so dim in my room.

"She always watched you like a hawk, Lenny."

"She did," I whispered. "God, she did."

"I miss her so much. It was in a moment of weakness that I thought I could drown in someone else to hush the aching, scream-ing need for her. It was the worst choice I've ever made, next to picking Vaughn just so you two could be here together and fall in love. But as it turns out, not all is lost."

I waited patiently for him to drop the bomb I had no doubt was coming.

"You got the Tate Modern exhibition spot. Vaughn dropped out," he said.

I couldn't breathe.

The sensation was foreign, unwelcome. I tried pulling air into my lungs, but I couldn't accept any oxygen. My body rejected it. It seemed to reject the very idea itself.

"Vaughn told me about your assemblage sculpture, said it was gorgeous and far more deserving than another piece of stone. I tend to agree with him on that point. He packed his belongings and left the premises earlier today. I'm terribly sorry, darling."

"Where did he go?" I jumped out of the bed, clutching Papa's shoulders as I stood in front of him.

He shook his head. "He didn't say. I don't think he wants to be found, Lenny. But I found this letter under your door when I walked in. Must've blown over to the other side."

He reached for his pocket and passed me an envelope. I wanted to scream.

How could he let him leave?

How could he let me—no, *force* me to fall in love with Vaughn, then watch as he left me?

But he'd never intended Vaughn to leave, had he?

And then the inevitable dawned on me, heavy as the rocks Vaughn fought with to create art.

I was in love with him, wasn't I?

He was psychotic, erratic, eccentric, and completely unlovable in any way…and that made me love him more. Because I knew how completely doomed he was. How much he needed it.

Our love was so much more than love. It stripped us of pride and anger and hate and insecurities. We were bare and beautiful and pure when we were together.

And now he is gone.

I clutched the letter in my fist, my hand shaking. The rest of me too. I was losing it.

Papa stood and brought his lips to my forehead. "All those months, I gave you time to figure yourself out, Lenny. But I never went away. I was always here. Always loving, hoping, praying. It's better to have loved and lost than never to have loved at all. I love you now. Then. Always."

———

Len,

The first time I saw you, you were reading a book, your back pressed against the fountain. It was an impactful moment in my life. Not because you were pretty (although you were very pretty but also very young—I don't think we liked each other the way we do today), but because I vividly remember being appalled by the cover.

It was a fantasy book. As such, the cover was full of colors, silhouettes, and faces. The composition was all wrong. I remember looking at it and scowling. It offended me on a personal level. I think that was the moment I realized I wanted to create symmetric, beautiful things.

The moment I found out I was going to be an artist, like my mom.

Then I looked up and saw your face, and again, it wasn't symmetric (I hope you don't mind).

Your eyes were huge, the rest of you small, which gave you an almost infant look. Your nose was sharp, your lips thin. Your blond hair twisted in curls that were not perfect or carefully brushed. Yet somehow, you were more beautiful than any beautiful girl I'd ever seen in my entire life.

I would later stumble across a line from Edgar Allan Poe that made sense of it all—he said there's no exquisite beauty without some sort of strangeness in the proportions.

That explained why I had to talk to you, even though it wasn't in my nature to speak to someone when completely unprovoked. I approached you, casting a shadow over your face, blocking the sun. I remember the moment you looked up and stared at me because once you held my gaze, I couldn't look away.

It wasn't a good or exciting feeling. It was terrifying. I gave you a brownie because I needed to do something. But when it came down to eating my part of it, I couldn't do it.

I was too nervous to eat.

From that day forward, I wouldn't eat much in front of people in general.

I always wondered where you were, if we'd meet again, and as crazy as it sounds, it always felt like we might.

You never came.

Until you did.

Until you showed up at my school senior year.

I'd be lying if I said I wasn't surprised when you didn't move with Poppy and Edgar. I took it as a personal offense. Was I not good enough? Were you disgusted with me? By me?

You were pure, beautiful, talented, and carefully tucked in your own rich world of art, books, and music. I was torn, miles away, in a rich beach town I hated, a kid who'd seen and felt way more than he should have.

A part of me wanted our worlds to collide so I could burst yours and tear it to pieces, and another wished we'd never see each other again.

And then you came.

Defiant, infuriating, and completely out of my control.

You stirred me to savagery at a time when nothing could move me at all.

You must understand, Len, that hate is nature's most flawless drive. It is infinitely renewable, reusable, and fuels people far better than love. Think about the number of wars that started because of hate, and the number that started because of love.

One.

There was one war in the history of the world to start upon the legs of love.

It was the Trojan War, and it was Greek mythology.

Which brings us right back to zero.

That's the logic I worked with, and fuck, did it do the trick.

I hated you because I had to feel something for you, and the opposite of hate was out of the question. Not on the goddamn table. Falling in love with a girl who hated me, who thought I was a monster who killed jellyfish and had been involved with a middle-aged man? No, thank you. Your face alone made me feel defanged, so I had to get creative. To bite harder.

We were an unfinished business, personal and always walking the tight rope between love and hate.

But we were always something, Len.

We will always be something.

You might move on and marry someone else, have his children, and get your happily ever after, but you will never be completely done with me. And that's the small chunk of mirth I allow myself. That's my half of the brownie. That's my one perfect summer moment in the South of France, watching the face of the girl I will love forever for the very first time.

Because Lenora Astalis, this is love. It's always been love. Love with many masquerade masks, twisted turns, and ugly truths.

I don't know where I'll go from here, but I'll be wishing you were there.

The internship has always been yours.

I blackmailed Harry for it at age thirteen, in the darkroom. Since your father was the deciding voice, I convinced him I'd give him something in return. You were always Alma's favorite. She chose you, but Harry and Edgar were the majority.

And so, it feels fitting that because the internship should have gone to you, you are going to show your sculpture at Tate Modern.

It is worthy and beautiful, just like you.

I wish I were strong enough not to do what I need to do.

I wish I could get the girl.

Because, Len, you are her.

You are that girl.

My safe place.

My asymmetric happiness.

My Edgar Allan Poe poem.

You are my Smiths, and my favorite fantasy book, my brownie, and summer vacations in lush places. There will never be anyone else like you.

And that's exactly why you deserve someone better than me.

Love,
Vaughn

CHAPTER TWENTY-EIGHT
LENORA

The weeks leading to the exhibition had been so busy, I was sometimes surprised I didn't forget to breathe. I certainly forgot to eat and sleep.

Papa and Poppy stuck by my side throughout, taking time off from their own schedules to assist me. It's like they could see the hole Vaughn had left in my heart when he packed his bags and vanished. Neither of them talked about him. He just hung in the pregnant air, suspended by strings of cruel hope and tragic impossibility. Heartbreak had a taste, and it exploded in my mouth every time I tried to smile.

I worked on autopilot, putting the last touches on my assemblage piece. I'd met with curators, designers, and the exhibition coordinators. I'd signed contracts and smiled for cameras and explained my work to people who oohed and ahhed. I'd interviewed, along with Pope and other young artists, with magazines, local newspapers, and even the BBC.

Pope visited me every other day, his face marred with paint and triumph.

His piece was good.

Real good.

We'd share a kebab and drink Irn-Bru and crochet our plans for the future. The theme for the exhibition was the most promising young artists in the world, and I was excited to be included. Although no matter how much Papa assured me I'd earned my place fair and square, doubt gnawed at my stomach every time I looked at my piece.

I wasn't supposed to be a part of the exhibition.

I was a last-minute replacement, second best, a fill-in.

And it wasn't the only reason my stomach always felt hollow.

Three days after Vaughn tore me to pieces with his letter, the news came out that Harry Fairhurst had committed suicide in his St. Albans mansion.

His death was met with cold, unnerving silence from his colleagues, close friends, and fans. Shortly before he was found dead in his bathtub, swimming in a pool of his own blood, some past and current students at Carlisle Prep had plucked up the courage to come forward and call him out for his sexual abuse.

Dominic Maples, a current senior, had led the petition against him.

Apparently, the posters I'd hung everywhere, combined with a traumatic experience involving my uncle, encouraged Dominic's decision. He explained in the news that there was something sinisterly liberating about watching Fairhurst's face on paper poked, dented, and smeared in paint, almost beyond recognition. It made him look less powerful, human. It occurred to me that many mortals were burdened with the false status of a god, and almost none of them enjoyed the power that came with it.

Vaughn Spencer, as an example.

While Poppy refused to believe the mounting evidence against our uncle and insisted on attending his small, intimate funeral, my father seemed furious and disgusted with his cousin. He refused to speak of him. We both opted out of any and all tributes and memorial arrangements for Fairhurst.

Father wasn't stupid. He must've connected the dots leading to Vaughn's disappearance. All the same, he never questioned Harry's so-called suicide.

But I knew.

I knew Harry Fairhurst hadn't committed suicide.

To put an end to your life, you must first feel acute regret, guilt, or unhappiness. I'd grown up next to my uncle. Not once did he look uncomfortable in his snakelike skin.

In the week leading to the exhibition, my art piece was shipped, right along with Pope's painting, to Tate Modern. I packed all of my belongings and said goodbye to Carlisle Castle for the last time. I returned my key to Mrs. Hawthorne, gave flowers to the staff, destroyed my student card and cafeteria pass, and threw out my cape. The finality of it frightened me to death. I was never going to live here again. I would visit, perhaps, but not often, and I certainly wouldn't be roaming the hallways with confidence, like I had before. I had no desire to return as a teacher. The idea crippled me. I didn't want to teach; I wanted to create.

Papa drove us to our house in Hampstead Heath, where I was going to live until I found my next gig. Like many artists, I still wasn't opting for higher education. I had the tools I needed from my studies at Carlisle Prep, and I believed in autodidactism. I wanted to work at a gallery, perhaps snag an internship with someone creative and patient, if I had any luck.

Everything was in motion, yet life had a stale feeling—like trying to run underwater.

"Tell me three things: something good, something bad, and something you are looking forward to," Papa requested in the midst of a traffic jam, drumming his fingers on the steering wheel of his vintage AC/Ace Cobra. I looked sideways, tapping the edge of the window. It was difficult to think about anything that wasn't Vaughn. He drenched my thoughts, contaminating everything else I wanted to focus on.

"Something good? I'm excited for tomorrow. Something bad? I'm frightened about tomorrow too. Something I look forward to..." I trailed off.

For Vaughn to come back.

But I knew that wouldn't happen. He said he'd disappear after he killed Harry Fairhurst, that once he had blood on his hands, he wasn't going to smear it on me or anything in my life. And he was a man of his word. I needed to come to terms with it. Although he was crazy if he thought I could truly move on with someone else.

"I'm looking forward to nothing," I finished quietly.

Nothing really mattered that much anymore. A journey without Vaughn was not worth taking. I wanted him to challenge my every step, to keep me on my toes. To drive me mad. To give me his laughs, his thoughts, his blood.

That didn't mean I wasn't going to do things with my life. But the aftertaste of nothing, the one I'd felt every day the past couple weeks, was going to chase me to the grave. I knew that with depressing clarity.

Nothing was going to taste as good as those brownies and chocolate.

I should have known they weren't divine because of some secret recipe—he'd sent them from different places, in different countries, even. They'd tasted divine because I knew, subconsciously, that they came from him.

Vaughn didn't stop sending me chocolate and brownies after he left, but I stopped taking them into my room. Frankly, it was a relief to move somewhere he couldn't send them anymore. He didn't know my personal address.

"That saddens me to hear." Papa clucked his tongue, his thumb brushing the steering wheel.

We'd had many intimate conversations since Arabella left. Her father had picked her up—I saw them from my window, hugging, shedding tears. I hoped he was in a better mental place, that he could be there for his daughters the way my father couldn't after my mum passed away.

"I'll get my groove back," I lied, feeling an incredible urge to down a bottle of gin. I understood alcoholics now. Numbness was far superior to pain.

"I know you will." He nodded and started talking about the weather. I rested my head against my seat and closed my eyes, drifting.

———————

I wore a black wool, one-shoulder bustier dress, which flowed down my body with tulle made of lace. It had been sent to me by Emilia LeBlanc-Spencer the evening before the exhibition in a special delivery, and it contained a note that made my fingers itch to call her and ask for the meaning behind the unexpected gift.

Lenora,

No act of kindness, no matter how small, is ever wasted.—Aesop
Thank you for giving my son a home away from home. You broke down his walls yet gave him shelter. I am forever in your debt.

Emilia LeBlanc-Spencer

Though I'd been in the same place as this woman several times over the years, we'd never been officially introduced. To me, she was a famous painter and Vaughn's mother. I knew of her gallery in Los Angeles and had admired her art from afar (and her son from up close). Why had she reached out? Had Vaughn been in touch with her since he disappeared? Had he told her about me?

The idea filled me with foolish hope that maybe he was missing me, thinking about me. That perhaps he'd changed his mind after all. The morning sweets deliveries almost felt like a force of habit at this point. An apology, perhaps.

Maybe he'll be at the exhibition. My mind raced into dangerous territory: hope.

The love declaration he'd made in his letter grew watered down by doubt with each passing day, but I had to admit, slipping into the dress Emilia had sent me felt like walking into his arms. I swore it had his scent.

It was gothic, chic, and enchanting.

Christmas hung in the air like an overripe fruit. The sweet scent of pastries wafted in the chilly London air, and white and red lights wrapped around the English capital like a bow. Tate Modern was a brown, boxy thing on the southeast side of London. It wasn't as posh and beautiful as Tate Britain, but today, it looked perfect to me.

Poppy held my hand, and Papa draped an arm over my shoulder as we walked across Turbine Hall toward the exhibition room. The minute I entered the space, I spotted my piece. It was impossible not to. It had been placed in the center of the room, surrounded by the other works of art, most of them pushed against the white walls.

Bursting from the bowels of the gallery with pristine brilliance and vivid colors, his tin face stared back at me in challenge. The Indian yellow of his cape battled for attention with the ruby red of his bleeding crown of thorns. He was alive, deadly, and godly.

My Angry God.

My heart beat faster when I realized a cluster of people orbited around it, staring. Some seemed to read the little explanatory sign underneath:

Angry God/Assemblage/Lenora Astalis

Material: nails, wood, thorns, paper, fabric, metal, glass, plastic, hair, blood

From the artist: When I started working on this piece, I had no idea what it meant to me. I wanted to immortalize the depraved ferocity of a beautiful man willfully marching to his own demise. The name, Angry God, derives from "Sinners in the Hands of an Angry God," a sermon written by the Christian theologian Jonathan Edwards and preached to his congregation in Northampton, Massachusetts, in 1741. It is said that Edwards

was interrupted many times during the sermon by people asking,
"What shall I do to be saved?"

   What will you do to be saved?

   Would you go so far as losing the love of your life?

"Come, come, the woman of the hour is here." Alma Everett-Hodkins curved her wrinkly, thin fingers around my wrist and pulled me into the throng of people, all of them sophisticated-looking professionals in black.

"I noticed her rare talent when she was merely eight." Alma grinned knowingly as my father and Poppy stood next to us, smiling proudly and cradling glasses of champagne. I would've killed for a drink, but I needed to remain professional and, unfortunately, sober. People asked me questions about the piece and gave me their interpretations of it. I answered dutifully, trying to cling to the moment, to be there, to experience the now, and to push Vaughn from my thoughts—at least for the duration of the evening. This was the height of my career, the peak I'd been waiting for. It wasn't fair that he was going to steal it without even being here.

Without even trying.

Pope stood on the other side of the room next to his floor-to-ceiling painting, talking to a cluster of young artists. There were many pieces of art in the exhibition, but most people were standing around my statue. Pride overwhelmed me. Maybe I really was good after all.

I craned my neck, stupidly looking for Vaughn among the crowd of people, but he wasn't here. It felt so fitting; it was hard not to hope he'd show up, like in the movies, storming in frazzled and lovesick, with a Hugh Grant smile and a stuttered-yet-charming monologue that would rip everyone's heart out, mine included.

"Did you have anyone in mind when you sculpted the face?" asked a stunning, blue-eyed woman with a brown chignon, the tips of her hair dyed lavender pink. She cradled a glass of red wine.

I turned to look at her and smiled. "What makes you ask that?"

"The cut of the cheekbones." She motioned with the hand that held the wine in the statue's direction. "The high brows, wide forehead, strong chin—it is symmetrical to a fault, more than King David. Almost godly in its beauty. I find it hard to believe a man like that exists." She tapped her lips now, musing. She looked familiar, but I couldn't put my finger on it. I would definitely remember if I'd met her before.

"Oh, he does," I said, running a finger along the cold, metallic side of his face.

"I know." She turned to me fully now, searching my eyes. "He's my son."

We both froze in our spots as I processed the information. My body prickled hotly, and my heart began to pound.

"Emilia?" I gasped.

She wrapped her arms around me, as if hugging were the most natural thing two strangers could do. I struggled to keep myself in check, knowing my tears were already planning their grand appearance. I had so much I wanted to ask her, yet somehow, I couldn't find my voice.

Once we disconnected, she cupped my cheeks and smiled down at me. She had a lovely smile. Not only because it was aesthetically attractive, but because her goodness shone through it. I could see why Baron "Vicious" Spencer was so madly in love with her. Rumors about the way he worshipped her, how he'd built a cherry-blossom garden for her in their backyard, had traveled throughout higher society in Todos Santos. She had this quality about her that made people do crazy things to please her—an invisible hold.

"How are you?" she asked.

I couldn't lie.

"Worried. Is he okay?" I dropped my voice so people around us couldn't hear.

Some moved to other pieces in the exhibition, but most waited patiently for us to finish talking so they could speak to me. I found the situation bizarre. The entire point of making art was so I didn't have to explain it.

She smiled but said nothing. She pulled me behind the assemblage so we couldn't be seen or heard.

"Lenora, you're about to be showered with proposals from gallery owners in approximately two minutes, but I wanted to be the first to offer you a spot in my gallery in Los Angeles. You don't have to answer now, of course, but I would be very excited to work with you. And I would like to take this opportunity to thank you again for all you did for Vaughn."

I swallowed. "Is he going to be there? In Los Angeles, I mean?" I eyed her.

I hated that I was desperate, that I still cared. No. Scratch that. I hated that he was *all* I cared about. At this moment, I didn't consider the merits of working in her gallery because it was prestigious or huge or offered a lot of work experience, God forbid.

Emilia shook her head. "I'm sorry, sweetie. Love is a trickster. It has a way of twisting you, doesn't it?"

My head hung low. "Yeah."

"The pain fades eventually."

"How do you know?"

"Once upon a time, I felt it too."

I squeezed her hand in mine. "All right. I'll think about it. Thank you."

She kissed my cheek and walked away.

The rest of the evening was a blur. I had business cards shoved into my hands, people asking for my number, my email, my *price*. By the time ten o'clock rolled around, my legs were trembling with exhaustion.

I leaned against Poppy for support, plucking a heel off for a moment and massaging my foot on a wince when she turned to me and said, "Papa called you a cab. Hurry up now."

"A cab?" I frowned. "Why?"

"He's taking Pope for a drink to close up a deal." She cocked her head toward the two of them, arching a meaningful brow. Dad and Pope were standing next to each other, shaking hands and laughing. I grinned. I was so happy Pope was going to stay close by, that we wouldn't become glorified strangers who sent each other the occasional Christmas card. I looked back to her.

"What about you? Are you coming with?"

She scoffed. "Hard pass. After Pope has a drink with Papa, I intend to have something else with him, so I'm tagging along."

"Are you serious?" My eyes widened.

"As a heart attack. Have you seen him? He is gorgeous, and he did a lot of growing up while we were in California. You don't mind, do you?"

"Of course not, you slag." I laughed.

She shrugged and strutted back to them. I shook my head. Rafferty and Poppy. Who would have thought?

In the cab, I let my mind wander to the fact that Pope had once touched me in a way I wasn't sure Poppy was going to appreciate. I shot her a quick text saying there was something I needed to tell her and perhaps she should hold off on the shagging session with my best friend.

Her reply came promptly.

Poppy: For God's sake, don't worry about us! Just go home.
Me: Pope and I did things. They meant nothing to either of
     us, but they still happened. I don't want you to be
     blindsided.
Poppy: Buh-bye!

Upon arrival, I shoved the key in, pushed the door open, and locked it behind me. Sighing heavily, I shouldered out of my coat and hung it in the foyer, kicking my heels off once and for all.

"Argh, never doing the high-heel thing again," I announced to the empty space.

After finding a glass of water, I went upstairs to my old child-hood room, which barely reminded me of my younger years now. I identified that period of my life with Carlisle Castle more than anything else. I pushed the door open. As soon as I did, the glass slipped from my fingers, dropping noiselessly to the carpet.

A yelp escaped my throat.

"We have to stop meeting like this," Vaughn said, perched on my bed, looking at me like nothing had happened at all.

Like he'd never left.

Like he hadn't broken and entered into my house for the thousandth time.

Like there wasn't a six-hundred-kilogram sculpture in the middle of my room—life-sized, gigantic, and absolutely gorgeous. I'd never seen anything like it. Violent shivers ran down my arms and back, and pure adrenaline dropped me to my knees as I tried to gulp a deep breath.

"It's..."

"*Us*," he said, standing from my bed and approaching me in measured, careful steps.

He looked good—healthy, tall, ripped, and still in his tattered black jeans and half-torn black shirt that couldn't dim his brutally stunning features. He stopped in front of me, offering me his hand.

Tentatively, I took it.

I stood, stepped forward, and examined the statue.

It was the two of us, curled against each other as children, lying on a bed. We were twelve and thirteen and looked just the way we had the day I'd caught him and Harry. Only in the sculpture, he wasn't standing above me, watching and threatening. Instead we were entwined together, his face partly covered by my hair. I was breathing into his neck, my arms protectively circling his shoulders.

Everything had been realistically carved, to the point that

it looked like a giant, living picture. I was sure if I put my fingers to our necks, I'd find a pulse. But when my gaze moved down to our stomachs, I noticed something weird. Our bottom parts were meshed together, mermaid-like, as if we were conjoined twins. We didn't have legs. We couldn't escape each other.

We were one.

The name of the sculpture was carved on its side:

GOOD GIRL

Vaughn took me by the hand and walked me to my bed, where we slipped under my blanket, legs entwined, mimicking the statue—his face in my hair, my nose pressed against his neck. *Home,* I thought, and everything became clear.

That's why Papa had taken Pope for an after-show drink. That's why my sister had stayed behind. She had no interest at all in Rafferty. They wanted to give us our privacy.

Emilia knew too. That's why she didn't tell me how Vaughn was doing.

It dawned on me that Vaughn and I had been ruthlessly patient with one another all those years. He'd waited for me to open up while I long-sufferingly watched as he crawled from behind the tall walls he'd built around himself.

"I started working on this statue before we were together. I started it before we'd even *kissed*. Before Jason. Before Arabella. Before everything, there was you," he whispered into my hair. "You came before art. Before life. Definitely before hate."

I shook with unrestrained tears. They were falling down my cheeks now, hot and furious and grateful. I pulled back reluctantly, catching his gaze.

"How could you think you are less than enough? How could you ever think that?" I asked, feeling my cheeks heating up with anger.

"I don't think that anymore," he said softly, caressing my hair.

"Or if I am, I don't care. I couldn't go through with it. I couldn't kill your uncle. I stood there with my weapon, and all I could think was what if he was right—if it was getting revenge or getting the girl…" He closed his magnificent blue eyes, taking a deep breath, opening them again. Determination zinged through them. "I'd rather have the girl."

I hugged him to a point of suffocation, laugh-crying. When we disconnected again, I frowned. "So who did it?"

I still didn't believe Uncle Harry had committed suicide.

Vaughn shrugged. "Perhaps another angry god."

I nodded, catching his drift.

"Why did you leave if you didn't killed him? Where have you been all this time?" A pang of pain slashed through my heart. Those weeks apart felt like forever. They'd stretched longer than all the years I'd lived without him by my side.

"I stuck around, admiring you from afar—but never too far." He took my chin between his thumb and index, bringing our lips together in a sweet, unhurried kiss. "Stayed at the cottage my parents rent downtown. I watched you walking into town with Rafferty, buying groceries, and hiking. I didn't come close because I knew that without me out of the way, you wouldn't have your chance to display your work at Tate Modern. And frankly, you were far more deserving of this spot. I've been your shadow for so long, Lenora. I wanted you to bask in the sun a little."

"My shadow?" I breathed.

He nodded. "Always there, following you, even when you didn't see. Remember the day Arabella, Soren, and Alice crowded you in that locker room and a door slammed in the distance, making them leave? That was me. And they paid for what they did. I stole Soren's Maserati and totaled it, causing his parents to almost disown him, and I planted cocaine in Alice's and Arabella's purses. Alice's parents gave her so much shit they decided to send her to rehab instead of college. With Arabella, I got even better results. She got hooked."

Silence.

"I've always loved you in my own fucked-up, destructive way."

I closed my eyes, relishing the word as it rolled off his tongue. So fantastically rare and forever mine.

"Say it again," I whispered to his lips, cupping his cheeks.

"I *love* you," he said, his tongue flicking my lips when he pronounced the L, opening them in the process. We kissed hungrily.

"Again," I growled into his mouth, clutching his shirt, knowing it was wet because of my tears and not giving a damn.

"I." He nuzzled his straight nose along my jawline.

"Love." He flicked my ear with his tongue.

"You," he finished, closing his mouth over mine in a passionate kiss that made my eyes roll in their sockets and took my breath away.

He moved on top of me, thrusting his groin into mine, pinning me down, and just like the sculpture, we became one again. He kicked his jeans off, I hoisted my dress, and a few minutes later, he was inside me, and we were perfectly tangled. He drove into me deeply, again and again and again, until I was delirious with pleasure and my heart soared and bloomed. I could feel my love cells multiplying inside my chest. More. More. *More.*

This. This was what I wanted and needed. Vaughn Spencer, of all people. In my bed. Protecting me from my favorite monster.

Himself.

EPILOGUE
VAUGHN

TWO YEARS LATER

It is the scent of cotton and lavender that gives her away.

I catch the faint waft of the feminine shampoo I'm so addicted to that I pathetically pack it with me in mini-bottles whenever I have to leave her to travel for work. Which, granted, isn't often. Either we join each other while traveling, or we don't travel at all. It's still fucked up to think we spent years away from each other while we were young.

I look up from the desk in the studio I share with Len, in the shed of our garden, and stare at the door. Nothing.

You can't fool me, Good Girl. You never could.

I put down the blue diamond I have in my hand and stand to walk outside. The air is humid and hot around me, even though the sun set hours ago. I check the time on my phone. One in the morning. *Fuck.* That's why she checked on me.

Has she seen what I was doing?

Of course she has, jackass. That's why she tried to slip away unnoticed—not to ruin your surprise.

I walk past our small garden and open the back door to our house. We live in a small villa in Corsica, France. We love that it's on an island, that it's within proximity to everything and everywhere we need to visit in Europe, and that our friends can visit us anytime, because who the fuck doesn't want to vacation in the South of France?

Padding barefoot down our dark hallway, I reach our bedroom door and pause. Our bedroom is the most glorious place in the house. Maybe the universe. It overlooks the Mediterranean Sea. Whoever designed this house was smart enough to put in floor-to-ceiling windows overlooking the wonder that is sunset in Corsica. I push the door open and walk over to our bed. Len is lying there, curled into herself like a shrimp, pretending to sleep, her eyelids fluttering.

I brush my thumb against her cheek, watching as goose bumps rise on her skin. This is how it all started, I think. A balled-up girl in the dark, begging not to be noticed.

No can do, sweetheart.

I tried so hard to ignore her existence when I saw her again after I gave her that chocolate because I knew how fucked I'd be if I let her in.

And she burst in anyway, tearing down my walls. I lower myself to her ear and breathe the words tauntingly:

"I know you're not asleep. Your eyelids are moving."

Her eyes pop open, and she rolls from her side to her back, staring at me defiantly.

"What if I am?" she whispers, challenging me. "What would you do?"

"That depends." I sit on the edge of the bed, removing a lock of hair from her face. "How much did you see back there?"

"Enough to expect either a ring or a swift yet very painful breakup if you give that piece of jewelry to someone else."

A simple *nothing* would have been sufficient. But of course, nothing is simple where my girlfriend is concerned. We've spent the last two years setting up a home in Corsica and traveling all around the world, following our inspiration. We spend six months at home, working and selling our art, and six months chasing memories and dreams and views most people only get to see in cheap pastel paintings at their doctor's office.

I said I wouldn't go back to Todos Santos, and I kept my word. We do travel there during the holidays, though. Sometimes Poppy and Edgar tag along. They're a part of my family now. You know shit's getting serious when you put up with a girl like Poppy Astalis. It practically feels like Len and I are married, but that's not enough for me. Every single time I see some random motherfucker checking her out at the airport, in a pub or a club, or even the goddamn fucking supermarket, I get an unexplainable urge to bash his head against the floor until both crack.

Considering this fact, it would be best if I put both the world's male population and myself out of misery by putting a ring on it, pissing on my territory, and making sure everyone knows Lenora Astalis is off-limits.

Because that's the essence of what I've been trying to do for years anyway, isn't it? Put my mark on her. Make sure people know she is mine.

"A quick and painful breakup is not in your future," I deadpan, expressionless.

She scoots up, leaning against the headboard and folding her arms. She is smiling now, that smile that disarms me of every negative feeling I have.

"What is it, then?" She raises an eyebrow.

"That depends on your answer," I shoot back.

"*That* depends on your effort," she retorts. "And right now you are cocking it up royally. Why don't you try when the ring is finished and find out?"

Not a no, then. Plus, she is playing right into my hands, thinking I'm some kind of rookie.

"Wait until the ring is ready?" I repeat.

She nods slowly, watching me. *All she saw was the diamond.*

"Fine." I go down on one knee in front of the bed, plucking the little box out of my back pocket.

Len perks up, cupping her mouth. "But I just saw you...I..." She blinks rapidly but stops saying whatever it is she is saying, because now *she's* the one fucking it up.

I put a hand on her knee, using my other hand to open the box. It was a bitch to make this ring. First of all, because I had to chase Edgar's ass to open up his safe in Switzerland and give me her mother's original engagement ring. Second, because I added to that ring every single rare diamond I could get my hands on, other than the blue one she just saw. No. That one is going to end up in a necklace the entire family is making for her. An engagement gift.

Things are going to get real awkward real fast if she says no.

"You saw what I wanted you to see. I think I always had this idea that you should be my savior, but naturally, the stubborn ass that I am, I didn't understand it. Now I do. I want you to save me today, and tomorrow, and in a month, and in a year, and in a decade. Save me. Give me your best and your worst and everything in between. I've always watched my dad loving my mom and thought he was stuck in a state of insanity. But he wasn't. Turns out, love really can be that fucking intense."

She has tears in her eyes. Happy ones, I hope. Although, there's really no knowing in my case. I know a lot of people who'd be brought to sad tears at the prospect of spending the rest of their lives with me. Arabella, for instance. Last I heard, she was in rehab, seeking treatment for a mental breakdown.

"Save me," I whisper, taking Lenora's hand and waiting for her to give me the okay to slip the ring on her finger.

"How did you know?" she rasps. "That I'd come out there now. It's the middle of the night."

"I didn't." I grab her wrist, kiss the inside of her palm. "I've kept the damn ring with me for months. You finally cracked and peeked."

"You've been acting mysteriously." She rubs my lower lip, back and forth.

"Not mysterious enough, as it turned out. We could've already been pregnant twice had it been up to me."

"You can't get pregnant twice at the same time. It's a one-time thing." She cracks up, covering her face. I think she's blushing, but it's damn hard to see in the dark.

"Is that a challenge?" I hiss, hooding my eyes. But my nonchalance expires a second later. "Am I going to kneel on one knee for all of fucking eternity? Not that I mind. Just asking for a friend."

"A friend?"

"Well, friends. My joints."

She full-blown giggles now. I try to bite down my smile, but I just want her to say yes and put me out of my goddamn misery.

"Fine." She rolls her eyes. "I'll marry you, Vaughn Spencer. But on one condition."

I frown. "Yes?"

"No children."

"You don't want any children?"

"Nope."

I don't pause to think about it. "Fine. Whatever. Fuck it. They're whiny and annoying and could grow up to be fucking serial killers. Who needs them?" I slip the ring on her finger and stand up, jerking her with me, holding her by the ass and wrapping her legs around my waist. She moans into my mouth, her arms linked around my shoulders as I kiss her.

I slap one of her ass cheeks with a grin. "Lenora Spencer."

"Lenora Astalis-Spencer," she corrects. "And I would very much like you to become Vaughn Astalis-Spencer."

This time I *do* think about it. There's a pause. Then she starts laughing again, wildly, covering my entire face with kisses.

"You're such a bloody eejit."

"And all fucking yours, baby."

LENORA

ONE YEAR LATER

"What happened to 'I don't want kids'?"

Vaughn is standing by the sink in the ob-gyn clinic, picking up a chart showing the fetus's growing stages and frowning at it with dry concentration.

He has the tendency to do everything gravely, and that makes me laugh.

"I said that just to see what kind of husband you'd be if you don't get your way. It was a test." I'm dangling my feet in the air, sitting on the examining table in a gown, waiting for the doctor to tell us the sex of the baby. The truth is, the idea of children had grown on me, like leaves on a summer tree, the more time Vaughn and I spent together.

But everything I thought I wanted or needed changed after we eloped in London's city hall three weeks after Vaughn's proposal, in front of our close friends and family. Poppy arrived with her new boyfriend, Jayden, whom Vaughn got along with surprisingly well. Really, we couldn't have done it any other way when you think about it. Vaughn wasn't one for fancy events.

Three weeks after the wedding, Baron and Emilia presented us with our wedding gift, a plush, six-bedroom beach house in Todos Santos. We thanked them politely but weren't going to do anything with it, of course. We loved our Corsica home. Then Emilia made the very good point that we could at least visit it and list it to be rented. We agreed.

The minute I set foot in that house, I knew I was born to live there.

The ocean called to me.

The sound of the waves crashing on the shore lulled me into drugging bliss.

Everything was open and beautiful and new. The air felt lighter and crisp. The four of us walked in—Emilia, me, Vaughn, and his father—and the minute I stood in the center of the living room, I knew it was my new home.

I turned to Vaughn with a smile. "Let's keep it."

Without a thought, he turned straight to his parents and narrowed his eyes at them. "Is it too late to rebel against your asses? Because you fucked me over real nice and good this time."

His father patted his shoulder with a patronizing smirk. "Watch and learn, Son."

"Not sure I'd be dedicating my life to screwing over my imaginary kids, if we wanted to have them," Vaughn countered.

He still thought I wasn't into the idea of kids. My silly, silly hubby.

"You'd be singing a different tune if and when they decided to live on the other side of the universe." His mother smiled sweetly, but there was no venom in her voice. She meant it. She missed us.

For the next few months, we lived at the Spencers', in hotels around Todos Santos, in San Diego, and with Knight and Luna Cole. We had to stay close while we worked on designing the house. And that left a lot of room for morning sex.

And evening sex.

And middle-of-the-night sex.

And, frankly, all-day sex.

I took the pill religiously and didn't take antibiotics or do anything to hinder their success. It was a fluke, but one I wasn't even a tiny bit annoyed with.

"Not sure I'm comfortable with something like this living inside my wife's body." Vaughn turns around to me now with the chart in his hand, tapping a pink blob the shape of a comma.

"Not sure you have much choice." I grin, sitting back on the bed. "Besides, if you think that's odd, it's about to get a hell of a lot weirder."

He pushes his lower lip out, coming to sit next to me. "Question."

"Yes?"

"What if I suck as a dad? I mean, I know you're one hundred percent going to save the situation, but what if I won't be enough?"

"Do you love me?" I ask him.

"To death," he says. "And that's not just a figure of speech, although I'd appreciate it greatly if you don't test me on the matter."

I already did, I want to tell him. *And you chose not to kill someone because of me.*

But that's not a conversation we have too often.

"Then you're going to love this baby twice, if not thrice as much. You're an amazing husband. Why wouldn't you make a fantastic father?"

We smile at each other, and the doctor walks in—the same one who delivered Vaughn, actually. I lay back and allow her to squirt ice-cold gel on my stomach. My stomach is poking out a little more than usual for how far along I am, but Emilia says it's because I'm tiny, so everything shows. Emilia is a bit like the mother figure Poppy and I needed after Mum died, and I would let that frighten me if it wasn't for the fact that my happiness is too raw, too real to let the past upset me.

The doctor stares at the monitor and moves the transducer around my belly. We all stare at the screen expectantly. Vaughn is holding my hand.

"How old are you again?" she asks as a way of making small talk.

"Twenty-one-ish." Vaughn answers on my behalf when he realizes I'm too stunned with joy and pride.

I can feel his foot tapping on the floor. He is nervous but happy.

"Why?" he asks suspiciously.

"How well do you deal with lack of sleep?"

Vaughn and I exchange amused looks.

"Quite well. We're not heavy sleepers. Besides, Vaughn's mother is going to help us a lot, and I'm taking a year off after the baby is born," I answer cheerfully, recovering from the initial shock. I can't understand anything I'm seeing on the screen anyway.

"Babies." The ob-gyn turns around and grins at me.

I blink at her. "Pardon?"

"When the babies arrive. Mrs. Astalis-Spencer, you're having twins. I'll take your mother-in-law's help and up you two part-time nannies."

I open my mouth to say something—although I really don't know what there is to say; we don't have a history of twins in my family, and neither does Vaughn—when my husband scoops me up in the air and kisses me in front of the doctor.

I laugh breathlessly as he puts me down, showering me with little kisses. He looks elated. Fantastically happy. The happiest I've seen him.

"Scared yet?" I smirk at him.

"With you by my side?" He grins. *"Never."*

BONUS EPILOGUE
VAUGHN

VAUGHN SAVING LENORA FROM THE FIRE, FROM VAUGHN'S POV

"She told us in the locker room weeks ago. Spilled it all out," Alice—also known as the walking, talking contraception advertisement of my school—tells me.

She is referring to Good Girl telling people my secret. Hey, the incentive is there. I'm making her life a living fucking hell at All Saints High. Short of making her run away from town, I've tried everything. And it's not because she's insufferable. She is actually *more* sufferable than most humans. And therein lies the problem.

"As much as I'd love to stand here and listen to you trying your hand at doing something with your mouth that doesn't include sucking dick, I have things to do." I let loose a frosty glare Alice's way, making my way to Good Girl's window.

There's alcohol, drugs, and mayhem everywhere at Lenora Astalis's pool party. The police are about to be here any minute, and Arabella just dropped a lamp all over the alcohol, creating a ring of fire around the pool. People are running toward the front gates, making their escape. But Lenora is locked in her room upstairs, and I'm not particularly hot on her dying on my watch.

Now, if she died on my dick, on the other hand...

Under her window, I look up and command, "Jump."

She shakes her head, swallowing hard. I can't blame her. I wouldn't jump on the opportunity to hurl myself out of a two-story window either. I check my surroundings, my heart beating like a jackhammer. Actually, my heart beating is enough to make me halt in surprise. Logically, I know it's beating because I'm alive (technically speaking). But I never feel it. My pulse is usually perpetually slow. Which begs the question—what the fuck?

Lenora is out of sight now. I can hear her clawing at her bedroom door as the fire spreads around me. The flames hiss and growl like hungry predators, smoke curling from yellow-red tips. Death can be so beautiful. It's crazy nearly no one sees it.

Without thinking, I place one foot on the first floor's outer windowsill, grabbing on to a spout and hoisting myself up. I plant my boots firmly on the wraparound roof below her window. Pulling my shirtsleeve with my teeth and wrapping it around my fist, I smash her window and slip into the attic. Shards of glass carpet the surface beneath me, crunching as I make my way to her.

Lenora turns around from her door and lets out a yelp.

"I'm going down first and then you'll jump into my arms," I instruct her. I don't know why I'm saving her. I don't know why I'm risking my life for her. What I *do* know for a goddamn fact is she wouldn't do the same for me. But somehow, impossibly, outrageously, *annoyingly*, it doesn't matter. This is not a tit-for-tat situation. Although, strictly speaking, I'm very interested in her tits.

"You can't catch me." She shakes her head anxiously.

"You do it my way or you burn to death. I really don't care. This is a one-minute offer. I'm not fucking up my life to save yours, Good Girl."

I slither out the window again, my blood roaring in my ears. I can hear Lenora running toward the window, and thank fuck she does, because we're running out of time. It's getting hard to breathe, and I can't see past all this black smoke.

"I didn't tell them your secret," she shouts through the window, half her body dangling from it. "Tell me you believe me, and I'll jump."

"What difference does it make?" I ask from my spot under her window, moving an inch left so I'm directly beneath her.

"Because it's the truth!" she cries out. I don't know if she is doing this for me to save her—if so, she's an idiot, because I'm already doing that—or because she hates the idea of anyone thinking she is less than perfect. I don't call her Good Girl for nothing. Either way, I'm getting bored of this conversation.

"I don't believe you, but I'll still catch you." My head hangs down in rage and defeat. "I will always catch you, the fucking dumbass that I am."

I wish I could purge her out of my system. That her life would mean as little to me as everyone else's. She isn't disposable, and I don't know what to make of that.

"What do you mean?" she asks from above my head.

"You soften me," I grind out.

"Why…?"

Is she seriously starting a goddamn heart-to-heart? We're about to be consumed by fire. Talk about shitty timing. "Because I don't want to fucking kill you!" I snap finally. "You're too fun to fuck with. Now get. The hell. Down."

She jumps with her eyes shut. Then she's in my arms. Her weight feels good in my fingertips. Exactly right. I'm not buff like Knight or Penn. I can't carry an entire human—no matter how small and slight— with the same ease I carry a backpack. But somehow the strain of taking Lenora all the way to safety doesn't matter. My shaking muscles. My burning flesh. All of this goes away because I know that she's safe.

Her arms are wrapped around my neck, and I can almost pretend she's holding me because she wants to and not because she is coughing tar and about to vomit a lung from all the smoke.

"You look like shit," I mutter, to balance out all that I'm feeling and thinking right now.

"Okay, but you look *splendid* right now. Straight to a catalog. Ten out of ten."

I press my lips together so as not to chuckle. The police burst through the front doors to the Astalis residence behind us. I can hear the sirens of fire trucks as they park outside.

"Why did you even care?" Lenora asks. "You said your father owns the police."

"I'd walk away unscathed. You, on the other hand…" I arch an eyebrow. Firemen are swarming her backyard now, but we're hidden from view, behind faraway bushes. The house is toast. Also fucking literally. Her dad's gonna blow a gasket.

"And you care because…?"

"I'm not done fucking with you."

Problem is, I don't only want to fuck with her. I want to fuck *her* too. And this need, this fire burning in my veins, is getting harder and harder to contain.

The Astalis mansion is not the only thing about to turn to ash.

So is my self-control when it comes to this girl.

SERIES INSPIRATION

Struggling to picture the characters? Here are the physical inspirations for each character:

Daria Followhill—Nicola Peltz
Bailey Followhill—Chloe Moretz
Penn Scully—Austin Butler
Knight Cole—Matthew Noszka
Luna Rexroth—Zendaya
Lev Cole—Patrick Schwarzenegger
Vaughn Spencer—Felix Mallard
Lenora Astalis—Jenna Ortega
Sylvia Scully—Lily Rose Depp
Hunter Fitzpatrick—Chase Mattson
Racer Rexroth—Andrew Davila

ACKNOWLEDGMENTS

This series has been such a ride. I wasn't sure if I should write the Sinners' kids' stories, but once I sat down and did it, I couldn't imagine NOT telling Daria's, Knight's, Luna's, and Vaughn's stories. I'm so glad I did. Some of the books in this series became the ones I'm most proud of.

And I couldn't write them without the help of the following wizards:

My amazing editors, Paige Maroney Smith and Jessica Royer Ocken for being so unbelievably talented and dedicated. Especially when I'm being super obsessive about each word. Thank you for putting up with me!

A huge shout-out to Letitia Hasser, who made this cover happen, and to Stacey Blake of Champagne Formatting for making the interior absolutely perfect.

Big thanks to my agent, Kimberly Brower at Brower Literary.

A huge, HUGE thank-you to my wonderful street team, my momager Tijuana Turner, who basically runs my entire life, and my beta readers, Amy Halter, Lana Kart, Vanessa Villegas, and Sarah Grim Sentz.

Special thanks to the people who put up with me on a regular basis, Charleigh Rose, Helena Hunting, Parker S. Huntington, and Ava Harrison.

Also, to the Sassy Sparrows, my reading group, and to my readers, who make me strive to become a better, more daring writer and artist. Thank you for pushing me in the right direction. Always.

On a personal note, I would be so grateful if you could leave a brief, honest review for the book when you are done reading.

All my love,
L.J. Shen

ABOUT THE AUTHOR

L.J. Shen is a *USA Today*, *WSJ*, *Washington Post* and #1 Amazon Kindle Store bestselling author of contemporary romance books. She writes angsty books, unredeemable antiheroes who are in Elon Musk's tax bracket, and sassy heroines who bring them to their knees (for more reasons than one). HEAs and groveling are guaranteed. She lives in Florida with her husband, three sons, and a disturbingly active imagination.

Website: authorljshen.com
Facebook: authorljshen
Instagram: @authorljshen
Twitter: @lj_shen
TikTok: @authorljshen
Pinterest: @authorljshen